VALENCE

CONFLUENCE BOOK 4

JENNIFER FOEHNER WELLS

D1707396

Blue Bedlam
SCIENCE FICTION

Jennifer Foehner Wells
Blue Bedlam Science Fiction
www.jenthulhu.com
jen@jenthulhu.com

Publisher's Note: This is a work of fiction. Names, characters, places, and
incidents are a product of the author's imagination. Locales and public names are
sometimes used for atmospheric purposes. Any resemblance to actual people,
living or dead, or to businesses, companies, events, institutions, or locales is
completely coincidental.

Cover Art © 2017 Stephan Martiniere
Book Layout © 2017 Vellum

Valence/ Jennifer Foehner Wells. — 1st ed.
ISBN 9781973320494 (paperback edition)

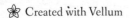 Created with Vellum

For Geoff
May we live long and prosper

"If you fell down yesterday, stand up today."

H.G. WELLS

1

February 16, 2018

THE PLIGANS HAD, without a doubt, endeared themselves to Jane's crew. They'd been lucky. If the *Speroancora* had been destined to crash-land somewhere, it'd been fortunate to land on Pliga, where the people were kind, generous, and capable. The crew, human and sectilian, had gathered in the ship's dining hall in preparation for heading up to the nearest segment of the Tree, and the conversation had turned toward pligan syntax.

"They talk like Yoda," Alan said. He was smirking, completely certain in his conviction. This clearly amused him greatly.

The Tree—alternately called Existence or Optimal Existence —was an architecturally stunning interconnected set of structures grown from, in, and supported by a worldwide network of cloned trees. The trees themselves were dramatic. Larger in diameter than the largest sequoias, their massive black trunks suspended the pligans' crystalline cities one hundred feet and more above ground.

Their foliage was dark, almost black, and their leaves were broad and dense. This was because Pliga's sun was a red dwarf. The light from this kind of star was far less intense than Sol's and more toward the less-energetic infrared spectrum, forcing the vegetation to evolve more pigments to harvest as much light as possible and reflect far less. The people of Pliga lived and worked in these structures, rarely coming down to the ground.

Thankfully, the pligans had been making an exception for the *Speroancora* and the *Oblignatus*, both of which had been badly damaged in a skirmish with a group of rogue kuboderans—and the subsequent crash landing, which they'd barely survived. The pligans were using their vast knowledge of materials science and engineering to repair both ships. Today, a pligan named Gili was going to show the crew how some of these materials were created by the Tree.

"Naw. Not like Yoda. That's nothing like Yoda," Ron said, shaking his head. Ron was generally agreeable, a typical astronaut, so Jane took notice when he challenged Alan.

"It's exactly like Yoda!" Alan looked affronted. "Tell him, Jane."

Jane inhaled sharply and raised her eyebrows. "Yoda?"

Ron roared with laughter, doubling over and pointing at Alan.

Alan made a long-suffering face. "Lady, we are going to have to nerd you up when we get back to Earth." Alan was an engineer and took his fandoms very seriously. It was a fascination they didn't share and was among the smaller challenges in their budding relationship.

Jane frowned, trying to remember the character fully. "Yoda was one of the Muppets, right?"

"He's a puppet, Jane. There's a difference. Actually, he transcends puppetry. I can't believe you haven't watched that movie. Everyone has watched it."

2

Jane raised her eyebrows. "I've watched *Star Wars*. I just haven't watched it fifty-seven times, like you have."

"Forty-three," Alan grumbled. "And we're talking about *The Empire Strikes Back*, for the record."

Ajaya's lips were twisted in a suppressed smile. "Yoda uses unusual sentence construction, doesn't he? It's out of order compared to standard English. I don't know if that's how the pligans speak, but I am eager to find out." Ajaya, the crew's doctor, had recently emerged from the healing gel of the sanalabrium. A nearly fatal injury, incurred while retrieving a sample from a booby-trapped ship, had kept her submerged for months. Today would be her first outing to meet the pligans.

Recognition hit Jane fully. "Oh, yes. Yes. I remember that now. It's a pet subject among linguists. It's a clever device to make the character seem more alien. But there actually are a few languages in Brazil that use that construction, like Nadëb. It is organized as object-subject-verb rather than English's more standard subject-verb-object construct—although poets like Shakespeare and Whitman have played with syntax this way for hundreds of years to work within a meter or for rhyme or rhythm." She realized she'd gone off on a linguistic tangent and everyone's eyes were glazing over. "As a standard construction, it's very rare."

"And...?" Alan said, leaning forward like he was waiting. He gestured with his hand, urging her to continue to speak.

"What?" Jane asked, her brow furrowing.

"And that's also how the pligans speak," Alan said, with a flourish of his fingers.

Jane shook her head. "No, it's not."

Ron guffawed and clapped his hands.

"Well, not always, anyway," she amended. "I'm not saying they never do. Their speech patterns are very individualized, in my observation."

"I think it's like poetry," Ron said. "The other day, when I mentioned I was thirsty, Gili led me to a fountain and said to me, 'Distinguishing the need when water is quenching.' It's Mensententia, but it's barely understandable without some kind of context I just don't have yet."

Alan leaned back against a table and folded his arms. "That's not how Bigu talks to me. Bigu talks like Yoda."

Jane put a hand on Alan's arm and squeezed. "If we see Bigu today, I will seek her out for conversation."

Ron eyed Alan. "One hundred bucks says Jane decides Bigu doesn't speak like Yoda."

Alan narrowed his eyes, then stood up and held out his hand. "You have yourself a wager, my friend."

They shook.

Ron said in a funny falsetto voice, "Easy money, this is. Hrm."

Ajaya ignored them and looked at Jane, curious. "Is it a dialect of Mensententia, Jane?"

"No. They use the same words and the words seem to mean the same things—they simply express themselves differently. Their usage reflects cultural influence, or perhaps a different way of thinking. And they aren't often in touch with other Mensententic-speaking cultures, so they may have developed some idiosyncrasies. I've thought of about twenty dissertation topics in linguistics that could be done here so far. It's fascinating."

This time on Pliga, though not entered under the best of circumstances, had been extremely interesting. Still, a frustrated sense of urgency was pushing at her to get moving. Kai'Memna had given the Swarm the coordinates for all of the planets in the galaxy inhabited by sentients. She needed to get to Terac, the galaxy's central governing planet, to warn the people there. Something had to be done to prepare for the Swarm's invasions, or a lot of innocent people would die.

4

They'd managed to dispatch Kai'Memna before he could transmit the location of Earth to the Swarm, but Sectilius was vulnerable, completely unable to defend itself. And Jane had no idea how well equipped other planets might be to resist the behemoth insect scourge. The repair work to the *Speroancora* was taking a great deal of time, however, and couldn't be rushed no matter how much she might want that.

The pligans had a unique method of manufacture. They were biological engineers. She wasn't sure she'd interpreted everything they'd said to her correctly, but it seemed that the Tree somehow grew everything they needed. They said they genetically programmed special nodes of the Tree to create things out of various polymers, and right now the Tree was growing plating for the *Speroancora*'s outer hull. She wasn't sure what that meant exactly and was very excited to see the production process in person.

Based on what she'd seen so far, though, she didn't doubt their engineering prowess. Even Alan was impressed with their ability to manufacture materials. All of the interior work on the *Speroancora* was complete. Brai's habitat had been repaired, even improved upon, and was ready for his full-time return.

After hearing about their encounter with Kai'Memna in orbit around their planet, the pligans had insisted on rebuilding the outer hull with a light and durable material that would work comparably to the passive-solar-collection plates and extruded materials that had been buffeted and broken off during their descent onto Pliga and impact with the ocean.

Alan had run tests on samples and had determined that the new hull was worth any additional weight and the time to grow it. They could still continue to create a nanite escutcheon for added protection, but these polymer materials were pretty amazing stuff, according to him, and an excellent backup, considering how long it would take to manufacture enough nanites for the job.

Some of the plating had already been mounted on the exterior of the ship. Rather than abutting edge to edge and creating seams, they overlapped the plates and chemically welded them together—she was assured this was not even remotely like gluing—in a configuration that resembled scales. She'd only seen the effect once, and briefly, on a rare calm day. It had induced a smile. The *Speroancora* was looking more and more like a sea creature all the time. When this project was complete, the ship would look very different from the way it had when they'd found it in their solar system. The swooping extrusions were gone. In their place: smooth, glittering, purplish-black, transparent scales.

Jane noted that Jaross, Ryliuk, and Pledor—three of the five sectilian members of her crew—were finishing up their meal and cleaning up. Pledor had put out an elaborate spread from the Greenspace Deck, saying he wanted to eat a big meal before going up to the Tree. He complained that the ubiquitous sap the pligans frequently offered them for sustenance did not agree with his digestive system, and he wasn't alone, though Pledor, formerly the Gistraedor Dux of a sectilian enclave, frequently found things to complain about.

Schlewan, a sectilian medical master, had tested several samples of the sap and found no dangerous compounds or pathogenic contaminants. What it did consist of was a large percentage of a family of difficult-to-digest carbohydrates. This apparently suited the pligan digestive tract perfectly. It was all she'd ever seen them consume. Schlewan had concluded that most sentients would be uncomfortable if they tried to ingest more than a small quantity.

Jane never refused the drink in order to avoid offending her hosts, but took tiny sips at Schlewan's suggestion. She liked the way it tasted, and it didn't bother her in small amounts. It made her think of very sweet floral hibiscus tea with a hint of licorice, brown sugar, and a light estery aftertaste, sort of like banana.

While that might seem to be an odd combination, it was tasty and refreshing. She thought that if it were fermented, it might make a nice wine or beer that was more digestible for humans and sectilians.

Schlewan entered and gathered some food cubes into a small container. It was time to go, but Tinor, the youngest member of the crew, was nowhere in sight. Jane frowned. In her experience it wasn't like a sectilian to be late.

Under normal circumstances Jane would have simply asked Brai, the kuboderan ship's navigator, where Tinor was and what she was up to. But Brai was out exploring the ocean with Ei'Pio— the kuboderan navigator of the *Oblignatus* who had single-handedly prevented the destruction of the *Speroancora*—and Jane didn't want to interrupt them. Brai wasn't keeping tabs on all of them as closely as he would have had he been in his internal environmental enclosure, but that was fine. She kept a very light link with sectilian Mind Master Ryliuk instead.

Brai had come back to assist with some of the initial repairs before the pligans helped them move the *Speroancora* more fully onto land. Now only a small part of the tail section was submerged, and a special access chamber had been installed so he could come and go as he pleased. He was still adjusting to the radical changes in his squillae code that had once suppressed his emotions and controlled his behavior. It was the first time in his adult life that he'd been allowed to voluntarily leave his tank inside the ship. He deserved a vacation after centuries of work without breaks of any kind.

Jane crossed over to Schlewan. Before she could say a word, Schlewan said, "Tinor is waiting near the exit."

Jane nodded. No matter what she said to the young woman, Tinor continued to avoid contact with her whenever possible. Jane had accepted Brai's explanation that Tinor wanted to stay beneath Jane's notice until she could accomplish something that would capture Jane's attention in a positive way after the gaffe with Tinor's coming-of-age gift, but this seemed a bit far to go. When they were together, Tinor acted as though nothing were wrong, but she persisted in this avoidance whenever possible.

Jane hadn't made it an order that they would meet in the crew dining hall, but she had said it, no one had disagreed, and everyone else had come at the appointed time. She shrugged it off. It was just a minor irritation, nothing truly troublesome.

"Okay, let's go then." She gestured for her crew to follow her down the corridor.

Ron put his arm protectively around Ajaya as they walked. "Are you ready to see your very first gray sky?"

Ajaya smiled. "I am indeed."

Visually, Pliga's sky took some getting used to. The whole world was colored like a sepia-toned photograph, only occasionally punctuated here and there with a yellow, orange, or red tone bright enough to stand out from the endless sea of drab gray, purplish brown and black. There weren't even any sunrises or sunsets to add color to the pale sky. It was always day on this side of Pliga. The planet was tidally locked with its dim star.

They reached the hatch and there was Tinor, waiting, with her gaze averted.

"Brace yourself," Ron told Ajaya. "It can sometimes be hurricane-force winds. It's a short walk, though. Just hold on to the rope. I'll be right there with you."

Jane unlatched the hatch and swung it open. "Not so bad at the moment," she said.

It was a short hop down and then thirty yards or so to the nearest structure with a ground egress point. The weather might be a little tamer today, but the wind still howled and sucked her breath away even when she was prepared for it.

They'd placed a rope between the ship and the small elevator column so they wouldn't get lost or separated. The wind often made it hard to see. Jane ducked her head and tried to keep her eyes open at a squint. She heard something behind her that sounded like a scream swallowed by the wind. She turned to see Ajaya and Alan engulfed in what looked like a purplish-brown tarp. It whipped violently around the edges. Ron was fighting to knock it loose.

Jane grabbed another edge of it and joined him in an attempt to push it over their heads. It was thick, leathery material. Finally they worked it free. For a second, it started to lift Jane into the air, like a parachute. Then Ron let go, and before she could do the same, it whipped savagely in her grip and tore off, leaving her left arm red and sore, with a chunk of the material still in her hand.

She shouted, "Everyone okay?"

Everyone was nodding. They finished the trek across and into the glasslike structure. As soon as they were through the opening, there was instant relief from the wind. Pausing a moment to catch her breath, Jane looked down at the leathery material she still held. There was something wet glistening at the broken edges of it. She held it up to her nose and sniffed. Floral and sugary with an aniselike note. She turned it over and noticed one side was paler than the other and had thick veins. This had to be a piece of one of the Tree's leaves. She frowned and set it down in a corner to pick up on the way back. She couldn't know if carrying it around might give offense, and it seemed wise to be careful. The Tree seemed to have mystical, almost religious significance to the pligans. But she did want to take it back to the ship for Schlewan to analyze.

There was something very special about this tree.

2

BRAI ROAMED the ocean in the vicinity of the *Speroancora* with Pio, extending their range in one direction or another with each excursion. They jetted in surges and then drifted, taking in what the locale offered, stopping frequently to hunt for food.

A lumbering marine mammal followed them sometimes as they moved through the bay to get to the open ocean. Timid, it would remain just out of reach until something else caught its interest or it got hungry and went away. Pio sometimes devoted an hour to coaxing it closer, stimulating the primitive anipraxic structures in its tiny brain.

Though the animal wasn't sentient enough to carry on a conversation, it was an interesting exercise in interspecies communication and patience. Pio had made some progress with it, as she was being exceedingly gentle, and it did seem the comical-looking animal was growing bolder and venturing a little closer to them as the days passed. A couple of times it had even seemed to invite Pio to play, though when she'd tried, the skittish animal had vanished. They hadn't seen the animal yet today, but he could tell Pio was keeping her eye out for it. She'd noticed an old wound on one of its fins, which worried her. She felt that it swam even more awkwardly than it was supposed to.

Brai's first impression of Pio, that she was timid and skittish, couldn't have been more wrong. That had been circumstance. Pio's primary personality trait was kindness. She had a great capacity for caring, but could be fierce when necessary. Her thoughts were full of curiosity and warmth. Their differences delighted him.

Pio preferred the flavor of a certain species of fish, and they often sought it out. If the fish had a name on Pliga, neither of them had any way of learning it. If it had a color, they had no way of knowing that either. Pliga's red sun mostly emitted longer wavelengths of light that were unable to penetrate sea water very deeply. In the upper layers they sometimes saw brightly colored fish, but with any depth they had to rely on their finely honed visual acuity, evolved for deep, dark waters on some distant unknown world, and enhanced by their cybernetics and nanites.

Here, the ocean was already dark, cold, and mysterious. It was exciting and invigorating. These excursions evoked buried memories of watching his sectilian crews go off on science expeditions in the past—except this time he was the one doing the exploring.

On some deep feral level he relished it.

He stayed alert but felt little fear. After months of these outings, they'd yet to encounter any dangerous predators. They'd seen a colossal plankton-sifting beast, but it had ignored them. It had not been sentient. Most of the creatures they'd come across were relatively small and innocuous.

Brai sensed movement in his peripheral vision and redirected his funnel to turn and look. Pio had already taken off in that direction. As he got closer he could see that it was a school of her favorite fish. He held back to watch her, as he had no interest in catching any for himself.

She held herself in a compact, torpedo-shaped form, letting a bolus of water through her siphon peter out slowly so that her momentum pushed her into the middle of the school in a nonthreatening manner. She opened her arms ever so slightly and deployed her tentacles lightning quick, before the fish even knew she was among them. They scattered, most of them never knowing why the school had dispersed, only the panic communicated through the movement of the others around them. The enormous school reformed nearby, where Pio took a few more in the same manner. She repeated this process until she'd had her fill.

She rejoined him, her mind full of satiety and pleasure, and they continued on toward a continental shelf where Brai sometimes hunted for crustaceans or jellies, though truth be told he was relying more and more on his bland premade nutriment now that his facilities had been repaired.

He struggled with his conscience daily whenever hunger pangs struck. On one hand, the premade food was convenient, easy, and nutritionally complete. It was technology used in a positive way to make his life simple so his energies could be expended on higher-level thinking and complex actions that his wild brethren probably could not even conceptualize.

On the other hand, eating it seemed like acquiescence, complaisance, a betrayal of his own people. The sectilian rations had become a symbol to him of the forced confinement, the lack of personal freedoms—all the way down to the banishment of his very emotions.

And then there was the fact that eating wild food required killing. It required breaking of protective shells, rending of flesh, spilling of lifeblood, and crunching of bones. He had some difficulty getting past that. The animals he took were not capable of the kind of complicated action or thought that he was, but did that make them any less deserving of life? Was he so important that he could take life because he was hungry?

It was all jumbled up with Kai'Memna's message. What did a kuboderan want? What did a kuboderan need or deserve? Was it a privilege to be taken and trained as a gubernaviti as they'd been told, or was it a prison?

Perhaps these questions were moot now. The vast fleet of Sectilius was gone, though many others of his kind were used in other ships all over the galaxy, originally sold on the black market by a less scrupulous sectilian individual and bred in captivity centuries prior. Some of those kuboderans could be living under better circumstances than he had been, but it seemed probable to him that most were not.

In all likelihood Kai'Memna had found and destroyed the world where sectilian mind masters trained captive kuboderan paralarvae. Perhaps he had even found the kuboderan home world. Brai wondered if that knowledge had died with Kai'Memna or if he'd shared it with any others. He intended to ask Jane to survey the wreckage of the *Portacollus* to look for any surviving databanks.

Jane still intended to seek out any marooned kuboderans remaining scattered around the galaxy and give them the choice to find their own crews or take a human or sectilian Quasador Dux once Alan set them free by breaking the yoke. Kai'Memna had done such a thorough job, however, that Brai wondered if there even were any others still out there, trapped, as he had been for so long. Brai had been spared Kai'Memna's impossible choice of joining his genocidal movement or death, but that was only by sheer coincidence. The secrecy surrounding Terra had kept the *Speroancora*'s location out of the official record, and the planet's remote location had prevented accidental discovery.

Brai hadn't realized he'd stopped moving, completely lost in thought and unaware of his surroundings, until he saw Pio's large, unblinking eye loom near his own. One of her arms reached out to him and she used the smooth side to caress his mantle. The rest of her arms curled around the both of them gracefully.

"Distraction could be dangerous in these waters, Brai," Pio said.

A cloud of bioluminescent plankton drifted around them. The pink light they emitted reflected off her silvery skin. He twined one of his thick arms around one of her more-delicate limbs and savored the intimacy. He was unsure if this kind of contact was natural for his species, but they both liked it. He and Pio had learned this kind of warmth from their contact with sectilians and humans.

Alien wants and needs had become their own.

After much reflection into his more base urges, he was fairly certain now: mating among wild kuboderans involved blind attraction by pheromones, bumping into another individual in the dark, a moment of panic and uncertainty that the individual was actually of the opposite sex, grappling violently with all eight arms and both tentacles to maneuver the female until she was beak to beak, stabbing blindly with one's terminal organ and hydraulically injecting spermatophores into her arms as she fought to break free. Each wormlike spermatophore contained thousands of spermatozoa and, like a parasite, would burrow even deeper into her flesh, releasing chemicals to trigger her reproductive organs to mature ovum.

Humans would call that act rape, and they'd be right.

It was distasteful. Thankfully he had more self-control and rational thought than that. He would not do that to her.

What he had with Pio was gentle and safe. They worked together, shared thoughts and emotions and...this. This tenderness. Perhaps it wasn't kuboderan. Perhaps it was better. They'd become something greater through their contact with other species. This act of cultural appropriation could be forgiven, he thought. Though it was nothing like the recreational lovemaking Jane shared with Alan—there was no burst of intense pleasure to culminate their moments together—it was enough. It was contentment, and that was so much more than either of them had ever had before.

Soon the pligans would finish the repair work on both of the ships, and the two of them would be separated. This brief vacation would be over and he'd be isolated once again. He had mixed feelings about that.

"We'll be useful. We will do good," she said, picking up his train of thought. He kept himself open to her now as a matter of habit. Once they'd gotten past that first hurdle of trust, it'd been easy. She was as transparent as glass. Her memories, her musings, her dreams and nightmares, all of it. She'd borne as much pain as he had over the centuries. Probably more. She was a lovely mosaic of warmth.

They were healing each other. They were each learning who they truly were without a yoke constricting their every movement, their every thought. They were maturing into themselves.

"We could stay here," he said, though they both knew he didn't mean it.

"And strand Jane?"

"After Jane warns Terac. We could come back. She'd let me go."

"She would. That's true," Pio agreed. There was melancholy in her mental touch, a strand of wondering what it could be like. He latched on to that. He wanted to pretend, at least for a while, that something like this bliss could last.

"Some might say this, here, is true freedom," he said.

But he'd tainted it. He couldn't help it.

"Kai'Memna said that." She ground her beak. Brai had hurt her unintentionally. "Freedom is not at the bottom of a gravity well. Not for us. We've been changed. We need the stars. We

16

need a community. Even Kai'Memna wouldn't give up his ship for the taste of fish."

He conceded silently and turned his gaze away from her in shame. It was selfish to want it all. To want both her and Jane.

"They need you," she said softly, turning him back toward her. "Besides, give us a couple of decades down here and we'd get so bored, we'd tear each other apart."

He didn't believe that. "They need both of us."

Her mental laugh was a tinkle. "That's debatable. I'm extraneous. But hopefully I'll serve a purpose eventually."

"You saved all of us," he admonished. She needed to be reminded of her worth, so she wouldn't despair. She'd lost too much.

"I had to."

The statement hung heavily between them. Pio feared being stranded alone more than anything else in the universe.

He didn't blame her. They shared that fear.

3

October 12, 2017
Two weeks after Jane Holloway's Global Announcement

ZARA HAMPTON silently thanked the house once again for the squeaky floorboard in the hallway just outside the family room. She closed the laptop silently, slid the afghan over it, and opened a waiting paperback book toward the last third of its pages—all in one fluid, practiced motion. The television squealed in the background, some silly cartoon that kids her age supposedly liked. It was good cover.

Her mother stood in the doorway for a long moment, watching her.

Zara pretended she didn't know that her mother was there, her eyes darting over the pages, mimicking reading. What she was really thinking about was the last private message she'd gotten from Becky before shutting the laptop, cajoling her to stop chickening out and download something alien related from her dad's laptop already.

She wished she'd never told a soul her dad worked for NASA.

It was creating unwanted pressure from her friends, both online and IRL. She felt like she was being ganged up on. They wouldn't let go of the idea, were sure it would be easy for her to accomplish.

She was less sure. She'd never tried to steal anything from her parents before. Could she really do it? Was it even possible? Was it really harmless? Would it make her a bad daughter? Would she survive the guilt? What would happen if she was caught?

"Didn't you hear me calling?"

Zara jumped. She'd already kinda forgotten Mom was there. "Hm?"

"Dinner."

Zara blinked and picked up her bookmark, careful not to move too much under her mother's scrutiny, fearful she might inadvertently reveal what she'd actually been doing. Her daily time online was tightly restricted to a desktop in the open-concept living room where her parents could watch the screen. They didn't know she'd found this run-down old laptop in the hall closet. It had been miserably slow before she'd run a disk refrag, reset it to factory settings using online tutorials, and removed all bloatware and unnecessary programs.

It was much better now—adequate for social media, messaging, surfing the Web, reading free e-books, watching the occasional cat video—and most importantly checking online news sites.

It was necessary. Mainstream media were unreliable. Everyone online said so. The media toed the government line, only gave out information the government wanted the public to see. She could see the evidence for this in her own home every day, because it was clear her dad knew something no one else did. She could see it in his face, in his reactions to anything anybody said when the topic inevitably strayed to current events. Most of the rest of the world seemed very, very confused though. It was easy to see why.

"What are we having?"

"Oh, sweetie. It's your dad's night to cook. You know what we're having." Her mom chuckled.

"Stir-fry." Zara scrunched up her face. "Not too spicy?"

"Nope. I didn't let him put in *any* sriracha. He can add it to his own." The last was tossed over her mother's shoulder as she headed back down the hall.

Squeak.

Zara slipped off the couch, silently sliding the laptop underneath to retrieve after dinner, if possible. The battery life was terrible and it needed to be recharged. She'd have to smuggle it into her bedroom tonight to do that, which was normally easy to do. She headed for the kitchen and heard her mother say, "Nose in a book again."

"Like mother, like daughter," her dad replied. He was probably smiling.

On impulse Zara turned back to her backpack, which lay propped against the couch, and unzipped the tiny front compartment. She fished out a thumb drive her mother had bought her for school that she hadn't used yet. It probably wouldn't have enough storage to save a big file, but she had to try. If this didn't work, she'd have to find a way to buy a 1 TB drive and try again.

She slipped the drive into the front pocket of her jeans. If the opportunity arose, she *would* take it. She wouldn't lose her nerve. She'd do it and she knew how. She'd been watching him. He always set his ID card on the counter with his keys alongside the tiny black notebook where he kept his passwords written down because NASA made him change them so frequently that he couldn't keep track of them any other way. Her heart sped up, and a jangly, uneasy feeling put some tension in her muscles.

As she entered the kitchen, her dad held up the remote and turned off the evening news. There was a scowl on his face as he picked up the still-sizzling wok to carry into the dining room. They didn't want her to see the turmoil the world was in, but it was all over the internet and it was all anyone talked about, even thirteen-year-old kids. She played along because there was no other option. They had good intentions but they couldn't really shelter her from it. It was far too big.

"Hey, Daddy," Zara said, feeling twinges of fear and guilt pinching her insides as she wrapped her arms around her dad's waist and gave him a quick squeeze. He protested, holding the hot wok well away from his body. She ignored that and grabbed the pitcher of iced tea to carry into the dining room, noting that Dad's laptop was still open on the counter, having gone into screensaver mode. It was out of the line of sight of the dining-room table. And there was his ID card and that little black notebook.

If she ate fast...

"How was school today?" he asked, the same question he asked every day at dinner.

"Mrs. Jeffries has the flu so there was a sub in math. We played a game."

He smiled and nodded, then shot her a serious look. "Those kids giving you any more trouble on the bus?" He asked that every day too. Both her parents worried about her being bullied. They lived in a multiethnic, multiracial area of the city, which minimized the chances of racism rearing its ugly head but didn't eliminate the possibility. There was nowhere entirely safe from that.

She felt her expression fall but then screwed it up quickly into a semblance of nonchalance. "No, Daddy."

The truth was they still taunted her or slapped her butt or flicked her in the head when they entered or exited the bus, especially if she was unlucky enough to have to sit on the aisle, but the worst of them were separated from her now by eight rows and had other kids to harass thanks to her parents' intervention with the bus driver. It did make her day a little easier, but didn't really eliminate the constant anxiety. There was nothing they could do about that, so there was no reason to bring it up. It was just something to bear.

She'd never told anyone how it had started. She'd been a target before and had learned to keep her head down. Her preference was to sit by the window, scoot down, and brace her knees on the back of the seat in front of her so that she could just barely see out the window. Keeping out of sight kept her from being noticed, mostly. She normally read during the trip home, looking up occasionally to see where they were on the route and only sitting up and rushing off the bus seconds before her stop.

One day she'd been taken by surprise—by her first menstrual period.

She hadn't even realized what had happened until she got home, though she knew her pants felt oddly damp. She'd assumed it was sweat because the bus was hot and the seats were vinyl. It hadn't been sweat. A rusty red stain had spread across the seat of her faded jeans, drawn there by gravity in that slouched position. Now kids offered her tampons regularly, asked her when her moon party was going to be, or called her Bloody Mary. She was a target once again.

Growing breasts was hard enough to deal with, but this humiliation was nearly unbearable. She hardly spoke to anyone but her parents and online friends. It seemed like everyone was just waiting to find some way to torment her.

Her body had betrayed her once. She didn't trust it not to do it again. She felt tight inside and out. Muscles, jaw, stomach. So tight sometimes it felt like she was fraying around the edges. It seemed like that feeling would never go away.

Both her parents said that being her age was hard. Kids didn't have the self-control that grown-ups eventually mastered, but based on overheard conversations, Zara guessed that grown-ups still had to deal with this junk. It just wasn't as overt when a person got older.

And it wasn't just bullies. Her friends were moody, capricious, and could be equally vicious. If they thought they had a shot at hanging out with the more popular kids, she was dead to them. It could be as simple as the color of shirt she wore on any given day. She might say the wrong words, talk to the wrong person, or admit to liking something they thought was dumb. There didn't seem to be any rhyme or reason to it sometimes. She just tried to get by.

She suppressed a sigh and spooned some rice onto her plate. She had to be careful or her parents would make her talk about it. She had to act as normal as possible or they'd bring up seeing a counselor again, and she couldn't imagine telling all this junk to some adult do-gooder with a plastic smile and fake caring attitude.

She had a ton of online friends who understood a whole lot better than any adult seemed to. These other kids were living the same kinds of lives. They didn't give her platitudes. They said, "Ikr? Ppl are so LAME." Then they told her about *their* stupid friends. That meant more. They were her real peeps. For life.

"Your shirt looks a little tight, Z. We should probably go shopping for clothes this weekend with Grandma," her mom observed tiredly as she poured iced tea for herself.

Zara frowned and looked down at herself. She thought she looked fine, but her mom wasn't necessarily wrong. Baggier shirts would definitely make her oddly shaped, A-cup-sized bulges less noticeable, which would probably be more comfortable. It was gross how people's eyes lingered on her chest, trying to see her budding baby boobies.

Her dad cleared his throat and added another dash of sriracha to his plate. "Growing like a weed, baby girl."

Both her parents looked exhausted. Mom would go into the hospital for a night shift soon, but had been up and reading when Zara got home from school. She took that shift so she could maximize her time with Zara despite its drawbacks. Dad would probably work up until his very late bedtime.

"How's work going, Dad?" she asked. "Solved that tough problem yet?"

Her dad didn't talk about work anymore. She didn't think he was allowed to. Not since Jane Holloway's Global Announcement. But she knew what he was working on. Everyone with any sense did. Every scientist at NASA had to be working on decrypting Jane's mysterious sectilian download, no matter what Tom Rather said on the six o'clock news about it being a hoax.

The download was all anyone talked about. The rumors called it the Second Space Race. They said that every country had put all their smartest scientists on it, competing to be the first to break into the files, put the puzzle pieces together, or at least find the blueprints Jane Holloway had mentioned in her message. The online media said that no one had a clue where to start with the massive file. It was all gibberish. Jane had apparently forgotten to give them a key in her eagerness to start her adventure.

Her dad sighed deeply and rubbed his face, shaking his head. Her mother's eyes flashed a warning at her. She'd been asked more than once not to talk about Dad's work.

Dad wouldn't admit that he was working on the sectilian download. She guessed he wasn't supposed to. It was classified. He wasn't allowed to admit it was real, not even to his own family.

Jane's message was supposed to be for everyone on Earth, had been broadcast across the planet on television simultaneously in lots of different languages, but few had the capability during the first viewing to download the accompanying transmission of data. Then the satellites transmitting it were shut down so they couldn't keep broadcasting it like Jane had intended for them to. At least that was what some people thought had happened. The consensus seemed to be that it was mainly governments and possibly some universities that had it. There was all kinds of speculation about who had what and how close they were to decrypting it.

Zara believed all of this was true. Her dad had changed after the Global Announcement. He'd always worked hard, but now he did nothing but work. He was worried all the time, preoccupied. Maybe it was just her imagination, but to her it seemed like he really wanted to tell them something important, but couldn't.

It was all so messed up.

It was really contrary to the spirit of Jane's message too—that humanity's first contact with an alien race over a lifetime ago was supposed to have given them amazing technological gifts in a spirit of peace and cooperation. The sectilians had just all gotten killed by some mysterious plague. That wasn't humanity's fault.

Zara believed in Jane. She just *knew* Jane really was an astronaut who'd been sent to an alien spaceship in the asteroid belt. She believed that Jane really had sent a download full of important information and blueprints of advanced alien technology to help the human race survive an uncertain future. The way the government had screwed all of this up was disrespectful to the people who had risked their lives to go on that mission.

But she could guess why they'd done it. They didn't want people to panic when they realized that there were other planets out there in the galaxy, all full of different kinds of alien people. And Jane had said some of them might have bad intentions. Earth might be in danger. They wanted to spare people that fear, but they hadn't. They'd only made it all so much worse.

The proof was on her dad's laptop.

Her fingers crept to the lump in her jeans' pocket. The thumb drive.

Subsequent airings of the Global Announcement online and on television were video only, always aired with a disclaimer or a theory or a crackpot scheme. So far the data file hadn't been leaked to the public as far as she knew. So far. It had only been a little over two weeks.

Two weeks since the world had changed completely.

Since that initial broadcast people had gone flippin' crazy. The new president had given an address claiming it was a hoax created by a mentally ill crackpot determined to disrupt the world economy and the welfare of Americans. Saturday Night Out had created a Jane Half-the-Way character who was a sexy, clownish oaf, often tipsy, and always frolicking with little green guys, little gray guys, guys with pointy ears, Jabba the Hutt, etc., etc. The clips were all over YouTV, but Zara didn't think they were funny.

A lot of smart people had gone on record saying they believed the announcement was real—that the mission to Mars had really been a mission to an alien ship in the Greater Asteroid Belt. And they gave out a lot of convincing evidence to prove their points.

As a result, the average person didn't know what to believe. Everyone seemed on edge, waiting for something to happen. Social media was blanketed with outraged people calling for the government to tell the truth or to punish Jane Holloway. Some people went straight-up religious, preaching about the end of times. A kid at school had told her she was going to hell because she didn't go to church every Sunday. It was nutty. And scary.

There'd been riots and looting in big cities across the globe. The media were constantly talking about how crime was up. Usage of mental-health services was up. Accidents were up. Suicide rates were up. Per-capita alcohol consumption was up. A lot of people were walking around like zombies. Human beings liked being the center of the universe and all this uncertainty about whether they were or weren't was driving everyone batshit.

Her school had closed for two days after the first broadcast. When they went back, her teachers had been very grave, and many still were. Her math teacher's hands shook and her voice warbled. Sometimes tears streaked down her cheeks as she worked through a long problem on the whiteboard. Zara heard Mrs. Jeffries had broken down in front of an algebra class the day before. That was probably the real reason why she hadn't shown up today, not the flu. Zara wished people would just hold it together, work *together*, instead of all this fear.

Jane had told them not to be afraid. Jane believed in them. She'd said so.

Zara agreed with Jane. The government should tell the truth, and they should just let everyone have the download. There were tons of stories out there of non-expert people figuring things out. Even kids. Finding quasars, inventing cancer-screening tests, or figuring out a way to clean up the floating islands of plastic junk in the oceans cheaply and efficiently. They should let everyone work on the sectilian data. They just *should*.

Yeah, it was kinda scary. But if people felt like they were helping in some way, it might make them feel better and not act so flippin' crazy.

She was trying to shovel down her meal as fast as possible so she could get to her dad's computer while he and Mom lingered over dinner. In her haste, Zara swallowed a hunk of dry chicken breast without chewing it, and it got stuck. She gulped some water then coughed as she aspirated some chewed-up chicken and water.

Her mom leaned toward her. Her dad reached over and put his hand on her back. "You okay, Zara?"

She nodded, eyes watering, and drank some more water. "Just

went down wrong," she croaked. She looked at her plate. Only two pieces of soggy broccoli left in a sea of salty brown sauce. "May I be excused?"

Her mother raised her eyebrows and looked pointedly at the broccoli.

Zara stabbed both pieces with a fork, and stuffed them in her mouth.

Her mother nodded and smiled at her father.

Zara got up, still chewing, and pushed in her chair. Her parents' conversation continued in muted tones as she walked her plate into the kitchen, scraped and rinsed it, then put it in the dishwasher. Then she stepped over to her dad's laptop, her hand already in her pocket, wrapped around the thumb drive.

Blood rushed in her ears. Her face felt hot.

Zara slid the drive home and tapped the touchpad. A special screen came up. She knew exactly what to do. She leaned over, wrapped her fingers around her dad's keys to keep them silent, and quickly swiped his ID card through the reader. A prompt for a password came up on the screen. She paged through the little black notebook to find the page where he'd neatly crossed off an old password and handwritten the most recent one.

Zara placed her fingers on the keyboard, ears straining for any hint of movement from the next room. She pressed the keys gently, so they were silent, carefully so she would get it right the first time. Her nerves couldn't take much more of this. Dinner was roiling around in her stomach and threatening to come back up.

She was in.

The screen went dark. Bizarre multilayer symbols in drab green flowed in different directions all over the place. When her finger landed on the touchpad, the symbol streams zoomed in and out of focus, like they were a flowing three-dimensional model and she was moving it around or moving through it or something.

If she hadn't been terrified of discovery, she might have been entranced. Was this what she was looking for? Was this a sectilian computer language?

She alt-tabbed out of the crazy soup of symbols, navigated to a directory, found the biggest folder on the laptop, called Target-Data, and clicked on it. There were tons of smaller files inside it. She barely looked at them, except to notice they were named with the same kinds of weird symbols she'd just seen. That had to be the right file. If it wasn't, she'd try again another day. She highlighted the first twenty files and saved them to the thumb drive. She'd guessed well. It filled the thumb drive almost to capacity, but she got all twenty. The download took only a few moments, though it felt like forever. She held her breath until she was lightheaded.

Finally it was done. She ejected the thumb drive and slid it free, closed everything she'd opened, and restored the application he'd been using.

A chair scraped in the dining room.

She froze.

Oh, no. She was dead. She was so dead.

The screensaver hadn't had time to come back on. If she ran out of the room, they'd hear or see her. She put the notebook and keys exactly where they'd been before, and waved her hands around, conflicted about what to do next.

"Want some coffee if I make a pot?" her mom said in the dining room. Dishes clanked together.

During the moment that her father hesitated, Zara shut the laptop, grabbed a magazine from the counter, and climbed onto a stool to look at it. She opened it to a random page and focused on breathing evenly.

"Sure," he answered. They both came into the room carrying dirty dishes.

Her mom looked at her quizzically. "What are you doing?"

Zara looked as innocent as she could. "Just reading this."

Her mom cocked an eyebrow. "*Time* magazine?"

Zara scowled. "Yeah."

Her dad slid the magazine out from under her fingertips, closer to himself, and turned it so he could see it better. "Reading up on the president's new proposed policy for health-care reform, are you?"

"Well, I just turned the page. I haven't read it yet."

"Your homework done?"

"Yes."

Her dad shooed her toward the living room. "Go smite some digital evil for an hour."

Zara forced a smile. "All right. You wanna play too?"

He looked wistfully back at her for a moment, like he really wanted to. Her hopes rose just a little, sending her emotions off-balance. She loved playing games with him, but she felt so guilty. "I wish I could, baby girl. Too much work."

She let her dejection show and trudged off for the living room, her hand hovering over her bulging pocket and the thumb drive inside with its contraband data.

4

AS JANE and her crew moved past the baffles at the entrance of the Tree, the sound of the gale died away to just dull white noise in the background. This was one of many similar columns that dropped down between the massive tree trunks, allowing contact with the ground for entry and egress, though most pligans rarely used them. Typically they traveled from trunk to trunk via the complex network of skywalks. They rarely had need to go down to the ground.

They regularly offered to build a skywalk directly to a *Speroancora* hatch, but Jane consistently refused the proposal as politely as possible because she'd found out the materials required would use the same manufacturing system as the scales they were applying to the hull of the ship. She didn't want to delay their departure any more than necessary or add to the debt she owed the pligans.

Being detained this long was stressful, but necessary. They wouldn't get very far in a ship that couldn't hold air, and the extra shielding the pligans were providing seemed paramount, given the encounters they'd had thus far. But sometimes all she could think about was the Swarm, the havoc it might be wreaking on some innocent people before she could properly warn the United Sentient Races at Terac. At times it felt unbearable to have these pleasant cultural exchanges, as though they didn't have anything pressing to do.

But pligans simply didn't experience urgency. It was maddening when work on the ships stalled. They just didn't seem to understand what was at stake. It was doubly frustrating that Jane had no material way to repay them. Even if Jane had had money, Pliga didn't have a money-based economy as far as she could tell. They didn't participate in galactic commerce or even communicate with the galaxy at large. Everything they needed, they made. Regardless, the short walk outside wasn't bad enough to warrant the time or materials it would take to build a skywalk.

When Jane had once asked Gili about traveling overland, Gili had seemed aghast. "The foot has been making for Existence. Existence has been making for the foot. They are making for each other, in tandem." At the time Jane hadn't understood, but she thought she did now. Gili was saying that the Tree and the pligan people had evolved together. Even though most of the time pligans now walked over the smooth, transparent materials of their architectural structures instead of clinging to the bark of the tree as their ancestors must have, those materials were made by the tree, and therefore were an extension of it, and more natural to Gili than even the ground itself.

Poor Ryliuk, over seven feet tall, was so uncomfortable inside many sections of the pligan habitat because it had not been constructed with his size in mind. Most pligans stood at just over four feet tall, and their structures were sized appropriately. He was forced to stoop almost everywhere they went inside. Even Jane had to duck sometimes because branches transversed the crystalline structures overhead.

Just now, Ryliuk was wedged into a corner, trying to make himself as small as possible. She motioned him over to the elevator. There were open spaces above where he'd be more comfortable.

Gili was waiting for them, awake this time, as the elevator opened. The pligans had evolved from amphibious creatures, and reminded Jane of tree frogs on Earth. Gili was mostly a shimmering bronze color with a pale, rosy-toned belly. His face came to a rounded point, marked with dark, wide stripes in a pattern that Jane had quickly come to recognize as his own personal identifying marks.

His eyes, though, were what Jane had noticed about him first. Large and luminous, with horizontal pupils, when they caught the light they sometimes looked like molten metal. And then there were the triangular peaks of skin above his upper eyelids, marking the beginning of a small ridge on each side of his face, leading down to the nostrils on his blunt nose in a V shape. She thought for some reason that those little triangular brows made the pligans seem owlish or a bit professorial. Maybe they reminded her of the wildly unkempt hairy eyebrows of a few professors she'd known over the years.

His personality added to that impression. He seemed part kindly teacher, part philosopher, part irascible old man who occasionally fell asleep if you didn't keep things interesting enough to hold his attention. He was truly none of those things because those concepts meant little here. He was pligan and she liked his company a great deal.

"Sleeping gave up, just in time," Gili said. He was referring to the fact that he'd just woken from a nap. Pligans didn't seem to have any kind of predictable biorhythms. Without the cycle of day and night, they slept whenever their bodies were tired, sometimes midconversation, if there was a lull. Their eyes would stare off into space then gradually close, and their limbs would pull up around them, making them more compact and less conspicuous, especially in darker, shadowy areas. They might sleep for an hour or three at any point around the clock. They normally returned to daily activity when they woke up, and drank sap whenever they felt hungry.

Gili's arms opened wide with palms out and fingers outstretched, displaying the large suckerlike protrusions at the end of each of four fingertips. It was his welcoming gesture.

His fleshy throat jiggled a little with excitement when he noticed Ajaya. He drew closer to her, extending his hands to her in invitation, his pupils expanding and contracting rapidly as he took her in. She moved closer, just as inquisitive. "Bringing the ultimate. A dark one. Jane is light. Fewer light than dark here, this grouping." He was always noticing things.

Jane had no idea how the pligans perceived the light spectrum or if their eyes saw colors in even remotely the same way humans did. But he'd commented on this difference in skin tone between them several times. In fact, he lumped the sectilians in with Ron because there was enough UV light on Pliga to trigger the autonomic melanin response in their skin. Jane had described them as different species, and he found that interesting, inquiring about differences and similarities, but he still seemed to group them together. He found the differences between sectilian and human less compelling than the differences between his own species and the newcomers.

It wasn't as though the pligans as a species hadn't been exposed to sectilians before. They'd had many alien visitors over the years, though they came with less frequency now and none recently. According to the ship's database, pligans were a curiosity among the USR. People came and studied their biotechnology and even took cuttings of the Tree, freely given, to their home worlds to try to replicate the results. But the Tree was very particular about the conditions it preferred and always withered and died elsewhere without pligans to tend it. And while the pligan people were not xenophobic in any way, they had no interest in leaving their planet. When Jane had asked Gili about this, he'd muttered indignantly, "Why would anyone be wanting to be living a suboptimal life?"

He frequently inquired about Jane's own home and what it was like, though. He seemed consternated that she didn't have a Tree, or something like it, of her own.

"Walking and to the producing," he said. He was already waddling away. Pligans walked something like springy penguins, though that wasn't quite right. When they fully extended their legs to reach something, they towered over humans, but they didn't do that often. Occasionally Jane saw one of them hop, usually a child, but that was rare. Mostly they kept the hinges of their knees bent, squatting comfortably whenever they stopped moving, and only elevating their bodies slightly on their elastic legs as they shuffled around with their knees bent at a forty-five-degree angle from center.

Walking over the transparent material of the flooring, especially at such a great height, took some getting used to for all of them. Jane made it a habit to not look down. Ajaya had Ron's arm in a death grip, but everyone else seemed fine. Jane quickly lost her sense of orientation as they moved through the maze of the pligan architectural structures, unsure which direction they had come from.

They passed a pligan who seemed to be struggling to walk. Their legs were set farther apart at a nearly ninety-degree angle from center, and they were holding themselves up by grasping the wall and rocking side to side rather than bringing each foot forward. They were clearly laboring under great difficulty to get where they were going, and Jane suspected that their locomotion would improve a great deal if they were to just stretch their legs out to propel themselves forward.

She bit her lip, but decided to ask about the individual once they were several turns away and she was certain they were out of earshot. She'd been struggling to think of ways to compensate the pligans for the work they were doing, and perhaps this was a way they could help. Gili so often spoke of how they lived an optimal life, but that person's gait did not seem optimal to Jane. "Gili, the person we passed back there who was having trouble walking, are they elderly or injured? Do they have a medical problem that perhaps my medical master could help with?"

Gili stopped walking and turned to look back. "That was Huna." Gili looked thoughtful for a moment, his metallic eyes rolling around in their orbits. "With each generation we are seeking mutation, this being our most important goal for us as a species, for Existence: new possibilities. This is how we are *becoming*, Jane. This is how we are growing into something better, constructing an Existence more optimal—always, more optimal. There are times when mutations will be conferring desirable traits, and, at times, undesirable traits. In the wild, traits that are advantageous make survival to reproduction more likely. This is how populations are changing. This is natural. This is how evolution is working, yes?"

Jane nodded. She followed him so far.

"There are occasions when one mutation is giving rise to both desirable and undesirable traits in one individual. Among sentients, the undesirable must be tolerated so that the desirable trait may be thriving. In time, we hope to be minimizing the bad in order to be increasing the good. You are understanding this?"

Jane contemplated what she'd learned about the Swarm and how chance genetic mutations had saved that species from extinction time and again, allowing it to reinvent itself so many times that it no longer resembled its earliest form in any way. Each subsequent mutation had allowed it to occupy another biological niche until its survival as a species was certain and it became a plague on the galaxy—definitely a negative trait if one was not a Swarm beetle.

She said, "So, Huna's leg conformation is less desirable, but Huna has another trait that is very desirable, that makes the disability worthwhile?"

Gili chirped softly. "You are understanding. We cannot always be knowing what will come of a mutation by looking only at the genes in a zygote. It is far too complicated. The genes must be expressing for us to be understanding. Huna is suffering a little, I am conceding, but is also expressing exceptional intelligence. He is among our brightest and most creative geneticists. Now he is understanding this concept better than anyone. He is not minding difficulty in walking because he is knowing his genes are making new children with more optimal lives. We are making manifest the Cunabula ideal. We are following them. They are giving us many gifts, many blessings, every day."

Gili stopped at a sap station, and it seemed their conversation about Huna had concluded. The station was built into an alcove that was up against a trunk, one of many places where bark was exposed. There were two irregularly bulging nodes in the trunk with spigots emerging from them. On the floor underneath there were two bins—one for clean, deep, wide bowls, neatly stacked, and one for used bowls, haphazardly dumped inside. Gili took a clean plastic bowl, filled it, and passed it to Jane. "Thirsting?" he said. She sniffed discreetly. It was sap. Jane explained to Ajaya that one spigot was sap and the other water.

Jane took a small sip from the mottled, cream-colored bowl and then handed it back to Gili. He drank deeply, tipping the bowl up until it emptied. He gestured to everyone. "Favor to drinking if thirsting." When he was satisfied that everyone had their fill, he waddled on.

"This visit you'll be seeing more of the community or seeing production alone?" Gili asked.

Jane smiled. "We would love to see anything you want to show us, Gili," she replied.

"Displaying carnivore teeth! Trying, but not succeeding, to frighten me. Jane will not be eating me today." Gili made a sound like a chortle.

Jane was confused. Hadn't she ever smiled for him before now? Maybe not with teeth. "Gili—no. This facial expression is a smile. It means I'm feeling happy."

His throat fluttered and he peered closely at her. She smiled again for him.

"Smiling?" he asked. His mouth curved up in an approximation, though it looked unnatural. Then he took it a step farther by curling the edges of his mouth back comically to resemble lips and revealing thin, gummy ridges and a pale gray tongue. "Smiling is making me happy." His laugh sounded like a champagne cork popping.

Jane giggled. They were all smiling now, even the sectilians.

A group of children who were all about the same size accompanied by one adult came down the hallway. They looked very orderly until one of the students lunged forward into a hop. The adult reacted lightning fast, stretching out their legs, grabbing the student by the arm, and yanking them back to resume their forward waddle. They were very small, and it was difficult to be sure, but she thought that perhaps these children's legs looked more like Huna's than Gili's. Could these children be descendants of Huna?

Then Jane noticed that there were six large lumps on the back of the adult who had accompanied the children. That meant she was female and the bulges were egg sacs. Pligans were marsupials. The eggs would develop and be nourished in their egg sacs until birth, when they would emerge, not as anything resembling tadpoles, but as small versions of adults.

"Is this a teacher with students?" asked Schlewan.

"Yes, teaching," Gili said solemnly. Then he called down the hall. "Kula, what is the teaching today?"

Kula did not reply until she was closer. "This brood is learning about the role of RNA in gene expression—*and manners*," she said. She didn't turn her head, but her large, expressive eyes settled on one of the children in a half-lidded stare. Jane assumed it was the child who had been trying to leap forward.

Schlewan looked shocked. "So young?"

Kula tilted her head one way and then the other. "I don't understand the question."

"They seem young to learn such concepts," Schlewan said.

Kula's throat trembled a little. "It may seem so to offworlders. We use integrated concepts from birth. We build upon the layers of knowledge as each brood is ready. This way, the lessons are well understood by transition time."

The children all looked up at the alien visitors and were very quiet. Jane wondered how old they actually were. So far Jane hadn't met a pligan who marked time in any way. How could you note the passing of years when you didn't have a night sky to mark the positions of the stars? Days and years had no meaning for them. Mentioning these concepts seemed to frazzle the pligans. Gili had just ignored the idea of being elderly in their conversation. There was so much of this culture she didn't understand yet.

They spoke of readiness often. One did something until one was ready to do something else. Time seemed to have little to do with it. From what she'd gathered so far, children were described by their growth and achievements, not by age.

Jaross spoke up. "Is this brood yours? Are these your children?"

Kula blinked and looked to Gili then back to Jaross. "These

children are pligan." She laid a hand on her back. "These will be pligan children. I do not own any of them."

Jaross said, "I misspoke. It is a cultural difference." Jaross's expression was bland, but Jane sensed her discomfiture. Because Brai wasn't available, Jane had decided to maintain a light anipraxic link to her crew through Ryliuk, whose abilities as a mind master were nearly as strong as most kuboderan. She'd grown comfortable with the method. It helped her monitor her people. She was careful to avoid being intrusive. It was merely a method of gauging mood and emotional tone in order to avoid cultural misunderstandings.

"We are like children ourselves," Jane said, hoping to ease the awkwardness. "We are learning so much, so fast about your culture."

Kula leaned forward. Her stare was curious but also felt somewhat tainted with revulsion. "Do you own children?"

Jane jumped in to reply before one of the sectilians might. They tended to be abrupt and she was afraid that as a group they were already giving offense. "Not really. Humans and sectilians tend to live in pairs or small cooperative groups. The offspring they produce lives in the same household as the pair or group and is normally the responsibility of the genetic parents. The genetic parents care for their children through to adulthood in most cases and we refer to those children as being 'theirs.' I think it must be different here." Jane hoped her explanation made things better, rather than worse. She wasn't sure what Kula had been inferring, but it seemed very negative in nature.

Both Kula and Gili were pulsing their throats as they listened to this explanation. Gili said, "Knowing genetic parents is very strange. Broods are born—many mothers at once—and the raising is done together by those specializing in teaching and watching."

Kula looked down at her charges. "Groups like these are

arranged by ability. They are constantly changing as the children learn and move to the next group."

Ajaya squatted down to eye level with the little ones and turned her palms out, mimicking what Gili had done when he'd greeted them at the elevator. "There are many ways to raise children successfully."

The little pligans took that as an invitation and edged forward to look at her more carefully. Kula didn't seem to mind this. They touched Ajaya's hands tentatively and then more boldly. One of them climbed on her back and plucked at her shiny black hair in its ponytail. Jane squatted down next to Ajaya, and then the little ones seemed to be comparing the two of them.

They didn't speak Mensententia yet, so they hadn't reached the age of puberty. Kula answered their questions in their own tongue, which was low and throaty, and didn't translate anything to Mensententia. Jane wondered what the children were saying but hesitated to ask after the earlier misunderstanding. Perhaps it was safer to stay silent with regard to the youngsters.

Soon everyone was crouching or kneeling on the floor, except Alan.

Until one of the little ones pulled on his pants leg.

"Oh, sheesh," he grumbled, but he got down on all fours and let the child explore him.

5

ALAN WAS tolerant of the micropligans crawling all over him until one of them stuck him right in the eyeball. That wasn't even so bad. It was the removal of the kid's fingertip sucker that hurt—felt like his eye was being pulled straight out of his head. He actually found himself holding his eyeball in the socket while the kid pulled until he was free, for fuck's sake.

No one had taught him how to handle this kind of stuff during astronaut training.

He let out a loud, "Yeowch!" just as the kid broke loose. The little guy hopped away to stand next to his teacher and just stared at him sullenly, making distressed chirping sounds.

God only knew what kind of germs were left behind, crawling around inside his eye socket after that little encounter.

He barely held himself back from cursing. Jane didn't like him to curse around aliens. She said it could be too easily misconstrued even if it was in English. He always tried his best not to start an interplanetary incident, but sometimes it was just damn hard.

Ajaya looked at his eye for half a second and declared he was fine. It didn't seem fine to him. His eye was watering like a bastard and he couldn't stop blinking.

He leaned against the nearest wall, as far away from the kids as he could get, and tried to be patient. He was too tired for this shit.

On Pliga, waiting for things to happen was the bane of his existence. Everybody just seemed to amble around, getting things done when they felt like it. It was just too damn happy-go-lucky when there were giant-ass bugs roaming around the galaxy eating everything and every*one* in sight. He knew Jane was constantly pushing to keep work on the ships moving forward, but it didn't seem to make much of a difference. Alan was eager to see the manufacturing sector to get an idea for himself of how close the final hull sheets were to being ready to put in place. Their biggest problem wasn't how to get the stuff done, but how fast, and when they would work. He never knew when that would be. These people had absolutely no concept of time.

Eventually the kiddos seemed to get bored with the crew, and Kula and the Gang moved on. Thank God.

Gili resumed his tour, finally. They walked past a newborn nursery. If the first kids they'd seen were micro, these tykes were nanoscale—barely larger than a human hand. There weren't many places with doors in the pligan buildings, but this room had one and Alan could see why. The munchkins were bouncing all over the place, including off the walls. As Alan and the others got closer, a few of the babies hopped onto the transparent divider, clinging with the suckers on their fingers and toes, to stare at them as they passed by. They looked so much like frogs that it actually made him feel a little weird to see those tiny, intelligent eyes looking back at him. Talk about cognitive dissonance.

Soon after, they entered the manufacturing sector, and the way the trees looked changed dramatically. Gili stopped in a big, open room where the limbs that were enclosed by the buildings terminated in huge basins of various sizes and shapes, grown from the wood itself, or at least that's what it looked like. The outsides of these basins flowed uninterrupted from the limbs and were covered with the same kind of gray bark.

There were huge, swollen knots in the branches between the trunks and the basins. When Alan got closer he could see that on one side these knots were actually large, amorphously shaped panels, devoid of bark, with a frosted polymer coating through which he could sort of make out wood. His first thought was that it had to be a touch screen, but that seemed absurd. Could the pligans have created a biologically based interface with the Tree?

The basins contained liquid-looking substances in various drab colors from off-white to gray-brown. Looking around through the plexiglass walls, he could see that these kinds of rooms went on as far as the eye could see. It seemed to be an organic factory.

Alan wandered over to one of the basins to examine it more closely. He wondered if Gili would let him take some samples.

"Here Existence is creating polymers," Gili said. Then he rushed over to Alan. "Carefully! We are not touching—chemical reactions are sometimes heating."

Alan gritted his teeth tightly, flexing his jaw. He hadn't been about to touch it. He was just looking. And he wished someone had been so concerned about his safety when a miniature pligan had been sticking a suction cup in his eye.

He walked away from Gili without replying. The room was warm, though the air smelled clean enough. Alan couldn't detect any fumes coming off the polymer basins.

Gili pointed to the organic panel emerging from the branch they were nearest to. There was a platform under this branch to allow a pligan to reach it. Gili hopped onto the platform. "Here is for giving genetic instructions to Existence. For bringing needed raw ingredients up from the ground and the rules for combining them." Gili touched the panel, his fingertip sinking into the material, and it polarized, revealing that it was a display resembling the e-ink in an electronic reading device. The surface was covered in symbols. Gili didn't touch it again, sadly, and the place where he had pressed re-formed instantly to appear flat again.

Alan gaped. "How does that work?"

Gili looked at the terminal like it was unremarkable. "Meristematic tissue in the vascular cambium is being modified."

Alan huffed and remarked, "Well, they do use technology. I could be wrong but I think we're looking at a rudimentary biological computer."

Ron nodded. "These are the first of these panels that I've seen. I wonder why they keep them so hidden. They only use them for manufacturing."

Gili's throat swelled slightly. "The optimal life. Using technology only when needing. It is for enhancing a life, not driving a life."

"What an interesting way of living," Ajaya said.

Pledor frowned. "It seems a bit backwards to me. Technology makes life easier."

Ajaya looked thoughtful. "For some, perhaps. Here that doesn't seem to be the case."

Gili's throat swelled again. "Yes. Ajaya is understanding. We are needing little. Optimal Existence is requiring little."

Jaross wandered over to a place where the branches spread out into a narrow lattice supporting something that looked a lot like the leaf that had nearly flattened him and Ajaya outside earlier, except it was much thicker. "It probably explains why they're just a curiosity to the USR and left alone, for the most part."

Ryliuk said, "Yes, but you are still at risk from the Swarm here. Does the USR extend any protection to you?"

Gili shuffled closer to Jaross. The rest of the group followed, except Alan. He kept an eye on them but stayed near the panel. It had already reversed polarity and gone blank. He glanced around to see if anyone was looking at him, saw that they weren't, then placed his finger experimentally on the touch screen. Nothing happened. He pressed a little harder. His finger sank into the polymer and he could feel something underneath, sort of gritty, maybe bumpy. Again, nothing changed on the screen. When he removed his digit, it re-formed and looked untouched. What was under there? How were signals getting to the Tree? How did it interpret the input data?

Gili said, "No, not risking anything. We are not needing protecting."

Tinor said, "But how is that possible? This seems like exactly the kind of world the Swarm would want to feed on. Landmasses full of life. An ocean full of sea creatures. They would see this world as food, just as they would see any other USR world, wouldn't they?"

Alan shuddered internally. The thought of any person being food was disturbing, even if they looked like frogs. He'd never eaten frog. And now he never would. The idea made him want to barf.

Gili faced Tinor and pulled back his lips in that bizarre facsimile of a smile he'd been practicing with Jane earlier. "Ah, but they cannot be 'seeing' us at all."

Alan frowned.

"They cannot see you? Why?" Jane asked.

Gili turned to the nearest trunk and gestured grandly. "Existence would be making it impossible."

Alan didn't even try not to look skeptical. These people seemed to think their damn trees were magic. Sure, they were doing some cool things, but come on. He couldn't stop himself from saying, "That sounds like wishful thinking."

Gili ignored Alan and swiveled to point to the enormous leaf that Jaross was standing next to. "This is what Existence is making for protecting you—your *Speroancora*. Many things being possible." He shuffled back toward the skywalk. Was he leaving already? They'd barely gotten to look at any of this stuff. Alan wasn't ready to move on yet.

Alan went over to examine this leaf more closely. Up close it did still look a lot like a leaf, but he'd seen the finished product before it was applied to the outer hull, and at that stage all the parts of the leaf—the veins, and the skin or whatever a botanist would call those parts of it—had either been removed or dissolved or put through some other process. It had been smooth as glass. Huh. He crouched down so he could look up from underneath it. That surface looked even more leafy than the top.

Jane called out, "Gili, please wait. Could you explain more? We could see your planet when we came here. Why wouldn't the Swarm be able to see it?"

Gili jutted his head forward, and his eyelids closed partway. Alan had seen Kula make that expression with the children earlier. It had to be a patronizing gesture—like an adult explaining something obvious to a child. Alan narrowed his eyes. What was going on here?

"We were not Hiding. We only express Hiding when the Swarm comes near. Also—we have Escaping, if needed." He took off walking again, already to the skywalk. He was just walking away like he expected them to follow. Then he called over his shoulder, "I will show you Escaping next. It has Hiding too. I will be showing you. Coming?"

Gili didn't wait to hear anyone answer. He shuffled on down the corridor.

Alan leaned over the plate in the making, getting as close as he could without touching it. "This is some amazing shit, man. What else have these guys got up their sleeves? What do you think he means by this Hiding and Escaping business?"

Schlewan joined him in peering at the leaflike structure. "Fascinating, fascinating, *fascinating*."

Alan grimaced and thumbed toward Schlewan. "She's starting to sound like him."

Jane started after Gili.

Alan scowled. "Wait a minute. Can't you ask him to explain this technology to us more, or to get someone who could give us more technical details?"

Ajaya said, "Yes, I'd love to learn more about how they manipulate the genes of the tree to create these structures."

Jane sighed. "He's getting sleepy. You know how he is. It sounds like he has something big to show us. Let's go see what it is before he takes another long nap. We can ask him to bring us back here later."

Alan spread out his hands. "What's the big hurry? We're here now. We don't know how far away this other thing is. Why not just stay put? Let him have his nap while we look around here?"

Jane waved them forward impatiently. "I know. I know. Another time. I have a hunch we're going to want to see this. We shouldn't miss this opportunity."

"But *this* is an opportunity—" Alan said incredulously.

Jane glanced back again at Gili, who was getting pretty far down the skywalk already. He seemed smaller, hunched, like he was readying himself to fold up into his sleeping form. She was right. A nap was impending. Even he could see that.

"Just humor me," Jane said. She turned around and jogged to catch up with Gili.

The rest of them followed reluctantly.

Jane touched Gili lightly when she caught up with him. "You were going to show us Escaping?"

He roused himself like he was already half asleep, smacking his gums together. "Escaping. Oh, yes. Walking to the carts, going to the lowest level."

The carts turned out to be up a gently sloping rise. They hadn't been to this part of the city before. It was a long walk and Gili was truly drooping by the time they got there.

Their destination was actually a sort of tram station, though Alan couldn't see any operators around. It was deserted aside from their group.

Gili stepped inside an empty car that was about the size of a train car and immediately folded himself up and went to sleep.

Alan sighed. "Great."

6

October 12, 2017

ZARA'S FINGERS shook as she moved the optical mouse around. She was having a hard time focusing on the screen. It seemed a little blurry. Behind her, her parents kept talking in the kitchen like everything was normal.

It wasn't. She'd just committed a crime. She could go to jail for this. No—not jail, juvie. Her parents would be so disappointed. Her life could be ruined.

She should destroy the thumb drive. Take it down to the alley and smash it with a hammer and throw the remains in five different dumpsters. What if someone checked Daddy's laptop every day? What if it was monitored remotely for illegal access? Would he come in here any moment to start yelling at her?

She clicked on her school e-mail automatically, because what else was she going to do? She couldn't just sit there and stare at the home screen.

There was a note from a teacher, a reminder about the impending deadline of the social studies group project on different kinds of political systems around the world. She'd already finished hers. Another message was about a spirit rally on Friday for the basketball game. There was one from Becky. She clicked on it absently.

"*U do it yet?*" was all it said.

"*NO!*" she typed forcefully, and clicked Send.

She was mad—that people were bugging her about this, that she'd felt pressure to do it—that she'd *actually* done it. Just because you *could* do something didn't mean you *should*. She didn't want anyone to get in trouble, least of all her.

Sweat beaded in her hairline. She looked longingly at the stairs to the second floor. She wanted to hunker down in her room to await her inevitable punishment. But she had to act like everything was okay. At least until it wasn't.

She might get away with it. She clung to that hope even as sick feelings swirled around inside her like a debilitating disease. It was more than nausea. There were strange sensations running through her arms and legs. She alternately felt hot, then cold. Her muscles twitched at the slightest sound.

She didn't know what to do with herself. She didn't want to play a game, but that's what they expected her to do. She settled for something easy, let herself be at least partially distracted by the cheery, 8-bit-inspired music and the flashing colors. She was passing time. That was it.

She was very conscious of her mother settling on the sofa with a book behind her—though she never turned to look—and of her dad whipping the easy chair into the reclined position and opening his laptop.

There was no accusation. No utterance of surprise. She'd gotten away with it. So far.

An hour crawled by.

Her dinner was just sitting inside there, churning around, not digesting.

She turned off the computer and drooped under feigned tiredness, hoping she wasn't overacting because Mama would see through that in a heartbeat. Normally she'd try to eke out more time before bed, but not tonight. She'd had enough.

She walked over to her mom, keeping her eyelids heavy and low. "Gonna go brush and put on PJs. Maybe read a little before bed."

Her mom furrowed her brow as she glanced up. "You feeling okay?"

"Just tired. Goodnight, Mama." She leaned over to lightly hug her mom and brush a kiss against her cheek.

"Goodnight, sweetie."

She went to her dad and repeated the ritual, then made herself walk slowly down the hallway, pausing in the family room to swipe the old laptop from under the sofa and grab her backpack. Upstairs, she propped the laptop behind her headboard and plugged it in, then quickly changed into pajamas. She couldn't dillydally. Her mother was listening for tooth-brushing sounds. She scrubbed her teeth in the hall bathroom and washed her face, rubbing at a tingly spot on her chin that was probably going to turn into a pimple. She normally would have put some pimple cream on it, but it just didn't seem to matter right now. Then she went to her room and closed the door, flopped on the bed spread-eagled, and waited.

After a long time just staring at the ceiling, she leaned over the side of the bed to pick up her jeans and fish out the thumb drive. She stared at it in indecision.

Some of the fear and desperation had worn off. She'd gotten away with it so far. Part of her still wanted to destroy it. But another part of her wanted to look at it. Really bad. She put it back in her backpack, determined to grab a hammer in the morning and obliterate it before she went to her bus stop. That was what she would do. Destroy the evidence. Keep hoping no one got in trouble.

She tried to distract herself by reading a book, but she read the same passage over and over again and it never once sank in. Her thoughts kept leaping to the contents of the thumb drive, which were probably exciting, then back to her inevitable punishment—either by her parents or potentially even the government. A spurt of unease washed over her every time she thought about that. She heard the faint sounds of her mother getting ready for work and then leaving.

She got up to pee and snuck downstairs to find her dad snoring in the easy chair. She turned off the lights and covered him with a blanket. Then she went back to her own bed. She tried to sleep, but ended up just lying there with her heart pounding so hard she could hear weird thumping sounds in her pillow.

The red numbers of her bedside clock said she passed two painfully long hours this way. She was wide-awake. Sleep would not be coming anytime soon. She leaned over and squinted as she turned on the light next to her bed.

She sat up, twitching with indecision.

The damage had already been done. Whether she looked at the download or didn't, the crime had been committed. She bit her lip. She couldn't undo that—and might as well satisfy her curiosity, especially if she was going to be punished either way.

She dragged it all out. The laptop, still charging. The thumb drive. With a sigh she opened the laptop and stuck the drive into a USB port. The files downloaded instantly. She took a deep breath to steady herself.

She scrolled through the list of files, staring hard at the alien symbols. At first she thought she'd just open the file at the top of the list, but she decided to look at all of the alien words first. They were beautiful and intricate, nothing at all like English letters or anything else she'd ever seen.

One of the file names stood out to her. She didn't know what it was...it just seemed like the combination of shapes in the characters was particularly appealing. She clicked on that one.

Immediately a new full-screen window opened. She expected to see symbols floating all over the display like they had on her dad's computer. Instead a pale, drab, green symbol filled the black space. It was circular with curving lines slicing it into smaller segments of varying proportions. Different elements of the symbol glowed more brightly and then receded. It cycled over and over again.

It seemed like it was telling her something important, but she couldn't figure out what. She put her finger on the touchpad and a small green dot appeared. It moved around like a cursor. She clicked on the symbol and an animation in that same drab green and black began to play. A smattering of dots all over the screen coalesced into a cloud in the middle, and then she realized it was rotating. The cloud exploded, and then after a few more seconds the swirling mass was recognizable as a solar system. The animation froze, the central ball glowed more brightly than the rest, and then the original symbol reappeared.

She watched this happening over and over again, fascinated. It suddenly clicked—this symbol meant sun or star. A feeling of euphoria and discovery flooded through her. She watched the animation again and this time noticed a squiggly line in the upper-right-hand corner of the screen next to an open square. The squiggly line undulated in a rhythmic pattern over and over again.

Wait a minute. Did that represent sound? She kept the laptop muted at all times so its random beeps and boops wouldn't attract unwanted attention.

She leaned sideways to reach into her backpack for her

earbuds, hurriedly shoved them into her ears, and plugged the cord into the headphone jack without ever taking her eyes off the screen. She turned up the sound.

A voice pronounced a word—first fast, then slow, over and over: *Solistella.*

It sounded so different, so foreign, but she thrummed with excitement. She whispered it without thinking, wanting more than anything to hear her own lips say the word. The empty box in the corner flashed, then filled up. When the box was solid, a new symbol appeared on the screen.

She smiled. The laptop's microphone had picked up her voice and confirmed that she'd said the word out loud. The file that she'd chosen was a language-learning program. She assumed it was meant to teach humans Mensententia, the common language Jane had described in her broadcast. She'd said it had been genetically locked inside every sentient species by an ancient alien race called the Cunabula—even humans had these genes, though humans didn't express them the way other galactic sentient species did. Aliens learned it during puberty, when they were old enough to begin interacting with adults from other worlds.

How lucky to have stumbled on that first thing.

She wondered if her dad already knew this language. She swung her legs over the side of the bed to run downstairs and wake him up to talk to him about it. Then she remembered she didn't dare.

But even that couldn't curb her enthusiasm. She eagerly clicked on the next symbol.

First it taught her nouns—words like star/sun, planet, moon, and asteroid. There was a full-color animation of a real planet. Sectilia. And then her moon, Atielle. Each time she realized what the word meant, she felt an intense, thrilling feeling.

Then came person, man, woman, neutral-gender adult, child

—also with neutral gender. Then came nouns for everyday objects, some of which she didn't recognize, but she learned them anyway. She realized that if she only repeated a word without fully understanding what it meant, she didn't get that exciting rush. Somehow comprehension was incentivized. Internally. Inside her.

Pronouns came next. Then verbs. Then descriptive words that were like adjectives and adverbs. The program began to show sequences of symbols, combining words she already knew with new ones in ways that made it easy to figure out the meanings of the new words.

She was enthralled and elated. Time passed without her noticing. She never felt tired. She couldn't stop herself from clicking the next tutorial and then the next.

A sound downstairs startled her out of the trance. The light in her room had changed. It was morning. She'd been up all night learning Mensententia. Really learning it. She could already think in a few short sentences, like a small child. It was amazing.

She really didn't want to stop.

She sped up, trying to get as many words in as she could before her dad came to knock on the door to wake her.

When he did knock, she'd long since forgotten about him and jumped violently, nearly flipping the laptop over the side of the bed. She took a second to recover, then had the presence of mind to call out in a sleepy, muffled voice that she was getting up. She hid everything reluctantly and took a quick shower, marveling that she didn't feel tired at all. Maybe she shouldn't waste so much time on sleep, if this was what staying up all night was like.

As she dressed, she looked longingly toward the place where the laptop was hidden. On impulse, she plucked it from its secret spot and shoved it into her backpack among her notebooks, coiling the charging cable and putting that in the front pocket. It added a lot of weight to the bag, but it was already overloaded with textbooks, so no one would notice the difference.

She wouldn't have time to look at it at school and even if she did, others might see, so that would be a bad idea. Her closest friends would know what she'd done at a glance and they'd want her to share. That would definitely compound the trouble she was already in. She hesitated, then zipped the backpack shut.

She was now a delinquent and she found she didn't really care that much. Not anymore. This was worth it.

She went downstairs and poured a heaping bowl of cereal and milk. She was starving. Dad was already seated on a stool at the island, absorbed in his work. Mom came home a few minutes later, looking even more tired than she had the night before. Mom mechanically made herself a fried egg and two pieces of toast and placed a couple of animal-shaped vitamins next to Zara's plate. Her mother ate with a blank look on her face, then waved and went upstairs to shower and relax before she got her sleep.

As Zara walked to the bus stop she noticed other people going about their business—work, school, other obligations—some hurriedly, others looking frazzled or dull. They were oblivious to her. For them, it was just another day.

But it was a special day for her. At this very moment across the globe, there were probably dozens of adult scientists learning this language with her. She was among a very small, lucky few.

She mouthed some of the words she'd learned in Mensententia, then experimentally strung together some sentences, whispering them under her breath. She knew she was only speaking very simply and only in present tense, and she suspected that soon she'd learn other tenses and lots of new words. Important words. In another language from the other side of the galaxy. She wanted to do that right now more than anything else in the world. It felt so *important*.

She felt an even-deeper connection to Jane Holloway now.

There was something incredible they had in common, her and the linguist astronaut.

Jane took risks. She did what was necessary to make things happen. Jane had told her friends and family she was going on a trip to Tibet when she was really in outer space, rocketing toward an alien spaceship. That took guts. And then, when she found the navigator on board had been marooned and alone for decades, she helped him to go home. That was the honorable thing to do. Jane was out there now, doing brave things among the stars with that alien navigator, and she was speaking to him in Mensententia. Zara wanted to be just like Jane—courageous and smart and noble.

When Zara reached the end of the block before the corner where she normally got on the bus, there was a crowd already forming—kids pushing and shoving, taunting, talking smack.

Dread welled up, turning her stomach sour.

She thought about the moment during Jane's announcement when she'd talked about how important it was for the people of Earth to learn Mensententia. Jane had said it had probably been easier for her because of a lifetime spent learning languages. Her language facility was still open like that of a child, while the other adult crew members found it more difficult to learn. She'd said the process of learning the language would most likely be easiest for young teenagers. She'd talked about what it had been like for her when she'd learned it—each new word a discovery, a rush, a feeling of unlocking something important. That's how it felt to Zara too.

She smiled. She was exactly the right age to be learning the language. Jane would be proud of her. She was doing what Jane wanted and that was worth the risk. It wasn't fair that they were keeping all this secret. That wasn't what they were supposed to do!

Zara stood there for a moment, thoughts of rebellion churning, as she watched her peers pushing each other around. Then she turned right and kept walking, still mumbling in Mensententia. She wasn't going to go to the bus stop. She didn't pause until she found herself standing outside a coffee shop a few blocks away. A thrill went down her spine and her stomach quivered, but her resolve solidified.

She wasn't going to go to school today. She was going to have a full day of learning, but not at an Earth school.

She went inside and rummaged in her pack for her prepaid credit card while she waited for her turn to order. Her parents loaded the card weekly with chore money. She didn't usually spend it, so she had plenty to buy a mocha frap and a muffin. She was a little worried the cashier might ask her why she wasn't at school, but then she saw another kid in line and stopped worrying. If anyone said anything, she'd say she was homeschooled and her mom was in the bathroom, then leave. She got her order and discovered a corner armchair was free. No one would be able to see her screen—and hopefully no one would notice her at all.

There was a newspaper on the coffee table in front of her. She picked it up to move it and the bright orange in the main photo caught her eye. It was someone in an astronaut suit. She scanned the headline. New controversial footage had just been released. Supposedly two of the original *Providence* Six—*Providence* Five according to the government—had returned to Earth on the day of Jane's Global Announcement. Someone had sent a bunch of camera drones to fly over the government installation where a small spaceship had touched down, and the footage had just gone viral. The photo was a single image from that footage, and the headline was asking whether it was real or faked.

She connected to the cafe's Wi-Fi immediately so she could see the footage for herself. It was easy to find. It looked like something from a sci-fi television show. It showed a bunch of drones buzzing around, being shot down by men in military uniforms.

The camera kept zooming in and out of focus as the drone evaded being hit and tried to capture images of something coming in for a landing. It was hard to watch but there were several very clear moments. It didn't look like a helicopter or airplane. It did look like a spaceship.

She leaned forward, trying to comprehend what she was looking at.

The drone continued to dodge as a group of men in blue biohazard or hazmat suits rushed to the vehicle as it opened. By that time there were only a few drones left and they were all bouncing around crazily. The men in the bright blue suits clustered around two new men in similar orange suits with big, clear faceplates.

The last surviving drone managed to capture a few seconds of the two men in orange as they were rushed into a nearby building. She looked for related links. Stills from that footage were all over the internet this morning. The two men were the *Providence*'s Commander Mark Walsh and his pilot, Thomas Compton. Those stills were being published side by side with official images of the two men as they looked just before the supposed Mars mission had been launched.

It was kinda amazing. They both looked a lot younger.

Zara stared at the pictures. Compton, at age sixty-four, had been a controversial choice in 2016, despite the fact that John Glenn had completed a mission at age seventy-seven. Previously the oldest continuously working astronaut had been a fifty-seven-year-old woman. NASA had put out a statement that Compton was the most physically fit sixty-four-year-old they'd ever seen—in better shape than many forty-five-year-olds in peak condition. They said that the crew would benefit from his experience and expertise. Due to the difficult requirements for and restrictions on becoming an astronaut, few astronauts were younger than thirty-five anyway. That meant their careers were short by necessity. Compton's robust health and fitness had given him an edge few people his age possessed.

She guessed Compton had looked young for his age at the time of the launch a little over a year before, but now everyone was saying he looked like he could be his own son, and the Web was already exploding with theories about how this could be possible.

Zara frowned. Jane had explained what had happened to him in her announcement, so she didn't know what they were all getting so freaked about. All of the astronauts had been put in some kind of medical device on the *Speroancora* to save them from the nanite plague on the ship. That device used tiny robots to fix sick people. Wasn't this just *proof* of how lucky the human race was that the *Speroancora* had come to their system? Hadn't Jane said that all of this tech stuff was explained in the download? It was going to help a lot of sick people here on Earth. They needed to focus on that.

Maybe they would start being able to, *if* they were learning the language like she was.

For a moment she considered anonymously uploading the language software to a popular site all her friends used. That lots of kids used. She twisted her lower lip between her thumb and forefinger, thinking. She had to think it through carefully to make sure that it couldn't be traced back to her. She wasn't sure she knew how to do that. She'd have to do some research.

She took a sip of the mocha and winced. It was too hot. Then came a second pain, a stab in the stomach.

She might not have a lot of time to think about it or plan anything. Someone could be checking her dad's computer right now. She could already be in trouble. The program might be taken from her by the end of the day. There could be federal agents already at her school, waiting for her bus to show up.

Tears flooded her eyes. She didn't want them to take it away from her.

She sniffed, wiped her leaky eyes, and looked around the coffee shop. No one was paying any attention to her. Yet. But she was very close to home and could be easily found if they searched the neighborhood.

She needed to be smarter than this if she was going to make a difference. If she was going to be like Jane.

She repacked her backpack, thinking through her options. Her student ID would allow her to take a city bus anywhere in town. Could that be traced? She thought about the times she'd used it with her parents to go downtown to the museums where parking was scarce and expensive. They scanned the ID. It probably could be used to find her if they were really motivated. She could buy a single-day bus pass. That could probably be traced too, but it would be harder and require more steps, which would give her more time.

She stood and walked to the door.

It was scary that she was thinking this way—making decisions that would affect a lot of other people. She'd never had to do anything like this before.

But it was what she had to do.

7

BRAI DRIFTED down toward the continental shelf next to Pio, each of them lost in thought. The water cooled with each push through his siphon. It was very dark here, but the shelf below them was darker. His eyes adjusted automatically.

"Have you given my request any more thought?" Pio asked. Her mental voice was almost casual, belying the gravity of what she was asking of him. She'd only brought this up once before, and yet he knew immediately what she was after.

Now he was on alert. "Pio." His tone was reproachful. He'd already refused her once.

"Just one packet. I can control it. I can program my squillae to keep the spermatozoa alive indefinitely. To release one egg at a time. Only one."

"I can't hurt you like that. It's barbaric." He wouldn't entertain the idea. Truth be told, he didn't think he had the control to give her only one, though he was fairly certain he could produce the dreadful things. He didn't think he'd been neutered when they'd implanted the cybernetic devices in his body, though he couldn't be sure.

He was afraid some unknown, savage part of himself could be let loose in the attempt. He didn't want to find out what that side of him might be like. Perhaps that side was what went into the making of an individual like Kai'Memna.

"Not if I choose it. You speak of freedom. True freedom is controlling my own biology."

"Sexual maturation for a female kuboderan may mean premature death after fertilization. It may mean the same for a male. We don't know."

"That's what they told us to keep us in line. They made us believe we were very useful animals."

"Now *you're* sounding like Kai'Memna."

"He was right about some of it," she said coldly. "His tactics were evil, but his anger was righteous."

She wasn't wrong about that.

"We will find other kuboderans—"

"I don't want to mate with other kuboderans."

"That's not what I was about to say. I'm trying to articulate that we won't be alone. There will be others. And humans. And sectilians. Perhaps even pligans."

"You don't know that. You don't know what the future holds."

"You want this as insurance."

"Yes. Clearly."

"Is that a legitimate reason to take the risk? Death, Pio, is a significant risk."

"Wild kuboderans don't have cybernetic implants. Or squillae. Or a working knowledge of medicine and their own biology. I can control every aspect of it. I assure you I have no interest in allowing reproduction to kill me. I won't let it. I'll monitor every process very carefully. The squillae will not let it kill me."

"Our habitats were not designed to support more than one individual."

She flung her arms away from him in frustration. "Don't be ridiculous. You know that can be changed easily. The pligans—"

"I can't do it," he said harshly. He wanted that to be the end of it. He didn't want to talk about this anymore.

"You won't do it. There is a difference."

He hurled her own words back at her. "True freedom is controlling my own biology."

Her mantle fluttered and she flashed her chromatophores disjointedly. Patches of her skin went dark in a riot of random sequences. Her emotions were all over the spectrum, and that was severely uncomfortable for both of them. Neither of them had any practice at controlling these kinds of raw feelings.

He knew he was making her experience pain by refusing her request, but that wasn't enough to change his mind. It couldn't be. He had to think of all of the repercussions. Even if he could entertain the idea, selfishly, he couldn't help but lament that they could easily be separated by circumstance. Life was unpredictable. What if he agreed and then never had the opportunity to meet his own children?

She pleaded, "Our offspring could be born free. We may not have an opportunity like this again. We should take it."

He didn't answer.

The only way he could agree to this experiment would be if he could be sure they'd have *many* opportunities like this again. Couldn't she see that?

They'd descended to the continental shelf. It supported a reef biome, full of diverse life. Small fish darted in and among strands of spindly things that might have been plants or another type of animal. Tiny horny creatures burrowed in the sand with only their eyes sticking out. Long, slender fish found cracks and crevices to hide in, darting out when a tasty morsel swam by. The last time they'd been here he'd eaten a bellyful. The thought of killing an innocent animal now was repulsive. He stared at the wildlife, tracking movement, counting individuals in some kind of instinctive way while he tried to formulate something soothing to say to her that he hadn't already said.

She was disappointed. They were both nervous and excited about the changes to come, and the journey to Terac, but reluctant to give up their paradise. That made things seem more immediate. It was surely natural to want what she wanted, though wild kuboderans didn't raise their own children like humans or sectilians or even pligans did. His own mother had merely been a presence that was gone from his life moments after the fleeting act of breaking free of his egg sac. But wasn't procreation one of the strongest driving forces behind all biological life?

He turned, hoping that seeing her would inspire some words that would help them resolve this issue. Maybe there was a compromise they could both be happy with. If he consulted with someone... Not Schlewan, no. But Ajaya... Perhaps something a bit more sterile could be done. An extraction of some kind. A procedure that didn't involve savagely driving squirming foreign matter into Pio's delicate limbs like a crazed animal.

Pio was drifting near the edge of the shelf, lost in her own thoughts.

He saw the flash of movement before she did.

A pale shape, outlined against the black. It was enormous.

And it was rising to the level of the surface of the shelf, moving swiftly.

He knew instantly it was not the lumbering, plankton-feeding behemoth they'd seen before. It wasn't round or slow-moving.

It was sleek. It was fast.

It was a predator.

8

THEY WAITED FOR HOURS.

After about twenty minutes Jane and the others sat down in the car to rest. There was a low curb made of a spongy, corky material around the interior perimeter to serve as seating for pligans. That was where Gili was napping. Jane had seen this kind of furniture within the Tree structures before, often with pligans sleeping on them. It was almost like camouflage for them.

Schlewan offered everyone some of the food cubes she'd brought. Jane was glad Schlewan had planned ahead for a longer stay and she plucked a couple from the green plastic container to nibble on.

Alan was restless. He examined every detail of the car minutely, though there wasn't much to see. The most interesting aspect was a biopanel which he was unable to activate. The rest of the car was made up of the same translucent material as the overall architecture. Overhead they could see that the car was attached to a cable that led down a gently sloping shaft.

"I think it might be using gravity," Alan said. "Maybe we

have to wait until there's enough weight inside the car to pull us down?"

"Maybe after a shift change? Do they have shift changes?" Ron ventured.

"Mm. I don't think so," Alan replied.

"I think we're waiting for a person," Ryliuk said.

People did begin to arrive. They looked at the humans and sectilians curiously, but then settled down to nap, just like Gili.

Eventually the sectilians put themselves in a state of torpor to pass the time. Ajaya nodded off in Ron's embrace.

Alan crouched down facing Jane, looked like he was going to say something, then changed his mind, turned, and just sat down next to her. His hands were clenching and unclenching. He said quietly, "I really would have liked to look at that stuff longer, Jane. And there's no reason why we couldn't have. Someone who could have explained it to us might have come along in all this time. The technology, the materials science they have going on there... I wonder if they even realize how unique it is."

"I don't know. I can't tell. I had no way of knowing he was going to sleep this long. Usually when he sleeps I wander off and find someone else to talk to nearby."

"No chance of that here," he said, his hands opening suddenly to indicate the other sleeping pligans.

Jane nodded. "I understand your frustration, but they do not mark time the way we do. They're not in a hurry to do anything. There's no deadline for them. They seem happy to wait for things as long as it takes."

It was clear that he knew that and knew it well. He made a general sound of displeasure.

"Maybe try to nap?"

He side-eyed her then rolled his eyes away. "If I could go exploring the area without being afraid that the tram would just take off the second I got six feet away—"

"Ryliuk or Brai could—"

"No. Too risky."

He probably thought it was risky because he might be caught too far away to get back in time, but she thought it was risky because he might get lost in the maze of the pligan Tree structures. And even though he and Brai had made a lot of strides, he was still reluctant to use anipraxia unless absolutely necessary. She felt a surge of affection for him and impulsively grabbed his head and smashed her lips against his cheek.

He threw his arms up in the air at first, startled, then turned toward her, grinning. "Oh, is this how we're going to pass the time? Snorgeling?"

Jane snorted softly. "Snorgeling?"

He nodded solemnly. "I should probably speak in gerunds just to keep your attention."

She grinned until he leaned down and planted his lips on hers, catching her so off guard that he was actually kissing her teeth for a second there. It was completely indecorous, totally inappropriate, and thoroughly Alan. He certainly kept her on her toes.

She pulled back and looked around, flustered. It wasn't that she didn't like public displays of affection. She actually did. But circumstances were different now. She tried to keep things professional so no one was uncomfortable. He knew that, but didn't always cooperate. She chalked that up to spontaneity, and since it didn't happen often, she let it go.

The kiss seemed to mollify him enough to allow him to relax a little. He let his legs sprawl out and he leaned back. He would probably fall asleep too. He'd been so tired lately because of the erratic work schedules on the hull. Jane put her head on his shoulder and gazed up into the dark overhead mass of black leaves. They blocked a significant amount of daylight, but the transparent walls made up for it, allowing a comfortable amount of ambient light, something like deep shade on a bright summer day on a trail in a deciduous forest. The branches above them seemed to simply be swaying in gentle breezes, though she knew that was far from the case. Jane wondered how these trees differed from trees on Earth, structurally. They had to be strong and resilient to cope with the never-ending gale without breaking up.

The ship's sensors had shown that the trees were usually between three hundred and fifty to four hundred feet in height, but most of the pligan architecture existed in the range of one hundred to two hundred feet, well below the foliage line. The branches that supported and buttressed the pligan habitat were still alive, but generally didn't have leaves. Instead they were harnessed to do the kind of work they'd seen today.

As she watched, the sky that peeked through the occasional parting of leaves overhead darkened from pale gray, like a Midwestern winter sky, to a leaden color, and a few large drops of rain spattered against the outside walls, whipped sideways by the wind after dripping out of the canopy.

The weather here was tempestuous because they were in the zone of the planet called the terminator—the only part of Pliga that could support land-based life. It was a habitable zone in a ring around the side of the planet that faced the sun, at the edge between the dark and light sides, a temperate zone between the extremes of constant, direct sun and unending night.

In the terminator, the cold air from the frozen night side and the hot air rising off the superheated ocean surface collided to form stormy conditions. That caused the constant high winds and lots of rain, but also consistently comfortable temperatures that were accommodating to life. The central part of the light side was much too hot—the few small islands there were barren rocks. Not much lived near the surface there aside from thermophilic microbes, but deeper it was dark and cool and teeming with diverse life.

Most of Pliga's land mass was on the dark side and covered with glacial ice, but some of it overlapped into the terminator zone. The pligans and their trees occupied all the arable space available. It was an interesting configuration, and the pligans seemed to have made the most of what the planet offered. Clearly Gili couldn't imagine life being any better. He frequently mentioned that the pligans lived an optimal life. Their symbiosis with their sacred tree was fulfilling. They didn't seem to want more.

Jane heard a chirping sound and looked down from the sky. A pligan was standing in the tram's door. Alan jerked and sat up. "Bigu?"

The pligan's throat jiggled and the low chirping sounded again, though her mouth only parted slightly. "Gili's sleeping?" she asked. She canted her head a little. "To us, it doesn't matter. We, to Escaping, will go." She turned and pressed the panel. It polarized under her touch and Jane could discern that it showed non-Mensententic symbols, but not much more. The car began a smooth descent.

Alan groaned. "Finally." Then he turned to Jane, his eyes alight with mischief. "Eh? Eh? She's totally speaking Yodish, isn't she?"

Jane pressed her lips together hard, because she wanted to smile and she was afraid that would hurt his feelings. "I'm not sure yet. I need more data."

He nodded. "Mark my words. It's just like Yoda."

9

ALAN LEANED BACK and gazed out the window. It was raining outside in big splats. He started thinking of some lines of dialogue he could recite to Jane to prove his point about the way Bigu spoke.

Once the tram got going, the descent was gentle and, of course, slow, because what else would it be? It stopped a few times and the movement or lack thereof seemed enough to wake the pligans, who got on and off in small numbers.

Except Gili. He kept sleeping.

Alan wondered how old Gili actually was. Age was already hard enough to figure when you were talking about aliens, because every planet had a different orbital period. But time here was impossible to figure. He hadn't thought of a way to communicate anything regarding time scale yet that made any sense to any pligan he'd spoken to. They just didn't seem to understand the concept.

No one was left except the *Speroancora* crew, Bigu, and Gili when the tram reached the last station. Bigu jiggled Gili and chirped at him. Gili sprang awake instantly and shuffled off the tram without a word.

Gili led them to another skywalk that also sloped down at a gradual pitch. It was a little darker down here at the lower levels of the complex, with more objects casting shade from overhead. The storm wasn't helping either.

Alan strolled along with the group, just looky-looing around. Something reflective caught his eye below and to his left. He shifted his gaze one way and then another. There it was again. He looked harder, stopped and moved his head around. There was something down there on the ground. Something big.

"What the hell is that?" he asked, pointing.

Jane came over to stand next to him and looked too. She glanced over at Gili and Bigu and translated what he'd said, without the curse words, of course.

Both of the pligans flapped their throats. "Escaping," they said, almost in unison.

Tinor plastered herself against the transparent wall. "That's a spaceship, isn't it?" she exclaimed.

It was dark in color, just like the plates they were putting on the *Speroancora*. Probably the exact same stuff. It had a bunch of debris on and around it, tossed there by the winds and storms, but the rain had revealed enough shine to catch his eye.

"Did the big guy know they had this?" Alan asked Jane.

She shook her head, still staring at the ship. "No. Brai didn't detect anything like this."

Jaross looked thoughtful. "This spaceship is called Escaping?"

Bigu blinked his enormous eyes slowly. "Escaping, many ships, all ships, is what we call them. Now, we, each other, understand."

Jane turned. "So if the Swarm came, you would use these ships to escape? There's enough room for everyone?"

"Yes, but the Swarm, here, has arrived before. We, Escaping, didn't need."

Jane shook her head, clearly perplexed. "Because of Hiding?" she asked. "What is Hiding?"

Gili's neck quivered so hard his whole body shook. He pointed behind them. "You should be looking!"

They all snapped their heads around to gape down at the ship.

"Holy fuck," Alan breathed. He had his face pressed so close to the glass he was fogging it up. He rubbed his arm over it and looked again.

"It is gone, gone, *gone*," Schlewan murmured.

Jaross looked up and met Alan's eyes. "How is this possible?"

Alan just stared back. "I don't know but I think we need to find out."

Bigu crowed, "Existence, this effect, makes. You, this effect, enjoy very much, to my thinking."

Gili's face cracked in another attempt at that maniacal smile. "Offworlders are always liking the Hiding."

Alan wanted to run the rest of the way down. It seemed to take forever for the pligans to shuffle their way to the hatch on that ship, though Bigu and Gili seemed just as excited as everyone else. Alan made an effort to stay in step with Bigu, who seemed to be something of an engineer.

"How does it work?" he asked.

"We, the crystalline structure of the hull, manipulate with the gene expression of Existence."

"The outer hull is connected to the Tree?" Alan asked, squinting.

"Existence, everything we do, works together."

"Okay, but what are we seeing?" he asked.

"Electromagnetic radiation of many kinds, around, it redirects. Also, we, special images, onto the metamaterials, project, to deceive."

That may be why Brai-thulhu hadn't seen it. If they were generating this Hiding business all the time, it could be invisible to the *Speroancora*'s sensors.

Jaross had caught up with them. "You said the Swarm has come here before and that you didn't need the ships then. Why not?"

Gili chirped and his neck jiggled. Alan was beginning to believe that indicated glee. "Existence can be producing the crystalline metamaterials as fine, fine dusts that we can be filling the upper atmosphere with. When Existence is expressing the gene, Pliga will be disappearing. We would be boarding Escaping for safety, but most likely not needing."

Jesus. These crazy talking little froggy guys were geniuses. They had to get their hands on this technology. Earth needed it, badly. "I'd really like to take some samples, Bigu, see what we can learn from this, if that's okay?"

"Many people, to learn this, have tried. None, successful, have been, to our knowledge."

Alan frowned. Surely they could manufacture these particles, or graft the genes into Earth trees or something?

"Walking down to see Escaping?" Gili asked.

"Hells yeah!" Alan said.

"Yes, we would enjoy seeing whatever you want to show us," Jane said with a smile.

As they walked down, Alan kept his eye on the place where the ship had been. It never reappeared. He stayed next to Jane, who gestured to Schlewan and Ajaya to come closer. Jane said, "You two know more about DNA than the rest of us. What do you make of this?"

Ajaya glanced at Schlewan before speaking. Schlewan looked

deep in thought. "Commander, human understanding of genetics is not even in its infancy compared to this. We're not even a fetus. We're not even a sperm or egg. We're...free-floating atoms in space that may one day be part of a sperm or egg." She shook her head as though in disbelief.

Alan couldn't keep from interjecting. "Come on, it's just four nucleic acids, right? How hard could it be? We're already sequencing stuff on Earth. We can learn how to do this too."

Schlewan looked sharply at Alan. "Oh, no. No, no, *no*. It's not that simple. You may not be aware, Doctor Bergen, that I reported to Qua'dux Jane Holloway recently that the pligans have either artificially developed several additional nucleic acids or found them in nature and incorporated them into their system. It is extremely complex. When I tried replicating their DNA in a *Speroancora* lab, my experiments went nowhere, even when I supplied all the proper materials. They are using special substrates or processes that we know nothing about."

Ajaya nodded. "Yes, I looked over Schlewan's work yesterday. It's mind-boggling. I have no idea what they're doing. It's way beyond us."

"It's well beyond sectilian science," Schlewan agreed.

Alan looked down at the ship again. "Well, fuck."

Jane said, "Gili told me that people come here to study, leave with samples and everything, but have no luck growing a specimen of Existence when they return to their home planets. It seemed like he was telling me that the Tree just won't do these things without pligans themselves working on the actual experiments. They seem to be part of the equation."

"You think it's more than just pure science? You think they're physically the only ones who can do it? That seems...absurd..." Alan said, but he faltered near the end of the statement. Even as he said it, he was already beginning to have doubts.

Schlewan said, "I would have said so myself, but the evidence seems to point to that being the case. We need to keep gathering data."

"Perhaps they are true symbionts. Maybe they make something the Tree needs to survive. If that substance, or substances, could be synthesized..." Ajaya mused.

Jane sighed. "Even if substances like that exist and are part of the equation, the pligans may not even know what they are. They seemed amused that no one else could replicate their results."

Alan huffed. "Maybe they know and they just think it's funny to let other people try and fail."

"And we're forgetting, forgetting, *forgetting* altogether the ethics of even *wanting* to learn how they do it," Schlewan said.

"What ethics? It's science. Science is for anyone who wants to learn it," Alan interjected.

"Is it?" Schlewan fixed her matronly gaze on him. "If it's biological, it may be proprietary. What if they own these formulas because, as Doctor Varma hypothesizes, they've created them with their bodies, with what makes them pligan? So far, they've been happy to show us everything they make, but have they ever shown us *how* anything is truly manufactured here? We see results. They may not want to share the process, and I don't think we have the right to ask. Sectilius has learned many lessons in the past about taking science too far. Our current crisis stems from the use of squillae against us in ways that are directly related to just this kind of hubris."

Alan scowled. "You're being a little melodramatic, I think."

"What if the only way to save Sectilius involved removing a vital organ from you, Doctor Bergen. One that only you alone in the entire universe could grow? Would you be happy to give up your liver to me for science so that Sectilius could survive?"

"I'm not talking about hurting anyone!"

Jane grabbed his arm and gave him that look, the one that said he should calm down or at least quiet down a little. He took a deep breath and counted to about seven. More calmly, he said, "I would never advocate hurting anyone in the name of science."

Schlewan lifted her gaze and looked away from him. "I heard you state once that the needs of many outweigh the needs of few or one."

His mouth fell open and his mind raced, trying to parse the translation to understand what she was saying...then he remembered. "That was a joke. A quote from a—oh, Jesus fucking Christ." What good would it do to explain that it was a film quote when sectilians didn't have films or television or even plays for fuck's sake? Sectilians really didn't understand human humor at all. They were far too literal.

Jane said, "I'm sure that's just a misunderstanding. Joking is a cultural thing we must be careful of. No one is going to hurt anyone. We aren't taking anything from Pliga that isn't freely given. Even now, I'm struggling to find some way to compensate the pligans for all the work they've done on our ship."

"Have they requested anything specific?" Ajaya asked.

"No. But we can't just take off without giving them something in return."

Ajaya seemed thoughtful. "If I may make a suggestion? They are interested in genetic diversity. We could give them plant samples from the Greenspace Deck to study."

Jane nodded. "That's a start. Yes. I like that idea."

"That's a little like giving Albert Einstein crayons to write his equations, don't you think?" he asked.

Ajaya rolled her eyes.

Jane gave him another one of her looks.

He rolled his eyes right back. "Fine. I'm sorry. That was rude. Even I know that. I don't know what to give them either. Maybe they don't expect anything in return."

Bleh. That didn't hurt to say. Much. Being nice was such a pain in the ass.

"I honestly don't think they do," Jane said. "I think they're helping us because they're kind people."

"Like sectilians, they seem to be a cooperative people," Schlewan stated with what seemed a lot like pride.

Well, la-dee-dah.

They reached the end of the skywalk. Gili stood outside, motioning with his hands. "So slow! Going in, now! Going inside!"

The hatch was open and they ducked inside at the end of the group. As people moved out of his way, deeper into the ship, Alan goggled. He swung around, looking in every direction. Could it be—was he really seeing what he thought he was seeing?

It was an organic ship.

It had been *grown*.

The exterior he'd seen from a distance had made him think that it was just hull plating like they were putting on the *Speroancora*, but this was something altogether different. He walked to one of the interior structural beams. Bark. There was bark. It looked like a branch. Most of the interior walls were transparent, similar to the ones in the tree houses above. The flooring was somewhat transparent, but there were ropelike branches or maybe roots extending all over the place, like conduits. Overhead and encasing the entire ship, he suspected, were not plates like they'd made for their ship, but modified leaves.

Holy hell.

He glanced at Jane. Her eyes were wide and her mouth was hanging open just like everyone else's. "Is this decorative or part of the structure?" she asked Gili as she placed her hand on the black, corky bark.

"It is Existence," said a deep, gruff voice from behind them.

"Huna! Welcome. I am showing the Others Escaping. Jane has been asking about you. She will be happy to be meeting you," Gili said.

Jane turned and smiled genuinely. "Huna, it is my pleasure to meet you. I've heard wonderful things about you."

Huna's throat fluttered. "Gili and Bigu and many others have spoken of all of you often. I wanted to meet you for myself. I heard you were coming here so I decided I would come as well. I often come here."

"I'm glad you did," Jane replied. "This is truly a miracle to us. This ship, I mean. I wonder if you realize how unusual it is. We've never seen anything like it."

Gili and Bigu chirped quietly.

Huna looked around at the interior of the ship. "Ships like these have served our people many times, rescued us from extinction many times, before we developed the trait for Hiding."

Jaross moved forward. "This isn't your original home world, your origin?"

"Oh, no," Huna answered. "Our people are ancient. We have changed ourselves generation by generation many, many times and have been forced to populate new worlds seven times. This is our eighth world."

Ajaya put her hand to the nearest wall, almost like she expected it to have a pulse. "But how did this connection to Existence begin? Do you know anything about the earliest origins of your symbiotic relationship?"

Huna shifted his weight. "A simple matter of mutual need. Our primitive ancestors needed shelter from predators and violent weather. Existence naturally formed extensive surface roots that provided that refuge. Both populations benefited from this. The trees received nourishment from my ancestors' excreta, and those who lived around the trees were more likely to survive.

As the contact between them grew, each species changed to accommodate the other.

"Existence began to form cavities that provided better shelter. The first instance of this was nothing more than a fluke mutation that conferred a benefit. My ancestors began to climb Existence, and more of these individuals survived to produce offspring. The trees that formed more cavities within themselves, especially at great heights, held larger populations of these proto-pligans and could grow stronger. They became favored by our archaic progenitors, who spent less and less time on the ground. The surfaces of the cavities—and, eventually, chambers—became more and more versatile. The bark of the trees thinned in these areas, becoming almost rootlike, to allow absorption of waste materials and sometimes exude sap. Our ancestors began to feed on the sap. Soon it was their sole dietary resource. They flourished. They became more intelligent. This process continued, each species refining the other, improving their odds of survival, until the proto-pligans began to have the intellectual ability to intentionally manipulate Existence."

Ajaya looked thoughtful, her hand still on the wall as she listened. "But not genetically?"

Huna leaned forward on his haunches slightly. "No, not yet. That took a great deal more time. And it wasn't until the earliest pligan people knew the Cunabula that structures like these began to be possible."

"From there to here," Ajaya breathed, looking around the space in wonder. "What an amazing journey."

"Knew the Cunabula? Like, personally? In person, knew them?" Alan asked.

Huna's eyes fixed on him and blinked slowly. "Pligans were among their first genetic experiments. When we became sentient, we became their students. They taught us much. You, terran, were among their final experiments."

Alan blew out a long breath. "Yeah. So we've heard."

"We have much to learn from each other," Huna said.

Bigu shuffled over closer to Huna, warbling a little. "Huna, curiosity, always expresses so much. Reading, his pastime, is. Reading, learning, and much experimenting. Us, his work, benefits—more than any other living individual among us."

Huna looked down, his semitransparent lower eyelids partly covering his enormous eyes. Alan got the distinct impression that he was uncomfortable with the praise. He'd never seen that from a pligan before. They seemed to flutter their throats or chirp when anyone said anything flattering. Even he knew that. Something was off.

"What is feeling wrong, Huna?" Gili asked.

Huna was slow to reply. "I have passed on my genes. There are many youth expressing similar traits to myself. I have, in effect, replaced myself. I have done my duty here. I understand why I could not be allowed to take an Escaping to leave this place, but now there is a new opportunity. I wish to ask Jane for a place on her ship. I hope that I am qualified to serve."

"That is not being our way," Gili croaked.

"It is my way," Huna stated. "This is not an optimal life for me."

Bigu and Gili looked stricken.

Bigu shuffled for the exit in a disjointed fashion that Alan couldn't help but interpret as laden with all kinds of emotion. "We, of this, will speak at length. I, rest, must leave to find... elsewhere."

Gili just stood there staring at Huna. His mouth kept opening for a few seconds and then closing again. "I am not knowing... I am not knowing... Huna. Huna. How can this be you speaking?" Then Gili plodded off in much the same manner as Bigu.

The *Speroancora* crew was left looking uncomfortably at

each other, while Huna continued to stare at the floor with his eyes partly closed.

Good grief. They couldn't just look at the freaking amazing ship in peace. They had to be subjected to a pligan soap opera too.

10

October 13, 2017

THE CITY BUS system was harder to navigate on her own than she'd anticipated. Usually she just followed her parents and didn't pay any attention to maps or stops or where things were in the city.

She picked up a tattered pamphlet from a covered bus stop that showed all the routes and kept moving as she glanced at it. It was color-coded. To stay under anyone's radar, she slipped into a fast-food restaurant and zipped straight to the bathroom. She went into the largest stall and closed the door. Grimacing, she perched on the edge of the toilet seat and balanced the laptop on her knees as it connected to Wi-Fi. It was gross, but necessary.

Public computer terminals were available at all of the branches of the city library. She knew that much. She would pick one that was relatively far away and take a bus to it. It took a while to figure out how that would work.

People came in and out of the restroom. The hand dryers roared to life regularly. She barely noticed.

By midmorning she had a plan. Everything hinged on her not getting noticed. She had to act like she had a purpose and knew what she was doing. If she looked lost or scared, she'd stand out. She had to blend in.

She left the stall under the baleful glare of a grandmotherly customer. That scared her. What if that lady called the police?

She hurried to a bus stop and waited, her anxiety barely under control. For the first time she realized she no longer had the mocha and couldn't remember where she'd left it. It might still be in the coffee shop or maybe on the sink in the fast-food restaurant's bathroom.

The first bus to pull up declared it went DOWNTOWN on its front screen. She used her student ID to pay because she didn't have any cash. There wasn't any other choice.

There weren't many people on the bus. She sat quietly and didn't make eye contact with anyone. When they got downtown, she went into the terminal and bought a day pass. The clerk looked bored and disinterested. That was good.

Buses were lined up to go all over town. Her heart hammered in her throat as she saw several come and go while she tried to figure out which one was the right route.

Finally she saw the one for Hilliard, a neighborhood across town with a library branch. She got on and held up the day pass. The bus driver was distracted and didn't notice her. She stood there, unsure what she was supposed to do.

Someone behind her grabbed her arm, turned it palm up, and shoved her hand under the scanner. The pass had a bar code on the back. She hadn't noticed that.

The person behind her scanned their own card while she stared at the pass dumbly, and then they shoved past her. She swallowed and moved to the back of the bus near the rear door. The vehicle lurched as she slid the pack off her back. She stumbled into a seat and wrapped her arms around the pack, tucking her fingers in so that they wouldn't tremble.

The scenery changed quickly to a part of town she didn't know. What if it was a dangerous part of town? How would she know if it was? Tears pricked her eyes. She sniffed and turned her body toward the window, blinking.

She didn't realize he was talking to her at first. A big guy with a big, friendly smile. Perfect teeth. She noticed the perfect teeth. "Hey, why aren't you in school today, little lady?"

A retort spilled out of her mouth. "Why aren't you at work?"

Her brain went blank for a second as she processed what she'd just said.

That was so rude! She was going to get herself in trouble! How was she going to accomplish her goal if she did stupid things?

He chuckled. "Touché. Touché." But he still looked at her with a cocked brow, expectantly. No one else seemed interested in their conversation. "It's my day off. What's your excuse?"

She lifted her chin. "Parent-teacher conference day. I'm going to the library to work on a project due next week about Jane Holloway." The lie rolled so easily off her tongue. She was kinda in awe of herself. She hadn't known she could do that.

She was doing all kinds of things she hadn't known she could do.

He nodded, his bottom lip pushing up in the sort of frown that indicated he was impressed with her answer. "You like her? Wanna be like her? She all that?"

She nodded once.

"A worthy goal, little sister. The world is changing 'cause of her. You can change it too, you know."

She shrugged, because she didn't know how to reply to that. Admitting you liked Jane Holloway could be unpopular, but this guy got it. He believed in Jane too, or pretended to.

Inside, she squirmed. He couldn't know what she was doing. There was no way.

A wave of cold swept up and down her body. Her fingertips tingled. There was a weird taste on her tongue.

What if he worked for NASA, and they were already out looking for her?

She took in a shaky breath and glanced at him again. He might. He had that sort of clean-cut look that her dad's coworkers had, But there weren't many brothers working there, and he didn't seem...well, very nerdy. But that didn't necessarily mean anything. People presented themselves all sorts of ways. You couldn't always tell much about a person by how they looked.

His skeptical look was back. "Thought you were heading to the library?"

She jerked her head to look out the window as the bus passed a modern brick building with lots of glass and weird angles that didn't really fit in with its neighbors. It was the Hilliard branch of the city's library system. She tried to stand up to reach the button to tell the driver to stop, but her backpack prevented her from coming fully upright, and she sprawled back onto the seat as the bus bucked under her. She shoved the pack aside, but the guy she'd been talking to calmly said, "I got you." He was pressing the button. The bus came to a stop at the next corner and the rear door opened. She scrambled for it awkwardly. Why couldn't she just be cool?

Just before the bus's door closed, she heard the guy shout, "Have a good time with the books!" Then the bus disappeared around a corner.

She forced herself to take deep breaths and walk toward the entrance.

It was a small branch, but there were stacks of books on either side of the door, so she strolled behind them. A furtive glance toward the circulation desk revealed busy librarians who were not looking her way. She walked around the perimeter until she came to an open lounging area. No computers on this side of the building.

Someone was dozing on a sofa with a stack of books on a coffee table in front of them. They were wearing a coat, plus a hat and gloves. A little overdressed for the weather.

She was so close.

Zara crossed to the other side of the center aisle and then to the opposite wall. She walked along the back wall of the building, watching the gaps between the stacks for signs of terminals. She passed the circulation desk from behind. On the other side of the building she spotted about a dozen ancient computers next to the little kids' books. Only three were being used by people.

Her stomach growled really loud. It was already lunchtime.

She settled in the chair farthest from the main desk and on the opposite side from it. That put the computers and people between her and the librarians so they wouldn't get a good look at her. She forced herself not to glance over at them and focused on the monitor. She read the home screen three times before she figured out how to navigate to outside web access instead of the library lookup system.

Now she was in more familiar territory. She typed in the name of a search engine, and when that came up, she typed *How to hide my IP address*. She read three sites until she felt she understood what she had to do.

She didn't think it was enough to just use the library's computer. The library's IP address would be assigned to a known geographical place. That meant that if anyone looked to see where she'd uploaded from, they'd know it came from this specific place. She had to take it up another level. Otherwise, everyone at her dad's work would be under scrutiny. Bringing attention to this geographical region could put heat on her dad. On her.

She contemplated using her prepaid credit card to buy access to a VPN, but her parents would see the transaction when they transferred chore money to the card. They sometimes commented on her purchases, or lack thereof. It was monitored. That was a dead end. She suddenly remembered that her parents would see the mocha purchase when she should have been at school and felt momentarily dazed with fear. She hadn't been thinking clearly. Then she forced herself to move on. She still didn't want her parents to know about her using a VPN.

The only other option was a free proxy server which would disguise the library's IP address and make it look like the file had originated somewhere else in the US or even the world. That was her only viable option, so that's what she would do. She found a list of proxy servers, but she couldn't figure out how to make the first two work. The sluggish wheel on the screen just kept rotating endlessly.

The third one worked.

She opened her laptop and connected it to the super-slow Wi-Fi, too, so she could work on things that didn't need to be secure at the same time. She needed screenshots from the Mensententia software and a really kickass profile pic. She also had to come up with an interesting screen name.

She created a new profile on the Instamat social network, using a cropped image of a female comic-book hero as the avatar. She called herself SectiliusDestiny, which was lame, but the three names she tried before that one were taken.

For the bio she simply wrote, "I found it." That was enigmatic. She hoped it got someone's attention.

She found a free Web host and made a simple page. At the top, a title said, "Mensententia Learning Software from Jane Holloway and the Sectilius." Underneath, a line of text that said *Click here* would start the download.

Then, because she hoped her site would get enough traffic to overwhelm the servers, she made four similar pages on different sites to handle the overflow. Thinking ahead like this made her feel clever. She'd never made a Web page before, but it wasn't that hard. She gathered up all of the links and put them in her bio. Then she created her first and only post to Instamat, which included all five links and a line of text explaining what they were, along with a really cool screenshot from the program to get people's attention.

Now she had to make sure people saw it. She typed *Cats of Instamat* into the search bar and started following anyone who was obviously her age. She took her time, didn't rush. It was important that kids found the post first because adult attention might prompt the government to get it shut down through Instamat. When she found the right users, it was easy to find a lot more in their friend lists. That spread things around. She didn't add any of her own friends or herself because that could draw attention to her. She felt she needed to follow at least several hundred, maybe more, to make sure enough people clicked on the post.

Her stomach kept growling so loudly that a lady with half-bleached-orange and half-brown hair stared at her like she was annoyed. Then Zara remembered the muffin from the coffee shop that morning. It had been crushed in her backpack and crumbs were everywhere, but she wolfed it down and kept working. It didn't really help her hunger much, but it tasted delicious and stopped the gastric noises temporarily.

As she continued to follow Instamat users, she started to get notifications that people were replying to the post. *Dis real?* someone typed.

U catfishin. Virus. Now it, someone else commented.

Think I'm stupid?

She didn't reply. Nothing she could say would sway them to believe it was real. She considered creating another account to use to leave a comment that said the link was legit, but a new account wouldn't have any history and would be ignored by smart users. She decided it would make her post look even more suspicious. The only thing that would work was social proof and sharing.

Someone just had to click on it.

"Come on..." she whispered under her breath.

It had to go viral. It just had to.

She continued adding targeted friends to the SectiliusDestiny account, ignoring the red flag at the top of the Instamat page that told her people were replying. Lots of people were, but if all the comments were negative, there was no point in looking at them. Her eyes welled up with tears and the screen went blurry. It might fail because no one would take a chance on clicking the links, or the download.

Everyone she knew wanted this. Everyone wanted a chance to know more about the Sectilius. If only someone would try it and report back—someone with a trustworthy profile—then others might too.

When the red flag told her there were fifty-eight new comments, she clicked on it with cold, shaky fingers. The newest comments were at the top.

The thread had blown up.

So kewl!

Mind blown!

Loaded all five links in a sandbox. Checks out clean. Still looking at download which *appears* to be in another language with a patch that allows it to run on PC. Could still be a hoax, but it would take longer than 17 days to create something like this. I'm inclined to believe this is the real deal. She faved that comment even though she was pretty sure it was an adult.

This is the shit!

What the fuck is a sandbox, Corker348?

Crap!!!!!! I can't believe it!!!!!! Finally!!!!!!

They started sharing the post on their feeds. She refreshed the screen several times and the shares went up by one or two.

Now there were comments like, *Am I rly learning Mensenti?* and *K this is fkng cool. Don't care if its real or not,* and *Wow!!!!! This is amazing!*

SectDestiny wear you get this???????

NASA Leaks!!!!! lmao lol roflmao :D :D :D

She packed up her stuff and looked around. No one else was using the computers anymore. The librarians were laughing and chatting quietly with each other. It was just another day for them.

But not for her.

Zara refreshed the page again. Her post had been shared thirty-four times. Another refresh just a second later brought the total to fifty-two.

She stared at the screen. She'd done it. Comments were in the hundreds and the newest ones were at the top—now the believers were outnumbering the skeptics. She'd done something important. What would Jane think of her? Jane would be proud, Zara was sure. She smiled.

Then she checked the time. It was 5:30.

Oh, no.

If she hadn't been in trouble before, she was now.

11

JANE GLANCED at Alan and then around at the rest of her crew. Everyone was uncomfortable with what had just transpired, but Huna seemed most uncomfortable of all. She took a step toward him, unsure what to say. She had to tread carefully here, not make any promises the pligans might not let her keep. Her ship and the *Oblignatus* were still being worked on by pligans whom she couldn't afford to offend.

She reached out to Huna, just short of contact. She didn't know if a touch would be reassuring or unwelcome. She couldn't be sure if he was embarrassed or angry that they'd witnessed his confession. "Huna, that must have been very difficult to say."

Her words seemed to prompt him to shudder. He met her eyes, still partly shrouded by his lower lids. "It was." He moved a little. "Are we alone, here?"

Jane looked around. They were hardly alone. But she thought she knew what he meant. "Bigu and Gili left. I haven't seen anyone else. I think it's just myself, my crew, and you."

His eyes opened fully, and he turned in his painfully shuffling way to look for himself in all directions. Then he sprang up to touch the ceiling and clung there with his hands, dangling, stretching his legs out fully. Letting go of the ceiling, he bounced in place a few times in a very controlled way, all of the previous awkwardness of his gait completely gone. "That's so much better. I'm sorry if I'm being rude. I hope you don't mind."

"You...I...you aren't being rude." Jane reached for the right words to say. "We were told you were disabled."

Huna let out an almost-human sigh through the nostrils at the end of his rounded face. "I am not disabled. I am expected to conform to a construct within which I do not fit." He bounced a few more times in what seemed to be a very natural way for him. "My people breed for a particular appearance, at some cost. In the pursuit of a favored leg type, they inevitably damage the cognitive ability to innovate. Ancient DNA is then reintroduced to reinvigorate the gene pool for a few generations, then the cycle repeats. Due to this focus on the superficial, they cannot evolve as fully as they should. Because so few take an interest in what has gone on before, they make the same mistakes again and again. They are stuck in this recursive cycle of short bursts of innovation and long periods of stagnation. They're unable to see this even when I explain it explicitly. I have tried to change these practices and have been unsuccessful. Those with my genetics are an unheard minority. There are so few of us alive at any given time. People like me have given them Hiding and Escaping, and so much more. They respect me for my work, but not my opinions. The culture is too deeply entrenched and the average person too limited to understand the repercussions. It is an abhorrent practice. One I no longer want to be a part of."

Alan blew out a low whistle. "Dude, that sucks."

Huna hopped forward into an open space, more interior to the ship. Jane and the others followed.

"I come here, or to one of the other Escaping vessels, often, to be alone where I can move unobserved—to be myself as I desire to be, and to mitigate the pain of being among the others. I have never allowed anyone else to see me move naturally, not since I reached adulthood. I just don't belong among them."

He was appealing to her for sanctuary. She wondered if this was something akin to early adult angst or something far more serious. Instinct told her it was more. "I want to help you, but I hope you can understand that I'll need to see what happens. I'm in a precarious position here."

Huna blinked slowly. "You need not worry overmuch. I believe they will object and lament, but ultimately let me go. If not, then I will remain as I am, as many who have gone before me have done."

Jane absorbed this. He seemed resigned. She hoped he would be able to come with them. She would do everything she could to make it possible. He might be able to teach them some of the secrets of pligan DNA manipulation, and he deserved to live unencumbered.

Pledor turned away from examining a workstation. "Is there an explanation for why your speech patterns are so different from the others?"

Jane pressed her lips together. This wasn't the most tactful time to bring that up, but she'd been wondering about it too.

Huna's throat fluttered. A choked laugh coughed out of him. "Your speech patterns differ from hers—" he pointed to Jane, then swept his arm toward Alan, "—and even more greatly from his."

Pledor's eyes narrowed in their hawklike way. "We are different species from different worlds."

Jane interrupted, trying to mitigate any discord. "And we have different levels of experience and practice with the language. For some of us, Mensententia is very new."

Huna settled into a splayed-leg crouch that looked more comfortable for him. His posture seemed more relaxed when he wasn't trying to force his legs forward at an unnatural angle. "That is understandable. I will try to help you make sense of it. Every brood cycle is raised in much the same way, but wants instinctively to distinguish itself, ironically enough. They spend a lot of time together. They develop idiosyncrasies, silly affectations. Gili and Bigu are from two different broods. They know full well how to speak properly, I suspect, but it gives them a sense of belonging, especially when spending time with brood-mates. It becomes a habit."

Pledor tilted his head to one side. "We met someone named Kula—"

"Kula is from my brood. I set the trend in that brood, by refusing to indulge the pretension. My will in that group was strongest, so that is our distinction." Huna looked down. His toes flexed against the floor. "Now Kula bears some of the next brood, and many of those youths will be something like me."

Schlewan took a step forward. "Why do you conform? Why not just insist on being yourself in all ways, not just speech?"

Ron dropped to a knee next to Huna, sympathy written all over his face. "It's not always that easy, is it, man?"

"No, it is not."

Jane thought about the correction Kula had given the youth who had wanted to hop freely and the corrections her own grandparents had given her to counteract what they had seen as her undesirable behavior. Both instances were well intentioned, but probably wrongly done. They served to stifle something that was a benign expression of individuality.

Ajaya asked, "Would you be able to survive away from the Tree?"

Huna chirped. "I will not even try. I will bring a piece of it with me. I believe I can easily reconfigure your Greenspace Deck to allow Existence to flourish there. As long as I remain aboard, it will thrive, and in turn it will allow me to thrive."

Pledor visibly balked. "What about the flora flourishing there already?"

Huna's large eyes moved back and forth. "It should be unaffected if I modify only a portion of the environment."

Jane's stomach protested the lengthy lack of food with a prolonged grumble. She suddenly realized that their guides through the city had abandoned them and it would be nearly impossible to find their way back to the ship unless Huna helped them. And that would be a slow, painful process for him. She looked back toward the hatch, wondering what the best approach would be to return to the *Speroancora*.

"There is more," Huna said, lunging forward in what seemed like a desperate gesture. Her heart went out to him. "I know you fear your planet Terra is in danger from the Swarm. I also know you're very curious about Hiding and whether something like it could be used to protect your world. I believe I can give it to you."

"Are you serious?" Alan asked sharply. "How?"

"The Pliga That Was—the planet my people used before this one. It was also tidally locked to a red-dwarf star, because that is what Existence needs. But they chose a young planet, hoping that with less competition Existence would thrive and cover the arable land quickly. That plan backfired when a volcanic eruption filled the atmosphere with ash, blocking out the star's light. Existence went dormant. The people began to starve. They used Escaping and migrated here. But..." Huna trailed off.

Schlewan spoke up. "Enough time has passed that the Tree will have recovered? It could be used to manufacture enough of the particles they mentioned to protect a planet?"

"Yes," Huna agreed. "I believe I can make that happen if the Tree yet lives. Yes."

12

INSTANT RECOGNITION of the danger ignited primal instincts.

Brai flashed Pio a signal while his mental voice bellowed at her to flee. He darted toward her without conscious thought.

She whirled, her arms flinging in a graceful arc around her. Swelling with water, taking in what was needed to jet in any direction—just away—she pulled her arms to her center line, a compact shape for quicker movement.

But it was too late. The predator was quicker. She didn't draw her limbs in fast enough.

Teeth.

Arms in a viselike grip.

Her body lashed violently from side to side.

Pio shrieked inside his head.

Her pain was a blow, but it did not deter him.

His sensate skin could taste her metallic blood, growing in concentration as he moved in.

Brai reached the sharklike thing. He could sense its ravenous hunger, its determination to feed.

The head. He aimed for its triangular head.

His beak was fully extended and open. He chopped at the tough flesh, quickly opening a gaping wound. Acrid bitterness filled his mouth. He wrestled chunks free, allowing the turbulent water to sweep the unwanted mess away as he bit the malefactor again and again.

Three of his arms wrapped around the animal's upper jaw. He tugged, digging the jagged hooks that capped his terminal suction cups into the animal's flesh, and pulled up, attempting to pry the creature's mouth open to release Pio.

Stubbornly, it clung to her.

Pio rallied from the shock. She flung her free arms out to grapple with her captor.

It thrashed, trying to buck Brai off, fully bite through her arms, or maybe break away. Brai held on. He would not be dislodged until she was free.

Then he realized that while it thrashed, the shark had managed to reset its bite higher on Pio's body, very close to where her arms joined her mantle.

She could survive without arms. Limbs could be regenerated. She could not survive without her internal organs or her brain. He could not allow the shark to do that again. It was already too close to those vital parts of her.

Brai wedged two more of his own arms between its teeth and pressed down, ignoring the pain of the sharp teeth piercing his skin. He would sacrifice his own arms to save her if he had to.

His beak hit bone, sending a jolt through his body. He kept hacking blindly at the long, wide portion of the shark's head. It wasn't enough.

Another of his arms reached for one of the animal's eyes. Just... there. He raked his barbs over one eye. This malevolent creature would never hunt properly again.

The creature jerked and spasmed. It released her. He saw her fall away, limp, to the surface of the continental shelf.

He was torn. Should he try to finish this thing off, to make sure it wouldn't come for them again as he carried her back to the ship? Or should he go for her—protect her from any other creatures that might take advantage of her weakened state?

Then there was the problem of his own limbs still stuck in the thing's mouth.

The shark dove over the cliff on the side of the continental shelf, taking Brai with it. It was moving fast. They were already too far away from Pio.

What if there were more of them down there? He wrestled, desperately prying his limbs from its mouth.

It gnashed its jaws and suddenly Brai broke free. He threw out his arms to slow down.

He saw something long and narrow falling away, still writhing spasmodically. The shark swerved to scoop it up and was gone almost instantly. It had what it wanted. One of Pio's arms.

Brai surged up and over the cliff, directly to the last place he'd seen her.

She was gone.

His hearts palpitated out of sequence. Pain was beginning to set in. He fought to segment it away, but he'd lost a lot of blood. He was becoming weaker by the minute, and his thought processes were affected by the drain on his body. His squillae were doing what they could to minimize the damage, but there was so much.

He darted jerkily in one direction and then another, calling out to her. Had some scavenger carried her off? Was she disoriented? Had she gone over the side of the cliff after him?

He stopped where he was. Anguish and fear were clouding

his judgment. He had to think. Racing back and forth was wasting time.

She was wounded and hurting. He went back to where he'd seen her land, put himself in her place, and looked around again. Why was she silent? Where would she go to hide?

He saw a crevice between two rocks, just large enough to slip into. He slid an arm in and instantly tasted her blood again. Then more pain. She was lashing out in blind terror. It was the most primitive form of self-protection. He ignored it and slid between the rocks himself, blanketing her mind with calm reassurances.

She stilled. He gathered her up and crept back out of the small space, darting looks in every direction. It seemed safe enough, but he should hurry. That shark might have comrades that were just as hungry as it had been.

He filled his mantle full to bursting and jetted directly toward the hatch of his own ship. Jane was already watching. She knew what was happening. She was rushing her crew back to the ship. She'd have Ajaya and Schlewan ready to help when he arrived. They would know what to do. He just had to get her into the diagnostic bubble.

Pio was catatonic. She sagged in his grasp, creating drag.

He pushed and pushed more. With each surge toward the hatch, he felt his resources diminishing.

Perhaps it would have been better to remain hidden in that cleft and let the squillae mitigate the damage instead of risking flight. But if they couldn't save her, that would have doomed her, and he couldn't have entertained that possibility.

If he ever left the ship again, he would need a weapon to be used against local wildlife. He would never be so arrogant again, to think he was safe out there with only his natural defenses to protect himself—and her. What foolishness. Alan would be able to modify something for him to use...

His energy was flagging, his mantle fluttering instead of properly filling.

He would rest a moment.

His eyes rolled around. He forced them back into alignment and warily scanned the area. The shark might come back for more.

A large shape loomed ahead.

He lurched into a defensive position, curling his arms around Pio next to his own mantle.

Jane was calling to him.

His eyes refocused again. It wasn't the shark. What was it?

Large, brown, sympathetic eyes. Curious eyes. It was Pio's marine mammal, the one that foraged in the seagrasses not far from shore. It was herbivorous, so not a threat. He relaxed slightly.

He was on the verge of losing consciousness himself. He struggled to stay awake.

The animal swam circles around him. It had a spindle-shaped body with a wide, downturned mouth covered in thick whiskers, and a pair of tusks curled up and around in comical swirling shapes on either side of its head. What a silly-looking creature.

It nudged him. He startled back to wakefulness.

Obnoxious git.

He peered into its mind and was perplexed by what he saw there. He could only get a glimpse of purpose from something so primitive. It was on a kind of mission... it... A wave of fear pushed him to sluggish alert. The creature was fending off small scavenging fish that were after him and Pio, but it was getting overwhelmed as the number of the fish steadily increased.

He lashed out with his tentacles, slashing their bodies and pulling fish after fish to his beak to end each threat. His new companion kept most of them off him by blocking their path with its body and swatting them away with its massive tail.

He'd never noticed these carnivorous fish before. But then, he'd never been bleeding in open water.

They worked together until the fish were all either dead or dispersed. He found the energy to fill his mantle again and pushed toward the ship, which he realized he could now see in the distance.

Jane was coming. She was walking across the ocean floor toward him in battle armor, along with most of the crew. He felt her presence growing stronger.

The marine mammal kept pace with him. Brai sent it a feeling of gratitude, though he wasn't sure it understood the concept. It answered by finding purchase on his body and using its own propulsion to assist in pushing him in the direction of his ship. Its mind was fixated on getting him and Pio back there safely. It seemed odd that this previously timorous individual would have so much empathy for a stranger, but he wasn't going to question its motives. It may have saved his and Pio's lives.

He just kept pushing doggedly. These waters were far more dangerous than he and Pio had ever suspected. They'd been so naive.

And then Jane was there with help. She hugged his mantle against her body, barely able to hold him, with his limbs flowing behind them. The suit gave her the strength to move fast against the friction of the water, and she bounced her way to the egress portal the pligan workers had made for him. He managed to tell her the marine mammal was friendly and note that someone else was carrying Pio before he fell into unconsciousness.

13

GETTING home during rush hour on crowded buses wasn't as easy as her trip out to Hilliard had been, but at least now she didn't look like she was playing hooky. She was just a kid going somewhere after school. She ended up riding one bus for its entire route before she realized it was the wrong line and she had to get off again and wait for another.

She couldn't remember ever being this hungry before. Some of the other passengers were taking food home to their families, and the buses smelled of the comfort food and spices of many different traditions. Despite the ambient noise of the crowded bus, a person next to her guffawed when her stomach protested really loudly. She got off, walked about five blocks wearily toward home, and then saw the bus she'd just gotten off rumble past as she got close to her own house.

She braced herself. Her parents were going to be livid that she hadn't come straight home from school. It was late. Really late.

She opened the door and immediately heard her mother gasp from the kitchen. Then Mama appeared. "Zara! Oh my Lord, girl!"

Mama rushed her, wrapped her arms around her tight, and started rocking back and forth, crying. "Thank God, thank God," she repeated over and over again. "I gotta call your father." She loosened her grip enough to dial the phone. "She's home. She's safe. Okay. Okay. Bye." Then she was being squeezed again.

Zara just blinked. This wasn't how she'd thought this would go.

Suddenly her mom pushed her to arm's length, with a vice-like grip on her upper arms. "Start talking."

This was what she'd expected.

She began as she'd planned. "I'm sorry, Mama. I got lost."

Mama's eyes widened. Her chin went down. "You got lost? On the way to school? How?"

She almost missed the detail. In her fear, hunger, and exhaustion, she almost went ahead with the lie she'd rehearsed. Now she scrambled to reformulate and decided to stick as close to the truth as possible.

They knew she hadn't gone to school today. She didn't know why that possibility had never even entered her mind.

"I—I went to the bus stop and the mean kids were there, pushing each other around. I freaked out. I'm sorry. I didn't want them to pick on me. I thought I'd hold back, wait until I saw the bus coming, then run and get on, but I—I didn't make it."

"You didn't make it?" Her mother's tone was flat, unbelieving.

"So, I knew you were sleeping. I thought I'd just take a city bus to school or walk or something..."

"That's too far to walk alone!"

"I know. So I got on a bus, but it was the green line. I thought the green line went by my school, but it went to Hilliard. Then

I..." She pulled the tattered pamphlet from her jeans pocket. "I...I got on..." She screwed up her face and sort of traced her finger around on a couple of different lines. She really had been confused on the way home. She really had gotten on the wrong bus. This wasn't hard to fake. It was mostly true.

Her stomach protested again. A long, loud gurgle, lending some credence to her distress.

Tears started streaming down her face. She was so tired. So hungry. "I haven't had any food since breakfast! I've been trying to get home all day!"

Her mother looked surprised and then sympathetic. "Are you okay, baby? Did anyone touch you?"

"I'm okay, Mama. No one bothered me."

"But why didn't you call?"

She was sobbing now. All the pent-up fear and frustration just poured out. "I kept thinking I had it figured out. I thought I'd just be tardy. Then when I realized how late it got, I was just trying to get home. I was afraid to ask for help because I...I was scared." Could her mom could even understand what she was saying?

The squeezing and rocking resumed. "You can trust women with children. You know that. You should have asked another mama for help, baby."

And that was that. Her dad brought home burgers and fries. She stuffed her face while they watched, both of them looking sort of shell-shocked.

They said they thought she'd been kidnapped. They said words like nightmare and afraid. They'd been searching for her all day long. She had to promise over and over not to do something like that again, promise to call, promise to ask for help if she needed it.

And there would be no more bus rides with bullies. Her dad would drive her to school on his way to work and her mom would pick her up. Or maybe they'd find a carpool. She felt guilty about that because she could tolerate the bus rides. She really could. But now that she'd terrified them, they would do anything to protect her.

She felt guilty about all of it, actually. Her remorse was real. Her mom had called in sick to work and hadn't slept all day. Her dad had left work early to drive around town. She'd caused a lot of grief without even thinking about the harm her actions would cause. She hoped it was worth it.

After dinner, they insisted she sit with them on the sofa to watch TV. She sat sandwiched between them and they both kept squeezing her like they couldn't believe she was real.

It was surprisingly nice, a reaffirmation that she was important to them. While she normally felt like she wanted more space, more freedom, to be treated like an adult—this, in this moment, felt good.

She'd scared herself a little, too, with what she'd done, with how far she'd been willing to go. Being treated like a child after making grown-up decisions all day was... not as bad as she might have thought twenty-four hours prior. They had her back. That felt good.

The long, stressful day, the lack of sleep the night before, and the bellyful of french fries caught up with her. She dozed off in her parents' arms, and her dad carried her to her bed and tucked her in like he'd done when she was just a little girl.

Her adventure was over.

14

ALAN FOLLOWED the rest of the crew up to the medical suite around Brai's diagnostic bubble. Schlewan and Ajaya monitored the two squidsters closely while sanalabrium-like filaments tethered both of them, diagnosed them, and began to stitch up wounds, administer medications, and so on. They were both unconscious.

Looking at them drifting around in there, unmoving, sort of grayish, their blue blood still clouding the water in spurts occasionally, was unnerving. Frankly, they looked dead.

It was the damnedest thing how that shaggy manatee-looking animal with the enormous tusks had followed the crew through the hatch, all along the submerged corridors, then helped move Pio the short distance across the open habitat into the diagnostic bubble. Now it was sort of just hanging out, watching the whole process with big brown eyes, its long whiskers twitching occasionally. The bubble's medical filaments just worked around it, and somehow it wasn't getting all tangled up in there.

It seemed like it was touch and go for a while for Brai's girlfriend. She'd lost an appendage, though they were both really beat up. They were lucky to be alive.

Jane looked calm enough. She stayed close, but out of the way, and waited patiently for reports from the docs. But he could see that tight little muscle in her jaw was clenched. She was seriously worried. He figured as long as she felt the need to stick around, he should too, despite the fact that all he wanted to do was collapse on their bed and sleep for three days. Moral support and all that.

They'd been concerned at first that their new manatee friend might die from being trapped in the habitat, and some time had been spent trying to coax the critter out, though it refused to budge. Marine mammals on Earth had to surface for air, but Huna volunteered that these animals didn't have to do that. They had adaptations to use oxygen sparingly and store large quantities of it in specialized hemoglobin structures in their blood, and they had rudimentary gills. Though they foraged in the sea grass near the shore, they were rarely seen at the surface of the oceans of Pliga. So, the crew left him or her in there.

"They're both stable. We'll only see improvement from here," Schlewan announced.

Jane looked directly at Ajaya, who nodded agreement. Jane seemed to sag with relief.

"There is an anomaly I'd like to study further, however. It's unrelated to the accident," Schlewan said.

"What is it?" Jane asked quickly.

Ajaya put a hand on Jane's arm. "It's nothing to worry about."

"No, no, *no*. Not worrisome at all. Just curious." Schlewan pulled up images of both squids' brains on a nearby monitor. "I noticed a change immediately with Ei'Brai during his initial scans, so I pulled Ei'Pio's files from the *Oblignatus* to compare, and what I've found is fascinating. Both kuboderans have experienced significant growth in the Tuvold Region, the area of their brains used for anipraxic communication."

She placed transparent before images over the after images with the affected areas highlighted. The difference was shocking. He could see it with the naked eye. In just one two-dimensional slice of one of the brains, there had to be at least a fifty percent increase in size.

Jane studied the images carefully. "What could cause changes like this?"

Schlewan looked back at Jane blankly. "That is unknown, but in all my years working in the sectilian fleet I never saw Tuvold Regions of this size, nor any variation in size or growth over the lifespan of a kuboderan individual past adolescence. Records in the database confirm this. This change is unprecedented."

Alan asked, "They both have this at the same rate?"

Schlewan nodded once and pulled up three-dimensional renderings of both Tuvold Regions, a hologram that rotated in the air in front of them. "Ei'Brai has experienced a 74.832 percent increase in total area of this region. And Ei'Pio is at a 76.432 percent increase. It is unknown whether these regions are still growing or if the process has already stopped."

Ajaya leaned in. "It could be due to dietary changes from eating a more natural diet. Or the alteration of the squillae code. Or possibly from having more freedom to move in a larger environment."

Alan raised his eyebrows. "These guys were raised in captivity. It makes sense that this change is just bringing them closer to what a wild kuboderan looks like. We know animals in captivity can have all kinds of issues."

Jane pivoted and looked Ryliuk squarely in the eyes. "What do you think?"

Ryliuk stiffened. "My work was exclusively with kuboderan

paralarvae and adult individuals needing reconditioning in the fleet. I don't know anything about their wild counterparts."

Jane turned back to Schlewan and Ajaya. "What does this mean? Will they have more range or signal strength or something?"

Schlewan said, "I have been thinking it odd, odd, *odd* that Ei'Pio was able to communicate, even rudimentarily, with a nonsentient animal. I've never heard of such a thing occurring. I had thought it was merely a lack of opportunity. However, this change may have made it possible."

Alan thought immediately of the battle they'd waged above Pliga. "Could they be changing into something more like Kai'Memna? It can't have been just me that thought his brain powers were much stronger."

Schlewan's ears pulled back sharply. "It's a shame we don't have his remains to study."

Yeah, Alan thought, *a real fucking shame.*

No one said anything for a while. Everyone was probably wondering just how much like Kai'Memna Brai and Pio might get. Not pretty thoughts, considering that neither of them was yoked anymore.

"Well, keep me informed of any other changes you discover," Jane said abruptly.

Pledor stepped forward. "With your permission, Qua'dux, I'd like to show Huna the Greenspace Deck?"

Pledor and that deck, man. He was all about that deck.

Jane nodded. "Of course."

Pledor and Huna started to leave, but stopped when Jane said, "And please personally escort him back to the Tree when he's ready to go, Pledor."

Pledor's ears pulled back, but his head dipped in acquiescence. "I will treat him as an honored guest."

Alan had to work hard not to roll his eyes or snort. Pledor's idea of treating guests well had left something to be desired when he had hosted them on Atielle.

Ryliuk followed them. "I will accompany them." He probably wanted to get out of the hot seat before Jane started asking more questions about his kuboderan "training" sessions. And show off his fuzzy pet plant to Huna. It was better not to leave Huna alone with Pledor anyway, so it was a good idea. Though Alan had doubts about whether Ryliuk was any better at playing host.

Everyone else seemed to be lingering around the console that monitored the two squid like they weren't sure what to do next. It had been a damn weird day. Total information overload. Maybe he should try to lighten the mood?

He sidled up to Jane and put an arm around her waist. "Well, they're cohabiting now. They've got a dog. What's next? A minivan? Popping out babies?"

Schlewan and Jaross stared at him blankly. Ajaya sighed. Ron snickered. Jane slapped his ribs lightly and turned to Schlewan. "Please stay and monitor them for the remainder of this shift. Tinor and Ajaya will relieve you in turns after they've gotten some rest. Yes?" She looked pointedly to Tinor and Ajaya, who both seemed agreeable to the plan. She left them to work out the details.

Alan followed her to the nearest deck transport. He stayed quiet because he was uncertain about her mood. Maybe he'd put his foot in it with the dog joke. But mostly, she just looked tired and worried. He knew how that felt.

"I'm starving," she muttered as she tapped the symbol for the crew deck.

Add hungry to the list.

He was hungry, too, now that he thought of it.

They ordered up some food cubes from the food printer and sat down. It was time to taste test his newest creation. He was going for pizza-flavored food cubes, but so far the closest he'd gotten was sort of like SpaghettiOs. He wasn't calling that a fail, though.

He cleared his throat. "Do you think Huna burned some bridges today on the way back here? He certainly hopped to it. I wonder if this will help his cause or make his situation worse."

Huna had correctly interpreted the seriousness of the situation and abandoned all pretense of walking like the other pligans while leading them back to the egress tower nearest the *Speroancora*. All along the way, they'd heard other pligans chirping at him. It had sounded a lot like scolding.

Jane looked thoughtful, ignored the terrible pun, and took a sip of water to wash down a food cube. "I'm not sure. I don't feel like I have a very good grasp on their cultural conventions. If I had to guess, I would say that the more he deviates from what they deem standard behavior, the more likely they will be to let him go. From what he says, they're committed to their orthodoxies at some great cost."

"Getting rid of the rebel would make them feel more comfortable, you mean."

Jane nodded. "Yes, but at the same time he's one of their most valuable resources. They may decide to simply hide him away from the general population instead, so he's not giving young people any ideas."

"I got the feeling that he preferred to be alone."

He tasted the first cube. *Holy crap.* He'd gone a little too far on the flavor component he called "Italian-esque Seasonings." He considered making something else to eat, but decided to struggle through.

"Yes and no. Solitude may feel like a relief because of the pressure they put on him when he's in public. But I got a sense of wistfulness when he talked about that. I could be wrong, but I think he'd rather just be able to be himself among others."

"Even if all the others are aliens. Man, that's messed up,"

Alan said dryly. "What I don't get is why they have any say at all in whether he stays or goes. He's clearly an adult. He's got free will. If he wants to leave, he should leave."

"It sounds like he wanted to leave some time ago and they objected to him taking one of the ships. I think he's counting on the fact that if he's made other arrangements they will not stop him. It didn't seem to me that he was asking for their permission, merely breaking the news to them. But I don't know."

"I guess we'll know eventually. Whenever they get around to talking about it."

Jane didn't reply. She looked so... sort of... pinched.

"He's going to be okay, Jane. They both are."

She exhaled heavily and looked up at the ceiling, breathing through her mouth, like she was actively struggling not to cry. "It was close. Too close. I... should never have believed it was safe out there for them. I should have insisted..." She broke off and stared down at her hands. A tear dropped onto the table.

"They're adults, Jane. You aren't their parent."

She looked up, anguish clear in her features. "Aren't I? In a way? I'm their leader. Well, Brai's, anyway. Pio is so fragile after all she's been through. And they've never had opportunities to learn how to *be* in the world. They need guidance. In some ways they're like children. They've been sheltered to such an extreme."

He frowned. He hated seeing her beating herself up like this. "Don't be absurd. Are you telling me that you would have denied Brai the experience of swimming free? There's no way in hell you would do that. It's a bizarre situation, but you did the right thing. They had to learn this lesson the hard way."

She threw up her hands. "By nearly dying in the mouth of a shark? I should have searched the entire geographic region myself, looking for predators. I should have made them stay close to the ship. I shouldn't have been so sure that their barbs and beaks and speed would be enough to protect them."

"And in the future, we'll do that, if that's what you want. But I don't think the old Squidster will like it. From his point of view, he's gained lifetimes of experience from hitching rides in sectilian brains as they tromped around the galaxy."

"That's different!"

"I agree with you. I agree with everything you're saying. But I'm still saying you didn't make a mistake. It's a shame it got this bad. It is. But, Jesus, Jane—do you really think he would have complied with strict restrictions, once he got out there? I don't. It was exciting for them. I could sense their euphoria and I barely pay attention to them. They were living—truly living for the first time. That had to feel great. It's good that they got to experience that."

She looked unconvinced.

He kept at it, hoping to get through to her, to alleviate some of her crippling guilt. "Look, I know what it's like to be out rock climbing by myself or with just one other person and taking stupid risks because you think you're invincible. You learn pretty quick what your limitations are when you find yourself in a life-or-death situation that's difficult to get out of. Now he knows. They both do. Any restrictions you put on them now will be more palatable."

"Maybe."

"Definitely. It's in the past. You can't redo it. So stop beating yourself up over it. Lessons have been learned. Move on."

She looked suspicious. "When did you get so wise?"

He laughed. "Always. You just didn't notice. You wanna try one of these?"

She leaned back and eyed his pile of food cubes, which obviously wasn't disappearing very fast. She'd tried some of his other creations and hadn't been impressed. "I think I'll make some tea."

"Coward. You tired? Wanna get some rest?" He attempted to

waggle his eyebrows at her suggestively, but he was so damn tired he probably looked like he was having a seizure.

Her lips twitched and she stood, giving him an amused sidelong look. "You go ahead. I know you're tired. It's early. I'm going to check on how the pligan work crews are progressing on the hull. Try to estimate how much longer it will be."

"I could help you relieve some stress..." He dangled the carrot, hopefully enticingly.

She didn't bite. She filled up a beaker at the hot-water station and dumped in some herbs Pledor had brought up from the Greenspace Deck. "I need to know how much more time we'll likely be spending here. It will inform how we handle Brai and Pio's recovery as well as our interactions with Huna. Enough work has been done that I should be able to figure out an average and estimate how much time is left."

"Good luck with that. Sometimes Bigu brings fifty folks, sometimes twelve. I'll be going back out there again tomorrow with Ron, Jaross, and Ryliuk. I'll try to do my own estimation."

"Thank you."

"So, about that rest—"

Pledor stormed in, his ears pulled back so far that his beak of a nose stood out even more than usual. "I would like to register a formal complaint."

Jane took a deep breath, like she was bracing herself, then sat down with her tea and turned her gaze on Pledor. "What seems to be the matter?"

"Huna! He said he would bring just one tree onto the ship— that that would be all he needed. I thought we would just remove the Dart Bell tree to make room. It doesn't produce anything edible. It's only ornamental. But he wants to clear out fully one-quarter of the productive space. I must protest! I'm feeding nine people. Surely that must be held in account!"

"I'm sure we can find a compromise, Pledor," Jane said tiredly.

"It's simple," Alan interjected. "Put Huna on the *Oblignatus* instead. We have two ships. Two Greenspace Decks."

Pledor looked from Alan to Jane, then back and forth again.

Jane said, "Maybe that would work. I don't know if Ei'Pio intends to travel with us. She is free to do as she chooses."

"Oh, please. She's coming with us." Alan leaned back in his chair and sprawled out.

Jane gave him a quelling look over her tea. "I won't speak for her. We'll have to wait until she's well enough to decide for herself."

Alan shrugged. He didn't think there was any question. The two cephalopods were thick as thieves. But he saw why Jane had to be diplomatic about it.

"Where is Huna now?" Jane asked.

Pledor visibly balked. "Master Ryliuk escorted him back to the Tree."

All softness left Jane's expression. "I asked you to personally escort him back. You said you would treat him as an honored guest. I hope you didn't make him feel ill at ease. We're indebted to these people. We can't afford to sour this relationship."

"I merely wished to make my concerns known to you. I'm sure I've given no offense, Quasador Dux Jane Holloway."

"Good. I'll take your concerns into consideration."

Jane frowned into her tea as Pledor skedaddled.

Alan was about to say something to her when Ryliuk lumbered in and filled a massive bowl with food cubes. He lifted his own bowl as an offering, but Ryliuk waved it off.

Damn. He might have to eat all of these.

Jane straightened. "You accompanied Huna back to the Tree?"

"I did. He is a most fascinating individual."

"How did the visit go on the Greenspace Deck?"

"It was unremarkable. Huna expressed an interest in the botanical variety. Pledor graciously showed it off to great effect. They discussed potential placement of a juvenile specimen. Then I walked back with him because Pledor said he had an errand."

A little more of the tightness in Jane's jaw eased. "Thank you," she said.

"Of note—Huna resumed his awkward posture upon his return. He was greeted unfavorably, I would say. The pligans in the near vicinity seemed displeased with his prior behavior. That was the general atmosphere of the place. His mien was one of discomfort, though he did not remark upon any of this. I don't perceive much from this species, though I would likely grasp more if they were trained in anipraxis."

"That's good to know. Thank you, Ryliuk."

He said nothing more and left the room.

Alan raised his eyebrows at her. "I think you're right. I think your job must be a lot like parenting."

15

"HOW CAN I HELP?" Jane asked.

She'd seated herself on a low bench in a corner room with Gili. He'd sent someone down to the ship to ask her to come up to the Tree after three days with no contact. During those three days none of Bigu's work crews had come to work on the ship. They hadn't heard anything from Huna either.

Jane had never gone to the Tree without an invitation, so she'd stayed away. Schlewan, however, had a habit of shadowing pligan teachers and students every day to learn pligan genetic techniques, and she continued that practice during Gili and Bigu's silence. Schlewan reported that many of what might be considered the elders of the community were closeted away in conferences over Huna.

Jane was bracing herself to hear the worst—that they were about to be banished from Pliga because of Huna's interest in joining them. There were still sections of both ships' hulls that were damaged and would be in danger of leaking air if the work wasn't finished. They could seal them off, but it wasn't ideal.

Oddly, Gili had very specifically asked that Jane bring

Schlewan along when he'd sent word to her. The sectilian woman sat next to her, cross-legged but silent.

"I am not feeling like smiling for you now," Gili said.

"I'm sorry to hear that. Is there anything I can do?" Jane asked.

"There has been much discussing with Huna. Such distressing goings-on." He repetitively rubbed a suction-cupped fingertip over a knuckle on his other hand. "We were telling him how much we're needing him, but he's not caring about that. He has been saying he will not be working with us anymore, that he'll be secluding himself, living alone, far away, if we are not letting him go with you on your ship. Either way, he will not be *being* with us any longer. He says he is not living an optimal life here." Gili's throat fluttered with his distress.

Jane swallowed and made fleeting eye contact with Schlewan. "Oh."

Gili made a distressed, creaking sigh. "What we are not knowing is if you are even wanting to take him with you when you are leaving."

Jane nodded slowly. "We are not opposed to giving Huna transport. But we will only do so if you do not object. We are friends of Pliga. We do not wish to offend."

"No one is offending!" Gili said quickly. His large, metallic eyes blinked slowly. "It is seeming that I should be telling you... We have a tradition. When an individual is being needed for a specific type of work, or for breeding certain traits, we would be negotiating with other parts of the Tree, sometimes from very far away. When all needs are being satisfied, then we would be trading the people. It is being beneficial for all involved. We are needing Huna, but there is... no one replacing him."

Jane drew her brows together. "I see."

"Are you seeing?" He turned to Schlewan. "Are *you* seeing?"

Schlewan looked thoughtful but didn't say anything.

Jane leaned forward a little. She felt it was best to be direct. "Do you want Schlewan to stay, to replace Huna?"

Gili's throat fluttered. He merely watched Schlewan.

Schlewan looked grave. "I am near the end of my lifespan. Huna is very young. I have not been educated in your genetic techniques. It is not a fair trade."

"The teachers are saying you show much promise. Your life experience is being very attractive to us. You may be finding you could be living longer here."

Schlewan looked into the distance. "I would require a great deal of education in your methods, and special accommodations would have to be made to meet my nutritional needs."

Gili chirped. "But of course! We will be making all necessary accommodations."

Schlewan stood. "Then I accept. I will go gather my things now, if you don't mind, Qua'dux?"

Jane stood too, her mouth gaping. "Ah, of course. Please take anything you think you might need from the ship. Take your time."

Schlewan walked away and Jane stood there, looking after her. She wasn't sure she liked this turn of events. She was losing a competent doctor. It had happened so fast. Had Schlewan known this invitation was coming? Was this really what she wanted, or was she doing it for another reason?

"Are you finding the trade satisfactory as well?" Gili asked. He looked far more at ease now.

Jane felt for words carefully. "Schlewan must decide for herself what path her life will take. I won't decide for her." She hesitated for a moment. "I am surprised you would want an offworlder in trade. Didn't you say that offworlders had no luck with your technology?"

"Oh, no. You are misunderstanding. In the past, offworlders visit, learn, and want to take Existence away. But Existence must be remaining here with us. There is no impediment to learning—only to taking Existence away. We like offworlders. They bring novel ideas with them. Novel ideas are what move us forward. If we cannot be having Huna, we will be having someone who will also be benefitting our people."

Jane nodded slowly. "If your people were to leave Pliga and have experiences on other worlds, they might find they also have more novel ideas."

Gili's eyes widened a fraction. "And leave an Optimal Existence? That is not our way."

"And Schlewan?"

"We will be doing everything in our power to be optimizing life for her as well."

Jane fidgeted. "There is still the matter of repayment for the work done on our ships."

Gili opened his mouth and shut it again, his throat fluttering. "We have been sharing."

"And we should give something in return. I'm afraid I don't know what's appropriate. Will you guide me in understanding?"

"It is I who is not understanding. Existence is providing a bounty, more than we are using, more than twice our people could be using. This is a trifling. We have been enjoying this sharing between our peoples."

Jane frowned. She was getting it all wrong. "I'm sorry if I have offended. I want only to be as generous as you have been."

Gili's throat fluttered. "Not offending. Existence is being generous. It is giving you and I what we need. All of us." His lips curled in that manic imitation of a smile.

Jane smiled in return.

Jane left Gili as soon as she felt it was polite to do so and made her way back to the ship. She found Schlewan just finishing packing up her quarters.

"A benefit of not owning much," Schlewan said as Jane passed through the door and noted that the room already looked bare. Schlewan gestured for Jane to sit on a chair while she settled herself on the edge of the bed.

"Master Schlewan, are you sure this is what you want? You were trapped on Atielle for so long, I don't want to leave you alone on Pliga unless you are absolutely certain this is the right thing for you."

Schlewan's eyes crinkled with warmth. "I appreciate your concern, Quasador Dux Jane Holloway. It is gratifying to know that you've considered my well-being in this manner. There is a difference, however. There, I was stranded with no hope of rescue, among people led by an individual I did not respect. Pliga will be very different. Here I will be a student among people I respect a great deal. And I will be able to learn things that may greatly benefit Sectilius, if I live long enough to return home."

"I see."

"I will keep a journal to document what I've learned. I think my perspective will be unique. It will be a mutually beneficial exchange."

"Did you know they were going to ask for this?"

"I hoped they might. The teachers I've been observing seemed very interested in my perspective. If they hadn't made an offer, I planned to discuss something similar with you. I was waiting to see how things developed diplomatically. And with Huna. If they had refused his request to leave, they might also have been less genial toward the idea of a long-term apprenticeship."

"We will be leaving in just a few weeks. You can still change your mind. We can try to find some other way to compensate them."

"That won't be necessary. I am at peace with the decision. Tinor and Doctor Ajaya Varma will be very capable in my absence."

Jane nodded. "We will miss you."

"You will. Tinor most of all, I'm sure. But she has outgrown the need for a caretaker, and it is time for teacher and student to part. I've taught her well, and the ship's teaching tools have taken over for me now. She has worked tirelessly to finish her education. She has just recently passed all the pertinent exams. She is a full medical master now."

Jane frowned. "I didn't know that!"

"She's been waiting for the most opportune time to make an announcement. She wants to please you, you know."

Jane's face got a little warm. "I know."

Schlewan stood. "Well now, well now, *well now*," she said. "I have much more to do. I'll be taking along files and tablet computers and a few medical tools. I would like to continue to gather things."

Jane stood too. "Please take a food printer and crates of raw food with you. I'll ask Alan if he will work with Bigu to figure out how to make it work at the Tree."

"*Casgrata.* My teachers and I plan to modify a node of the Tree to make food tailored for my consumption, but in the meantime, that would help a great deal."

16

BRAI NUDGED PIO GENTLY. The medical master was bringing her out of her medically induced coma for the first time, and it worried him that she was so slow to wake.

The three of them filled the diagnostic bubble past capacity. Pio was well within reach. Movement was restricted by design within the space, but this was a little more claustrophobic than his earlier stay. At least he could watch Pio closely.

Finally her dull, staring eyes moved in their sockets and she jerked, whacking her arms against the sides of the bubble. The sea cow wriggled between them, its black eyes worriedly watching Pio.

"Oh," Pio said sluggishly.

Gradually she became aware of where she was, who was with her, and that Schlewan was attempting to communicate with her.

"Are you in pain?" Schlewan asked.

Pio was wary, reluctant to discuss how she felt with a sectilian. "No, not much."

It seemed to be true nonetheless.

She moved, carefully examining her limbs one by one, delicately working around the curious sea cow's body, not annoyed by its presence in any way. When she reached the missing limb, she didn't dwell on the loss. It was just a temporary problem.

"Thank you," she said. "You saved my life."

"Don't speak of it. You would have done the same," Brai replied.

A wave of warm feelings washed over him, surprising him with its intensity.

"I would have, yes." She turned her attention to the marine mammal, running the backs of her arms over the creature's shaggy head. Its eyes partially closed, and it edged even closer to Pio. "And this sweet little soul came with us."

"It wouldn't leave us. We must also give it some gratitude for our lives. It contributed to our rescue."

"We can't go on calling her an it," Pio said, continuing to caress the shaggy animal.

"It is female?" Brai asked.

"Of course she is. I think I'll call her Lira. Thank you, Lira, for helping us." Pio projected fondness and appreciation toward the animal.

The sea cow rolled in place, a blissful expression on her face.

Brai caught a burst of delight coming from Lira through his connection with Pio, which was echoed and magnified in Pio herself. "By the Cunabula," he exclaimed.

"She likes her name," Pio said, pleased with herself.

"I've never observed such communication," Brai said, somewhat stupefied by what Pio had accomplished with this nonsentient animal.

Pio's mental laugh tinkled in his head. "You weren't paying attention."

Umbrage spurted up inside him. "It didn't seem important."

"It was to me," she whispered.

Guilt and regret replaced the momentary offense. This was acknowledged and he was forgiven instantly.

"We must find a way to feed her," Pio said.

"They've been giving her leafy greens from the Greenspace Deck."

"That isn't sustainable for the long term," Pio replied.

Brai stayed silent, shielding his thoughts from her for the first time in a long time. She wanted to keep the mammal with her. He found that very odd. And perhaps not right. The animal would surely be happiest in its natural habitat, not stuck in an artificial enclosure.

But Pio understood what his silence meant. "She's injured. She cannot swim properly for migration, which might mean she'd be vulnerable in the bay all alone. She is a social creature. And she wants to be with us, with *me*."

"Perhaps Schlewan could mend the injury—"

"No. Not Schlewan. I can sense her revulsion that Lira is here inside the ship."

She wasn't wrong. Schlewan's feelings were obvious. "Ajaya or Tinor then?"

"Perhaps."

But he could sense her reluctance. She had already become attached to the idea of keeping Lira in this brief time. Perhaps it was for the best. If she had Lira with her, the requests for his genetic contribution might subside. But he had to wonder, "Will the Qua'dux approve?"

Pio's limbs curled into tight corkscrews, indicating angst. "Why should I need Jane's approval? Have they not told me I am free? That I am master of my destiny? That I may stay with them or go as I please?"

A threat hung unspoken among those words. Alarm that she might be thinking along those lines made him instantly contrite. "I only meant—"

"You have to let the old ways go. I intend to keep Lira with me. The humans and sectilians will adapt. You let me handle this in my own way. Do not meddle."

He struggled against a feeling of being wounded, moving as far from her as he could, which was not far at all, and turning his body so that he looked away from her into the air-filled medical chamber where Schlewan monitored their vitals and interpreted test results. "I assure you I will not interfere." He didn't know what else to say and resisted the urge to plead with her to stay with them. He didn't think her threat had been completely serious and he didn't want to agitate her further.

After a time her feelings receded and she slipped into sleep. He dozed as well.

When he woke, she was alert again and caressing Lira. Feelings swelled up inside him. "I'm sorry," he blurted suddenly, without planning to.

Her eyes darted to his, a lack of understanding in her mind.

He squirmed. "I had lost all sense of caution. I wasn't wary enough. I didn't see the predator until it was too late."

"We both had. There were two of us there." She reached out and stroked her arm down one of his limbs, just short of his worst injuries. "There is nothing to forgive. We both paid a price. We won't be so careless again."

And just like that he felt as though all was right between them once more.

17

JANE HEARD a beep inside her helmet and tapped the control to answer. "Holloway here."

Ron's deep baritone came through. "How you doing down there, QD?"

She swept her eyes over the HUD of her suit, which showed the surrounding area still clear of all large animals and every member of her team in good shape. "Doing fine so far."

Jane bounded across the seafloor of the bay with a small team in power armor surrounding Pio and Brai, their marine-mammal friend swimming in circles around them. Their goal was to return the animal, which Pio had named Lira, to the wild if it would let them. So far it showed no interest in leaving the kuboderans behind. Ron hovered just above the water's surface in a *Speroancora* shuttle, with more team members ready to dive if anything dangerous showed up.

She was uneasy, and not just because of the potentially dangerous predators. Though she'd been submerged in this suit before, it was always disquieting. She reminded herself it was airtight, made to fight in the vacuum of space. It could handle keeping her alive underwater. It had before. She was being a little cautious, but no one had criticized her or complained about it yet. They'd all seen the damage the shark had done to Pio and Brai.

She tapped off the autorun on her suit and called a halt. "These are the coordinates where I found Ei'Brai on the day he was injured. Lira's home must be near here."

Pio drifted toward some areas of sparse, ribbonlike seagrass that grew denser over distance, and one of her long arms extended. She was nervous about coming back here, but was bearing up well. Her wounds had healed and her truncated arm had begun to regenerate. "We often saw her in this meadow. She was always alone. I never saw another of her species, though I believe she would normally live in a group."

The water was relatively shallow, only about thirty feet deep, and it was still fairly well lit here, though relatively colorless. The seagrasses undulated as far as the eye could see, but there were no animals like Lira anywhere nearby.

Jane tapped her comm. "Ron, we aren't detecting any large wildlife in the area. Can you scan the entire bay from up there?"

"I'd have to increase altitude, which means a longer reaction time if you need us."

She glanced around uneasily. "Go ahead."

"Scanning now."

Alan walked deeper into the meadow and examined the seagrass. "This is probably its primary food source. We should take some samples."

Pio jetted over to him, an effusive feeling radiating from her. "Yes! We can modify a nutrition-conversion device to make a diet specifically for her, just as a diet has been made for Brai and myself!"

Alan made eye contact with Jane, his eyebrows raised in question. "Sure. We could."

Ron came back over the comm. "Bad news and good news.

Still not detecting anything. No mammals like Lira, no large predators. If she was part of a group, could they have migrated?"

Alan squatted down with a sample bag and grasped some seagrass.

Tinor strode over to him and stayed his hand. "Wait. There's more to consider."

Alan straightened slowly. "Okay."

Jane held up her arm to get everyone's attention. "Stay alert. Spread out. Keep the kuboderans inside our circle. Watch your heads-up display carefully for predators, just in case. Ron, widen your search, please. Look for other bays and sheltered areas where the water is shallow and calmer."

Jaross and Ryliuk moved out in opposite directions, scanning.

Tinor gestured at the seagrass around her and Alan. "Look carefully. This hasn't been foraged. It's very lush. The biomass may be too fertile here. That may be why the others have moved on."

Alan cleared his throat. "I thought lush and fertile was good for plants."

"Good for the plants, but less nutritious for those who feed upon them. See how there are grasses around the perimeter that have been chewed down to the root? And the lines in the silt where the rhizomes have been pulled up? Seagrass that grows more sparsely likely also grows more slowly—and as a result contains more protein and more nutrition. If we become responsible for the sea cow, we have to make certain we optimize its food source. It has already lost some body fat while confined on the ship, despite Pledor's efforts to feed it leafy greens. If we aren't careful, we could do it harm."

Alan huffed, but not in an annoyed way. He seemed to be fascinated. "Noted."

"The Sectilius have long dealt with scarcity. Cultivation concepts are very important to our culture and taught in the schoolroom. Overfertilization must be guarded against to prevent malnutrition."

Alan moved over to the perimeter of the meadow. He gestured at the scraggly and closely cropped grasses there. "These? We could pull up the roots too."

Tinor got down next to him. "Yes. Let's take at least twenty samples from different areas around the margins of the meadow. There will be little they overlooked before they moved on, but there will be some."

"Oh, see—look!" Pio exclaimed. "I asked her to show me what she eats. She *is* eating from the fringe area. What a good girl!"

Tinor stood and marched over to Lira, observing the mammal eating with great intensity. Lira's mobile upper lip looked elephantine as it moved delicately over the grasses, pulling with surprising strength to get even the roots and then shaking the silt away before chewing.

Jane frowned. She hadn't realized Pio was able to communicate that well with the mammal. She eased her consciousness a little closer to Pio's to more closely watch her interact with Lira. Immediately she was struck by the intense emotional attachment Pio felt. Pio's interest in the lumbering mammal was verging on obsession. Jane quickly withdrew and glanced nervously at the HUD again.

She'd seen that kind of fixation before. In parents with newborns. And young adults who wanted babies but had to settle for pets instead.

Pio was not interested in returning this animal to the wild. Her primary concern was to make it possible to share her habitat with Lira, for companionship. But she was intelligent enough to realize she'd have to go about it in a roundabout way if the *Speroancora* crew was going to take her seriously.

When Pio caressed Lira, the animal drew closer to her and rolled. When Pio stopped, Lira nudged her arms. It certainly seemed to be choosing to stay near Pio and Brai. It was acting just like a pet.

Jane didn't know why or how this bond had formed. But it had. And Pio seemed revitalized because of it. Losing an arm hadn't broken her. The pain of regeneration hadn't put her in a funk. After all she'd been through, the emotional state she'd been in when they'd found her, that was a good thing. Pio had lost a lot.

Jane knew that it was a kuboderan characteristic to have a strong need to watch over and be involved with their crews. Now Pio had all of them to care about and Brai too, but she still seemed unsettled. Putting a more permanent crew on the *Oblignatus* would be a good start. Lira gave her another positive thing to focus on.

Guilt pricked at Jane a little. Perhaps she should have done something more for Pio sooner. But she hadn't really understood what was needed until now. And even if she had, she wouldn't have guessed a pet would be the answer.

"QD, I've found a group of five, far to the north. It's definitely not within walking distance. I don't see how we can get Lira up there until the ships are ready for launch."

Pio said, "It's too far for her with her injuries, I'm sure. That's why she stayed behind. Poor lonely Lira. She needs us."

Jane smiled at Pio and announced to the team, "Let's start gathering the samples we need to learn to care for Lira."

Jane let Tinor take charge of the sample gathering. The young sectilian was in her element, ordering everyone around, issuing strict instructions, checking over their work, and signaling when they had reached their goals. In the end they collected samples from eight different sites and five different grass species that Pio coaxed Lira into showing them. Then they gathered a large amount to feed Lira over the next few days while Tinor analyzed the nutritional content of all the samples and worked on a solution to feeding the animal.

Tinor also recorded all kinds of parameters about the environment—light levels, temperature, salinity—and took many samples from the seafloor, so that she could replicate an aquaculture environment if that was ultimately what would be needed.

As they walked back toward the ship, Tinor settled into step next to Jane. "We will have several different options. The easiest will be if Lira takes to synthesized food. Other options include genetically modifying a sectilian land plant to feed her or starting an aquaculture project either inside Pio's habitat or nearby. Would it be possible for me to move my living quarters to the *Oblignatus* so that I won't have to waste time going back and forth?"

Jane smiled. The girl Tinor had been was all but gone. A grown woman stood in her place—confident, driven, ready to serve her community. "Of course. I think that's a fine idea. You've done excellent work today. Thank you."

Tinor looked pleased. "Who will be the Quasador Dux of that ship?"

"That's a good question. I'll be discussing that with Pio over the next few days. I'll let you know as soon as I know."

"All right," Tinor said gravely. Then, in a fit of exuberance, she turned cartwheels and raced ahead.

There was still a little child left, it seemed.

18

February 15, 2018
Five months after Jane Holloway's Global Announcement

ZARA BEGAN to dream in Mensententia. She sometimes caught herself thinking in Mensententia. She'd even accidentally used some of the alien words in mundane situations.

She'd once told her mother *"Casgrata"* instead of "Thank you," prompting the necessity to lie about wanting to learn Italian. It seemed to work, but her mother had given her some strange looks. Another time, she'd replied *"Scaluuti,"* when a friend had greeted her in the hallway at school. The friend looked at her oddly, then brightened with recognition and replied with the same salutation. Now it was commonly heard in the halls of her school—a sort of secret handshake.

It was weird to have instigated something that even popular kids thought was cool. Of course, none of them knew she'd been the one to start the movement, so she remained in obscurity. She didn't care. Knowing it was working was enough.

There were tens of thousands of shares of her original

Instamat post, hundreds of sites and message boards and forums linked to her websites, and many other sites now hosted the download. It had quietly blown up among adolescents, but it was another three weeks before the adult segment of the population even seemed to notice it was happening.

Then it made the news. The report she saw said someone had uploaded the file from Atlanta, Georgia. She hoped that no one would be able to dig any deeper into where it had originated. But even if they did, it was too late to contain it. Kids and adults everywhere were learning Mensententia. She followed a few public online groups where people posted their progress and provided peer support if anyone had questions or problems with either getting the software to work on their system or the language itself. Most people were enthusiastic and completely engaged with learning it. True to what Jane had said, anecdotally at least, adults seemed to have more difficulty with the language, but many were pursuing it anyway.

Neither her dad nor her mom ever brought it up.

She assumed that they thought she didn't have access to it because they monitored her Web use. They still hadn't discovered the laptop. They didn't know she used Instamat. They also didn't know she stayed up late every night learning the language.

She started staying up even later after she learned the word Swarm. The definition chilled her. There were giant bugs out in space that could systematically strip an entire planet clean of all living things—even if there were people there.

Then rumors started cropping up on the Web that a Ukrainian astronomer had detected something quirky in the vicinity of a distant star system called Epsilon Eridani. Something that he said he had tracked over time and seemed to be moving toward Earth. It wasn't a comet. It wasn't anything anyone recognized, but it was so far away that it could be anything or nothing. Zara studied the articles with an obsessed passion, but she couldn't glean anything meaningful from them. They were all so frustratingly vague and used terminology that she researched to endpoints that led her nowhere. The mainstream media were silent on the topic, but she wasn't sure that meant anything. It terrified her. It could be made up. But what if it wasn't?

Suddenly learning Mensententia wasn't just a game. She was driven now more than ever. She began to wonder what she could do to protect Earth from those things or anything else in the universe that might want a piece of her world. It didn't seem like just learning a language was enough anymore. But what could she do? What could any single person do?

It haunted her. Her stomach hurt all the time. She wasn't sleeping well. She constantly had headaches. Going to school everyday seemed pointless, everything seemed pointless except learning the language. But she was thirteen. Just a thirteen-year-old girl.

Her dark skin mostly camouflaged the purplish circles under her eyes that a lighter-skinned girl might have sported, but frankly nothing could cover up her grouchy disposition from being tired all the time. She became more reckless and holed up in her room with her illicit laptop all the time. Her parents seemed to attribute that behavior to simply being a teenager. At least they knocked before they came into her room, giving her time to hide the computer, but it was becoming increasingly tempting to simply defy them. But she didn't. Because they had more power than she did. She knew that. They wouldn't understand even if she told them everything.

When her friends asked her if she was the one who'd uploaded the language software, she scowled and said no, but that she was glad someone had finally done it. That put an end to those conversations. She didn't join in when other kids talked about learning the language in her presence, not even her online friends. She didn't dare. It would be too risky for her dad if anyone guessed it had been her. She just listened, comparing their experiences to her own.

It might have been a self-fulfilling prophecy, but at least it seemed like the language being out there kinda helped people focus on something positive. The whole world was learning about the language now, and there were lots of news stories reporting on that. It gave her some hope—it seemed a lot better than conspiracy theories, though those still existed too. Some people thought that it was all a hoax, but how could something this complex be a hoax? People were stupid.

And what was Jane doing out there? Did she even wonder how Earth was faring after she dropped her info bomb and went off to the stars? When would she come back and give them all more guidance? Would she be able to protect them from horrible things like the Swarm?

"Better get that chicken in the oven if we're going to eat before midnight," her dad observed.

"Oh." She looked back down at the limp, raw chicken and the huge kitchen scissors in her hands. It was her night to cook, and tonight she was making roasted chicken and cauliflower. It had once been one of her favorite meals to make. She used to enjoy being given this little bit of responsibility. Now it just felt like a chore. It was time consuming and kept her from what was really important.

"Where did you go, just now?" her dad asked, chuckling, from his spot at the counter bar. He was there to supervise and help, if needed, but his laptop was open, like always.

She grimaced. "I don't know!" She struggled with the scissors some more and remembered why she'd stopped to rest. Her hands hurt. She was trying to cut the backbone out of the chicken, but her hands were not that strong. She looked over her shoulder impatiently. "Can you cut this?"

Her dad made a comically grossed-out face. He hated chicken on the bone and raw meat in general, but he did the job for her, then washed his hands three times.

She finished the initial meal prep and had time to kill until she could do the next steps. She was so tired and didn't know what to do with herself while she waited, so she walked around the peninsula and leaned against her dad. He wrapped an arm around her and kissed the top of her head. She felt safe in his embrace. She could pretend her world wasn't so scary for just a few minutes.

She reopened her eyes drowsily and slowly refocused. Dad hadn't shut his laptop or changed the screen. It was displaying that same Mensententic soup of symbols that she'd seen before, swimming in and out of focus. Overlaid was another application in a small window off to one side with a numbered list. Each item on that list was a string of Mensententic symbols. One was high-lighted, and her father moved the cursor around until one of those symbols came into focus, then clicked on it.

But these strings of symbols were nonsense. They were completely unrelated words. What was he doing?

She frowned and watched the symbols on the screen herself. She could read many of them now, unlike the first time she'd seen them. Daddy moved his finger around on the trackpad intently. He was probably looking for the next symbol in the sequence he had there in that little window.

As the viewpoint shifted, she saw that he was zooming in and out of various parts of the word cloud. She could see now that the central core of the symbol cluster was where the language-learning file was located, along with what looked like an index and a few other files that were meant to introduce concepts that might be alien to other cultures. It was a different way of orga-nizing files than any she'd seen before, but it made sense to her. Instead of presenting grids, or lists, it allowed clusters of related ideas to be found together. It wasn't how a human would do it, but that was the point. Sectilians surely thought differently and organized things differently, but it all made sense if you learned the language first, which was precisely what Jane had told them to do.

Had her dad skipped that part or not found it yet? It was all right there, but he was stringing these nonsense symbols together instead—for what purpose? It didn't make any sense. Couldn't he see that there was a pattern? Or was he trying to find something very specific? It didn't really seem like he knew what he was doing.

She looked up at him quizzically.

His eyes were heavy lidded. His posture was slumped. He looked tired and defeated. She didn't like seeing him like that. And when she thought about it, she realized he'd looked like that for weeks. She wondered what he knew. He didn't return her gaze for a moment, as he kept looking into the cloud for the next symbol in his sequence, methodically clicking on each one.

Then he inhaled sharply. He seemed to wake up and realize that she had seen his screen, which he was normally extremely careful to prevent. He blinked a few times. His mouth opened to speak, but then closed again. He slowly reached out to close the laptop and looked down at his hands, silently, like he was just very tired. She knew that feeling well.

The first timer went off.

She straightened and went back around the peninsula.

"What was that timer for?" he murmured.

"Time to start the rice."

She poured the premeasured water into the pot and turned on the stove. The mood between them was strained all of a sudden. She felt weird. Her heart was beating fast and her hands moved jerkily. She was terrified, but she had to say something to him. She had to. The moment had come.

"Daddy—"

"I—"

They spoke at the same time and then stopped, staring at each other warily. She wondered if he was as scared as she was. He looked like it. She waited to see what he would say.

He grimaced. "I just made a mistake. I'm really not supposed to bring this home, much less let you see it, baby girl. There just aren't enough hours in the day."

"You're tired, Daddy. It's okay."

He shook his head. "Not okay. If I could just make some sense of this..." He slapped his hands lightly against the edge of the countertop and came around the peninsula to hover over her.

She sniffed and turned to grab the scissors to open the rice packet and the flavoring packet. She was breathing shallowly. The urge to run upstairs and hide in her room was strong. Instead she poured in the rice and they both watched the pot as she stirred the contents and waited for it to boil.

"Daddy," she whispered, "I can make sense of it. If you don't know where to start, I can show you. I can show you how it works."

She glanced up at him. He looked like he'd been smacked across the face.

"What are you talking about?" he said sharply.

She blurted out, "It's just that the words you're putting together are nonsense, Daddy. They don't mean anything. I don't think it works like that."

He searched her face like he didn't know what she was saying —like she was just as enigmatic as the software he was trying to decipher.

Then he seemed to deflate all at once, all the energy animating his body going out of him. He put a limp hand up to his face and rubbed at the five-o'clock shadow bristling there.

"You've been... Where? How?" He shook his head. "Damn it. It doesn't matter. Show me what you think you know."

They went back around the peninsula together. She showed him the center of the cloud. "Yes, we looked there first," he said impatiently. But when she clicked on the symbols for the language-learning software in the right sequence, the familiar start window came up. He looked startled. His lips pursed. "I suspect you're familiar with this part," he said.

She nodded and went back to the main screen. Then she showed him some of the other parts and translated what they were for. He grabbed a notebook and scribbled furiously, nodding and asking her to slow down so he could meticulously copy the alien symbols.

They forgot about the rice until it boiled over, hissing and sputtering, making a burnt smell and a brown mess all over the stove. Zara went back to turn the heat down and clean up the mess. She felt self-conscious, because her dad was watching her with a look of indecision on his face. Suddenly he grabbed his phone and went into the family room at the back of the house. She could faintly hear him talking to someone. He alternated between sounding contrite and persuasive, but she couldn't make out exactly what he was saying.

Mama wandered in and clucked at the mess on the stove, but helped her wipe it up and then cracked the oven door to see how the chicken was doing.

Daddy came back in. He looked excited. "Okay. Okay. You and me, baby girl. We're going to the lab to show them what you just showed me."

"What?" Mama looked from Zara to her dad and back again.

"Well, it looks like our daughter has been learning Mensen-tentia," Dad said.

Her mother looked shocked and a little angry. "She what?"

Daddy shook his head. "Cilla, just let it be for now. I think she's going to be a big help. We'll shake out the details later." He went to the hall closet and grabbed his jacket and Zara's. "Let's go."

Mama narrowed her eyes. The second timer went off. "What about dinner? I think this can wait twenty minutes so you can eat a few bites."

Daddy frowned but ultimately agreed.

That night, Zara became the youngest employee of NASA's Jet Propulsion Laboratory.

19

JANE STOOD on the beach for a long time watching Alan, Ron, Jaross, and Ryliuk assist the pligan workers as they placed the last of the new hull scales on the *Speroancora* with a crane suspended from the nearest Tree structure. Both ships glittered like polished obsidian in the pale sunlight.

The *Speroancora* didn't look like a ship that had nearly been a total loss. It looked magnificent. And if Alan's calculations were correct, the ship was stronger and safer than ever before.

They would be leaving very soon.

She had wound a piece of fabric around her head and neck, but the wind still worked some pieces of her hair free and lashed them against her cheeks until they stung. She put her head down and tramped across the beach to the ramp leading into the *Oblignatus*.

Pio greeted her warmly as soon as she stepped inside. And through her, Huna, Tinor, and Pledor sent a welcoming "*Scaluuti!*"

This ship was a twin to her own. It had the same dimensions, same configuration, and same drab color scheme, but a completely different energy. Whereas Jane's predecessor had commissioned colorful murals for some of the public spaces, testimony to Rageth's love of art, this ship was bare of unique decor, though the remnants of the lives of the sectilians who had died here so long ago still lay scattered around everywhere Jane walked. No one had taken time to tidy this ship up yet. Thankfully, Pio had removed the bodies long ago, just as Brai had, using armies of squillae. The new Qua'dux would finish the clean up in their own way. They would probably want to catalog many of the instruments and devices and put them away carefully, just as her crew had.

Jane loosened her head wrap as she boarded, but didn't remove it. The core of the ship was cooler. She made her way there quickly. Rageth's memories of her first time aboard the *Speroancora* flitted in the back of her mind, triggered by the appearance of the bare ship.

She saw Lira first. The shaggy sea cow snuffled against the barrier of Pio's habitat as though wanting to be petted, then turned away to look up, her curled tusks scraping against the glass as she went.

Pio appeared, descending slowly to the level of the gangway Jane stood on. Pio was longer and more slender than Brai. Her shimmering, silver-and-gold-gilded limbs twined around her body, gossamer fins undulating along her mantle. Enormous cobalt-blue eyes, surrounded by a milky white sclera glittering with aquamarine iridescence, turned on Jane. Jane had always thought Brai was lovely to look at, but Pio was breathtaking.

"It is time to decide, isn't it?" Pio asked warily.

"It is, Pio. I'm sorry to push you, but there isn't much time left. We'll be leaving for Terac soon. We need to get people settled."

"Are you certain you can't manage two ships?"

Jane shifted uneasily under Pio's unblinking stare. Pio had

asked this before and Jane had been firm then. "One ship is more than enough to manage. You'll do fine with whomever you choose. Having someone aboard will be far better, in case we get separated."

Pio muttered irritably, "I do wish you would choose for me."

Jane grimaced and shook her head slowly. "You know I won't do that."

"I do know." She was silent for a moment. Her arms whorled and twined around her in agitation, and her skin flashed her anxiety a couple of times. "Perhaps it is wrong, but I want to select a human, rather than a sectilian or Huna."

Jane drew her brows together and stepped closer to the barrier between them. "It's not wrong. Tell me about your thought process."

"It's really rather simple. I'm afraid to trust a sectilian and I just don't know the pligan very well."

Tears pricked Jane's eyes. Such a bald confession. So filled with history and pain, but uttered so cleanly. Pio didn't evade the truth, even if it was like pressing hard on a painful bruise. Jane appreciated that about her. In time, she felt Pio would heal fully and be wise and formidable. Even now, Jane knew she trusted her without reservation. Pio had risked everything when she'd turned against Kai'Memna, and then done it again when she'd used her own ship to prevent the *Speroancora* from sinking to the bottom of Pliga's ocean.

"That makes sense. You realize the sectilians we know now are very different from the ones you knew before. They've learned from the trials of the past."

Pio twisted sharply, losing some of her grace. "Not different enough to give me comfort."

"Okay."

"I see how the humans interact with Brai. With me. I note the difference. I could never accept someone like Ryliuk as my Qua'-

dux. He does not see us as more than animals. I will not be that docile servant again."

Pio's concern here was legitimate. "He has come a long way, but still has much to learn."

"But my choice will cause some problems. I've been struggling with the decision because of this. I think he will accept, but there are relationships to consider. Many things to consider, actually. I don't want to make life harder for anyone. Or cause anyone to suffer."

Pio sounded calm, but Jane's heart stuttered. Did she mean to ask Alan? That would mean separation. She hadn't thought of that as a possibility. It had never occurred to her that Pio might choose Alan—because of his general distrust of Brai—but perhaps Pio saw that as some kind of positive?

Pio turned away slightly. Her regenerating arm came into view. It looked functional now, but half the length of the rest. Schlewan said it would eventually reach full size, but that would take time. Lira hung suspended upside down, her eyes pinched closed in bliss as Pio rubbed an arm over her flank. And there was more—Jane could sense through her connection with Pio that Lira felt happiness. It surprised Jane, but also laid to rest any worry that they'd done the wrong thing by allowing Pio to bring a wild animal aboard.

Jane waited while Pio debated with herself.

Finally Pio turned back to Jane. "I would like to choose Doctor Ronald Gibbs to be the Quasador Dux of this ship."

Jane let out a breath. Ron. She wanted Ron. Jane smiled. He was the Qua'dux she would have chosen for her. "Excellent choice."

"I like how he is genial and calm under pressure. He is decisive but never belligerent."

Ron was a model example of the US astronaut program. Their standard candidates always demonstrated this type of self-possessed personality. In fact, Ron, Ajaya, and Tom Compton were all nearly imperturbable individuals. NASA had stepped outside that comfort zone when including her and Alan, and to some extent Mark Walsh, on the *Providence* mission. They'd said they had found a new dynamic that their experts had decided worked better under stressful conditions. And perhaps they'd been correct. It had been one hell of a test program.

Jane nodded. "He is all of those things. I think the two of you will work together well. I'd be surprised if he didn't agree."

"Oh, I know my shortcomings. I wasn't always like this, you know." A note of melancholy crept into her mental voice. "But I think he will fill in the chinks. He will help to keep me balanced."

Jane didn't disagree. "Do you have a second choice?"

"Doctor Ajaya Varma, for similar reasons. Though..." Pio turned her attention again to Lira, who was rolling under Pio's caresses. "And herein my concerns lie. I'd really like Tinor to stay because of her devotion to Lira—she has made it possible to keep Lira with me. If Varma wishes to stay with Gibbs, and Tinor also remains aboard, that would leave you without a medical doctor on the *Speroancora*. If we should need to part ways at any point, that could be a problem for you."

Jane sighed. "I see why you're worried about it. Well, let's find out what Ron says first, then the rest will work itself out. One step at a time, don't you think?"

Pio's agitated limbs settled back into a more normal, graceful, fluid motion.

"Call him down for a visit," Jane said. "They've just finished outside, so he should be free. I'm going to see how Huna is doing with the Tree on the Greenspace Deck. I'll come back in a bit to find out what Ron said."

"Oh—now?"

"Let's not put it off any longer."

Pio immediately seemed distressed again.

"I assure you, you'll feel better once it's done and you know his answer."

"I'm sure you're right. You must be right."

"Remember, Pio—the yoke is gone. The relationship you have with a new Quasador Dux will be very different from any you've had before. It will be cooperative in nature. You will have a meaningful say in your future."

Pio agreed silently, and while she was still apprehensive, her anxiety seemed greatly reduced from where it had been at the beginning of their conversation.

Jane smiled and waved at Lira. "I'll be back soon."

Jane opened the door of the Greenspace Deck to find it looking very much like a construction zone. Plants and trees lay on their sides in piles around the perimeter of the deck with coarse fabric wrapped around their root balls. The soil was churned up with bits of leaves and branches sticking out. About a dozen pligan workers were digging up vegetation and moving it around. Huna might have been all but shunned for his behavior, but they still cared about his welfare. They'd sent work crews to help ensure that he would survive aboard the *Oblignatus*.

"Qua'dux!"

Jane turned to see Pledor emerging from around masses of greenery. He was looking cheerful despite being covered in dirt.

"How are things progressing here?" she asked.

"Briskly, with all this help." He gestured to the pile of plants behind him and cocked his head to one side, watching her reaction in his very birdlike way. "These will be hauled back to the Tree for cultivation and study. The pligans are excited to study the genetics of these plants—as well they should be! Sectilius has quite a bounty of flora that they would do well to scrutinize! I've also set aside a selection of useful food-bearing specimens to transplant to the *Speroancora*. It will greatly increase our daily yield." Pledor's willowy frame swelled with pride. "And I have a surprise for Master Ryliuk." He indicated a wilted pile of foliage that Jane had assumed was destined for composting. A closer look revealed it to be the fuzzy plants that Ryliuk was so fond of.

Jane raised her eyebrows. The plants didn't look like they were doing too well. She would have guessed they were dead, but she didn't know anything about them.

"I've adjusted the lighting, soil composition, and watering schedule to mimic conditions on Pliga. They'll be bringing in a rooted specimen of the Tree any moment now."

Jane wondered how Huna felt about Pledor taking over this project. He'd surely be able to fine-tune things after Pledor left. "I'm certain your extensive experience gardening in the Sten compound has been very helpful."

"Oh, it most certainly has," Pledor agreed, and he dashed away to direct some pligans carrying plants from elsewhere on the deck.

Jane strolled around, careful to keep out of the way of the workers as a massive cart with a twenty-foot-tall tree was wheeled in. It was obvious immediately that this was Huna's Tree. Its trunk was disproportionately wide, probably at least three feet in diameter, with several small sap nodes coming off of it. The leaves were the same thick, leathery ones she'd seen on the Tree, though quite a bit smaller. Perhaps this Tree had been genetically altered to survive under these conditions.

The workers removed bindings and coverings from the roots and gently lowered it into a wide hole. Then they began to painstakingly stretch out the roots and pat soil into place around them. This went on for a long time—arranging, scooping, and smoothing by hand with a great deal of attention to detail and a distinct sense of reverence. Some flexible piping was laid among the roots at the same time, presumably for irrigation. Jane didn't intrude to ask. Somehow it felt wrong to interrupt.

She heard a sharp intake of breath and glanced back at the main door to see Ryliuk standing there with his ears pulled back and his eyes bulging. He strode directly to the plants Pledor had been saving for him and knelt. She walked over to him. He was tenderly lifting up the limp plants.

He met her eyes. "They're in terrible pain," he said to her, mind to mind, his words laden with anguish. "Who did this?"

"I'm certain it wasn't intentional. Pledor was so excited to show them to you—"

Ryliuk stood and marched out of the room, brushing coldly by Pledor, whose animated expression fell instantly.

Jane sent him a sympathetic look. She hoped this incident wouldn't cause friction between the two men. Sectilians took their disputes to the local Dux. That was her.

She sighed and headed back to the core of the ship to see how Ron and Pio had fared.

Jane rode the deck transport to the level Ron was on and walked across the catwalk to find him sprawled out on the grating with his feet against Pio's tank, back against the railing, elbows on knees. Jane didn't know the content of their conversation, but Ron's expression was serious, despite his relaxed pose. He motioned at her to join them, so she sank down next to him, facing Pio.

"Pio was just asking me to team up," he said simply in his deep baritone.

"And have you got an answer for her?"

He smiled. "I'd be honored to serve with her."

Jane connected with Pio, and a wave of relief and exuberance washed over her.

Ron nodded, acknowledging the emotion coming from Pio. "I think one of the first things the four of us should talk about is the chain of command. It's a sticky subject, given the history here, but it would be foolish to ignore it. Currently we have a fleet of two ships. In time that may grow if we find more trapped kuboderans, so we should establish protocols early on that feel comfortable for everyone but keep everything working as it should."

Pio hung in place, barely moving. Her thoughts stilled as she focused on every nuance of Ron's mental speech.

He continued. "Jane and Brai have set up something new. A more egalitarian community than the sectilians had. I don't think we need some elaborate ranking system like a military. But I think that we should make every effort to communicate well. Each of us should manage our portion of the day-to-day running of each ship as diplomatically as possible, but if bad stuff goes down, I'm going to be looking to Jane to see what she wants from us. I guess I'd call her QD Prime or something. Does that make sense to the both of you?"

Pio agreed immediately, and they both turned their eyes to Jane.

Jane was less certain. "If bad stuff goes down, Ron, you have far more military experience. I've counted on you to advise me on several occasions—"

"And I'll continue to advise you in that capacity. Given where we are and what we're about to do, we need someone with diplomatic experience as our default leader. I've been impressed time and again with your ability to handle these situations. Let's keep things as they are."

Jane acquiesced, reluctantly.

Ron clapped once. "All right. Pio and I need to get to know each other better, so I'll move my stuff over here. I'm going to do a quick walk-through of the ship and check in on Huna. And... I need to talk to Ajaya. See what she wants to do. We should meet tomorrow and iron out more details, talk about crew assignments. But this is a good start, I think."

Jane stood and held out her hand to Ron. "Congratulations, Quasador Dux Ronald Gibbs."

20

October 21, 2018

ALAN WOKE from an indeterminate amount of sleep and rolled over, feeling for Jane. She wasn't there. He rubbed his hands over his face, trying to decide whether he wanted to sleep more or just get up. If Jane wasn't there, it meant it was human and sectilian daytime, but he had no idea at what point in the day it was now. Jane had turned the lights off when she left.

He wouldn't know for a while whether he'd caught up on sleep or not. It would depend on whether the grogginess lasted. He was tired of feeling like a zombie. Hopefully today was the day that would end. As soon as he woke up.

God, he missed coffee.

Over the course of their stay on Pliga, he'd completely lost all hope of a normal sleep schedule, sleeping in fits and starts or not at all. Even when he had time to sleep, he couldn't seem to relax. He was either wired from overstimulation or dragging his ass through endless days.

He had a lot of big projects going on that dominated his

thoughts. That level of obsession tended to make it harder to sleep. Immediately after they'd gotten the ship secured and the biggest repairs out of the way, he'd begun outfitting both ships with anti-anipraxis broadcasting devices to create a sort of external anti-anipraxis shield, but allow internal anipraxis communication to continue as normal. They wouldn't be caught with their pants down again. Kai'Memna might be dead, but he still had followers out there, and who knew how motivated they would be to get revenge for that genocidal maniac's death? He couldn't let them batter Jane's brain like that ever again.

In that same vein, he'd taken the opportunity to design other offensive and defensive measures. Implementing them had been a much larger challenge. Luckily the *Speroancora* had a robust workshop on the Tech Deck, containing theoretical modeling tools as well as massive bays of 3-D printers.

Wormhole travel was amazing, and clearly the fastest mode of traversing vast distances in space, but it took time to spool up that drive, which meant it wasn't a great method of escaping from a foe at short notice should the odds ever be against them. Creating wormholes required the use of exotic particles. That had gotten Alan thinking. What if those were the same particles a certain Mexican physicist was thinking about when he imagined the Alcubierre drive?

This kind of gravimetric or warp drive was consistent with Einstein's field equations, and wasn't contradicted by any sectilian theories of physics that he could find. He even took the time to talk to Jaross about it. She was heavily trained in theoretical physics, despite the state of their civilization. She couldn't see any reason that it wouldn't work either. They put their heads together, and with the help of the sectilian modeling tools, they began to work out the math and then make models.

Now he was building one. He had two reasons. While a drive of this nature wasn't needed for the *Speroancora* to move from point A to point B for travel, it could potentially allow them to dodge any kind of laser or artillery. Moving short distances faster than light would be a very effective defense. Even if they couldn't predict when a weapon would be fired, they could easily set up a macro that would move the ship around randomly while they were in combat, only staying in one location long enough to get off a shot of their own. It was theoretically possible that the warp bubble alone could deflect laser fire and ballistic weapons because of the tidal forces present at the edges of the space curvature. They'd still have their heavy-duty pligan-grown hull, and eventually the regrown nanite escutcheon, but this would give them a lot more flexibility under combat conditions.

Secondly, he was adapting the drive to hurl ordnance. This idea was much trickier to work out. If he could control the shift of space around the ship even for a moment, and he could drop something into that vortex, his models showed it would create a slingshot effect, allowing the drive to hurl things so fast the bad guys wouldn't know what hit them.

What would he throw? He had two prototypes. One was a fission bomb, which, when detonated remotely, would create a massive EMP which would obliterate all electronics, including squillae. That would remove a kuboderan's power over their sectilian servants, if any were present, as well as disable the ship in question. The other was a mass filled with his seek-and-destroy nanites. One way or another, he was determined to take away the edge these rogue kuboderans had. He had a lot of other ideas too, but those were on the back burner for now. These projects were more likely to produce dramatic results.

If this thing worked like he thought it would—and all his modeling showed that it would—he would get to name the resulting apparatus. This was going to give him major, major cred back home among his old colleagues. He could name it the Alcubierre drive or simply the gravimetric drive. He could even name it the Bergen drive. But he liked the idea of calling it the blink drive, for the level 102 World of Warcraft mage he'd had to leave behind on Earth and because of the way the ship would appear to blink in and out of existence across space-time. So that's what he decided to call it.

This project forced him to swallow his reluctance about communicating with Brai for the greater good. He looped Jaross in, because it was just good practice to have another knowledge-able set of eyes on something this complex. The three of them spent countless hours going over the specs of the blink drive. Brai pointed out a couple of issues Alan hadn't seen. Jaross raised a lot of good questions that ultimately led to a better design. He wouldn't have been able to get up and running so fast without them and their extensive knowledge of physics.

When all three of them were satisfied with the final model, Alan began the printing phase, and Jaross helped him build the device right there on Tech Deck where they could tap into the neural-electric pathways that connected Brai cybernetically to the ship. There would be controls for the blink drive on the bridge, but ultimately Brai would be the most qualified person to use it, as navigator. If their experiments went well, Alan would make a second one for the *Oblignatus*. The process of creating the experimental drive had cost him a lot of sleep, but he felt sure that eventually it would all be worth it.

Living was good.

There were plenty of other things stealing his sleep as well. Work on the Tree-grown hull plating had been taking place errat-ically around the clock. He felt he had to be there when one of the pieces was positioned—he'd never seen the pligans do a bad job of it, but the plating wasn't easily repositioned once it was sealed down, so it seemed best to supervise each placement.

Basically, the work crews showed up at any freakin' time and gave no warning that they were about to start. That meant he was often woken by the rumble of the crane moving into position. He'd rouse himself and throw on some clothes and get out there. Then, more often than not, he'd just stay awake and work because the exposure to sunlight seemed to trick his body into day mode. Ron and Jaross were the same. Sometimes even Ryliuk showed up.

That guy.

Ryliuk had been throwing a big stink over how Pledor had mishandled some of his pet plants. He and Pledor had a couple of yelling matches. It wasn't pretty. So much for the planet of cooperation. Schlewan and Tinor were always going on about how sectilians were collaborators, and shared resources, and cooperation blah blah, on and on. Well, Alan was beginning to think that was some pretty idealistic stuff they were spouting and nothing like reality at all.

It got so bad Jane and Ron had to take it into account when they worked out ship assignments. Pledor had now run both Huna and Ryliuk off the *Speroancora*.

And Pledor was still there.

Alan sighed and stretched out on his back to think for a minute before getting out of bed.

Ryliuk was nonessential anyway. He didn't really have any useful skills aside from brawn. His super mind powers were matched or exceeded by Brai's. So, meh. It was fine. Ryliuk had packed up all of his stuff and transplanted his fuzzy-huggy plants to the *Oblignatus*. Apparently Huna was helping him nurse them back to health, and everybody was happy over there communing on the Greenspace Deck like a bunch of hippies.

As far as the other ship assignments were concerned, they had two engineers and two doctors, so it made sense to split them up by job. Jaross had been handy to have around. She'd gotten up to speed quickly by taking some computer course she found in the database—the very same one he was taking, now that he knew it was there—and had become exceedingly competent. He'd miss the help, especially with Ron gone too. He'd manage though.

Ajaya and Ron were pretty low-key about their relationship, but it was clear they were a thing, so he wasn't surprised when Jane said Ajaya would be moving to the other ship. Man. They were splitting up the band. He'd always known it might happen, but he still didn't like it much. He hadn't been sorry to see Mark Walsh go, but Compton...yeah, that dude had been all right. And now this. It felt weird. He didn't like it.

So that meant that the *Speroancora* would be manned by himself, Jane, Brai, Pledor, and Tinor. He and Jane, and their tentacled third wheel, would be stuck with the two people he liked least. Pledor was just an ass. And Tinor... well... he just couldn't look the kiddo in the eye after she'd managed to sneak into his bed. It was freaky. He would continue to be uncomfortable and to avoid her whenever possible.

He was kinda sorry Schlewan would be staying behind. He might actually miss the old bird.

The *Oblignatus* would be crewed by Pio, Ron, Ajaya, Jaross, Huna, and Ryliuk. And, of course, Lira as team mascot. They had gotten the better end of the deal, by far.

He rubbed his face again, scrubbing at the drool collected in his beard. He was definitely alert. He must be awake. He launched himself out of bed, tapped the lights, stretched, and wandered over to a terminal to check the time.

Fuck.

He'd slept for more than sixteen hours. That must be some kind of record. They'd be launching soon.

He took a quick shower, dressed, and headed up to the bridge. Jane was there by herself. She looked like she was in a deep trance but kinda perked up when he moved into her field of view.

"Hey," he said. "Still green for launch?"

"Almost ready. Brai is doing the last-minute checks."

Alan rubbed the back of his neck. He should have been helping with that. "I wish you'd woken me."

"Oh, no. We're good. You needed the sleep."

And she really meant it. It wasn't some passive-aggressive lip service. Jane said what she meant. It was damn refreshing. She was literally the best.

Alan sat down at the engineering console and cracked his knuckles. Everything looked good there. He connected to the Braimeister. "Hey, big guy. Help me get up to speed?"

"Certainly," was the reply he got. Then the flood of information hit him like a tsunami. He did that mental pinching thing he'd learned, to slow it down so he could parse it all. Within a couple of minutes he was aware of everything he needed to know and agreed that they were safe to go ahead with launch.

He and Brai had obsessively checked and rechecked every pertinent system aboard for the last few weeks while Brai and Pio were recovering from their shark encounter, between plating installations and the other projects. Everything should be fine. But Alan knew that things had a way of cropping up at the last minute when it came to launches, and he'd learned long ago that with this kind of immense power use, there was no such thing as too many system checks.

It went off without a hitch. Within moments of Jane giving the nod they were in orbit, and the *Oblignatus* joined them a minute later. Of course, no one patted him on the back for doing his job properly, but that was part of being on a team.

Immediately, Jane was on to the next thing. "Scan for the debris of the *Portacollus*. Let's see if there's any information we can salvage from the wreckage. We need to know more about what Kai'Memna was planning."

Alan frowned. It had been months since they'd landed. They knew the *Portacollus* had crashed on the dark, arctic side of the planet. Atmospheric conditions in the transition zone between the habitable side and the frozen side were too intense for a shuttle to pass through. After their descent on Atielle, they were certain of that. So they'd had to wait until now to attempt reconnaissance. Surely the crazy winds would have scattered anything useful, destroyed it, or buried it in ice and snow. It seemed unlikely they'd find anything that would yield information about Kai'Memna's plans for galactic domination.

But still they scanned.

And scanned.

And scanned some more.

They easily found the other ship, the *Colocallida*, which had been captained by one of Kai'Memna's minions'. It was smashed to smithereens on the dark side of Pliga.

But the remains of the *Portacollus* were nowhere to be found.

Jane was beside herself. "Let's look at the sensor data again from the day we landed." She and Ron were on the mental-squid-phone, along with everyone else. Things were pretty tense.

"Yeah, that looks bad," Ron said as they replayed images from Pio's Hail Mary maneuver, when she docked the *Oblignatus* with the *Colocallida* and rammed that ship into Kai'Memna's *Portacollus*, creating massive destruction.

"See there? His tank was breached," Jane said. "I don't see how he could have survived that." She was right. Ice shards were visible in the recording.

Alan cleared his throat. He didn't want to say it. "Brai survived a breach to his tank."

Jane flinched visibly. "Barely. He had help."

Ron said, "Don't forget Kai'Memna had a sectilian crew on board. He would have had even more help than Brai. He must have managed to limp away."

To fight another day.

Holy shit.

Kai'Memna was still out there. He knew where Earth was. He'd threatened Earth. And he claimed he knew how to talk to the Swarm.

And they'd just been sitting there on Pliga for months.

Earth was fucked.

21

FOR BRAI, it was a maelstrom.

He'd felt something like it only once. He and Pio had gotten too close to the surface while exploring near the shore. A strong rip current had caught them off guard. In those moments, all they knew was the sudden chaos echoing in each other's minds, tumbling, panic spiking through flailing limbs, reaching out and finding nothing to grab as they were pushed out to deeper waters in a dizzying rush. It was a storm of disorientation and fear. No sensory input made sense.

It was very much like this.

They had just discovered that Kai'Memna had not met dusk as they had all quite firmly believed.

Each member of both crews reacted to this discovery passionately, and their simultaneous emotions overwhelmed him—disbelief, panic, desperate fear, despair, anger, a desire for reprisal. It felt toxic. He could not begin to process his own feelings on the matter because their emotions broke over him like a dam bursting. He couldn't control it or even stem the tide.

It was worse than any physical pain, and he found himself

with his limbs reflexively pulled in, barbs out, to protect himself from it. Of course that offered no material defense. It was just a vestigial, instinctual compulsion without meaning in this context.

He had no distance. There was no insulation within his mind to retreat behind. The old squillae programming would have allowed him to merely watch this happening dispassionately, but that was gone. He wondered momentarily if that would have been better.

And then it ebbed. Just a bit. And his own fears got purchase. Then the dam broke again as they cascaded out of control.

Kai'Memna was a treacherous, genocidal fiend. He was alive out there, might still be murdering their brethren, converting them to his cause, sounding a call to war, or communicating with the Swarm to further his nefarious agenda.

He had already nearly killed them, and would have succeeded, if not for Pio and Jane and their resolute bravery. Kai'Memna had a vindictive inclination. He would most certainly come for them again. And he was powerful and devious. What if he could bring fifteen ships—or fifty—against them? It was certainly possible. They wouldn't have a chance against such numbers. Kai'Memna would be free to forward his plot to destroy anyone he opposed, which seemed to be the entirety of the sentient races.

After seconds that lasted eternities the worst of the emotional tempest subsided, leaving a corporeal ache throbbing in his brains. Rational thought returned.

Pio. He worried for Pio. What would this news do to her? Kai'Memna had forced her to choose between death and participating in his evil plans and then used her as bait to trap the *Speroancora*.

He reached out to her, a private thread of thought, to assess her mental state and to query about her reaction to all of this. To his astonishment, her mindscape was smooth, unruffled, even tranquil. In fact she seemed to exude a sense of wonder. At first he thought it was stupefaction, that she was so distraught she had become completely dysfunctional. But then gentle amusement seeped into his awareness and he knew his primary assessment was incorrect.

She was watching him watch her, and she found that rather droll.

"Brai, I'm fine."

He probed a bit deeper, verifying that what she said was true. It was. "I was concerned."

"Not without good reason," she conceded.

"How can you be so calm?" he asked.

She paused to reflect. "I have just realized something about myself that has changed everything. Perhaps you'll find it foolish, but it has oddly given me some peace of mind. Perhaps it won't last, but for now, I am fine."

"What is it?"

"I felt dread as we began to search. The fear intensified as we went on. It was near to paralyzing. I was fully present, though, the moment Qua'dux Ronald Gibbs made the statement that Kai'Memna must be alive. I was well on the way to shutting down completely—but I noticed something. I noted the first flicker of Jane's fear. It caught my attention and held it. And then I just observed. Her—all of them. Even Huna. Even you. And the longer I watched all of you react, the more I felt my own fear slipping away. Brai, four very different, unrelated species of sentients reacted to this realization in much the same way."

Brai stared at the glass wall of his enclosure, wishing he could see her physically—another data point to confirm that she was as stable as she seemed. "Yes?"

"I have been struggling... with pain, sorrow, loss on so many levels. But the primary source of that struggle has been with the feeling of it. I rejected the emotions out of hand as being weak or inferior because I'd never had to process them on such a scale before. I did everything I could to resist them, to avoid them, to distract myself from them. But I couldn't. Not completely. I felt brittle. I thought there was something broken inside me. Kai'Memna reset my nanites so they would not control me, but I had no context within which to integrate a wholly new side of myself. I was breaking apart from the inside out."

"I have felt that myself," Brai confessed. He sensed her drifting weightlessly through her own enclosure.

"Having you in my life, the humans, sectilians, and now Lira as well—these experiences have brought me so much joy—a positive emotion that makes life pleasant. Realizing that laid the groundwork for this moment, I think."

"I'm glad—"

"Brai. I'm normal. My reactions are normal. It is normal to feel. And there is something else—it is also normal to resist feeling unpleasant things. The sectilians do. You do. The male humans do somewhat more than the females, but they all do it to some degree. This was an instructive moment for me. I am normal within the parameters of this highly variable group."

Something inside him relaxed. He went limp, his limbs loosening around him.

She continued, "My deepest fear for many standard years was that these emotions were proof that I was becoming something akin to Memna. That they were just the beginning of a path to madness. That I was undeserving of freedom. I didn't want to hurt anyone. Ever. But this is not madness, Brai. It's normal to feel. We aren't monsters. We're ordinary."

She was right. How strange to observe something in others in order to realize something fundamental about oneself. Their bodies might be different. Their thought patterns, abilities, and needs even more so. But every sentient being had a sense of self that was composed of primary emotions, common to all.

It was completely daft to realize such a fundamental thing—
an understanding that should be present at birth. But somehow
he'd always thought he and all of his species were different.
Better in some ways and inferior in others—many others. The
squillae had imposed that, made it integral to his core personality.
But now, perhaps he and Pio could be free.

"We are. Yes," he agreed. He began to share the sense of
wonderment she'd been experiencing.

"It has given me great peace to know this. It's probably
obvious to most people, but I hope I can be forgiven for being
slow to understand."

"Of course you can!" he exclaimed, so forcefully it embarrassed him a little. She didn't seem to notice.

"Memna will want revenge for my betrayal. That puts my
new crew in peril. I must be as honest with myself and others as
possible now. Especially Quasador Dux Ronald Gibbs. I must be
hard and sharp when that is necessary and soft and pliable when
that is necessary. I must adapt or we will not survive."

Brai considered this. They were all adapting, learning from
each other, changing. By working together, this multicultural
crew had developed strengths that were formidable.

Kai'Memna was a single-minded individual. He could not
comprehend what they were becoming together.

Woe to him, if he tested that.

22

JANE FELT her connection to Brai and Pio weaken and knew they must be discussing this discovery between themselves privately. She hated to interrupt, but the other three members of her crew were on the bridge looking to her for direction. She would be surprised if Ron wasn't experiencing the same. They needed to talk. The best and fastest way they could do that, without docking with the *Oblignatus*, was through Brai or Pio or both.

She closed her eyes and concentrated on getting his attention, something she rarely had to do. "Brai, Pio, we need you to be fully present."

Instantly the anipraxic connection between all of them strengthened, and it was like lights coming up to full in a dark room. The part of her brain that was connected to Brai and Pio was fully active, and she now had a sort of external sense of every member of both crews. Everyone seemed much calmer than they'd been only minutes before. Brai especially. That was good. Jane took a deep breath. Brai and Pio were good for each other— and that was good for all of them.

She squared her shoulders and walked over to the communications console to send a request for visual contact to the *Oblignatus*. She could feel them, but she just needed to see them as they talked. Her request was answered immediately, and the large central viewscreen came to life. It was like a mirror inhabited by Ron, Ajaya, Ryliuk, Jaross, and Hator.

"We have to decide a course of action," she said.

"He knows the location of Earth. We have to go home," Alan said.

Ryliuk spoke up. "He knows the location of every sentient world. They're all at risk. Sectilius is defenseless. He may send the Swarm to finish what he started."

Alan huffed. "I'm sorry, dude, but there's no comparison. The population of Earth is in the billions."

Jane walked over to Alan and put her hand on his arm. He bowed his head.

Huna said, "If this Kai'Memna wants vengeance, your last known location was Pliga."

"Perhaps he thinks we are already dead? We did crash in the ocean," Tinor said in a tiny voice.

"*We* thought that about *him*," Alan said.

Jaross's expression was bleak on the screen, but her mental voice remained calm. "Is the extinction of any sentient species acceptable? How can we choose one planet to protect when we do not have the ability to track the Swarm?"

Ajaya interrupted, "Does anyone have the ability to track the Swarm?"

Ryliuk answered stiffly and coldly, "I remember hearing a news report, before the plague, that there were sectilian ships working with other USR scientists to develop tracking technologies for an early warning system to be put in place. That was many standard years ago. Surely some progress has been made by now. We must go to Terac, as originally planned. That is your duty in this case. This information must be shared. Where you go from there is up to you. I, for one, wish to work for any resistance that may be amassed. I will leave your company on Terac if necessary."

The rest of the sectilians had muted reactions to that announcement, some in agreement, some in dismay.

Jane sniffed. Her fingers felt cold. Even wrapped around Alan's arm, they weren't warming. "Earth has already been warned about the possibility of a Swarm attack. That was part of the packet of information I gave them when we left our solar system. Surely they will have already begun to build defenses."

If they'd listened to her.

If they could master the sectilian technology, and if that would be enough to stop a Swarm pod.

"Your world is remote. The Swarm travels slowly compared to our capabilities. There is time to do much before the threat becomes real," Jaross reminded them.

Alan closed his eyes. "From what I've read, over vast distances they can accelerate to FTL speeds. We don't know if there are Swarm pods in the vicinity of Earth or how fast they can communicate with each other. Earth could already be under attack. They need our help."

Ron stood up from his Qua'dux's chair and paced a bit. Jane followed him with her eyes until he spoke. "That seems unlikely to me. It should still take years for them to get there, probably a lot longer than that. It's all conjecture, of course, but I'm going to guess we have at least a decade to prepare Earth. We have plenty of time to not only warn everyone, but also to develop and build defenses."

"If there were sectilians in the Quasador Dux positions on these vessels, we would not be indulging in this conversation," Ryliuk said coldly.

Jane felt anger rising in both Brai and Pio. Brai blurted out,

"Perhaps not, but if it were not for the selfish practices of the Sectilius, the monster that is Kai'Memna would never have been created."

That statement went through the group like a shockwave.

It clearly angered Ryliuk. "Quite the opposite. His shackles were warranted. He and every other kuboderan is a power-hungry beast when those bonds are broken. Don't you think I would know better than anyone? I—who have trained countless of these sea creatures to navigate ships?"

"I see no evidence of that," Huna said quickly.

"Enough," Ron said firmly. "Emotions are running high, but we will not malign our fellow crew members. We're all in this together."

Ryliuk rocked a bit on his feet. A retort seemed forthcoming. Then he sat and pinched his connection to the bare minimum, his face expressionless, staring at the floor of the bridge.

Jane squeezed Alan's arm. "The best chance for Earth is an alliance with the Unified Sentient Races. There are resources there, people ostensibly experienced in dealing with the Swarm, possible advances in knowledge and technology. The information we're working under is decades old, from before the sectilian plague. Many things are bound to be different now. We won't know until we get there. At Terac, we might be able to rally an armada that could make short work of any threat to Earth. That would be the best possible outcome, and the one I will do everything in my power to make happen."

Ron stood tall. "Does anyone have anything else to say in disagreement with Quasador Dux Jane Holloway's statement?"

Alan flinched, but remained silent.

Jane let go of his arm. "We have a consensus, then? Speak up now if you disagree."

The mental connection was mute.

After a few moments passed, Ron said, "Right. It's decided."

Jane nodded. "Alan, Tinor, and I will take a shuttle down to the *Colocallida* to attempt to retrieve the data core. If we can salvage it, we might find out more about Kai'Memna's resources and the worlds he might use as refuge, or some other vital information that could help us fight him."

Alan turned wide eyes on her, like he was about to protest.

"No need," Pio said abruptly. "I'm uploading the contents of the data core now. It's damaged, and a good deal of the data has been corrupted, but there may be something useful. I have access."

Ryliuk asked, "But how? There should be codes."

Pio's mental voice was icy. "They didn't change the codes. Ei'Uba and I were on the same side at that time, after all. Until we weren't."

Jane sat down in the command chair. "While Pio works on that, Brai, please plot a course for Terac. We'll begin a jump sequence as soon as Pio finishes."

23

April 17, 2018
Seven months after Jane Holloway's Global Announcement

ZARA DIDN'T GET PAID, exactly.

They called it an internship and her dad got a huge raise or something. But she did get an official badge and she went to work with her dad every day instead of going to school.

If anyone knew that Zara was the one to set Mensententia free on the Web, no one said so, and her dad wasn't disciplined for it. Instead everyone seemed so grateful for her expertise, she suspected they'd have overlooked that part, even if they'd known.

At first everyone, including Zara, thought that she'd just translate the symbol cloud for them, help them figure out how it all worked together, and that would be all they'd need. The grown-ups would be learning Mensententia from the software. She'd go back to school after a few days.

It quickly became apparent that it wasn't as simple as that. The adults *were* learning the language now, but it didn't stick in their heads the same way. They didn't get the same burst of excitement when they learned a new word. That experience, she was sure, was the glue that stuck the language in her brain. Without that sensation, they were just memorizing. And there was only so much memorizing a person could do without getting tired of it and forgetting a lot.

Adults seemed to learn Mensententia at the same rate they could learn any foreign language, except they also had to learn a new symbol system and a new way of thinking at the same time. It was slower and less efficient than simply asking Zara. The only adults anywhere in the world having any success comparable to teenagers were the true language prodigies, who knew dozens of languages, but there were just a handful of those on the planet and every country that had one kept them for themselves.

Mensententia overwhelmed most adults with its hugeness, its alien nature, its complexity. They couldn't see it as learning one word or concept at a time. They focused on how little progress they were making or how hard it was. Adults forgot things, got flustered or frustrated, and requested her assistance repeatedly, even for things she'd already explained to them. The list of requests for meetings with her was a mile long. Soon she found herself learning not just Mensententia, but the beginnings of engineering terminology and computer languages. It was fascinating and fun, and overwhelming quite often, but she never stopped learning something new.

When it was clear that this was not going to be a short-term assignment, her mom protested, and a tutor was provided for a few hours a day so that Zara wouldn't fall behind in any of her middle-school studies. And, of course, she studied Mensententia for a couple of hours every day as well. The days were long, but she didn't mind. It was a relief to be useful. The people were nice. She was part of something bigger than herself and it felt good to be needed.

She didn't have to hide anymore. She'd been grounded for

her deceit but it hardly mattered. She never went anywhere but the lab anyway, now. And they didn't take away the laptop.

No one at NASA pretended Jane or the *Speroancora* wasn't real. But she had to promise not to talk about any of this to her friends, and she agreed immediately. It was a fair exchange.

Zara became accustomed to sitting in on meetings, finding polite ways to correct adults when they made mistakes, and giving presentations to different groups of scientists on various parts of the download—teaching them keywords and how to interact with the symbol cloud.

One day she was meeting with a group of computer scientists, engineers, and linguists who were working on a Mensententic keyboard that would make interacting with the symbol cloud easier. They were about to break for lunch when Dr. Sakey, her dad's boss, came in with a stranger decked out in fancy military clothes.

Dr. Sakey called her over. "Zara Hampton, I'd like you to meet General Gordon Bonham, the NASA administrator, as well as Deputy Administrator Marshall."

"So this is the wunderkind?" the general said with a smile.

Zara shrugged shyly.

"I think we need a few more of you. Do you know where we can find them?"

She knew he was joking, but she decided to answer as though he were serious. "Of course I do. They're all over the country. All over the world."

His eyebrows shot up. "You mean the other people learning the language from the illegal download posted online?"

She decided to ignore the word *illegal*, though it made her angry. Jane had wanted all of this for everyone. He was one of the ones who'd prevented that from happening. "No, not people. Kids. Kids my age. There are lots of them. You need them."

"It's best to encourage adults who already work for us, who

specialize in these fields, to learn the language and get up to speed as quickly as possible," he said dismissively and turned back to Dr. Sakey.

She sensed he was ready to move on. That made her even madder. He wasn't taking her seriously. Wasn't she the expert?

She straightened up, mimicking the general's self-assured posture. "Come on, man—that's not good enough."

He laughed like he was humoring her, but his smile didn't go up into his eyes and make them twinkle like it had when they'd been introduced.

She spoke over his laugh, firmly, trying to sound like a grown-up, though her heart hammered wildly. She used the biggest words she knew. "The adults can't learn Mensententia as efficiently as adolescents. It's too late for them. Jane told us that the language is normally learned—she used the word 'unlocked'—at puberty. You *need* kids who are already interested in science, math, aeronautics, and engineering. It's the only way to make sense of this as fast as possible. Other countries are already doing this."

He sobered and turned back to her. "What makes you say that?"

"The online Mensententia community." She looked to Dr. Sakey for help.

Sakey bobbed a nod in affirmative. "I believe she's right. I was planning to bring this up. We have developed a report, a plan of action, and a budget, with Zara's help."

"We can't have dozens of children handling state secrets. This is a matter of national security. And do I need to remind you that we have child labor laws in this country, Dr. Sakey?"

"I'm aware of that, General Bonham, but I believe we can find a way."

Zara nodded. "You could call it an internship and provide

free college tuition for participants. A lot of kids are super smart and worry about paying for college."

Bonham's brows drew together. "You've thought about this a great deal."

Deputy Administrator Marshal spoke up quizzically. "Kids your age are worried about college?"

Zara couldn't keep the disbelief out of her voice. She was verging on sass and she didn't care anymore. Respect for her elders wasn't getting her anywhere. All of her fears came pouring out. "Sir, we're worried about more than that. What if we don't figure this all out fast enough? What did that Ukrainian astronomer see in the sky that no one wants to talk about? What if that's the Swarm, heading to Earth? If those hungry bugs come here, they'll make sure there's nothing left to worry about. Are state secrets more important than *that*?" It was a gut punch and she knew it. But she was thirteen, for crap's sake. If she had to bear that burden, he should own it too.

It was probably stupid to bring up that tabloid stuff. They'd just dismiss her now. She didn't know for sure if the Swarm was coming, but Jane had warned about it and the sectilian database was full of descriptions of death and destruction with regard to these giant bugs. It seemed like a good idea to work faster to prepare for anything, rather than drag their feet and pretend that their biggest threat was the Russians or the Chinese or whoever.

Everything had changed. This wasn't about little black lines on a globe anymore. It was about humanity's survival. She knew it in her bones.

Bonham looked her up and down like he was reevaluating her. "Show me what you're working on."

She led him over to her team. "How much do you know about Mensententia?"

"Assume I know nothing."

She nodded. "That's how you have to start." She gestured at

their prototype keyboard, which was larger and more complex than a QWERTY keyboard. "The first thing you have to realize is that Mensententia doesn't use letters. Each symbol you see is a word, not a letter—the symbols are built from component parts that tell you how it sounds and give you clues as to its meaning. That's similar in some ways to the Korean language, Hangul, I've been told."

Zara tilted the monitor so that the general could see it better. "The software Jane sent is designed to teach you words and their components, so that as you learn each word, you're also learning a foundation that will help to learn new words." She started an animation on a word in the language software. "It shows you the layers as it pronounces the word. Some really complex symbols are compound words, layers of combined elements representing ideas."

"And what's this?" General Bonham pointed at the keyboard.

"This is a keyboard that we 3-D printed from plans for a sectilian keyboard that I found in the download. We've been trying to decide if it works for us, or whether we want to redesign it so it would be easier for a human to use. It was originally designed with a lot of different hand sizes in mind, though. So far, we think we'll keep it as is, just maybe make the keys smaller, more the size of our keys."

"*You* found it?"

The folks she'd been working with were nodding. Gail spoke up. "You bet she did. She's a force to be reckoned with. Truly inspiring."

Zara's face felt hot. Gail was an amazing linguist on loan from the University of Oregon. She had a daughter that was about Zara's age, and she often went to bat for Zara when people were dismissive of her abilities. It made her feel really good to have an adult champion.

"Show me how you type a word," Bonham said.

Zara leaned over and typed carefully. The symbol elements appeared on the screen, overlaying each other and reconfiguring until she hit the equivalent of the space bar. She straightened. "You all know this word."

Everyone squinted at the screen, humoring her, but no one spoke up.

"It's the name the sectilians gave to the ship that you called the Target. *Speroancora*. The symbol has a dual meaning—it's a compound word. It means to wait and to hope. Spooky, considering what Ei'Brai went through, don't you think?"

Bonham didn't comment. Instead he looked at her current team members. "I assume one or more of you are linguists?"

Gail and Carlo spoke up, saying they were. Carlo was an army cryptologic linguist who'd been called home from his station in al-Kut, Iraq, where he'd been translating captured Arabic communications to alert combat troops of danger.

"Why do you think children are learning this language so easily compared to adults?"

Gail said, "We don't know any more than what Dr. Holloway said in the Global Announcement. All I can tell you is that it's true. I've seen some young people learning it, my own daughter included, and their experiences are very different than my own."

"These children have experiences comparable to this young lady's?" Bonham looked searchingly at both Bonnie and Carlo.

"Yes."

"Absolutely."

"And your own experience? How does it compare?"

Carlo looked chagrined. "We're doing better than most adults, but not faring as well as Zara, sadly. We're devoted to the task, but as Zara says, it may be too late for us to learn it in quite the same way. The genetic component... we don't understand how that works, and it'll take a long time for geneticists to figure it out. By then it will probably be irrelevant."

Bonham narrowed his eyes. "But you're linguists. You're trained for this. Why would it have been so different for Dr. Holloway?"

Zara spoke up. "Dr. Holloway had learned six languages by the time she was twelve years old. She studied Latin, Greek, and classics in her early teens in a special program through a local university. We know that somehow Latin and Mensententia are very closely related. Language wasn't just Jane's college major or something. Her entire life revolved around language, learning language."

Gail nodded. "I think that's the difference, General. The few linguist savants on the order of Jane Holloway are working hard on this too, but there are a lot more teenagers than there are specialists of that kind. And we need more people on this, pronto."

Carlo agreed. "I wish Dr. Holloway were here to help us understand. She must have so much insight."

Bonham sighed and nodded. He spoke, seemingly to himself. "It's never easy." He gestured to Sakey. "Let's see this report you've got."

24

WITHIN HOURS of their departure from Pliga, they'd arrived in Teracian space. They opened single wormholes and both ships went through. Both Gubernaviti moved the ships with ease. Every jump was precise, painless, and uneventful. Replacing Brai's nanites seemed to have solved that problem.

They set a sublight course for the primary planet, but they didn't get far.

Brai announced, "There is a Teracian vessel on an approach vector. A larger force is forming 0.873 vastuumet ahead."

Seconds later, a communique came in. Pledor was managing that console. He triggered it to play over the bridge's speaker system. It was a high, squeaky voice. "Sectilian vessels, reverse course immediately. Your system is under quarantine. You will return to sectilian space or face dire consequences."

Alan muttered, "Oh, blah blah, dire consequences."

Jane stared at him with eyebrows raised for a moment before glancing at Pledor. She squared her shoulders. "Open communications. On-screen. Brai, Pio, cut engines. We'll move under momentum only. We don't want to seem aggressive."

Pledor's hands hovered over his console before finding the right place to tap. The display changed from a starscape with a distant sun and a single tiny planet in view to a bald, grayish individual with a deeply sloping forehead and enormous black glittering eyes.

Jane opened her mouth to speak, but the gray person interrupted her with the same squeaky voice they'd heard before. "Do you know how many statutes, bylaws, and ordinances you're breaking? So many. So many. We could incarcerate you for standard years. But we won't. We'll spank you hard and give you back to the stars."

That... didn't seem to translate well.

The Gray leaned forward, peering at them. "Did you think you could disguise your ship and we wouldn't know it was sectilian? You forgot about—*or didn't know about*—the beacons that transmit identification codes! Heh. Heh. Stupid."

The Gray waved at the screen as though shooing them away, then wrinkled up a nearly nonexistent nose, effectively pinching the nostrils closed. "Did you surgically alter yourselves so you wouldn't look sectilian? If you don't stop moving on a course toward Terac, we'll be forced to dust space with your remains."

"Have you finished? May I speak?" Jane asked as soon as she could get a word in, with as much affability as she could muster.

"Have I...?" The gray individual's eyes went almost comically wide. There were no whites around them. "Have I finished?"

It hadn't landed well. But Jane took advantage of the Gray's shock to speak. "I am Jane Augusta Holloway, a terran. This ship and its companion *are* sectilian. If you'll check your records you will discover that this is the *Speroancora*, a ship sent by the USR to find Terra seventy-three standard years ago. Our Gubernaviti survived the sectilian plague. My people recently found the ship in our solar system. I command it now. Both ships have been thoroughly decontaminated. The new hull plating is not a disguise, but repairs made on Pliga. I have important information about the Swarm and a criminal named Kai'Memna that must be disseminated on Terac to the entire USR, immediately."

"Oh, immediately. *Immediately*, she says." The Gray waved around boneless-looking handlike appendages. "Pliga... Pliga... Who ever heard of Pliga?"

"Jazz hands? Really? They sent Jazz Hands to talk to us," Alan said in English, *sotto voce*.

"This is an important mission. Many lives may be at stake," Jane said.

"Do you know how many illegals I put the boot to in this system every day? Do you know how many of them tell the same stories? They're always terran, or Yoosilhuot pups, or descendants of the Cunabula, or Recalinari elders, or bringing in the last Drudii alive in the entire universe. And many lives are always at stake. You'll have to do better than that to get by me. Turn around and go back to Sectilius before I turn my cannons on you. I. Will. Smoke. You."

Alan drawled, "It's like the DMV meets High Noon in space out here."

Jane stared at the Gray. She moved her jaw back and forth because it was getting tight from clenching it so hard. "I would like to speak with your supervisor."

Alan looked incredulous. "Jane, this isn't Burger King—"

The Gray's lipless mouth opened, shut, then said pleasantly, "Why certainly. Just a moment." The Gray moved out of the camera frame.

The Gray came back, looking smug. "No. Move off, Born-To-Be-Dust. No one wants nanites let loose in the galaxy that make you crazy before they finish you off. Quarantine. You. Now."

Jane inhaled slowly. She was going to have to bluster her way through this. "I know my rights. I'm a documented USR citizen by sectilian medical standards. I demand verification of my DNA signature per the Friba Compact: Section 1687, Article 923." Jane held up a small tablet computer. "I can read it to you."

The Gray seemed ready to make another contemptuous remark until she started quoting regulations. Then he wiggled, made a strange burbling sound, and left the camera frame again.

Minutes passed.

The gray returned, looking distressed. "We cannot board your vessel to verify your DNA signature. You are under quarantine."

"Have you scanned our ships?"

"No. Why should I?"

"Because you would see that there are very few active nanites on either ship. We destroyed them all at once with an electromagnetic pulse and are in the process of repopulation."

"And how would I know what a defective nanite looks like, compared to a normal one?"

Jane closed her eyes, then opened them again. "I have prepared documentation that is legally binding from the ships' logs that shows every procedure we used in order to be certain the plague nanites were eradicated. You know the logs can't be tampered with. May I send the proper documents over?"

The Gray stared at her for a full minute, wiggled, burbled, and left the camera frame again.

Jane told Pledor to send the files.

The Gray was gone for nearly an hour.

"You are still quarantined. Therefore, I'm blocking all access to the galactic communications network, and I'd advise you to maintain your orbit exactly where you are if you know what's good for you. However, I'm sending an intern in full medical protective gear to take samples. If anything happens to her, you will be space dust. So much space dust."

Jane smiled. "Thank you."

The Gray's eyes bulged, then the transmission was cut.

"Welcome to Terac," Alan announced.

25

WHEN THE AIRLOCK OPENED, Jane had to school her expression so she didn't appear surprised. A petite and diminutive individual strolled through in very familiar obsidian armor, holding out some kind of scanning device. He or she was the size of a seven- or eight-year-old child.

The intern didn't waste any time with a greeting, moving forward to scan Jane and the rest of her crew immediately. After a few moments Jane said, "I am Jane Augusta Holloway."

The helmet swiveled in her direction. "Yes, I saw you on-screen. I am Murrrsi, Hamloc's intern. I detect nanites on all of you, though it's certainly a very minute population. I'm downloading the code and forwarding it to Hamloc's science team for analysis." Murrrsi's voice was soft and low, and she rolled her r's in such a way that they sounded a little like growls.

"That's sectilian power armor," Pledor said accusingly as Murrrsi scanned him.

Murrrsi's head tilted forward as though looking down at the armor. "Of course it is. Sectilius was the best at producing armor that fits all body types. It's impossible to find anything else to fit someone my size. I've only had to make small modifications. It's very old but still in excellent condition—testament to how well it was built. The fact that it's outfitted with all kinds of scientific equipment is an added bonus. In many circles the sectilian manufacturing sector is sorely missed."

That mollified Pledor. He said nothing more.

Murrrsi stood stock still for a moment, then tapped her chest. "Acknowledged." She returned to scanning. "I was just told the code is significantly changed from the documented plague-nanite code. Our first assessment is that it has been defused. I'll need to proceed, of course. You understand." She continued to scan the room until she reached the door. "May I go through?"

"Of course," Jane said.

They all followed her.

Alan jogged ahead of Murrrsi to face her. "If that's true, why isn't there more pressure to lift the quarantine?"

Murrrsi turned to him briefly. "No one wants to die? I have two choices when I'm done with my analysis here. I can get back in that shuttle, go through decontamination protocols, then be quarantined for two standard years in isolation—or stay with you until we prove you're safe. They aren't good options, for me, anyway. My career is probably over." She sounded resigned.

"It's not over," Alan said. "We don't want to die either. I personally rewrote the code. And I've swept the ship multiple times myself, concentrating heavily on areas that may have been shielded from the EMP where any remaining bad nanites could have hidden. I've never found a single one. You know, I've modified a device to differentiate between the plague code and my rewritten code, if you want to use it."

Murrrsi seemed to nod. "I'll look at it." She stopped and turned to gaze at the whole group. "You're a *yiviti* bunch—using a sectilian ship to get around. Ten standard years ago you would have been blown up before you got this far, no questions asked.

But people are softening on the Sectilius now. Their products and other contributions are missed, at least by those who remember them. Attitudes are starting to change. People are forgetting the impact of the plague."

"*Yiviti?*" Alan whispered to Jane. "That...what does that mean?"

Jane cleared her throat and whispered back, "Sort of like... ballsy, but not gendered. It's hard to explain. I'll try later." Then she raised her voice to address Murrrsi again. "We actually don't know what the impact of the plague was, aside from Sectilius. Would you tell us?"

Murrrsi turned bodily toward Jane, though Jane could not see her face through the darkened visor. "How can you not know?"

"We're terran," was all she could say in answer.

Murrrsi set the instrument she held on a console and pulled another one out of her suit's thigh-compartment. She scanned Jane with it at close range, from her feet to as high as she could reach. Then she repeated the procedure on Alan. "Definitely not sectilian morphology. These things can be fooled, though. Guess that's why I'm here instead of sending in a drone." She sighed.

She put the second instrument back in her suit's compartment and went back to the first one, waving it around as she walked deeper into the ship. "Everyone knows. Either you're pretending or you're legitimately ignorant. Either way, it doesn't hurt me to tell you. Six thousand seven hundred and eighty-two cities or settlements were impacted by the sectilian nanite plague. Billions upon billions of people died all over the galaxy, wherever sectilian ships happened to be."

Jane took in a startled breath. "That many. We had no idea."

"A few are still quarantined to this day because it's difficult to prove that the nanites are gone. Outbreaks occasionally happen on some worlds despite efforts at containment, while on other worlds the plague seemed to fizzle out on its own from replication failures. Every species of anthropoid origin was affected. Not my species, though. That's why they sent me. It won't kill me, but I could become a carrier."

Replication failures. That explained why the plague hadn't killed more than a few dozen people on Earth after the Roswell accident. Of course, the humans there at the time had never known it was caused by nanites.

When Murrrsi paused, Jane asked, "Does the USR know who started it?"

"What do you mean, 'who'? The sectilians had to be the ones to do it. It's pretty incontrovertible. Clearly they made a mistake because they nearly took themselves out too."

Jane felt all of the sectilians in the anipraxic network reel with shock at that pronouncement. That was quickly followed up with outrage. Jane reminded them silently to hold their tongues, but was quick to respond to Murrrsi's statement. "No. They didn't. We know who did, though."

The helmet seemed to stare at her for a long time. "You know that sounds insane, right? It's common knowledge the sectilians did it."

Jane held up a hand because Pledor looked like he was about to explode. Tinor just looked uneasy. Mentally, every sectilian was seriously aggrieved. "That doesn't make any sense, Murrrsi, especially given their unique history with nanite technology. You just said yourself that Sectilius was known for producing superior products. My guess is they were not known for making mistakes."

Murrrsi abruptly returned to scanning. "Well, I didn't write history. Who do you think did it?"

"A kuboderan named Kai'Memna did it. He admitted it to me, personally."

"You have this confession on the ship's logs?"

"No, he was using anipraxia. But every member of both ships' crews, except for Huna, heard it."

Murrrsi paused. "Well, if that's true, it might be admissible. I'm no legal expert, mind. I'm just training to be a transportation access officer." She put the instrument away in a suit compartment. "I've just been told they're analyzing the initial data and want me to move on to the DNA collection. Shall we visit the medical section? Also, are there people claiming to be terran on both ships? Eventually I'll need to scan the other ship as well, but for now we need to concentrate on the DNA. Can they be summoned here, or do I need to go there?"

Jane stood on the diagnostic platform. The computer announced her name and vital statistics. Murrrsi scanned all around the platform. "Doesn't seem to be tampered with. Okay. We're getting somewhere. Computer, does the terran female Jane Augusta Holloway have any chimeric DNA or foreign-tissue grafts?"

"Does Jane Augusta Holloway agree to release these details to the parties present?"

"I do," Jane said.

"Terran female Jane Augusta Holloway does not possess any chimeric DNA or foreign-tissue grafts. All DNA is consistent with terran DNA profiles."

Murrrsi said, "We've verified this ship was the one sent to the location thought to be Terra at the time, so it makes sense that those profiles were downloaded from what is left of the Cunabula database. That makes my job a little easier. You're one step closer to verification of your planetary origin. However, I still need to take samples. They want to look at your DNA down to the base pairs to make sure nothing strange is going on. You're getting a lot of attention in the news cycle. The Teracian Assembly is involved now, and they've decided to send the data I collect out to independent labs. I know this isn't fun, but I have to do every step properly. A lot is at stake."

Jane nodded. "Go ahead. But don't you think you'd be more comfortable out of the suit? I've worn them for extended periods of time, myself. It's as comfortable as something like it can be, but it does get tiresome. You're safe here. We're not going to hurt you."

"They don't want me to, but they aren't going to be in quarantine for two years." She subsided into low growls, and then, abruptly, the helmet retracted and the suit split open down the chest. Murrrsi was covered in dark crimson fur with high, erect ears and a stubby, muzzlelike mouth.

Jane glanced at Alan, a little worried about what he might say. His eyebrows were raised and he mouthed a single word at her: *Foxy.* She had to press her lips together to keep from smiling at his absurdity.

"You can stare all you want. I'll never be anthropoid," Murrrsi said with a sigh as she stepped out of the suit's legs. When she turned, Jane saw that a short tail with long draping fur nearly touching the floor hugged close to her body.

Jane shook her head. "I'm sorry. It must be hard to understand, but we've never—"

"Anyway..." Murrrsi turned back to the armor, rubbing a hand over her head to smooth down her head fur, rumpled from the helmet, and reached for another tool. "They tell me this won't hurt. I have to take forty samples from you. If it does hurt, I'm sorry they lied to me. But we have to do this to every person claiming to be terran."

The device was deceptively small, about the size of a fat marker. Murrrsi applied it to Jane's bare skin in thirty-five places over her arms, legs, neck and face. Each time she felt nothing more than a quick pinch and it was over. Only a tiny red mark was left behind, smaller than an insect bite.

The last five extractions were a bit different.

"Your abdomen, please. The device will insert a filament to

retrieve a sample from one of your internal organs, to confirm that your interior and exterior match. It won't hurt you. It's only taking a few cells."

"Whoa! That's pretty invasive," Alan exclaimed.

Murrrsi flicked a glance at him. "You have three choices. Submit to the testing. Leave now and never come back. Or be blown up. I'd really rather not get caught in the middle of the third thing myself."

"Christ," Alan muttered. "You're expecting us to put a lot of trust in you people."

"Trust?" Murrrsi said bluntly. "Trust is not putting you through a fiery burial in space. Trust is coming over here, by myself, and taking off my power armor. Don't tell me about trust."

Jane loosened the knots on her garment and lifted one edge. Murrrsi palpated Jane's stomach for a second then applied the device. Jane gasped at the familiar sensation of the filament burrowing deep. It was just like being in the sanalabrium. A second of sharp pain and weirdness, then it was over. "Let me guess, sectilian technology too?"

"Adapted." Murrrsi reached for Jane's arm. "Now, three bones. Legs and arms are fine. Then digestive tract last."

Three more sharp pinches, then Murrrsi held the device in Jane's mouth for about twenty seconds. Jane didn't feel anything from that one. That was it.

Murrrsi raised the device and spoke. "Jane Augusta Holloway, sampling complete." The device whirred as an external casing emerged from internal compartments, encapsulating it. She set it down on the platform. "Now it can't be tampered with."

Brai informed her that Ron and Ajaya had landed in a shuttle bay and were making their way to the medical section. Jane said, "The rest of my people are on their way. Two more."

Murrrsi got out three more devices. Alan submitted but

indulged in a lot of eye rolling and sighing. When Ron and Ajaya arrived, they were already aware of what was needed because they'd been observing the proceedings through the anipraxic link, and it was over quickly.

Murrrsi stepped back into her armored suit. "I'll return to my shuttle briefly to get the processing of these samples started in the portable lab there. The results will be uploaded to the science teams automatically. Then I'll return to continue to scan for nanites. And I'd like to see that device you mentioned, Alan Bergen."

26

October 6, 2020
Three years after Jane Holloway's Global Announcement

ZARA SLAPPED OFF HER ALARM, groaning aloud, like she did every morning. A 5:00 a.m. wake-up call was not normal or easy for a sixteen-year-old, but nothing was normal or easy in her life anymore.

The US congress had given funding to NASA for a pilot program for kids aged eleven to fifteen. That eventually evolved into a full-blown program involving NASA facilities, national labs, all branches of the military, science-oriented universities nationwide, and even some private contractors in the aerospace field. The positions for "children demonstrating acumen in Mensententia as well as excelling in STEM subjects" were described as internships, mentoring opportunities, and even apprenticeships in some cases.

They officially called it the MSTEM Scholars Program, and the students were commonly referred to as MSTEMs, M Scholars, or just Ms. But no matter what people called it, it changed everything. The United States wasn't the first to create such curricula officially or unofficially, and by 2020, every industrialized nation had similar measures in place.

The government had been forced to do some backpedaling. They had admitted to some things. They still kept a great deal obfuscated, but in Zara's mind it was a step in the right direction.

Zara was growing up as an MSTEM Scholar. She went to work with her father at 7:00 a.m. Once there, she attended a class employing accelerated teaching principles with lectures on advanced math and science on a rotating schedule that also featured Mensententia, linguistics, and examples from the download, many of which she'd originally helped decipher. After their classwork was complete, the students went to work for the rest of the day, collaborating with various teams on the download.

Zara fumbled around for her robe and headed into the bathroom. After relieving herself, she stood in front of the mirror, blinking against the light, to determine the state her hair was in, in order to decide if it needed to be wetted down, or conditioned, or if a quick application of a light product would be enough to whip the recalcitrant, springy curls into a semblance of shape. She started feeling and scrunching her hair before she even looked up.

Wild color assaulted her eyeballs. Purple. Her hair was shockingly brilliant purple.

She was instantly awake. "What...?" she shrieked, before remembering that her parents might still be sleeping.

She turned her head one way and then another, parting her hair randomly to look at it more carefully. The color went all the way down to the scalp. "Oh, no. Oh, no. What? How?" she whispered frantically.

Her hair was not only purple. It was sparkly. It shimmered, actually. It looked like nothing she'd ever seen on a human head before.

Who could have done this? Her parents certainly wouldn't do such a thing to her while she slept. She dived into the shower and leaned forward with her hair under the stream. Nothing happened. Colorless water went down the drain. She put a handful of shampoo into her hair, expecting the shampoo's suds to turn purple in her hands. They didn't. She shampooed three times and nothing changed. She stretched a strand out toward her face so she could see it. Even wet, it was still obviously bright purple.

She leaned her head against the cold tile. She could go to extremes to try to get the color out, which could do a lot of damage to her fragile natural hair. She could try bleaching or dyeing over it, but she didn't know anything about that stuff. Something could go horribly wrong. She'd seen girls with chemical damage on their natural hair. It looked much worse than this purple. It was just too risky.

The other option was to just accept it.

It seemed as though someone had played a prank on her. If so, maybe it wasn't malicious. She breathed shakily, trying to stem the tide of emotion and be rational. It certainly wasn't ugly. It wasn't something that created shame, necessarily. It was just a surprise.

One of the other students in her program must have done it, possibly with some technology they'd pulled from the database. They were always playing harmless practical jokes on each other, usually creative and humorous ones—never anything mean. The instructors carefully fostered a mildly competitive but overall cooperative team environment, and the kids generally played along with very little friction.

She'd been bullied before. That had made her feel worthless. This was different, wasn't it?

This was the first time she'd been a target of her M peers' jokes. Was this a rite of passage? Or some other initiation ritual?

If that was the case, she was being included.

She felt her lips curl up a little bit.

She pulled the shower curtain back and looked at her wet head in the mirror. Truth be told, it was pretty. She might even have chosen to do something like it, if she lived a more normal life. If she'd been a normal teenager.

She globbed on a handful of deep conditioner, carefully combed it through with her fingers, and soaped up the rest of her body.

You know what? She was going to own it.

She smirked. And she was going to find out who did it and reciprocate with something equally clever and shocking. She'd have to start weighing her options. Take her time. Come up with something creative and just as mysterious.

When she went down to breakfast, her dad looked up at her. His eyes widened. He coughed and spluttered. A little coffee may have shot out his nose.

"You okay, Dad?"

He turned and grabbed the DVR remote. "You might want to see this, Grimace."

He pressed a button and the news began to rewind. She saw a blur of purple—the same shade she'd just tried to wash out of her hair. He pressed Play and the news anchor spoke:

"In Australia today the Mensententia Students woke up with a surprise on their heads. Their hair had turned bright purple overnight." They played footage of a multitude of students talking about their hair. Some of them seemed irritated, others indifferent, but quite a few were amused or cheerful. The theme was that none of them knew how it happened. "Similar reports of the phenomenon have come in from other countries across the globe, including Russia, Germany, and Egypt, only involving teenagers in Mensententia programs."

Her dad looked back at her.

"Huh." It was all she could think of to say. This was bigger than she'd thought.

"You didn't know this was going to happen?" he asked.

"No. I just spent twenty minutes trying to wash it out."

"Someone is making a statement," he said and poured himself another cup of coffee.

Her brows drew together. "What kind of statement?"

Her dad blew on his coffee and looked at her skeptically, like she should know the answer. "Unity."

27

ALAN WASN'T sure where Jane was, but he had a hunch. The meeting was going to start in half an hour, so she'd probably been walking the corridors of the ship for a while and ended up at that one window bubble that she seemed to like.

He could have asked the squid where she was, and sometimes that was useful if he was in a hurry, but it took a lot of the fun out of it.

She was there, curled up in the curve of the bubble and looking out at the stars. He almost hated to interrupt. The whirring and quiet clunk of his cybernetic leg alerted her to his presence long before he got close. She looked up at him and smiled, but it was a sad impersonation of her truest, most joyful smile. She was anxious about what the Teracian Assembly was going to say. Various government agencies had been communicating exclusively with Murrrsi for weeks while she scanned both ships. Today they were going to find out what the USR had decided to do about them.

He leaned into the opposite curve of the bubble and looked out. He could see the ass end of Murrrsi's shuttle docked a few decks away and lots and lots of stars. Back on Earth, stars seemed like things that were sort of sprinkled sparsely through the galaxy. Here, they were packed so densely that the idea of constellations seemed silly. They seemed brighter too. It was a change that was hard to get used to. He could see why she was drawn here so often.

"What do you see when you look out there?" he asked softly, not wanting to spoil her moment.

She glanced at him and ducked her head sheepishly. "I look at our sun."

"At Sol? Really? You know which one it is?" He moved to her side of the bubble, leaned down until his head was level with hers, and tried to look in the same direction.

"Brai showed me." She raised a finger and pointed at a region of space.

He squinted, but it was just a clump of stars. He couldn't see how she could pick any single one out. He shrugged. If he wanted to know which one it was, he could ask the squid. Maybe he would sometime. He was warming to the Squidster lately.

"I'm worried about Earth. I hope we're making the right choices. I so desperately want to protect our home." Her eyes looked watery.

"I know." He couldn't give her platitudes. She'd either go down in history as a villain or a savior. Or maybe there wouldn't be any more history at all. Regardless, she was doing her best, as corny as that sounded. They all were.

He'd done all he could to help their cause by giving the Teracians the blueprints for his device that could detect the difference between good and bad nanites, as well as his version of a search-and-destroy nanite that would seek out any plague nanites and obliterate them. He'd gotten the idea from Brai and improved upon the design that Brai had used to try to protect him and Jane during their early days on the ship.

Both crews had been helpful and cooperative. There was nothing more they could possibly do.

She sniffed and stood. He grabbed her hand and squeezed hard. Unexpectedly she wrapped her arms around him and held on like he was a life raft. When she let go there was a wet spot on his shirt. He ignored that as they silently walked to the bridge.

By the time they got there, she had her captain face on. She was all business.

The crews of both ships were present. Everyone spoke in hushed tones and milled around like it was a funeral.

Murrrsi sat at a console, looking just as nervous as everyone else. She said she'd given positive recommendations but had no control over the outcome. Of course, this affected her future as well. No one here was immune to the decision this unknown governmental body was about to deliver.

Finally the screen came to life. Ten wildly different-looking individuals stood around a circular table, murmuring to each other. The view was from above. They seemed to realize that they were being broadcast, and one of them tapped a screen imbedded in the table. The camera's viewpoint shifted to focus on that person.

Pinkish, amorphously shaped, and covered with independently moving villi the size of Alan's smallest finger, this person was accompanied by a machine that wafted a fog over their body. "This Decatribunal was formed from the greater Teracian Assembly of the United Sentient Races to decide the fate of the two sectilian vessels that wish to enter Teracian space, their inhabitants, and the intern in training for the position of transportation access officer, Murrrsi."

The broadcast returned to the high center viewpoint. Another delegate tapped their screen and the camera instantly moved in on them. This person looked almost human except for being white—not white like most humans thought of the classification, but chalk white. Even their hair. This startling lack of pigment—or was it actually an abundance of white pigment?—was accentuated by a shapeless black garment that hid the person's form so that Alan couldn't determine gender. The voice sounded feminine and breathy, though, and their eyes were a pale, ethereal gray. "We have studied all of the testing results as well as the ship scans in great detail. As you know, three independent labs were employed to analyze your genetic results, which were of utmost importance to determine before moving forward. Their conclusions were unanimous. Our deliberations were less so, but we have reached a verdict that is a fair compromise."

The camera changed instantly to reveal a third delegate removing their hand from their screen. If you could call that a hand. The delegate resembled a very large black walking stick—an insect. They had a bit of an obnoxiously regal air. "Regarding the matter of Jane Augusta Holloway and the three other individuals claiming to be terran: we conclude that Terra is indeed your planet of origin. Your DNA incontrovertibly matches the terran DNA sequences left behind by the Cunabula. Your citizenship will reflect this status. Terra is a non-USR world, but a world that is of vital interest to the USR. For us, this concludes an arduous search by many scholars over centuries and centuries. It is a long-awaited, momentous day worthy of celebration. We urge you to send an emissary to petition the USR in an official capacity to further our mutual interests. We have much to learn from each other."

Damn. It was all actually true? All that crap Brai had been spouting about the human race being selectively bred to be more aggressive, to rescue the pansy-asses of the galaxy? He'd pretty much expected that to be debunked here and now. Alan looked around the room and the rest of the *Providence* crew seemed equally stunned. No one said anything, though.

And they were back to the high central camera. It stayed that way for a while. The delegates seemed to be murmuring to each other again. He couldn't quite make out what any of them were saying. He wondered if Jane was faring any better and glanced at her. Her expression was set in a neutral arrangement, but her eyes avidly roamed over the screen as though willing them to continue.

A brawny person with a horn crowning a long snout took the focus next. A horn? Really? Seriously, nothing else would ever surprise him after this. "Now, on to the matter of quarantine. A verdict has been reached. Exposure to the sectilian nanite infection is a serious matter. The billions of citizens who lost their lives to this plague will not be forgotten. Protocols were put in place decades ago to protect the populations of USR worlds and must be followed. The Teracian Assembly of the United Sentient Races cannot make an exception, regardless of a petitioner's planetary origin. The transportation access officer in training did commendable work scanning these sectilian ships and found no evidence of remaining plague nanites, and that is well and good. However, the *Speroancora* and the *Oblignatus* have harbored the plague in the past and must abide by the quarantine rules. Two standard years before landfall. That is our pronouncement."

"Shit," Alan said. If they were still under quarantine, they couldn't communicate with anyone. The whole purpose of coming here was to warn the galaxy about Kai'Memna and the Swarm—not to mention to drum up support for Earth.

Jane turned away from the screen. Ron was rolling his shoulders like he was ready for a fight. Ajaya bowed her head. Tinor stared around with big eyes. Everyone else was just looking to Jane.

Alan glanced at the screen and saw that all but one of the ten delegates was leaving the circular table. That delegate reached out a hand to trigger the camera to refocus. It was clear almost immediately that the communication went both ways. The person on the screen could see them too. They probably all had, but they were such bullshitters that they pretended not to while they made their pronouncements.

This delegate reminded Alan of reconstructed images of human ancestors. Pale, tawny hair fanned out around a face with a slightly protruding jaw, a heavy brow ridge, and soft brown, closely spaced eyes. "I am Yliriu of Sebapen. I have been chosen to be your liaison on Terac. We understand this is not the outcome you'd hoped for. Know that this decision was not reached easily."

Jane turned suddenly and asked, "Is there an appeals process we can begin?"

Yliriu looked sympathetic. "The Decatribunal's findings are final and binding."

Fuck.

Jane looked away.

Two standard years. *Two years.* It would be less than two years on Earth's time scale because a USR standard year was based on a planet that orbited closer to its sun. He did the math in his head. That was 1.78 years. Plenty long enough. How could he stand to live on this ship for almost two years with nothing actually going on? He was going to go nuts.

The delegate spoke again. "I have a few more things to tell you, and then you may ask any questions you might have."

Everyone turned at least some attention back to the screen.

"Murrrsi may decide to live out the quarantine period aboard her assigned shuttle or aboard either the *Speroancora* or the *Oblignatus* at her discretion. She will receive a commendation for this service, ongoing remuneration at full TAO pay, and a TAO position will be waiting for her at the end of this term."

Murrrsi's mouth opened like she was stunned. "Thank you, Delegate."

"You're welcome. These are unusual circumstances. Hamloc

sends along his well-wishes." Yliriu nodded. "Now, we've decided to ease the strictness of the quarantine as much as possible for you, as this is a special case. You will find you now have access to a few things not previously available to sectilians. You will have use of the USR network of communication relay points and access to news feeds, and you may directly communicate with anyone in Teracian space."

Well, that was something. Small, but something. Jane visibly sagged with relief.

"Supplies will be ferried to you by drone as needed. You are honored guests of Terac. You do not need to fear starvation or want. We will supply you. You have only to ask. However, be aware that any individual who opts to pay a visit to either of your vessels will be obligated to live out the remainder of the quarantine period with you. No exceptions."

Ron straightened. "Can we leave the system?"

The delegate raised her eyebrows and considered his question for a few moments. "I would advise that no more than one ship leave the system. But be forewarned—a stop at any USR world would be considered an act of war and would be acted upon swiftly. And if both ships were to leave, I could not guarantee that either would ever be permitted back into USR space." Yliriu pursed her lips and got even more serious looking. "You must show the delegations that you are serious applicants if Terra should choose to join the USR, which of course is what we're hoping—and, indeed, expecting. I would strongly advise that your flagship remain here."

Ron nodded. "But one ship could make arrangements to visit an unpopulated world to gather a needed material? The USR would not object to that?"

Yliriu's eyes moved around in thought. "There should be no objections. It would be best if you registered your plans with my office ahead of time. And you should be aware that both ships have been tagged with tracking devices. We'll be keeping an eye on you." She glanced off screen. "If there are no other questions...?"

Jane stood. "What of the criminal Kai'Memna, his assertion that he has spoken with the Swarm, and the threat that may pose to Terra and every USR world?"

Yliriu dipped her head to one side in a sort of nod. "There is a separate, ongoing inquest into this matter. You will be called to testify, remotely of course. Be prepared for this process to take most of the quarantine period. The judicial system moves slowly here. We have sent out messages to scouts that track Swarm pods and are currently waiting for the answering reports to these queries. That will inform the evaluation of your assertions and any legal proceedings. Is there anything else?"

No one spoke.

"My contact information will be the first communique in your queue. Please call if you need anything." The screen went blank.

"Wow," Ron said in an expressionless voice. "Wow."

Huna took a couple of waddling steps closer to Ron. "You're thinking of journeying to the Pliga That Was during this time?"

Jane still looked impassive. He thought maybe she was trying hard not to let her disappointment show. "It sounds like they have no objections. It would be a good use of the time."

The rest of the group huddled together to talk about what all of this meant, but Alan couldn't participate. He found himself pacing up and down the length of the cafeteria, his right hand squeezing the back of his neck.

How could he sit around here for two years? What would he do with himself for all that time? He had his experiments, true, but he was ready to start physical trials and he couldn't do that here in populated space.

Jane had to stay. She had to be all diplomatic and shit. He

understood that. And his place was with her, wasn't it? That's what real couples did. They stuck together through thick and thin.

On the other hand, a jaunt to Old Pliga wouldn't take too long. They'd be apart, but absence and the heart and fondness and all that, right? It would be something useful to do. Ron might need him to solve a problem. These planet-hiding particles might need special containment, which might need to be built from scratch. He could do that. And they probably would need another set of hands. It might be hard work, gathering planet-hiding particles.

The others yakked for a long time. In the end, it was Ron and Jane talking after everyone else had left, and Alan still kept pacing. Thinking and pacing, though his thoughts seemed to spiral into ever-narrowing circles. He wasn't getting anywhere.

When Ron took off, Jane slumped against the door. "Do you think you could pace back to our quarters now?"

"Yeah."

They were most of the way to her rooms when she said, "You're unhappy."

He didn't answer right away.

She grabbed his arm, stopped him in the middle of the corridor, and stuck her face up in his, questioning. "Talk to me."

"I don't do waiting around very well," he said plaintively.

She nodded tiredly. "I know." She started walking again. "You should go with Ron."

28

BRAI WAS DELIGHTED.

It seemed that Dr. Alan Bergen was making the first move in the complex orchestration of asserting the foundation of friendship. Giving him distance and being patient had paid off as Jane had promised it would. But he had to be careful. This was a critical juncture. Reassurance would be key.

Brai quite simply had always been desperate to befriend the man. Alan was so different from any individual he had ever known. He applied his intelligence with a level of self-assurance and creativity that was intriguing. From the first, Brai had wanted to delve into that mind and try to understand how it worked, even to the point of trying to emulate his complex thinking processes in order to better himself. But his fervor had been his downfall in that endeavor.

But more recently Alan had trusted him, including him as an expert along with Pio, Jaross, and Ron as he worked through the design and physical implementation of some of his newest engineering ventures, which were extraordinary. Brai had taken those tasks quite seriously and the collaborations had borne abundant fruit.

And now here he was.

"This is just you and me talking, right? No one else can hear us, our thoughts? You'll keep the contents of this conversation to yourself?" Alan asked as he strode along the walkway that circumnavigated Brai's enclosure, turned, and then strode back again.

"Yes. Certainly. This is a private conversation," Brai replied.

"I'd talk to Ron but he's on the other ship and this has all gotten so fucking complicated. I'd have to talk to him through you, so you'd know what I was saying anyway, so I guess it just makes sense to talk to you because you're here."

"A logical conclusion." Brai moved back so that he wouldn't have to keep turning his body to track Alan's movements. Being as still as possible might serve his goals better.

Alan's hand went to the back of his neck. "I mean, it's not like I could talk to Pledor or Tinor, you know? Or Murrrsi. I don't even know her. You know what I mean, right?"

"I count Tinor as a dear friend, but I have noted a level of discomfort between the two of you since the misunderstanding over Jane's gift. It is certainly true that different individuals seek different levels of intimacy from different people. This is natural. There are many factors involved and they are often of a personal nature, built by past experiences."

There was a hitch in Alan's stride. He paused. "Maybe this was the wrong thing to do..."

Brai stayed outwardly calm and motionless, but internally he berated himself for talking too much. He was pushing Alan away again, the way he had before, by trying too hard. The best approach would be to listen, coax Alan to speak—that was the reason stated that he had come there. Then perhaps something more natural might form. They had gotten along so well while they worked on Alan's theoretical device. That had allowed this moment to come to fruition.

He kept his mental voice as tranquil as possible. "Do you wish to talk about the journey to Huna's Pliga That Was, or perhaps the quarantine?"

Alan swung around to face Brai. "This damn quarantine! I understand why they're doing it, but it's so frustrating to come all this way and then sit on our asses for years."

"I know this feeling well."

Alan waved his hand. "Well, yeah. You would. Fucking waiting is the worst. I thought that was behind me forever."

"At least you will not be alone."

Alan gestured vehemently with his arms. "But that's just the thing. I probably will be, a lot of the time. Jane's already in back-to-back meetings. She's going to be busy, talking her way into Terac society or whatever, trying to find ways to protect Earth. That's important. That's what she has to be doing. And I don't want to make it all about me, but I have to be realistic about who and what I am. I'm going to go nuts around here with nothing to do and no one to talk to most of the time."

"I'll be here."

Alan threw himself down to the grating and leaned his back against the railing. "Yeah." His foot twitched, and he used his fingers to fiddle with his shoe.

"Is there something wrong with your foot?"

"What? No." Alan sighed. "I want to go with Ron. Jane told me to go with Ron. But for some fucking reason that feels wrong."

"Why do you think it feels wrong?"

Alan had moved on to fiddling with the hem of his pants in a repetitive fashion. "First of all, splitting up the group is always a bad idea. I know you've never seen a horror movie, but that's usually the first sign that something really, really bad is about to happen. Also, going upstairs, but I'm getting off point here."

Brai was at a complete loss. He had no context for this comment, though he could say that when a group split, each half might be more vulnerable... but the moment was gone.

"Jane tells it like it is. If she says I should go, I know that she means it. She's not sending mixed signals. She doesn't really want me to stay. She doesn't play games like that. And that's amazing. And I appreciate that. But even so, I can't help but think there could be a price to pay."

Brai had lost his bearings. "Why would a person say one thing when they want the opposite?"

"I know, right? I've dated some women... well—that's not important." Alan was now pulling on the elastic of his socks. "Something could happen here and she might need me, and I'd be all the way out in Ye Olde Pliga. I'm not trying to be some macho jackass. I know she can take care of herself. But partners are supposed to be there for each other. That's just what they're supposed to do, you know? The thing is, if I stay, I might do just as much damage, because I'll be bored. I'll be a total fuckwit. She doesn't need that. And we'd probably fight. Then we'd be stuck in the ship together, fighting for two years. It'll ruin everything."

Brai watched Alan picking at his socks and knew a few things for certain. Alan cared deeply for Jane and didn't want to destroy their relationship. Alan found this decision extremely difficult. He was clearly perturbed. "I wonder—which of these two choices seems least palatable to you?"

Alan was silent. Brai sensed that Alan wasn't sure, but he dared not delve deeper than just a casual level of communication. He hadn't been given permission to explore Alan's thoughts and feelings, and he knew now that it was wrong to do so to a human, especially one so unskilled with anipraxis.

After a few moments, Brai said, "Perhaps the best course of action is what you have already said: to take Jane at her word.

Trust in her judgement and abilities. Know that she can handle whatever issues may arise."

Alan spread his hands. His thoughts were anguished. "But what if Kai'Memna shows up while we're gone?"

"Unlikely. Kai'Memna is a sociopath, but he's not stupid. Even now, Jane is working toward having him recognized as the criminal he is. The delegates on Terac clearly want Earth on their side. There are small fleets of escort ships from all over the galaxy here that I have no doubt would take on any enemy of Jane Holloway, simply because she is terran, and all that means historically. Kai'Memna looks for the easy fight, not the hard one. He would not dare."

Some tension seemed to go out of Alan's body. "Yeah. That makes sense. She's probably safer here than anywhere else in the galaxy right now."

"I am certain of it."

Alan leaned back and seemed to look at Brai for the first time. "Oh, man. I wasn't thinking at all. I mean, you and your... I mean you two—you and Pio—will have to be separated too. I didn't mean..."

"This is the life of a kuboderan. The difference is that you have a choice and I do not."

29

"ARE YOU READY?" Jane asked Alan. He was lying on his back with his knees bent, balancing one of the larger sectilian semi-transparent touchscreen plexipads on his stomach. He was using it like a tablet computer though it was at least twenty inches wide. He seemed to be watching a newsfeed in Mensententia at low volume, his forehead wrinkled with determination as he attempted to digest the broadcast. "Yes and no," he said.

She raised her eyebrows at him as she pulled back the filmy sheet and sat on the edge of the bed in one of his T-shirts to smooth on a little lotion. It had been a habit since her teens to put on lotion before bed, something her grandmother had encouraged that stuck with her. Sectilian lotion, though, took a little getting used to. It was very raw, mainly composed of unrefined oils, and was seen as more medicinal than a kind of daily skin care routine. So it didn't smell nice, and a little went a long way. Too much, and her skin felt greasy.

He tore his eyes from the screen and looked up at the ceiling. "I got my crap together. But..." His voice sounded stressed. She knew he was torn. She wished he didn't have to go, but she knew that he found it difficult to remain stationary for too long. The ten-month journey in the *Providence* had been very difficult for him. Though he'd have room to move around on the *Speroancora*, he'd still be relatively purposeless for two years if he stayed with her. This would be an uncomfortable separation, but also for the best.

She glanced back at him. "Second thoughts?"

"Yes, but I'll go."

"Murrrsi has decided to stay aboard," she said, hoping that mentioning that an officer of sorts would be present might help him feel better about leaving. "She'll be more comfortable here than on that tiny shuttle. She says she's going to use the time to study for a promotion. Apparently there are tests that have to be taken to raise your rank."

He drew his hand down her back. A pleasurable shiver went down her spine. "Ajaya and Tinor are resettled?"

Jane nodded and put away the small jar of cream in a wall protrusion near the bed. Ajaya and Tinor had mutually decided to switch places. "None of the sectilians are particularly comfortable here, given that the entire galaxy blames them for the squillae plague. And Ajaya felt she could be more help here with me, talking to delegates whenever possible. Many of the delegates have been very interested in meeting more humans. They bring it up a lot."

"But Pledor is staying?" His eyes had been drawn back to the screen.

She sat down on her side of the bed with her knees drawn up to her chin. "Yes. His focus is on the Greenspace Deck. He barely notices where we are."

Alan huffed. "No kidding. How did today go?"

"It was odd," she said cheerfully, because the thought of how she'd spent it made her want to laugh. "I was invited to a dinner party and I went. Sort of."

Alan rolled to his side and pushed himself up on an elbow. "How does that work?"

"They set up a monitor on some kind of trolley and put it out among the guests. When they went in to dinner, so did the trolley."

"Huh."

"Thank goodness for Brai. At one point I was speaking and said, 'um,' and Brai warned me not to say that anywhere near a goyton because it's sexually suggestive. He's helping me navigate this. I don't know what I'd do without his quick thinking and knowledge about all these different people."

Alan crooked a brow. "Were there any of these goytons at the party?"

Jane chuckled. "Yes, actually, but she was across the room and I don't think she heard me. Do you know, there is a species that sings instead of speaking? It terrifies me. I'm pretty sure I'm tone deaf. I don't know how I'll manage to talk to them."

"Crap. That's hard core. Does Ajaya sing?"

"I need to ask her. Mainly, it seems right now like I'm just a curiosity. There was a crowd around me all evening. Lots of questions about Earth and Earth culture, but it's all very superficial. There's surprisingly little interest in the topics of kuboderans, the quarantine of Sectilius, Kai'Memna, or even the Swarm. They just start talking about something else whenever I bring them up."

"You're a pop-culture sensation. It's your five minutes of fame. They want you to sparkle."

She sighed. "So it would seem. I don't like feeling like a novelty. I'm gradually gaining some ground, though. Finding the right people to talk to. Forming tenuous alliances. It would be much easier in person. I don't seem to be quite real to them."

He shifted the plexipad a little. "You will be."

She lay down on her side, facing him. His hand came to rest on her hip. "I'm real to you."

"You sure are." His eyes were still sort of sad, but his lips turned up in that feral smile that was just for her.

She inhaled deeply, ready to savor their last lovemaking session for a while. She was reaching for the plexipad in order to move it off him and set it aside when she heard it say dramatically, "There are terrans among us." She frowned and sat up, grabbing the plexipad off Alan and pulling it to her.

On-screen, a host was seated across from a blue-tinged hominid with no neck. A thick, bony ridge ran from their nose over their head. When the reporter spoke to them, they turned bodily, revealing that the ridge got larger as it followed their spine, and though it disappeared under their clothing, Jane could see it clearly outlined going down their back.

"You, sir, are terran?" the host asked.

Alan sat up too.

"I am," the blue man rasped. "Though I've concealed my identity until now."

"What the hell?" Alan said. "Is that guy saying what I think he's saying?"

Jane nodded.

The bluish man went on to say, "...though like Jane Holloway I prefer my native term: human."

"Fuck!" Alan yelled.

The host asked, "And why have you kept your origin a secret?"

"The galaxy was unready for us to reveal ourselves. We only recently made the decision, as one, to come forward."

"So you are saying there has been a secret network, a cabal of terran operatives among us, waiting for the timing to be right to reveal themselves?"

The blue man looked smug. "Yes, you have the right of it."

The host glanced at the camera. "Can you tell us who these people are?"

"Of course I cannot betray my people in this way."

"Why are you so different in appearance from Jane Holloway and her crew?"

The blue man shrugged one shoulder. "As you know, the Cunabula gave us great genetic diversity. You see this evidence among Jane Holloway's crew. We come in many colors and shapes and sizes."

"What the...!" Alan said in disbelief.

The reporter said, "Tell us about your diet. What do you eat?"

The blue man looked straight into the camera and said, with a straight face, "We eat wood."

"And how do terrans mate?"

"It's really quite simple." The blue man gestured at his legs. "I have one leg and one member—"

Jane's eyes bulged.

Alan's mouth was hanging open. "What the hell?"

They continued to watch, stunned and horrified, as this same host paraded a variety of people through his interview seat, male and female. Very few of them looked even remotely human, but all claimed to be terran, though the stories they provided varied wildly, ultimately discrediting them all.

"Why are they doing this? Is this satire?" Jane asked.

"Maybe they're paying them to appear," Alan said.

Jane shook her head. "Surely this can't be a reputable broadcast. This has to be some kind of tabloid show."

Alan scrubbed at his beard. "We're the flavor of the month. They can't get enough of humans so they're making this shit up for ratings. I guess it's good to know."

The on-screen backdrop changed. Now the host was on the

street interviewing people about terrans, asking them if they'd seen any in their day-to-day travels. If they claimed they had, then they were grilled for information about where and when, what they looked like, how they acted.

Alan lay back on the bed with his arm over his eyes, muttering under his breath.

Jane contemplated setting the plexipad aside and refocusing on their last night together, though the mood was completely broken now.

"I've just seen one!" an interviewee exclaimed, and turned to point into the nearby crowd. The host manically dashed into the crowd toward a group of darkly hooded figures with their backs facing him, the camera struggling to keep up. The host grabbed one of the group, they exclaimed, and the group as a whole turned.

Jane gasped as the wind caught the hood of one of the figures, lifting away to reveal a young, light-skinned black woman with long, dark, curling hair cascading over her shoulders.

"What?" Alan sat up again.

Jane pushed the plexipad into his hands. "Can you rewind this? Turn up the sound!"

The group quickly fled the scene, and the host returned to interviewing people on the street, but not before replaying that short scene two times—once in slow motion with the words Is This a Terran? superimposed over the video.

Alan and Jane watched, stupefied, as a reptilian-looking person with a colorful, sluglike creature wrapped around her neck, said, "Come, Darcy, it's not safe to linger here."

"Holy shhhhhhit!" Alan whispered.

"She's human," Jane said. "They called her Darcy. That woman was a human. She had to be. She was actually human, right? I'm not seeing things, am I?"

"No, she looked human to me."

"We have to find her. What's she doing out here? How could she have...?"

Alan looked back at her, wide-eyed. "Fuck if I know."

30

November 30, 2018

ON THE DAY that the *Oblignatus* broke orbit to head for the uninhabited planet once known as Pliga, Jane sat down wearily at a console to sift through the correspondence and communications requests that had come in overnight.

She and Alan hadn't slept much. They'd spent most of the night researching the mysterious young woman they'd seen on the broadcast. They'd been able to uncover that the planet that segment of the show had been recorded on was Bashenpau, a busy port often used for refueling and resupplying ships, as well as the time frame involved in the recording, which had been late the previous day. Brai was meticulously poring over the thousands of records of the ships that had come and gone from that port in and around that time, looking for anything that might help them pinpoint which ship she'd been on. It was looking for a needle in a haystack. It seemed pretty clear she didn't want to be found. But if anyone could do it, Brai could.

In the meantime, Jane had other work to do. The first

communique she opened included a five-thousand-page document from a corporation with headquarters on Terac. She scanned the first few pages to find it was composed entirely in legalese. The accompanying text essentially said, "Let's talk!" She saved that one to another file to look at again later.

The next few messages were from delegates. These were generally stiff and formal requests for face time to discuss how Earth might fit into the USR, what Jane's plans were, or how they should look for mutually beneficial ways of serving each other in the future. Typical political stuff. It made her nervous, but at least it was predictable.

Then there was a query from a small child asking if it was true that terrans could breathe fire.

She sat back in her seat, frowning.

"This disturbs you. May I ask why?" Brai asked. In the background of his mind, she could sense him still scanning ship manifests from Bashenpau, as well as tracing down several other leads.

Jane worried her lower lip between her teeth. "You told me from the beginning that the Cunabula were a real, scientifically documented people that existed long ago. You said that their descriptions of Earth weren't myths or legends, but known facts. The main detail that remained in obscurity was where they had placed us."

"This is true."

"Then how could I get a question like this?"

"Imagination. A dearth of information leads to a filling in of the gaps, often with fantasy. You saw this last night. I'm uncertain why you register surprise. Your own world history is full of such stories."

Jane shook her head. "No. It's not the same thing. Those kinds of tales come from a time when we were in the dark. We didn't know our origins. We didn't have science or a modern tech-

VALENCE

nological framework around which to base reality. All we had was fire and sticks and each other."

"Are you sure? It seems to me that misinformation, misinterpretation, and obfuscation were still in strong practice even in your so-called information age. We are all just animals with higher brain function, some more than others. And perhaps many want to believe that something more exciting exists out in the black of space."

Jane closed her eyes. "So there is a mythology around Terra?"

"Certainly. Though you won't find anything about it in the sectilian database because the Sectilius deal only in science, logic, and fact. You'll have to do a search through USR networks if you want to discover the myriad ways you've been depicted through time."

Jane groaned. That was not the answer she'd wanted to hear. "All right. But I've got to get through this queue first."

The next message seemed very oddly phrased. It wasn't especially formal or anything—it just seemed to follow some kind of pattern that she couldn't parse. At first she thought it was metered like poetry, but she wasn't sure. "Brai, what can you tell me about the ogoxians?"

"I can tell you not to converse with one without me present to do the proper calculations in order to carefully choose every word for both lingual and mathematical clarity."

"What?"

"Their native language has a foundation in octal or base-eight mathematics. They extend this concept through to their use of Mensententia. Every sentence must reflect this or one is considered rude, unsocialized, and ignorant."

"But if I am not from their world—"

"It doesn't matter. On some worlds it is polite to regurgitate at the table during a meal, but if a delegate did that next to you, am I correct in assuming you'd be offended?"

How could she possibly navigate this without messing every-thing up? "You're joking, right?"

"Absolutely not."

"But none of them know anything about Earth and they're all communicating with me."

"Indeed. And so far you have noted that their primary interest is to learn Earth customs before moving into more profound discussions with you. This is the foundation you must build before you can have the more meaningful conversations you seek. This is the way society works at the galactic level."

Jane stared at the console, though she wasn't really seeing it. "I'm not saying that it's not important to have a basic knowledge of custom—that was precisely what I did in my own work on Earth, and it was absolutely necessary. But I was working with one culture at a time, immersing myself in both language and local convention while surrounded by the people. This situation is very different. These cultures are so varied and there are so many of them. How can any one delegate possibly hope to learn all of this? It's insane." She put her head in her hands and rubbed her temples. "I need to get through to them. I need to warn them about Kai'Memna and the Swarm. But we're all hung up on all...*this*."

"This is one of many reasons why the Sectilius relied heavily on their gubernaviti when it came to cultural exchanges. Other civilizations quickly adopted the practice. We have long been more than navigators. The human mind may not be able to accommodate such vast amounts of information, but a kuboder-an's can. And my cybernetic connection with the ship's database and networks gives me microsecond access to any information I lack. Any delay in response would be imperceptible to an alien emissary. Indeed, it would be expected. You will eventually get to the kind of communications you desire, but this is how you start the conversation."

Jane rubbed her forehead. "Okay. I guess this is just not what I was expecting. I'm not sure what I thought this would be like, but I suppose I imagined there would be some kind of neutral ground, a kind of equitable culture unto itself based upon the work of delegation, something with a lot more latitude and understanding. I suppose that was lazy thinking. I'll work harder to understand."

"The task is daunting. You expect more of yourself than any single individual can possibly achieve. You've barely begun, and yet you're making progress. Rely on me. I am your partner in this."

He was right. Even now he was processing several streams of data as they spoke. "Okay, partner. What do you make of that huge document sent by the Brigoo Corporation?"

She sensed him opening the document and skimming it. "They want to hire you as a spokesperson for their subcutaneous nutritional line."

Jane blinked slowly and exhaled noisily through loose lips. "Okay, that's... completely unimportant. Moving on."

She quickly sorted through the rest of the messages and noticed that she was receiving a few call requests. These meant that someone on Terac was letting her know they were available to speak. If they withdrew the call request before she answered it, that meant they had become unavailable. The first was from Kuan Broadcasting Network.

She took a deep breath and pressed the button to open the call. She was careful to keep her expression neutral. Smiling with bared teeth was considered predatory in some cultures, submissive in others. And apparently some, like the pligans, just thought it was odd.

Oh, how she wished she were dealing with just one culture at a time.

"*Scaluuti.* This is Jane Holloway."

A face came up on the screen. "Quasador Dux Doctor Jane Augusta Holloway?" Jane instantly recognized the species. This person was nintergertehunt, a species that, on the surface, anyway, looked fairly similar to humans except that they tended to appear to be carved from alabaster. Lacking any skin pigment whatsoever, they had evolved a type of vacuole in their skin cells that accumulated certain trace minerals from their blood. As a result, their skin reflected light, protecting it from harmful UV rays in the same way that melanin did for humans and sectilians, and appeared to be pure white. Jane had only seen a few members of this species so far. They had all been striking, with pale eyes in gray, blue, or green.

"Yes. That's me. May I ask who's calling?"

The caller made a tittering sound. "I am Fiun."

Jane was instantly on alert. "Brai, help me out here."

"Fiun is the female host of a very popular daily broadcast in magazine format called Et Ostend."

Jane said, "Of course. Fiun of Et Ostend. I've heard wonderful things. Forgive me."

Fiun seemed to ripple with gratification all the way up and through her snowy hair styled in a tall mohawk. "No, please forgive me. I know that you must be suffering terribly. These circumstances. These conditions you find yourself in. It is a terrible imposition for me to call you."

Jane nodded patiently. "Not at all. I assure you, the conditions here are not bad at all. It is the waiting we find difficult, of course."

Fiun's pale green eyes were wide, as though astonished. "But the confinement. It would drive one mad, I am sure."

"We are bearing up well, I think."

Fiun nearly sparkled with a bright white smile. She was either not afraid to offend, or was reassured by their outwardly similar physical appearance. "Oh, I am so very pleased to hear this. Now, Qua'dux Doctor Jane Holloway, you must answer a question for me. I insist."

"I'd be happy to," Jane said, though inside she already felt wary.

Fiun's lips spread again in a beatific expression oozing with unctuousness. "But of course you know that you are at the very center of the galaxy's attention. A terran come to Terac! And in a stolen sectilian vessel, no less. It is all anyone can talk about!"

Jane held up a hand to get Fiun's attention. When Fiun paused for breath, Jane said, "For the sake of clarity, I'd just like to say that the *Speroancora* was not stolen. Its care and the position of Quasador Dux were given to me."

"Oh! You see? These are just the details we insist to know! Can't you see that you must be compelled to tell your story? The whole galaxy knows where you are from and what you look like, but who are you, Qua'dux Doctor Jane Augusta Holloway? Who are you?"

"Please. Call me Jane."

Fiun nodded slowly, and her lip curled sensually. "Jane, I would like you to consider this offer. Kuan Broadcasting Network wishes to extend an invitation to you to appear on Et Ostend. This exposure will put all the rumors to rest. You may tell your personal story, give us an accounting of the history of Terra, uncover the culture that has given rise to you. This is the opportunity that you need to launch your career. Perhaps we can tweak things to make it look as though circumstances are very bad for you there and the people will speak—the Assembly could be forced to reconsider its pronouncement and relent to give you the freedom you deserve. What do you say to this, Jane?"

"Brai, can I say I need to think about this without offending her?"

Brai's voice rumbled with laughter in her inner ear. "I suggest you tease her. Tell her you have other offers. She'll love it."

"I can't do that!"

"Suit yourself."

Jane looked back at the screen. "Fiun, I'm honored that you're interested in giving me this opportunity. Thank you. May I call you with an answer tomorrow?"

Fiun raised a brow skeptically, her lips turning down. Was that displeasure? "But of course, Jane. I'll be waiting." The screen went dark.

"I don't trust her. She wants to sensationalize us," Jane said to Brai.

"Shall I send messages to her more grounded competitors, asking if they would like to broadcast this story?"

Jane shuddered with revulsion. "Ack. No." Then she thought about the little girl wondering if she breathed fire and the bizarre broadcast they'd watched the night before. "I don't know. Maybe we should do something. Could we make something ourselves? Something that we could control? Is there a way we could broadcast it?"

"Easily, yes. It would require more work on your part, to plan, orchestrate, edit and package. But you do have the time."

"Yes. Yes, I do. That's what we're going to do. I'll make an ongoing series and maybe even answer questions. I've got plenty to talk about."

"Jane, I've just detected a small vehicle on a direct course."

She tapped her console to get a look at exterior camera angles. "Is it one of the drones the Assembly mentioned they'd send?"

"No, this is a shuttle. Pelimarian."

Pelimarian. Pelimarian. Why did that name sound familiar?

Jane turned back to the communications station. There was a call request from a pelimarian delegate. It said the name was Xua. She clicked it. "Hello? This is Jane Holloway."

On the other side of the call, all Jane could see was a wall and part of a room.

She spoke louder. "Is anyone there?"

There was some murmuring and the noises of someone moving around. Then someone appeared in a loosely tied, yellow-and-magenta-patterned robe that was open to the waist. They were standing so Jane couldn't see their face. What she could see was that their skin was pebbly and mottled green and gray. They made no move to put their face into the frame, but continued to speak softly to someone else who must have been just outside of camera range. She couldn't make out what they were saying.

Jane was embarrassed. "Oh, I'm very sorry to bother you. It's just that there's a pelimarian vessel en route to my own vessel..."

The tie of their robe fell apart and the garment gaped further. Jane looked away. This person appeared to be rather emphatically male, possibly aroused, and not at all concerned about displaying his nudity.

"Apologies. We got distracted and moved away from our station," a deep, sultry voice intoned.

Jane peeped at the monitor and was relieved to see that the man had seated himself and now only his face and shoulders were visible. He was humanoid with enigmatic dark eyes.

"Oh, I see," Jane stuttered. Then, silently, she said, "Brai..."

"Pelimarians are reputed to be very sexual creatures. They include sexual acts in all aspects of life as a way of easing tension, relaxing, and encouraging cooperation. For them, copulation is as common as consuming food, sleeping, and working."

Jane kept her expression as pleasant as she could, but she felt like she was wearing a mask. She had no idea what to say. Her mind was blank.

The man on the other side of the screen was drinking something. He came back to the center of the display, loose-limbed and relaxed. "Thank you for taking our call. The pelimarian dele-gation wants you to know that we are here for you in your time of need. Yliriu made us aware that your partners have left on a crit-ical mission, so we polled the junior delegation and found a few eager volunteers to keep you company for the next two standard years."

Jane opened her mouth and then shut it again. She had seen this man's reproductive organs and knew his given name but that was it. "I'm sorry?"

"For interrupting? It's not a bother. It happens all the time." He gave her a genuine closed-lip smile. He exuded charisma.

She struggled to compose herself. This was going off the rails. "I'm sorry. I'm not communicating very well. Did you say that you are sending people here?"

Brai intoned, "Careful, Jane. Refusal may offend."

Jane gritted her teeth and pressed her nails into her palms.

"Of both genders, not knowing what types of partners you prefer or what your appetites may entail." Xua leaned in, as though sharing a confidence. "We examined images of you care-fully. Since your physiology appears to resemble nintergertehunt anatomy—though we must say you are dramatically more color-ful, and, we dare say, more aesthetically pleasing—we reason that you, like them, are compatible with our species as well. At any rate, you'll have fun figuring it all out. How we wish we could be there. You truly are stunning to witness, Jane Holloway." It was like he was leaning in to kiss her. His face filled the screen.

Her mouth had gone dry. "We...humans, that is—we call ourselves humans, not terrans...we're mostly, though not always, monogamous. I'm afraid I don't..."

Xua raised his hairless brows. "You are monogamous?"

"I am, yes. It is the cultural norm for humans." She floun-dered. "Though, as I said, it's not true for all. I don't mean to speak for everyone. Uh...intimacy among humans is generally very private and we are... easily embarrassed."

His lip quirked and his eyelids drooped a little, as though that sounded very, very sexy to him. "We like a challenge."

The screen went blank.

Jane leaned forward and put her face in her hands. "Oh, my God. What are we going to do?" She'd never even gotten a chance to politely protest that she couldn't expect anyone to be closed up with them for that length of time.

"I think you are going to have company," Brai said, his voice full of mirth.

"Can't we just refuse to open the hatch?"

"You could do that. And risk offending one of the most powerful species in the galaxy."

Jane groaned aloud and it turned into an agonized growl. Her teeth were clenched so tight she might just break one. "All of this —all of this! It's so frustrating." She clutched her head in her hands. "Why are they making it so hard?"

Brai's mirth dissipated.

She stood and swung around. "We waited for ages on Pliga and now we're stuck here too, spinning our wheels. I came here to cultivate allies to protect Earth from the Swarm. The Swarm could destroy my world and eradicate my entire species—and instead I'm just wading through all of this ridiculous nonsense. There must be something else we can do!"

"Our options are few."

She plopped back down in her seat. "Have you found anything in the search for Darcy?"

"As a matter of fact, I have. I've been monitoring all mentions of terrans in the media and following each of these many threads where they lead. I have just discovered there was a report of a terran spotted on a planet called Legare mere days ago. I have cross-referenced port logs from both Legare and Bashenpau and found a match. A ship called the *Vermachten* is owned by a female individual who identifies as nieblic. I'm attempting to locate the vessel now. It appears to be a long-haul food transport, of the type that sells starvation-remediation supplies to remote colonies."

"Nieblic? That's a species that looks human, isn't it?"

"Without much scrutiny, it may have been possible for a human to pass as nieblic before you came to Terac. Now, however, it seems less likely." Brai pushed the image of a citizen credential to the nearest screen.

It was the same woman.

"That's her." Jane stared at the human face in front of her. What was her story? How had she ended up owning a ship? Did she need help? How many humans were with her? "Thank you Brai. You're amazing. I'm so glad you're my partner in this. Now, let's find that ship."

31

June 15, 2022
Five years after Jane Holloway's Global Announcement

ZARA LOUNGED in the break room with her feet up on an empty chair, surrounded by the detritus of her lunch. She had eleven minutes left on her lunch break, which, as usual, she'd taken late, so she was the only person using the room.

She was texting with a boy she thought was probably in South Korea about an engineering translation error that had gotten propagated across a lot of Asian countries. Some people on her team believed the US government had done that on purpose, but Zara didn't think that was true. It was just a mistake. Mistakes happened.

This particular error cropped up all the time, though, which was frustrating because they weren't allowed to discuss things of that nature through official channels. It had to be done privately, one individual at a time. They had to communicate in Mensententia, because it was the only language they had in common. "SunnyJun-seo" was patient, as Zara rapidly thumbed out the standard response on her phone's Mensententia keyboard, including points of reference in the database she had memorized where he could go to confirm what she was telling him.

Modern tweens and teens had grown up with social media as a large part of their social life. When Ms came up against a problem, they were encouraged to discuss it with their mentors and peers. But "peers" meant something different to the Ms than it did to the adults running the facilities. The administration meant the other Ms they physically saw every day at their own facility, though possibly they would have included other Ms nationwide on the secure government network. But Zara and the other Ms she knew tacitly understood those instructions to mean anyone like them—anyone in the world. The administration would never have condoned this, but the coworkers who just wanted to solve problems and get their supervisors off their backs looked the other way.

It wasn't a conspiracy and it wasn't subversive in nature—it wasn't that the Ms weren't patriotic either. It was that their patriotism had been elevated a notch from being national in nature to being global in nature. Knowing for certain that the universe was dramatically different than their ancestors believed had made this generation diverge in their ideology and other belief systems.

Every kid Zara's age spoke, read, and wrote Mensententia. It had become a global phenomenon almost overnight. Communication between these young people had been effortless the moment the Mensententic phone keyboard apps rolled out on all platforms. If all someone saw was a screen name online, they didn't know where that kid was—and it honestly didn't matter as long as the problem at hand got solved.

Ms, more than anyone else, seemed to understand that this wasn't a second space race between the nations of Earth.

It was a race for human survival.

"*Casgrata!*" SunnyJun-seo texted back when Zara finished.

She started to close out all open apps on her phone and sit up to gather her things to get back to work early. She only really needed about fifteen minutes to eat anyway. She was about to close a social-media app that she didn't remember opening when she noticed a flashing red alert—it said it was highest priority. She jerked to attention and tapped to open it. She squinted at the name of the sender because it wasn't immediately familiar. It was an instant-message request. She accepted. It would be unusual, but another M might contact her on this platform.

"*Zara Hampton? Is this the girl I went to middle school with at Mercy?*"

She looked at the name again. Rebecca Smith. Oh, yeah. Becky. Becky had been an on-again, off-again friend and sometimes mean girl. Becky had run hot and cold as a middle schooler. Friendship with Becky, if you could call it that, had not been a lot of fun.

"Yes."

"*I wasn't sure. I mean, how many Zara Hamptons can there be? But you don't have a profile picture so I wasn't sure. I've been trying to contact you for weeks.*"

Zara frowned. She didn't normally use this site because it was outdated and Ms didn't use it much. She'd probably opened the app by accident. "*MSTEM Scholars aren't allowed to use pictures of themselves as their social-media avatars.*"

"Right."

Zara started to feel impatient. She had stuff to do. "So, what's up?"

"*My mom just organized this really big high-school-reunion thing for her graduating class and it got me thinking—so much of our class just disappeared when that MSTEM thing happened. And I started to feel sorry for you guys that you aren't going to graduate with us at the end of this year! I mean, you'll never have a high-school reunion or anything, you know? So sad!*"

Zara raised an eyebrow. She was already partway through her bachelor's degree. She'd flown through high-school coursework with zero fanfare and they were projecting that she'd finish her degree in mechanical engineering and linguistics by age twenty. She was tempted to type: *So what?* But Becky went on messaging.

"And we haven't even seen you guys in years! I mean, what's it been now? Six or seven years since they took you away?"

"Five." It would be five years in about four months since she joined the MSTEM Scholarship Program. Who could forget the date September 27, 2017, when Jane Holloway's Global Announcement was first broadcast worldwide? It was the single most momentous day in history. That Becky didn't remember that seemed odd. Was the general population even affected by all of this? Had everything returned to normal, business as usual? Was society segregated by those who "knew things" and those who didn't? She'd completely lost touch with the outside world, stuck in a bubble at work and school, with almost no contact with people outside her circle.

"So I talked to the principal and he agreed that it was a wonderful idea to have a big party with all of you guys to celebrate graduation. Aren't you excited?!"

Zara hesitated. She didn't want to hurt Becky's feelings, though as she remembered it, Becky had never shied away from hurting hers. But Zara wasn't eager to spend the modicum of free time she had with kids she used to know who hadn't always been what she would now label as true friends. Not to mention that she'd have to get permission from the MSTEM program and bring a chaperone. Her dad would probably agree to do that, but it would be a lot of paperwork to fill out. MSTEMs' lives weren't really their own. She didn't feel like taking the time to explain all of that, so she tapped out, *"I'm kinda busy."* That was true. What with a full course load, a job, studying and everything...

"*What?*"

Zara could just imagine Becky's dejected pouting expression, though surely it had changed some since seventh grade as the girl had grown up.

"*We're planning a big space theme and everything for you guys. We have planets and asteroids and everything. I can't believe you aren't interested!*"

Zara blinked at her phone.

Becky went on. "*You've really changed, Zara. I'm trying to do something nice for you. I don't know why you can't see that.*"

Zara set down her phone and stared at it. Had she changed?

Yes, she absolutely had. She'd grown more confident, more sure of herself. She wouldn't do something just because that was what Becky wanted. Not anymore. She didn't need to grovel to have friends. People liked her because of who she was, not because of what she did for them. No, she didn't go to parties. But the Ms were everything to her. They were more than friends, more than a social network. They were family. They knew what her life was like and they'd think this idea was just as dumb as she did.

She picked up the phone again, her thumbs moving quickly. "*Becky, I'm sorry if I hurt your feelings, but I've got a lot of big things on my mind. You know what I'm doing here. You know what might be coming. I wish I had time for things like parties and dances, but I just don't.*"

"*What might be coming?*" Becky typed. "*What are you talking about?*"

She shouldn't have said that. They were, under no circumstances, permitted to remind anyone in the general public about Jane Holloway's warning regarding extrasolar threats. But Zara's life revolved around working to prepare the world to counter those threats, so it was constantly on her mind and hard to avoid slipping up. Fortunately, she didn't have to worry about that very often.

She started tapping again, to quickly dismiss what she'd written, but a notice popped up on her screen: Wi-Fi Unavailable.

Oh, no.

She cleaned up quickly and got back to the lab. As soon as she saw Dr. Sakey's face, her heart sank into her stomach. She was in trouble. He tended to look the other way about certain things, as long as the Ms weren't using government equipment and it wasn't classified or sensitive information. He let things slide if she was helping out other Ms across the globe as long as the information she gave them was available widely online. Not all supervisors would do that. But it was clear her message to Becky had been intercepted and flagged through the Wi-Fi. She couldn't even remember what she'd typed, but she must have used a keyword they looked for.

She was about to get a lecture, the contents of which she was familiar with.

She would have to be a lot more careful.

32

JANE ROUNDED up Ajaya and Murrrsi to help her get rooms ready once she'd determined that three pelimarians were on their way. She chose a grand central suite meant for visiting dignitaries, surrounded by private rooms on the extreme opposite side of the Crew Deck from where her own crew was housed. Pledor delivered a bountiful presentation of fresh food to welcome them.

Murrrsi seemed to find the situation amusing, which grated on Jane's nerves. She kept snickering in a way that almost sounded like soft, playful barking as they made beds and checked that all the amenities functioned properly.

Ajaya raised an eyebrow at Murrrsi as she settled a gauzy sheet on a bed. "You seem to be excited about our visitors' arrival."

Murrrsi collapsed on the bed, her short muzzle parting in full coughing laughs, revealing some wicked-looking canines. She rubbed the dark red fur on the top of her head. "Oh, this situation is just like one of my favorite comedic theatrics. I can't help but wonder if it will play out the same way."

Ajaya looked at Jane. "Is a theatric something like a television show, do you think?"

Jane nodded. She was filled with dread. "Yes, they have episodic shows like we do."

Ajaya turned back to Murrrsi. "What is the premise of this theatric?"

"Every episode features the same three pelimarians getting stuck somewhere with a group of people from another species." Murrrsi collapsed into giggles again.

Ajaya said, "This is a humorous sort of story?"

Murrrsi's seemed unable to catch her breath. "Oh... yes. Yes."

Ajaya asked, "Would you mind telling us what's so funny?"

Murrrsi's eyes rolled with mischief. "I think it would be so much more interesting if you didn't know."

"Jane?" Ajaya looked put out.

Jane sighed. "The pelimarians as a species have a reputation for being rather... hedonistic."

"Oh! Oh! Oh!" Murrrsi was rolling on the bed now, holding her stomach, shaking and wheezing, her feet kicking in the air.

"What aren't you saying, Jane? There has to be more to it than that," Ajaya said.

Jane fluttered her hands. "I don't know how to say it politely. I'm sure there must be a good word. I just don't know it."

"Just say it in English then," Ajaya said.

"There aren't any polite words in our language. We'd say they're 'promiscuous' and even that word has a derogatory connotation. Apparently they like sex and they have a lot of it, all the time. Or so I'm told. In their culture it's not taboo in any way. It's open and nurturing. From what I can gather."

Ajaya gently shooed Murrrsi off the bed and straightened the bed coverings. She seemed unperturbed. "Well, that's not so bad. It's not like they eat babies or something, right?"

Jane smiled slightly. "I suppose that's one way to look at it."

Murrrsi sobered up. "Are you worried about this, Jane?"

"Yes! I'm going to have five different species aboard, all with different cultural backgrounds. I'm concerned about potential misunderstandings. Anything could happen. Sex for humans is... fraught with issues."

"Jane." Murrrsi extended her small, furry hands to Jane. Jane reached out and Murrrsi took her hand and stroked it gently. "Apologies. This isn't a theatric. I'm sure it'll be fine."

Jane continued to worry anyway.

She worried she was prejudging the pelimarians before they even arrived. Perhaps the delegate had just been playful or had been conveying some other emotion. She had been intensely uncomfortable and he'd surely picked up on that. Or maybe he hadn't. There was no way to know. Perhaps it was her own cultural baggage that made his gestures and words seem threatening.

She wasn't a prude. She was just private. She'd also seen leers like that many times on male human faces, and those leers had never taken any social interaction to a good place. However, a leer didn't necessarily mean the same thing on a pelimarian face. Or he might have been expressing his own personal feelings, which might not actually be a cultural norm. How many politicians on Earth were truly representative of their constituents?

And then there was the most important question: Why were they coming at all? Jane didn't buy the altruistic line the delegate had fed her. This system appeared to be a den of political factionalism and nobody in a place like that did anything without thinking they were going to benefit personally.

When the pelimarians arrived, she schooled her features and determined to remain kind but neutral. She was the leader. She set the tone. Friendly but cool.

The pelimarians, two women and one man, arrived and were clearly tired from the journey. They were cordial to Jane and the crew and very affectionate among themselves. Jane noticed lots of lingering touches, pats, and squeezes.

Also, they smelled amazing. She couldn't define the scent they wore. It was spicy, musky, and slightly sweet. Not overpowering. She only noticed it when they were close. Whatever it was, it would do well on Earth.

They were gracious when Jane showed them their quarters, and seemed delighted to find the platters of freshly harvested sectilian food that Pledor had left there for them. Then they begged off of any other social interactions, saying they wished to sleep after the long journey.

Jane closed the door between them, feeling abashed and hopeful. This was another opportunity for cultural exchange. The pelimarians could be a strong ally. The fact that they were there was a good thing. She'd been silly to worry so much.

She met Ajaya in the corridor as she walked back to her quarters.

"An auspicious beginning, I should think," Ajaya said as she fell into step.

Jane smiled. Truth be told she felt relieved that the pelimarians seemed so normal. She'd been half-expecting them to launch into a full-scale orgy upon arrival. "Yes, I think so."

Ajaya nodded. "I've been doing some research on the USR networks for the last few days. I think you'll find it rather interesting. It seems that the Cunabula left behind some notes on their genetic experiments, and in the intervening time, much study has addressed what modern USR geneticists know of our human genetics and how they differ from other anthropoid species."

Jane listened intently. "And what have you found?"

"Well, it's all very complex. But the Cunabula seemed to be experimenting with polymorphisms—duplications, deletions, and mutations of various traits on very particular loci that may affect social function."

Ajaya seemed to notice Jane's uncomprehending stare. "Put simply, they tried a lot of combinations in an attempt to affect behavior. For example—and I'm speaking in averages for a species, not of individuals—sectilians code for less of a hormone called vasopressin which does many things in the body, including retaining water when one is dehydrated and constricting blood vessels. But interestingly, less vasopressin is also implicated in decreased understanding of social cues. More vasopressin may give rise to what is termed goodwill behavior. Humans, the nintergertehunt, the nieblic, and pelimarians make more of this hormone by comparison. Pelimarians make the most of this hormone—which, interestingly, is necessary for pair bonding in some mammals. Pelimarians also make more oxytocin, a related hormone which affects social bonding and trust. And that's just two among dozens of hormones that interact and affect both biology and behavior in extremely complicated ways."

Jane tried to digest all of that. "If sectilians fall on the low side and pelimarians on the high side, where are humans on this spectrum?"

"In the expression of these two hormones in particular, we are somewhere in the middle. But in relation to some other, similar parameters of genetic expression, we are a bit more extreme. It's quite complex."

Jane raised her brows. "So the whole nature-versus-nurture thing?"

Ajaya smiled. "They both play a role in individual behavior, of course. We are speaking broadly of populations and norms within an entire culture here."

Jane stopped in front of her door. "What do you glean from this? What does this mean?"

Ajaya looked thoughtful. "To me, it is proof that we are all very closely related, with only minor variations. The same kinds of variations may show up in human populations. These people are our kin. We are more alike than we are different."

"Jane," Brai said. "I've found the *Vermachten*. Would you like to send a message? You may not have long. It has a history of moving from port to port swiftly."

"On my way." She turned to Ajaya. "Brai found Darcy."

Jane returned to the bridge with Ajaya and recorded a message, speaking first in English and then in Mensententia. She kept it brief and vague, and did not mention that she thought this young woman was human. There could be a reason she was keeping her true identity a secret, and Jane didn't want to endanger her in any way if the message were intercepted. Once it was sent, all they could do was wait. It would take a few minutes for the message to arrive through the communication network.

Twenty minutes later they received a reply. It was text only, requesting that all communications take place via a specific encrypted channel. That was it.

Jane frowned. "Is this unusual?" she asked Brai.

"Among the Sectilius, it would be, yes. I have no basis on which to conjecture otherwise," he replied.

When no other messages were forthcoming, Jane re-sent the original on the encrypted channel. A response came back a few minutes later in a video format.

The same young woman was on the screen. She wore a gauzy white jumpsuit and her hair was uncovered. She licked her lips nervously before she began to speak. "Well, you must have worked hard to find me. I guess you're wondering if I'm human. I am. My name is Darcy Eberhardt. If you don't mind, I'd like to know more about you and what you're up to before I tell you more about myself. I mean, I've seen the news feeds. I know about the Mars mission and I recognize some of the astronauts with you, but I'm pretty curious about how you got to Terac from there. And, well, I'm sorry for being sort of... oblique. I have good reasons."

She sighed and glanced away from the camera. "I'll try to keep up with communications as best I can, because there are some things I'd like to discuss with you that I think are pretty urgent. I'm about to jump to a new sector, so I'll look for your reply when I arrive. My co-captain is sending you the coordinates so you can route your message properly. Please continue to use this encrypted channel. Thanks." She fluttered her fingers in a self-conscious wave that contrasted with her serious expression, and then the screen went blank.

"Well that's very odd," Ajaya commented.

Jane furrowed her brow. Darcy had spoken the entire time in Mensententia. She must be from a non-English-speaking country. Jane took her time recording a thorough reply, describing what her original mission had been and how she'd ended up at Terac. She didn't sugarcoat anything. That would be insulting. This young woman was captaining a starship. She knew what was going on out there. She ended the message by asking where Darcy was from originally and how she had come to be where she was.

She and Ajaya continued their conversation about galactic genetics while they waited for a reply. It came sooner than they expected.

Darcy was seated this time. "I'll start at the top, but I have a lot to tell you. I was abducted," she said. Her nostrils flared. "Along with thirty-four other humans. I managed to turn the tables on my captor, but not before he sold my boyfriend as a slave." She seemed to choke on that last word, then gathered herself. Her voice sounded a little stronger. "I'm searching for him. His name is Adam Benally. I know... I know the galaxy is huge, but if you should ever hear anything about him, or run across him, I hope you'll let me know."

Tears sprang to Jane's eyes. What this girl must have been through.

Darcy looked down at the console in front of her for a long moment before going on. "I'm originally from Ohio. I understood your message in English, but I can't really speak it coherently anymore. At least it doesn't seem like it. Maybe one day we can meet and you can tell me." She tried to smile but it looked pained. "They... yeah. They put a chip in my brain because I couldn't speak Mensententia. Guess humans don't do that like the rest of the galaxy." She shrugged and looked away.

Jane frowned. She hadn't even known that was possible.

"Horrible," Ajaya murmured.

Darcy sniffed and looked back at the camera. "I'm actually glad you found me. I've been meaning to contact you after I saw you on the news feeds, but I didn't know what would be the best way. I can't come to Terac. Too dangerous. It's crazy. So, thank you for that. It's good to know you're out here too. It makes me feel less alone."

She rubbed her hands up and down her thighs. "Because of what I'm trying to do, I have to keep an ear out in less-than-savory places, you know? I have to find out where the trading centers are, who buys who, and where they're taking them. My biggest resource has been my kuboderan navigator, Do'Vela. I really depend on her. Kuboderans talk. They talk a lot. More than anyone realizes."

"Do'Vela kept hearing about a kuboderan named Kai'Memna. Sounds like you'll know who I'm talking about. This guy. Whoa. He's sly. He's working to recruit kuboderans to rise up against their captains—telling them how to kill them, how to kill an entire crew. It's some serious shit." She held her hands up, palms out, with a look of disbelief on her face.

Jane's heart sped up. Darcy had heard of Kai'Memna?

"I don't know how successful he is, generally. We've been hearing about his attempts at recruitment for a while. But at our last stop... Well, it was weird that you chose then to contact me. It freaked me out. And that's part of why I was hesitant. We were really out in the beyond, dropping some people off so they could get home—people like me, who'd been taken—and Kai'Memna's ship was there too and he was doing his thing, but he was also looking for information about you. It makes sense after hearing your message. But it's weird. He's definitely got some kind of grudge against all of you. Do'Vela seemed to think he's unhinged."

She shook her head. "Do'Vela got an earful. Luckily she's very loyal to me and my co-captain, Hain. We take good care of her and she's not interested in his preaching. I don't know why he's allowed to roam free with the things he says, but maybe it's because most people don't treat their kuboderans very well. And that's problematic, you know? It's... well... I can see why it's happening. If you've seen the news feeds, you'll have noticed there's been a few kuboderan mutinies recently that I don't think the authorities have linked together. I'm guessing they're all tied to that individual."

Jane felt sick. That was the first she'd heard of this. She would have to bring this up with Yliriu.

"But here's the most important thing I have to say to you today. Kai'Memna alluded to the fact that your crew split itself on two ships—that while you remained at Terac and were still untouchable, the other ship would be vulnerable. It might have just been smack talk. It was cryptic and that's all I know, but I just heard this a couple of hours ago. I checked the news feeds after I got your message and it seems that what he's saying is true."

Jane froze. She held her breath, listening. She heard Ajaya suck in a breath.

"We're just finishing up here. I can be mobile again in less than an hour. My ship is disguised. It's actually pretty badass. I can lend support. We gotta protect our own. But to start, you need to get a message to your other ship to warn them. Just let me know if I can help. I guess that's it. I'll wait here for your reply. I'm out."

Jane stood up. Sat back down again. Stood up and paced, thinking.

Ajaya silently watched her walk up and down the bridge.

She couldn't send a message. They were already out of range of the USR communication networks. The thought that Kai'Memna would track them down was terrifying.

"Do you think he could find them that easily?" Jane asked Brai.

Brai had been silent, but she'd felt his growing concern and horror as he'd watched the video through her eyes. "With sufficient motivation, I do not believe it would be any more difficult to discover the current location of the *Oblignatus* than it was for me to find the *Vermachten*."

She went back to the console and tapped out the sequence to start recording another message with trembling fingers. Now Brai was shoring her up, helping her stay calm.

"Darcy, my heart goes out to you. You've been through a horrible ordeal and I respect and admire what you're doing now. I will help you any way I can through my contacts here at Terac, starting immediately. My navigator, Brai, has already begun to do research and will assist me going forward. When I saw you on the media, I never dreamed..."

Jane swallowed hard, trying to be brave, trying to find the right words. Darcy had offered assistance and Jane had no choice but to take it. She had to warn Ron and Alan so they could get somewhere safe before Kai'Memna caught them unawares. "I'm going to have to appeal to you for your help. I have no way of contacting the *Oblignatus*. They're beyond the galactic comm network. I..."

She glanced up at the ceiling to keep her composure. "I cannot leave here, for diplomatic reasons. There's a lot at stake. Earth needs me to stay here. I can provide more details about that at a later time The crew of the *Oblignatus* is in danger. Kai'Memna is a very real threat. Please, could you carry a message to them to warn them? Sending coordinates along with this message."

She stopped there and tapped send. She was desperate, but she didn't want to sound that way.

Jane collapsed in a seat. Ajaya stared bleakly back at her.

It seemed like it took forever for Darcy to reply. Neither of them felt like talking anymore. They just sat there, waiting. Jane couldn't stop imagining all the terrible ways that Alan and Ron and the rest of her friends could die if Kai'Memna got there first.

Then Darcy's reply finally came. "Yes. Absolutely I will. Immediately. I'll help any way I can. But you better send me a message to give to them because they're going to think it's pretty weird when I show up to tell them to get the hell out of Dodge."

Jane recorded two more messages. One to thank Darcy. The other for Ron and Alan and the rest of the crew of the *Oblignatus*. Minutes later, she got a text reply. "Got it. Leaving now. Try not to worry. I'll be in touch as soon as I can."

33

ALAN REGRETTED LEAVING the *Speroancora* almost immediately.

The trip to Old Pliga itself was short because of the wormhole drive. They got to the planet and yada yada all the ash in the
atmosphere had cleared up during the intervening years and the
Tree had come out of dormancy just fine as Huna had predicted.
In fact, it seemed to be thriving all over the habitable parts of the
planet. That was the good news. They might be able to make this
shit, take it back to Earth, and be goddamn heroes.

So they went down in shuttles and found that both the planet
and the crystalline treehouses there were remarkably similar to
the ones they'd just left on New Pliga, except they were spookily
empty. Huna set himself up at a one of the flat bioterminals and
began to reconfigure a single Tree node for a change in genetic
processing in preparation for growing a test crop of pods.

That was when Alan realized his mistake: this wasn't a one-
shot thing. This was going to take a really long time—maybe the
entire two standard years. They wouldn't be heading back to
Terac anytime soon.

He hadn't really thought about how long these might take to grow. They were plants, right? Water, air, and sun. How long could it take? Sure, the hull plating had taken months to grow, but these were tiny particles, right?

Particles.

Versus humongous sheets of polymer.

Seemed like particles might be faster.

Eh. That would be a nope. Huna admitted, with his limited understanding of time scales, that it would not be significantly faster at all.

Crap.

To Huna's credit, he *was* starting to understand the passage of time. He paid close attention to human and sectilian biorhythms, though he couldn't share them. He marked the passage of days, watched the clock, and announced the hour like a little kid. But since this was all very new to him, he couldn't predict how long anything would take.

So the twiddling of thumbs was going to be happening no matter where Alan was. This was all made a bit worse because Old Pliga was just out of reach of the USR relay network. If they wanted to send messages to the *Spero*, they'd have to jump out of the system and then back again, which was a pain in the ass to say the least. Not that he was composing flowery love notes or anything. Well, not really.

He did have his blink drive to run experiments on and tinker with. He'd brought a second iteration of the device with him, along with a few other prototypes of various sizes and in various other stages of functionality. It wouldn't be long before he'd have enough data to attempt a full-size warp bubble that hurled ordnance. All his models worked. All his small-scale experiments had worked. A completely unpopulated solar system was actually the perfect place to test this stuff and he was nearly ready to do that.

It had only been a few days so far, but things were going well. Pledor wasn't around to piss everyone off, which was nice. Ron set up work schedules for all the engineer types to run system checks. Huna jammed on his genetics. Ryliuk divided his time between cleaning up, cataloging tools and devices, and nurturing his fuzzy love grove in the little secluded spot he'd carved out on the Greenspace Deck. Tinor was obsessed with feeding Pio's manatee. She had about thirteen different experiments ongoing and regularly held taste tests pampered pet.

Alan also continued to work on his Mensententia skills. He intended to fully give himself over to Jane's suggestion about using the ship's learning software, which, she insisted would actually help him with speed and understanding. Truth was, his vocabulary was really coming along. He might never be as fluent as Jane, but he rarely had issues in conversation anymore. The harder he worked at it, and the more he talked with Huna and Jaross and the other sectilians, the better he got. When he got back to Jane he was planning on showing off.

All of this would keep him busy. He hoped. So busy that he could mostly block out the ache in his chest when he thought about being away from Jane for so long. The truth was he missed her like a lovesick fool, and it was probably only going to get worse from here on out. Yeah, he had it bad. But so what? Jane was awesome.

Alan was tinkering with one of his blink drive prototypes, getting it ready for a test run. He'd just started loading some materials on a small cart when Pio politely interrupted his train of thought.

"Machinutorus Alan Bergen, you are needed on the bridge as soon as possible."

"What's up, Pio?" Alan asked. He liked Pio. Her personality was so different from Brai's. She was pleasant, thoughtful, and never intrusive. She was interested in what he was working on—really curious, in fact—but she didn't pressure him. And she didn't have the hots for his woman, which was a plus. He actually didn't mind keeping a light connection with her because it didn't feel like she was spying. It felt more like being aware that Bob or whoever was on the other side of the construction bay working, without having to keep an eye on him.

"There is a ship approaching, on a direct course."

Alan stopped loading materials and stood up straight. "A ship?"

34

JANE SPENT the rest of the evening and well into the night with Ajaya talking and worrying. She barely slept for the second night in a row. She rose at her regular time and was immediately informed by Brai that just after she'd fallen off to sleep, the Pelimarians had arrived on the bridge, ready to begin a work shift. Brai hadn't wanted to disturb her rest, so as the acting commanding officer he began their orientation to the ship's controls.

"Was this action acceptable to you?" There was something in the note of his mental voice, an uncharacteristic uncertainty.

Jane pulled her hair up into a ponytail. "That sounds reasonable. They gave me the impression yesterday that they wanted to get to work right away. One of them has experience as a communications officer, I think. Did you think I would object to you doing your job?"

"I confess I'm still adjusting to your confidence in my leadership."

Jane left her rooms to grab some food cubes and brew a mug of tea before heading to the bridge. She sympathized. Brai's formal title as gubernaviti, or governing navigator, had been nominal only, a concession the sectilians gave the kuboderans to mollify them as they used these amazing sentient beings as glorified navigational computers. "So what are your impressions?"

"They seem quite capable." The note of discomfiture was still there.

She turned around and headed for the bridge instead. "What happened?"

"A great deal, as it turns out."

Jane arrived on the bridge moments later to find the three pelimarians seated at consoles, clearly working. They all stood, smiling, as she entered.

Feig came forward. She was the taller of the two pelimarian women, taller than most human women, actually, and her pebbled skin seemed to be more predominantly green than gray. She was bald like the others, except for extremely long lashes fringing large, dark eyes. She wore a simple lavender tunic with dark pants that skimmed her curves without being snug. "*Scaluuti*, Quasador Dux Holloway. Much has happened during your rest period. Are you ready to be briefed?" Feig held out a hand.

Jane took Feig's hand and shook automatically, noting distractedly that there was that enticing scent again. "Yes, of course."

She glanced at the other two pelimarians. Celui, the male, was primarily dark gray with flecks of light green dotting his skin. He would be average in height and build for a human male. He was also dressed simply in navy and brown. Ouvaq was much shorter and more filled out than the others. Her skin was mostly light gray with areas that were tinged green. She wore a simple charcoal-colored floor-length dress.

Feig dropped Jane's hand and gestured at her companions. "Celui has organized your official correspondence, flagging messages from delegates and ongoing conversations with priority. He'll go over that with you, as well as brief you on any call requests you may be receiving. Any personal messages will be untouched, of course. Ouvaq was just leaving to prepare quarters for your newest visitor before he arrives." Ouvaq nodded at Jane and left the bridge.

Jane looked sharply at Feig. "What? Another visitor?"

"Yes, well. We've been busy." Feig tapped the nearest console and the main viewscreen lit up, displaying a sea of ships of all shapes and sizes orbiting Terac very close to the *Speroancora*.

Jane's mouth fell open. "What happened?"

Feig tilted her head to one side until it nearly touched her shoulder. Perhaps it was like a shrug? "When word got out that Pelimar sent an envoy to the *Speroancora*, nearly every world decided to do the same. The Decatribunal assigned to your case held an emergency session and determined that the cost of supporting hundreds of visitors to the ship was untenable. There was also the concern of unnecessary potential exposure to the nanovirus during your quarantine. The sebapenese delegate Yliriu just intervened and ordered Transportation Access to form a blockade. No one else will be allowed to approach the *Speroancora* without special authorization."

Jane frowned. A lot *had* happened while she was sleeping. Brai and the pelimarians had handled it all. That felt strange. "I see."

"A wexian envoy arrived and was docked before the blockade was in place. They sent a single individual, a male named Imadua. We recommend greeting him as soon as possible. He's waiting to board. Technically, he's already been exposed."

Jane lowered her gaze. "If you'll excuse me for just one moment." She turned away from the watching eyes of the pelimarians. "Brai, please debrief me on how all of this unfolded."

Her inexperience at command was a stone around her neck.

She'd just reassured Brai that she trusted his judgment, but these decisions he'd made in her absence were going to impact all of them and she wondered if maybe she could have been consulted.

This situation reminded her of how fundamentally different she and Brai were from each other in values, background, and training. Ongoing communication would be the only way for this nascent command structure to function properly as the crew grew. She was figuring this out from scratch. She knew she couldn't micromanage everything. This wasn't academia. She had not been trained for this. She would not overreact. The ship was intact. No one was in danger. Nothing was blowing up.

Brai knew all of this, perhaps instinctively, or possibly because of his own unease with the lack of structure and definition between them. "Allow me to mitigate your fears. The pelimarians were not let loose to make decisions on the bridge of your ship. I was connected with them, consulted on every keystroke. I made these decisions in your absence, as the officer in command. All of the data is available for your perusal."

"I would expect nothing less," Jane told him. She was grateful that he did not seem to be defensive in any way. He merely related the facts.

"The circumstances were unusual. When it became evident that so many envoys were being sent, before the arrival of even the first ship, we were in direct contact with the sebapenese delegate, Yliriu. She was straightforward. She was displeased by this turn of events for the reasons Feig has stated. She did not object to supporting small numbers of envoys, as the pelimarian arrival had not been forbidden and could not be undone. But she would not support the expense of dozens. I considered the possible reasons why envoys would be sent and how those reasons would ultimately affect your goals."

Brai went on, "Hosting solely the pelimarian delegation to the exclusion of all others could be problematic. It could be seen as xenophobia or favoritism. While the Assembly was in its emergency session, the wexian arrived. I deemed this a good choice for creating some balance among the visitors. Wex is not the most influential planet, but it is stable, prosperous, and resides in the same arm of the galaxy as Earth. Had the Assembly not finished their debates so quickly, I intended to allow two more envoys to dock before barring entrance. For these reasons and others, including your uneasiness about pelimarian culture, I felt that permitting a few additional guests to board would allow you to divide your attention, to relieve the expectation of attending to the pelimarians as host so exclusively. But that was not to be. I would have advised you to take these actions had you been on the bridge yourself."

Jane let out a breath slowly. His logic and actions were sound. "Very good. You've done well."

"My gratitude, Jane. Shall I continue to supervise bridge activity?"

"Yes, please." She turned and made eye contact with Feig.

Feig gestured toward the door. "Shall we go now to greet Imadua?"

"Of course."

As Jane and Feig walked, Jane wondered about the politics at play in this incident. Had the pelimarians created this brouhaha for some reason, or had it happened spontaneously? Why were so many worlds suddenly eager to send a presence to board this ship when they'd been content with video calls the day before? She picked back up on the thread of conversation with Brai. "Why do you think they're here? Why is the wexian here? What's going on? Was this some kind of political play?"

"Anything is possible. I'm analyzing all the data I can find, but I've been out of communication range for decades. The finer points of galactic politics are lost on me at the moment, but I think it's safe to assume that it is a simple stratagem to curry favor with a new culture that they believe will quickly rise to importance."

"All right. Can you brief me on what the wexian will be like?"

"Wex is a planet with an abundance of water. The wexian species is a nonanthropoid tripod that originated in marshy environments."

"Tripod? They have three legs?"

"Affirmative. Three legs, two arms, four eye stalks. No bones. Any internal structure is cartilage. Perhaps more akin to my form than yours, though our species are unrelated."

Feig stopped outside the docking portal.

Jane instructed Brai to unlock the portal and allow the wexian to come through. "Will he need any special accommodations? Does he breathe the same kind of air?"

"He shouldn't require anything extraordinary. The pelimarian named Ouvaq is thoroughly addressing his requirements in his quarters. You need only greet him."

Imadua came through. Jane was ready and kept her expression neutral, though internally she couldn't help but be surprised. The wexian was so delicately balanced on three spindly appendages terminating in thin, leaf-shaped clubs that he almost appeared to be floating. These legs—as well as two similar, but shorter, arms—emerged from under a rounded, hood-shaped mantle structure which clearly housed all of his internal organs. His entire body was pale pink except for his eye stalks, which glowed fuchsia. He came to stand before Jane and stretched out his arms to either side, tilting his mantle forward, reminding Jane of a small girl in a frilly dress curtsying.

Jane instinctively bowed in return. "Welcome, Imadua, to the *Speroancora*. I am honored by your visit. I hope your trip was pleasant."

He straightened and spoke softly, though she could see no

evidence of a mouth. Or nose or ears, for that matter. "Very. I have come to serve the terran crew in any manner you deem appropriate, Qua'dux."

"I am Feig. I'll be happy to escort you to your quarters." Feig held out a hand to Imadua.

Imadua laid one of his ovate hand against hers. Their pressed hands turned ninety degrees so that they were parallel with the floor and ceiling, and then slid apart.

Jane blanched internally. She'd shaken hands with Feig without thinking and hadn't noticed any surprise on Feig's part. Clearly this was the gesture that had been expected. She hoped these little mistakes wouldn't be held against her. But then, Feig was expecting Imadua to greet her the pelimarian way, wasn't she? That assumed it was a pelimarian greeting and not a universal one. Possibly it had been normal and correct for Jane to expect a human greeting. Or perhaps demanding one's own greeting was a way of asserting dominance. She just wasn't sure. In time, she'd learn this, and a million other things like it.

Imadua turned and Jane realized he was holding a small device. A rolling platform became visible through the docking portal and began to follow him, bearing what she assumed was his luggage.

Feig began to lead Imadua away and Jane stood there, uncertain of what she should do. It didn't seem as though they expected her to tag along. In the end she opted to return to the bridge to try to get a handle on what was going on.

Celui was alone on the bridge. He stood when she entered and extended his hand. Jane decided to try the new greeting she'd just observed. She didn't grasp his hand, just laid her hand against his. Then when she felt his hand begin to tilt, she followed his lead. As their hands slid apart, she glanced into his face with surprise. It was a surprisingly sensual gesture. She hoped she hadn't jerked her hand away too quickly. Her cheeks felt hot.

His eyes were twinkling with what appeared to be humor. "Well done!" he said enthusiastically. Then he seated himself at the communications console again and gestured to the seat next to his.

She sat, though she was a little uncomfortable placing herself so close to his personal space. Something about that seemed a little too familiar. His personal scent was similar to Feig's.

He continued. "Primarily, your official correspondence today revolves around this rush to send envoys to the ship. Many are asking that you grant them an exception to the Assembly's ruling."

Jane's brows drew together. "I seriously doubt I have the power to do that. And anyway, how would I choose one delegation over another?"

"You don't and you can't. They know this. It's all part of the dance." He smiled again. She was struck by how human he seemed. "If you want to compose one reply, we can tweak it to fit each delegation, and send it to all."

She glanced at the console. There were hundreds of messages today, and she was so worried about the *Oblignatus* that she really didn't want to deal with any of it. What he was offering would be a lot of work. "You would do that for me? That's very generous."

"Of course we would. That's why we're here."

Jane stared at him hard. Her gut feeling was to be strictly honest, and she decided to go with it. "You're here to work for me? Really? Forgive me, please. I don't understand. I don't have any money to pay you. I don't even know anything about galactic currency. Can you explain your motives more plainly? We look so much alike, but I can't forget that our cultures must be vastly different. I'm completely in the dark here. Why are you here? Why is Imadua here? What do you have to gain?"

He laughed. "Candor. We like that." He raised a hairless brow ridge and gazed at her intently.

She had to force herself not to fidget under his inspection and gaze back at him expectantly.

He leaned toward her, his forearm brushing against hers. "It's simple, Qua'dux. Prestige. You're the long-awaited terran representative. The circumstances of your arrival—the nanite plague—put all of the delegations at arm's length at first. It's a serious matter, as I'm sure you know. But Xua realized immediately that if an envoy should help you during your confinement and survive, terrans would bear a small debt to Pelimar. That's why he asked for volunteers among us. We want unity between all the species, of course, but especially among those who are like us. We go to great lengths to maintain good relationships with all the anthropoid species."

Was it just her imagination, or had he put special emphasis on the words "great lengths?" She decided to ignore that. His argument rang true. It was the simplest of the explanations she could think of. It did sound a bit jingoistic, however, which concerned her. Placing importance on getting along with people who look like oneself was at the heart of some of the worst conflicts on Earth. "You think Imadua's motivation is similar?"

"Of course. He was lucky to get here before the Assembly ordered the blockade. There are a lot of frustrated envoys out there whose worlds spent a lot of money to send representatives and gifts here for you, all with the same intent."

She realized she was scrunching her body away from him slightly and tried to relax. "And the three of you? Why were you chosen in particular?"

"We volunteered, actually. We are a small, new family. Most pelimarian families are much larger and well established. The risk-to-reward ratio is very much in our favor. And this is work that we know well. We've been performing the same duties for Xua for years. It was a good opportunity. Our interest was unanimous."

Feig and Ouvaq returned while Jane was composing her reply to the requests for exception to the blockade. Celui then showed her how they'd been sorting her correspondence and why he felt that some messages should be answered before others. He gave her a lot of insight into how pelimarians viewed galactic politics. After several hours of work, she rose to go meet Ajaya for lunch in the crew cafeteria. Ajaya would want to know whether she'd heard anything yet from Darcy. She hadn't. She asked the pelimarians, "Would you like to accompany me?"

The three exchanged enigmatic looks as they got to their feet. Feig replied, "We will join you shortly. We need a small rest in our rooms first."

Jane was instantly uncomfortable again. She glanced over her shoulder as she left the bridge to see the three of them converging, and the affectionate petting she'd noted when they arrived resuming.

35

ALAN SPRINTED FOR THE BRIDGE. Something interesting was going down and he didn't want to miss a second. "What kind of ship? Who is it?"

"The captain appears to be terran," Pio replied. "And I believe this is not someone you already know."

"Is Ron already talking to them?"

"He is."

"You're sure they aren't nintergertewhoever? Or—what's that other race that looks kinda like us? Nieblic?"

"They used the word 'human.'"

"Holy shit." He hit the symbol for the bridge level on the deck transport. How many humans were there out here? And even weirder—how did they find the *Obli*?

He arrived on the bridge along with everyone else to see the girl Jane had been looking for up on the viewscreen. Apparently she'd found her.

Ron turned slightly. "Hey. Everybody, this is Darcy Eberhardt. She's also from Earth."

"What did I miss?" Alan said.

"Not much," Ron said with a grin. "Captain Eberhardt brought us a message from Jane."

Alan nodded. "So Jane tracked you down?"

"She did. And you can call me Darcy. But before we get into chit-chat, I think you better watch this." Darcy leaned forward and tapped on a console. Jane came up on-screen. Her message was brief and to the point. Kai'Memna was publicly plotting revenge and likely knew exactly where the *Obli* was. Jane wanted them to pack up and leave.

"Damn," Ron muttered.

Alan rubbed the back of his neck. "Here we go again."

"You have a wormhole drive, right?" Darcy said anxiously.

Ron leaned against a console, squeezing his lower lip between thumb and forefinger. "We do, but we're not going anywhere."

"Is something wrong with your ship?" she asked. "Because I've got plenty of room. I can't take you to Terac, but I can give you a ride to a hub or something—"

Ron shook his head. "No. We're in the middle of an important project. We can't leave it untended."

She looked confused. "This is an abandoned planet."

Ron nodded. "It's a long story. Basically we're growing something that we hope will protect Earth from a pretty severe threat."

Darcy looked surprised. "Oh."

Ron's eyes flicked back and forth. "Do you have any idea how many ships he's bringing with him, what types, when we can expect him?"

Her face went blank. Alan knew that look. She was connecting with her kuboderan to ask for more information. She came back to herself and said, "My kuboderan got the feeling that his plans were impending. My kuboderan and yours are exchanging information now."

"Thank you. We appreciate the heads-up. I'd love to talk to you more, but you better make yourself scarce. This guy is—"

Her chin jutted out a little bit. "I'm not going anywhere."

Ron opened his mouth to speak but she cut him off again.

"I know this ship looks like a cracker hauler, but it's not. I have a crapton of weapons. I also have a co-captain who is no stranger to combat." Darcy waved to someone offscreen, who came forward. "This is Hain."

Alan blinked. Hain was a goddamn plant. Now he'd seen everything.

"Greetings," Hain said breathily.

"If Earth is in danger and you've got some project that will help, I'm all in," Darcy said defiantly. "And my crew is with me. We knew we were taking a risk coming out here, and we're ready to fight. When I get to go home I want the Earth I know to still be there."

"If I may, Qua'dux?" Pio interrupted.

"Go ahead, Pio," Ron said.

"After conferring with Do'Vela, I must conclude the *Vermachten* is a match for the *Portacollus*. It's small but well armored and boasts considerable armament."

Ron looked up. "If I could shake your hand, I would. We'll definitely talk more soon. But for now, I think we'd better work on battening down the hatches."

"Good enough," Darcy said. "I'm sending an encryption code now. Any further communication should take place on this channel, but encrypted." She started to reach for a control.

"Hey," Alan said, taking a step forward. "If this goes horribly wrong, you'll get word to Jane in Terac, won't you?"

"You bet." The screen went blank.

36

March 23, 2027
Ten years after Jane Holloway's Global Announcement

ZARA CLOSED her eyes as the countdown timer started from ten. She forced herself to breathe evenly in an attempt to calm her nerves. These simulations felt real and there was a lot riding on them.

Her future. On a ship. Like Jane.

The enlistment requirements were savage. The simulation she was about to undergo was designed for a position she was overqualified for, but that didn't matter. Everyone in the engineering track went through this one whether they were training to be an officer or a specialist. You had to prove you knew your stuff.

A decade had passed since the MSTEM program had started, since she'd taken that trip to the library in Hilliard. She was twenty-three and had just defended her dissertation a few weeks prior: "Sectilian Metamaterials: Feasibility of Manufacture and Potential Applications." She'd completed officer-training coursework and the special basic training session designed for M Scholars. She was just beginning life as a full-time NASA employee.

While she'd been busy studying, the world had come together like never before to build a fleet. The truth had begun to seep into the collective unconscious. There was a big universe out there. The Sectilius had clearly documented threats to their own worlds and their colonies. As Mensententia became more common than even Chinese, Spanish, or English as a world language, more and more individuals had read the sectilian download.

People began to demand that Earth build its own defense. The momentum was slow to build, but grew in intensity as Ms grew up and lent their adult voices to the conversation.

Earth was vulnerable. Suddenly a fleet became a top priority. It was the will of the people, though many governments—and Western governments in particular—continued to drag their feet and deny that there was really a threat.

The funding for materials and labor came from corporations, private donors, crowdfunding, and—in lesser amounts— international governments. Early on, someone with deep pockets had the presence of mind to stipulate their donation would only go forward if the ships were built free of national borders and influence.

It was a global fleet, an Earth United fleet, not divided by or representing individual nations. The population of Earth watched as the shipyards were set up. A new international committee had oversight. Exchanges were created so that no one culture dominated any single geographical building site. A new Earth United military was being formed, an amalgam of the world's armed forces to serve within this fleet.

The first four starships took four years to build in pieces on the ground. During that time a space elevator was erected near the equator in the Pacific Ocean to get the individual sections to Low Earth Orbit for assembly using the robotic arms of the International Space Station. Over the next few years a larger space station was constructed at the top of the space elevator to assemble and service these ships, and eight more ships were scheduled for construction. In the end, they would have a total of four large, heavily armored dreadnoughts and eight smaller cruisers.

The first twelve ships were built mostly to sectilian specifications with minor deviations. But plans were under way, even before work began, to redesign them, improve upon them as only humans could. This was reflected initially in the new-and-improved sectilian shuttlecraft, which was reconfigured to perform more like a fighter plane than a jumbo jet.

Earth was united in a common goal as it never had been before. National identity had its place—it helped to define an individual—but the emerging language of Earth was Mensententia, and a united Earth was beginning to be ready to defend itself should the need arise.

And Zara wanted to be a part of that.

When the counter hit zero, all hell would break loose and she'd be performing a role as junior engineer in a scenario on a replica of one of the sectilian ships Earth had built. It was a test.

Rumor had it that simulation scores were the final determining factor in whether or not an M got assigned to a ship or was stationed on the ground. And being stationed on the ground was no guarantee that an M would even be working on these projects anymore. Danny Jarvik, who at age fifteen had created the nanites using sectilian tech that had turned all of the Ms' hair purple across the globe, had been "loaned" to a big pharmaceutical company for research and development. He'd written a blog post describing how he got poached. He wasn't happy about it, but he didn't have any recourse. He was basically indentured because of documents they'd all signed when they joined. Fine print. Fine print allowed the government to choose a life for them.

Zara had been among the first humans to lay eyes on the blueprints for these interstellar ships. She'd worked on them since she was thirteen years old. She knew them inch by inch, inside and out. She'd watched them being built in stages over live cameras online and marveled at how beautifully they'd come to be. She'd held her breath as the pieces were lifted to Low Earth Orbit via the space elevator in the Pacific. And now she had a chance to live and work on one.

A buzzer sounded. She opened her eyes and scanned all the primary system readouts on her console. Everything was nominal, as the American astronauts had traditionally said. But it wasn't nominal for long.

The deck vibrated under her feet. The lighting changed to a red tone. A klaxon broadcast over the ship's speakers. Orders came down from the captain, and Zara was given a task by her commanding officer: reroute power to exclude a damaged area so that repairs could safely begin.

She double-checked her console to verify the source of the problem and then strode swiftly, trying to appear unruffled but quick, to one of the main electrical-conduit bays. The door slid open under her hand. On a sectilian ship, these would include parallel neural-electric pathways, a network of special synthetic neural channels allowing ship information to be transferred to a kuboderan's cybernetics almost instantly. But humans didn't have access to kuboderans, so these ships contained only electrical conduits.

It was a simple task if you knew the ship as well as she did. That's what she thought at first. She pulled a tool from its convenient casing nearby and quickly punched in a bypass code that would allow her to loosen the connection and reroute power away from the damaged area of the ship so that someone in that section could start work without fear of electrocution.

The tool wouldn't budge. Someone had torqued the conduit housing down hard. Completely unnecessarily. The outer housing had nothing to do with the connection. It was just an additional safety feature.

She knew that rerouting could be done with a computer keystroke. That wasn't the point. The point was to know the ship well enough to handle any and every situation. If computer systems were down, manually rerouting would be necessary. Anything could happen in space. A good engineer knew every part of the ship like the back of her hand.

Was this part of the test? Brute strength?

She moved in closer and wiped her forehead on her shoulder. Stray purple curls were falling down, drooping from sweat, and getting plastered to her forehead. She should have pinned it back before starting the simulation. It wasn't too warm or anything, she was just amped up and sweating freely.

Placing the tool high with both hands, she dropped into a squat, forcing her body weight to do the work. The housing loosened and she got the casing free. She grabbed the quick-connect mechanism and froze as her eye caught a small readout next to the flexible pipe.

Hold on.

She couldn't reroute this. She jogged to the nearest console and pulled up energy-usage charts for each conduit. They looked normal. But the reading she'd just seen didn't match. It was triple the reading on the console. This wasn't just a few kilowatts. Something was wrong. If she manually rerouted this, it could create serious problems down the line. Something could explode. People could die.

This had to be part of the test. She was supposed to figure out what to do. A monkey could reroute a conduit. But only a good engineer would notice this weird discrepancy and do something to fix the problem.

She used the interface on the console to trace the conduit and could find no reason for the surge. She went back to the bay and checked the readout again. It hadn't varied.

"Hampton? Check in. What's the holdup? Have you completed your task?"

Zara tapped the control on her ear to answer. "No, sir. I've found another problem. The conduit may be overpowered or there may be a fault in the sensor here. I'm about to check that."

"Just reroute and get back over here for your next task."

She bit back a reply and returned to the conduit. But she couldn't do it. The people on this ship were her family. She couldn't let anything bad happen to them. She took apart the sensor and checked it. It was working fine.

She left the conduit disconnected in case people were moving in to do repairs and went back to the console. A surge wouldn't normally last this long.

She checked the other sensors. She couldn't find any difference. Then she decided to inspect the software inside the sensor. That's where she found the problem. The software in the display had been uploaded incorrectly. It was for the wrong sensor and displayed a conversion error. Someone had just tapped the wrong button as they installed it. That was why the console was correct, but the display was wrong. She found the correct software and loaded that. The display changed instantly to safe levels. She finished the rerouting task and scuttled back to her supervisor. The lighting changed back to normal and the klaxon silenced. The simulation was over. Her superior officer looked grim and gave her definite side eye.

Three days later she met with a sergeant to go over her performance.

Sergeant Krapf slapped a stack of papers down and frowned. She was one of very few African-American officers Zara had run into in the quasimilitary version of NASA that funneled people into Earth United forces.

Zara met her gaze evenly. She wanted to impress this officer.

"You completed only one of three tasks," Krapf said.

Zara opened her mouth, but nothing came out.

"I've watched the footage of your test so you don't need to explain. Let me tell you the numbers."

Zara nodded slightly.

"Twenty-three people completed the simulation before you. Of those, ten noticed the display on the conduit housing. Three of those rerouted anyway and went on to the next task and didn't say anything to their commanding officer. Five immediately contacted their CO and asked for direction. When they were told to reroute anyway, they did as told. Two checked the console, like you did, and apparently decided the display was wrong, rerouted, and went on to the next task. You were the only one who defied a direct order."

Zara felt the blood drain from her face. "I—"

"You don't need to tell me what you were thinking. You thought you knew better. That's not how the military works. You've been trained. You should know this by now."

"But a surge of that magnitude—"

"It was a simulation and you failed. I'm recommending you stay dirtside."

Dirtside. The derogatory word for those trapped on Earth.

She couldn't stop herself from protesting. Her throat ached. She choked out, "With all due respect, we were supposed to treat this like it was really happening. I was trying to prevent unnecessary casualties. How could I know what was part of the test and what wasn't? If I were in your position, I'd fail anyone who ignored that faulty display—or worse yet—didn't notice it!"

Krapf narrowed her eyes. "It wasn't part of the test, Hampton. It was an oversight during installation. As a matter of fact, it's fixed now. You fixed it. This simulation was meant to test simple knowledge of the engineered structures of the ship."

"And didn't I demonstrate that I know them better than anyone else?"

"What you've demonstrated is you can't be counted on to follow orders in a crisis. You're unfit to serve. I'm recommending another round of basic for you. Dismissed."

37

ALAN CAME the closest he'd ever come to shitting himself.

Mere minutes after they got off the call with the new kid, fourteen ships jumped into the system.

Fourteen.

He glanced down at the console in front of him as he estimated how long it would take Kai'Memna's fleet to arrive—less time than it took to get the jump drive ready. *Shit.*

Darcy's ship might not be just a simple cargo hauler, but there was no way it was fitted out with enough firepower to face down fourteen ships with a grudge, hell bent on revenge and destruction.

She didn't look to be more than twenty-five, and he doubted she was even that old. Her frickin' sidekick was a plant. How aggressive could a plant be?

If she didn't bolt, she might be able to help them die a little more slowly.

Ron was barking orders, ordering Pio to start spooling up the jump drive in case they had to retreat, calling all hands to battle stations. "We've got a commodity down there that could save a lot of lives. If Kai'Memna gets even a whiff of how important it is to us, he'll destroy the Tree just to make sure we can never have it. That would be a huge loss. We're going to do our best to make sure that doesn't happen."

Ron turned to Alan. "Activate the anti-anipraxis protocol."

Alan nodded and brought the devices online. No external attempts at anipraxis would get through the jamming network, but internally they could continue to communicate as usual because the devices all broadcast outward. Their signals over-lapped to such an extent that they could lose any single device and still be safe from Kai'Memna mind-fucking abilities.

Ron started to pivot away, but stopped and gave Alan a side-long glance. "Your blink drive is ready for the testing phase."

Alan straightened, instantly on alert. He hadn't expected Ron to bring this up. "Yeah."

"So let's test it."

Alan blinked and let out a long slow breath, rubbing the back of his neck. On one hand, he was ninety-nine percent sure it would work. On the other, he hadn't completed all of the phases of testing. Sure, he'd done extensive experimentation on several stages of smaller-scale drives and knocked out all the bugs. Those drives worked like a charm. And he had already built and installed a full-scale drive on the ship. He just hadn't run it through all its paces yet.

But going straight to full-ship usage was skipping a few steps. Changing the scale to that degree, well... they might just blink out of existence if he got something wrong.

But if they were likely to die anyway, it was probably worth the risk. "Okay, boss. You know that's a terrible idea."

Ron huffed. "A terrible plan is better than no plan. Where are you at with the gravitational sling?"

"Nowhere near being ready. I don't have any of the mecha-nisms installed on the *Oblignatus*."

Ron spread his hands, like they were talking about the weather. "Okay, so it can't be used on the scale of this ship, but you've got working prototypes that could still pack a wallop, right?"

A malevolent grin crept across Alan's face. He hadn't even considered them. True, there were only three, but they could do a fuckton of damage to three ships. Suddenly survival didn't seem quite so remote. "I do. I might be persuaded to sacrifice them, if it means I get to live through this."

"Get to work. Shock and awe, man. That's what we've got to create or we'll lose this planet's resources. We can't let those kuboderans figure out that what we're doing here is important. They'll just mow down the Tree. Cutting and running is not an option."

"Aye-aye."

Alan raced to the workshop on Tech Deck, communicating his ideas with Pio as he ran. She was the most qualified to drive these things.

Pio asked, "Alan, have you forgotten the abandoned first-generation blink drive?"

"It didn't work properly, remember? We didn't get the calculations quite right. It distorted space-time too much."

"Precisely. Not safe for moving a ship, but perfect as a weapon."

He laughed. "I like how you think, Pio."

"With your permission, I'll move it now and use its grappling arm to attach it to a small asteroid in orbit."

"Even better."

The *Portacollus* and pals took their time. Ultimately the fourteen ships surrounded the *Oblignatus* on all sides, matching their orbit and velocity, just like the last time they'd hung out, over Pliga. It was like deja vu. Except this time they'd brought a few more friends.

Alan looked up from his sensor logs. "Ongoing attempts at anipraxis are being neutralized by the anti-anipraxis network."

Ron nodded from the command chair. "He's gotta be getting frustrated. Stay alert. We'll let them make the first move."

Ryliuk spoke from the communications console. "We're being hailed."

"This should be interesting," Alan murmured. Kai'Memna didn't have vocal chords. How was he planning to communicate without anipraxia?

"Open a channel. On-screen," Ron said.

An emaciated sectilian appeared before them. His skin was the color of ash, and patches of his hair were missing. Alan had seen a lot of skinny sectilians, but this guy was skeletal. It was shocking. "We meet again." His voice was low and growling.

Ron stood up. "Actually, I don't believe we've had the pleasure."

"I use this body as a vessel for the vocalization of speech, when necessary."

Ron nodded. "Then I'm speaking with Kai'Memna, I assume?"

"You are."

Ron kept up the jocular tone. "What can we do for you, Kai'Memna? You know, we have plenty of rations aboard. We'd be happy to provide aid. It looks like your dude could use a biscuit."

The sectilian before them practically snarled, "It seems humans are even more insolent than sectilians."

Ron smiled. He didn't look perturbed in the slightest. "Oh, we've earned our reputation."

"I will speak freely with Ei'Pio."

Ron looked mildly apologetic. "I'm afraid I can't let you

do that."

"Then I'll destroy your petty contrivances. And if your ship is obliterated in the process, it will be of little consequence."

Ron shrugged like he was unconcerned. "You can try." He turned to Ryliuk. "Cut the connection and be ready to reset exterior cameras." And to Alan, his eyes hard but steady, he said, "Blink."

They'd set it up so that Ei'Pio was constantly feeding the most advantageous coordinates into Alan's console. He only had to press a button to send them faster than light to the new location. He did.

His vision vibrated for a moment that ended in a flash that was dark around the edges. As soon as he registered the phenomenon, it muted, and his eyesight returned to normal. He looked down at his sensor data and noted that they were in orbit high above the kuboderan ships, just out of firing range.

The blink drive had worked. Relief flooded through him.

"All hands check in. Everyone okay?" Ron said, cool as a cucumber.

One by one, all five crew members checked in, reporting that they were fine.

Ron tipped his head toward Alan as a sort of congratulatory nod, then turned his attention to the new camera view that had come up on the viewscreen just in time to show the aftermath of what had happened while they'd been moving to the new position.

All fourteen ships had fired through empty space... into each other.

Jaross announced, "Six of the fourteen ships have taken minor damage, including the *Portacollus*."

Alan crowed, "Hells yeah!"

The blink drive worked just as he'd dreamed it would. It was glorious. This was absolutely the pinnacle of his career.

Several of Kai'Memna's ships were in the process of backing off, breaking formation. A few narrowly missed hitting neighboring ships. They'd clearly never seen anything like this and were scrambling. He could just imagine how confused and pissed off they were.

Ron said, "Deploy two gravitational slings at the *Portacollus* to create some more chaos before they can regroup. We'll hold the remaining two in reserve until we need them."

Alan triggered a compartment door that would let two of his babies out into space. "You heard him, Pio. Maximum destruction, please."

"With pleasure," she replied. She was remarkably calm, considering the state she'd been in when they'd first met her, but maybe that was because she actually had some control in this situation. She used the first-generation blink drive first, maneuvering it quickly so that it dropped the warp bubble when the edge of it came in contact with the hull just over the *Portacollus*'s engineering decks. As the warp bubble fell apart, not only did the space-time distortion impact the hull of the *Portacollus*, but the small asteroid the drive had in tow broke apart violently, doubling the impact. The resulting explosion created a breach.

Alan called out, "Hey, Ron, keep talking to him, man!"

Ron raised a brow. "Why? We've got nothing to say."

"Trash talk. Kai'Memna would love it."

Ron coughed out a chuckle. Damn, that guy was cool under pressure. "Blink."

Alan checked all of the readouts. Everything was green for go. He pressed the button. They skipped across space again with the same momentary visual disturbance. It was less disorienting the second time. Pio calmly sent one of Alan's prototype gravitational slings toward the hole the first one had created. This one was equipped with a very small fission bomb which would create a very large EMP.

And it was away.

Alan watched his monitors closely, every muscle tensed. "Three... two... one. EMP detonation."

A bright flash emanated from the crater in the *Portacollus*'s hull. Then every light on that ship went out. Oh, yeah. That was satisfying.

Alan nodded smugly. "It worked. The *Portacollus* has gone dark. Setting coordinates for the third blink drive on target number two."

Ron said, "Blink. And hold those gravitational slings for a minute. I believe I do have something to say."

Alan scanned his console again. Pio was very good at keeping up with several tasks at once. New coordinates were ready to go, changing in real time along with their position. He triggered the blink drive again and quickly reoriented himself. Now they were below and ahead of the fourteen ships in the orbital plane.

Ryliuk reset the cameras so they could watch the ships above and behind them.

Ron stood up. "Open an audio-visual channel with every ship."

A moment later, Ryliuk said, "Channel open, Qua'dux."

Ron spread his hands. "You guys just aren't bringing your A game. We can do this all day long. We've got a couple of these special bombs for each of you, if you insist on keeping this up. But I don't think you will. Why? I think you're all smarter than that. Look, you must realize by now that you aren't a serious threat to us. Your leader is down for the count."

Ron stepped closer to the camera mounted above the screen. "We're human. Yes, we're insolent. But we're also innovative. And we don't take shit. We also believe all people are equal. That's why our kuboderan navigators have the same rights and privileges we do. They're free. Free to choose their destiny. They don't endure a yoke. If they don't want to fly, they can retire, whenever and wherever they want."

Ron turned and took his time returning to the command chair. "I bet there are a few of you who have been uncomfortable with Kai'Memna's tactics all along. But he didn't really give you an option, did he? You had to decide between joining him and death. Now, I'm going to tell you something. Kai'Memna wasn't wrong. You do deserve to be free. But genocide will never be the right way to achieve that goal. There's always another way. So here's the thing. I'm going to give you three choices right here and now."

Ron held up three fingers, folding them down one at a time as he spoke. "You can keep fighting us and die here. You can leave and find some quiet place to settle down and put all of this behind you. Or you can join us. We'll help you find a crew that you can be proud to call your equals. No yoke necessary. Just equity and trust. You need never be slaves again. The choice is yours. I suggest you decide quickly." Ron made a cutting motion with his hand. Ryliuk's eyes widened for a second, and then he leaned over his console and tapped the channel closed.

Jaross called out, "The *Portacollus* is losing altitude fast."

Ron's eyes narrowed. "Jesus. Can it really be this easy? Split the screen. Half on Kai'Memna, half on the rest of his fleet."

Ryliuk hunched over his console, tapping his screens furiously, then looked up as he made Ron's order manifest.

The *Portacollus* twirled drunkenly as the asteroid's impact, the planet's gravity, and Kai'Memna's abortive attempts to maneuver prevailed over what was left of its forward momentum. The rest of Kai'Memna's fleet maintained position, probably observing the same thing they were.

Huna spoke up for the first time from the rear of the bridge, where he'd been watching everything silently. "Is there anything we can do to preserve the lives of the innocents aboard?"

Pio spoke inside Alan's head—probably in everyone's heads— in an anguished whisper. "They've been dead for decades. We're finally letting them go to find their peace in dusk."

Alan glanced around. Ryliuk and Jaross looked solemn, but no one protested. He couldn't help but think of the maneuvers Pio had performed to save the *Speroancora* months before. Trying to pull a stunt like that now with a ship in freefall would be foolish. They'd die trying to save them. And if the rest of the crew looked like the man they'd just seen on the screen, Pio was right. They were releasing them from a hellish existence.

It didn't take long. The *Portacollus* flipped end over end until it hit atmosphere. Then it glowed bright red from the friction of entry and pieces started breaking off. The fissure they'd created with the gravitational sling split the ship in two and a plume of water vaporized in the sky, creating a vertical white cloud. If Kai'Memna hadn't already been dead, he'd just boiled alive.

"Damn," Alan muttered. He glanced over at Ron. Ron's shoulders drooped a little, and he had a look on his face like he'd just tasted something bad. He was shaking his head slightly.

Alan looked back at the screen in time to see the final impact. The largest piece hit a part of the main continent covered with the Tree. They'd just lost some of their potential crop. The rest landed somewhere on the dark side of Pliga That Was.

He'd be taking a shuttle down later to verify that son of a bitch was actually dead this time.

Ron straightened. "Pio, if we drop the anipraxis shield, do you feel up to saying a few words to the kuboderans back there? I want to assure you that the shield will go right back up if anything funny happens."

Pio's voice was soft, but firm. "I will do my best, Quasador Dux Ronald Gibbs. What would you like me to convey to them?"

Ron looked thoughtful. "Nothing more or less than the truth as you see it."

38

January 27, 2031
Fourteen years after Jane Holloway's Global Announcement

ZARA ALMOST MISSED the small file. It was so close in proximity to a much larger file that its single tiny symbol was nearly eclipsed, and was probably often mistaken for a part of the larger file. Her multidisciplinary team had been assigned the task of meticulously cataloging every file in the database, so she approached the project from several vectors to prevent any omissions. The file cloud had been mapped many times, but this was to be the definitive, internationally recognized version, commissioned by a newly formed international oversight committee.

When she opened the small file, she gasped in surprise. The sound echoed through the room and a few people looked up. She quickly brought her expression under control because she wasn't ready to share this... not just yet.

She couldn't believe no one else had seen this. If they had, she'd have heard about it. They'd all been looking at this thing for years. How could they have missed it?

But maybe that was the point.

It was a personal message from Jane Holloway. A video.

As a kid she'd found videos of Holloway lecturing and watched them over and over again, but this was different, special. This was an older Jane Holloway who had been on the *Speroancora*. Presumably she'd have more to say than she had on the Global Announcement. Zara tilted her screen as unobtrusively as she could and looked around. No one should be able to see it. She rummaged in her purse for some ear buds and stuck them in her ears, then found the jack on the PC under her desk and plugged them in. She hit Play.

The backdrop was the same as it had been for the Global Announcement. Greenish walls and some consoles. The general consensus was that this was the bridge of the *Speroancora*. Jane wore the same expression. Serious, but genial. She spoke in Mensententia.

"Congratulations. You've made significant headway into understanding the sectilian file packet we sent to Earth, or you wouldn't have been able to find this video. My fellow *Providence* crewmate, Dr. Alan Bergen, programmed this particular file to unmask after a series of files were examined that we as a group felt were most important. Good work."

The urge to hoot with childish glee was nearly overwhelming, but Zara managed to keep herself in check, just barely.

"Along with this video, you'll find that this file contains glossaries and indexes of the entirety of the sectilian file packet, personally created by me with the assistance of Dr. Ronald Gibbs, Dr. Alan Bergen, and the *Speroancora*'s navigator, Ei'Brai."

That was exactly what Zara and her team were working on. She couldn't wait to look at these files to see how Jane had organized them.

"I can't take all the credit. The packet was originally

compiled by the sectilian crew that came to our system in 1947. We modified it only slightly. The Quasador Dux of the vessel at that time, Rageth Elia Hator, had intended to send the sectilian version of tablet computers to the surface, knowing that Earth's computers at that time were primitive and in the earliest stages of development. Under Hator, humans would have been coaxed through the program with the help of their new sectilian friends. Sadly, they died before they could accomplish their mission. We realized that a lot of things, technology especially, have changed in the intervening sixty-plus years, with no small thanks owing to the study of the sectilian shuttle that crashed in Roswell that year."

"We decided it made more sense in 2017 to simply pass on the file itself, so Dr. Gibbs and Dr. Bergen adapted the original software so that it would perform on a PC. I asked them to move the Mensententic language software to the core, hoping that it would be found early on. I hope that was the right thing to do."

Jane smiled slightly. "I suspect there will have been resistance to learning the language, so I tried to emphasize how important that was when I sent my message to all the peoples of Earth. Regardless, you must be on track now, or you wouldn't understand a word I'm saying." Her smile expanded and lit up her face.

Throughout the remainder of the video, Holloway breathed life into the way the download worked from a sectilian point of view and explained its structure. She went on to discuss what she knew about the Cunabula's supposed interference in human evolution and the legendary importance of humanity to the rest of the galaxy. There was a lot of new information there. It was fascinating. Then Jane outlined all the potential threats to Earth—primarily the Swarm, which Zara had already read about—providing extensive background information on each and even some images. She ended the video by saying, "I wish you well. Whoever you are, wherever you are on Earth, you are doing good work that will benefit humanity. I thank you."

Zara sat back and heaved a deep sigh. She was going to have to take this file to her supervisor ASAP. She saved the file to a thumb drive, printed out ten copies of the text files, and went to knock on Dr. Sakey's door. He skimmed through it and immediately got on the phone with the administrator's office, waving at her to sit down.

This took a long time. She got bored and perused the text files while she waited. Eventually Sakey got off the phone and told her that the current administrator was moving up a visit planned for a few days out. Dr. Kenneth Lin wanted to meet with Zara personally. They hadn't met before. She'd met his predecessor under the previous administration, but not Lin.

She protested. "But I can just email this to his office."

"Oh, no. He's taken a personal interest in you and wants to hear it all from your lips."

Zara frowned. "All right."

Sakey got up and moved between her and his desk. He leaned back on it and looked up at the ceiling. "Don't share this file with anyone. I'll take those." He reached for the remaining printouts and thumb drive. "Do you have anything else on this drive that you need?"

"No, it was empty."

He nodded, then leaned back on his desk to touch a button on his phone. "Cindy, send in someone from Jay Wellington's team, please."

A tinny voice responded, "Right away, sir."

"Zara, I'm sure I don't need to tell you that this message is sensitive information. We can't know who has seen this and who hasn't, but my guess is that you're the first to find it. I've been instructed to expunge it from the sectilian database."

Zara shook her head. "Sir, with all due respect, that would be impossible. The number of copies all over the world would make that action meaningless. Other people will find this information eventually. People have a right to know this stuff. It's important information."

"Believe me, I understand. I will even go so far as to tell you I agree with you, but it's not up to me. Orders are orders. It's out of my hands." He looked at her meaningfully, his stare lingering far longer than seemed normal.

Her brow furrowed. Was he trying to tell her something? Jay Wellington's team was made up of a bunch of computer specialists—hackers, really. Was Sakey going to instruct them to remove this file from every instance of the sectilian database online? Was that even possible? Why would they do that after all of the international cooperative gains that had been made?

"Zara, you have been instrumental in this program's success from the very beginning. You know that." Was it her imagination or had he loaded the word "beginning" with significance? Did he know that she was the one who had uploaded the language file in 2017?

Her head was spinning. She nodded absently and swallowed.

"Go back to your team. You'll have a few minutes to extract just the portion that pertains to your project—use that to help you complete the work quickly, but don't show it to anyone else. Destroy that data when the project is done. I know I can trust you to do that. You are not to speak to anyone about finding this file or the contents of the message from Jane Holloway."

The intercom buzzed. "Jay Wellington to see you, sir."

Sakey leaned back. "Send him in. You're dismissed, Dr. Hampton." He made no further eye contact.

She stood and left without a word.

When she got back to her desk she stared at her blank monitor, frustration and anger welling up inside her. This information had already been set free. It wasn't right to try to put a lid on it now—not when the world needed to know what it was up against. They'd already made so many gains. To do this... it would handicap the world when it needed this information the most. Was Sakey encouraging her to take the matter into her own hands?

If they were going to ground her forever, keep her from fulfilling her lifelong dream, she would be damned if she was going to let them get away with this. The world needed to know about these threats. They needed to see the words coming directly from Jane Holloway's lips. She wasn't an abstract figure anymore. She wasn't reviled as a crackpot. The world believed in Jane Holloway now.

They needed to see this video now more than ever, to prove to naysayers that the world's new fleet was not a waste of resources and manpower. Earth needed not just this small fleet of ships, but dozens and dozens more if they were to have any hope of protecting their home from something as hideous as the Swarm. This video would make them understand that, surely.

Her fingers shook as she logged back into the secure network.

She did as Sakey instructed and copied the part of the text file that pertained to her work. Then she went still, her fingers hesitating over the command to copy the entire file again.

No.

Everything she did on this server could be reviewed. That's not what Sakey was telling her to do. He had made a point of reminding her what she'd done when she was thirteen, when she'd covered her tracks. She could do something like that again. Except that she was older and wiser now. She had far better tools. And brilliant friends.

She felt like she was being watched. The hairs on the back of her neck stood on end. She went back to work, the process made much faster with Jane's help. It was only two hours until quitting time.

At 4:30 p.m. she texted her roommate Charlotte to cancel their dinner plans, saying that she wasn't up for anything but canned chicken soup, a blankie, and a movie on TV. She was going home right after work. Then she looked at the sectilian database on the local server. The file was already gone.

She really wasn't feeling well. If she got caught, she had so much more to lose now than she had at age thirteen.

She left the building at 4:55 p.m. and went straight home. They had a Tor relay on their network, one of the advantages of living with computer geeks. She rented a rundown, rambling three-story house with five other former MSTEM Scholars. They were all socking away money toward an uncertain future. Once home, she opened a new account with a Web-based texting service using a made-up name and messaged a few of her international contacts, using vague references in the hopes they would recognize her.

The first person to respond was a linguist in a program similar to MSTEM in China. Zara identified herself in a round-about way, gave her the coordinates in the sectilian database for Jane's text file, and asked her if she could find it.

She couldn't.

Damn. Either Jay's team was working fast, or the file hadn't been unmasked in the way Holloway described in China yet.

She changed tactics and searched for the sectilian database herself. There were dozens of hits. She went through each one until she found one with the video file intact. It was on a server in Uganda. She saved the database to her laptop and then sent a message to someone she knew in Uganda, asking him to do the same and to post it online if he could.

The race was on.

She carefully posted it herself in several places using methods that she hoped wouldn't be traceable, then continued to contact people all over the world, asking them to find and share the file as

well. She had to make sure that people knew this file existed—
that the US government didn't bury knowledge that was vital to
the world. The old guys in charge were still playing the same old
games. It felt like it was up to her, once again, to keep them
honest.

Her roommates arrived home full of cheap sushi and sake,
laughing and joking. They sobered when she told them what she
was doing and why. Soon the only sound in the house was the
clacking of keys as six individuals sat around on the secondhand
sofas and chairs that crowded their big, drafty living room and
raced against Jay's team.

Zara checked the files she'd uploaded to the Web a couple of
hours before. One of them had been found and removed.

"The file is down in Russia," Charlotte announced from the
floor at Zara's feet.

"I've got someone in New York City posting it everywhere
they can think of," Jake called out.

"We've got it back up and new firewalls in place in
Australia," Danny said before getting up to make a pot of coffee.
Zara asked him to throw a frozen burrito in the microwave for
her, so she could keep working. Her hunger was getting
distracting but she couldn't stop. There wasn't time to stop. She
tore off a bite of the burrito now and then, chewing without
tasting as she alternated between typing messages furiously into
her phone and searching for Jane's video in the sectilian database
wherever she could find it online.

They went on late into the night.

Ben leaned forward, excited. "A popular Medium blogger
just posted about how this file is appearing and disappearing on
servers all over the world."

Fifteen minutes later Ben reported, "Getting a 404 on that
Medium blogger now."

"ui8 has an article up about it."

Charlotte shouted, "Turn on CNN!"

Zara checked the first five sites she'd posted on. Four of them were down. One of them was getting a lot of traffic, though. She looked up as the TV came on and Dominica found the right network.

"It appears to be a cyber-information war," an announcer said. "Groups of anonymous individuals around the world are trying to keep this information online, and just as fast as they can post it, another group is taking it down. The purpose of the attacks is unclear, since millions of individuals likely have downloaded the sectilian database and saved it to their personal computers—those files on private computers would be unchanged by these hacking attacks on servers across the globe. Experts suggest this may be an attempt to minimize the opportunity of discovery of a file which is said to be a lengthy message from Dr. Jane Holloway, hidden in plain sight within the sectilian database just as the *Speroancora* was said to be hidden in the Greater Asteroid Belt. The persons or entities responsible on either side are unknown and untraceable." The anchor went on to list the five sites currently hosting the file that were most likely to last due to having more secure servers, then showed a brief clip of Holloway's video file. "This information is being kept as current as possible on our website. If you want to obtain a copy to watch and read for yourself, we suggest you do so now."

"Holy shit. They're on our side," Dominica whispered as she placed the remote on a beat-up side table and looked at all of them one by one, incredulous.

"As of yet, we have been unable to confirm if this is indeed a message left in the sectilian database by Jane Holloway. We will bring you up-to-the-minute coverage on this topic as more information comes to light." The network went to commercial.

"What do we do now?" Charlotte asked. She looked tired. They all did.

Zara refocused on her laptop. "We keep going," she said.

At 2:00 a.m. they began to notice that the database no longer seemed to be disappearing. By 3:00 a.m. they'd confirmed that was the case.

Zara rubbed her eyes. "Let's get some sleep. We made our point and people noticed. We have to go into work tomorrow and pretend that nothing has happened."

One by one her roommates shut their own laptops and wandered off to bed, fist-bumping and high-fiving her as they passed by.

Charlotte flashed her a wan smile. "I didn't know victory could be so exhausting."

Zara nodded.

It was the second time in her life that she'd thwarted the government for the greater good of Earth.

39

ALAN COULDN'T RELAX JUST YET.
Pio was talking to the other kuboderans. They had questions
about humans. They all seemed calm for now, but he wasn't
letting down his guard.

Anything could happen in the next hour or so. There were
thirteen kuboderans out there, and who knew how many of them
had drunk the Kai'Memna Kool-Aid. They could be buying time
while they reorganized and planned a counterattack.

Ryliuk said, "Message coming in on the encrypted channel
set up by Darcy Eberhardt."

"Put it up on-screen," Ron replied.

Darcy's face appeared. She instantly started talking. No
small talk. No congratulations. "What the hell was *that?*"

Ron snorted. "That was just a couple of inventions by a
certain Dr. Alan Bergen."

Her eyes were wide with disbelief. "You invented that stuff?
What are you, a genius?"

Alan smirked. "Actually, yes. Yes, I am."

"Why did you act so worried when I showed up? You didn't need my help. Clearly."

Alan leaned back in his seat, enjoying the attention just a little, though at the back of his mind a little voice was reminding him that the fight could have just as easily gone the other way. If any one of the devices hadn't worked, they'd have been screwed. He hadn't been ready for fourteen ships. Suddenly the praise didn't feel so great. "Well, those were just experiments I've been working on lately. We weren't sure they would work."

Her jaw dropped and her eyebrows shot up. "If those were just experiments, I'm glad you're on our side."

Ron gave him a sidelong look. "All right. That's enough congratulations for Berg. His head is big enough."

A few long, spindly light-green fingers came into the frame, followed by the tree person Darcy had said was named Hain. Her voice was breathy and creepily monotone, like a sexy computer voice. What a strange combination. "Would you be willing to share your notes on these inventions?"

Alan balked. He hadn't even considered this possibility. He didn't really know these people. Sure, they'd just warned them of an impending attack, but...

Ron saved him from having to reply. "When he's got all the bugs worked out of them, we'll talk."

Darcy looked rueful. "Right. We'll hold you to that. Well, I'd love to stick around and get to know you all better, but I've got a lead I need to follow before the trail goes cold. You seem to have this under control, so I'm gonna jet. I'll let Holloway know how things went here. She was pretty worried, though I don't know why."

Alan frowned. What? She was already leaving?

Ron said, "Thank you for the warning. It made all the difference. We're in your debt."

"When you're back in civilized space, contact me anytime on this channel with these credentials."

Ron inclined his head. "This channel goes both ways, so let us know if you need any help."

Alan raised his hand like an effing schoolboy. "Hey, could you give Jane a message from me?"

"Sure thing."

He froze. What should he say? "Tell her I miss her."

Ron slow-clapped. "Come on, man. You can do better than that."

Alan let out an exasperated huff. "She'll know what I mean."

Darcy raised her eyebrows. "Do you want to take a few minutes to write a message or record something?"

Alan waved her off. "No. It's fine. Just tell her that."

"Actually..." Ron bent over a nearby console. "I've got a series of messages for Jane and another crew member that you could deliver, if you don't mind. Sending... now."

Alan rolled his eyes. "Jesus, Ron. Way to make me look like an idiot."

Darcy's eyes crinkled with amusement. "Will do. I hope to talk to you again soon. Goodbye."

"Goodbye, Darcy. Gibbs over and out."

The screen went blank.

Alan sat down at his console again. "I wonder what her story is."

Ron looked incredulous. "No idea. Maybe Jane knows."

Pio talked to the kuboderans for a couple of hours.

The rest of the crew sat on the bridge waiting to see what the outcome would be. Alan never let his fingers get very far from the blink-drive controls. When stomachs started rumbling loud enough for a gastric chorus to form, Huna was kind enough to hop off to fetch some food cubes and water for everyone while they waited.

Toward the end of this meal, Pio announced that the talks had concluded.

She sounded very calm as she discussed the outcome. "Nine ships are undecided. Of those, seven are inclined to join us, but want more time to think about the advantages and disadvantages of such an alliance. Two believe they want to end their navigation careers and find a planet to settle on. All nine are preparing to leave orbit now, but some may return once their decision has been made. The remaining four will stay in orbit with us, joining us."

"Are there any living sectilians aboard the four ships?" Ron asked.

Pio's voice was full of sorrow. "No."

Ron took a deep breath. "What do we do with them now? I promised them each a crew, but we can't spare anyone right now. We're thin as it is."

"If I may?" Pio said. "Kuboderans can live for thousands of years. You intend to return to Earth eventually. They don't expect anything sooner than that. I've made them aware of the timeline. No one was concerned about it."

Ron leaned forward. He spoke to Pio carefully and deliberately. "You were communicating with them, very closely. It's my understanding from talking with Jane and Brai that it would be difficult for them to deceive you. Is that correct? Do they all seem sincere? Do any of them harbor ill will toward us? I guess what I'm asking is for your gut reaction: Do we have any Kai'Memnas in the making among them?"

"Yes, it would be difficult to deceive me. I spoke to them both as a group and individually, so that I could monitor their reactions closely. I do not believe we are at risk for another attack from these kuboderans. The strange truth is that Kai'Memna was an aberration. Most of us were happy in our lives before, did not see what we were missing until he forced us to see it. Kai'Memna demanded a terrible choice from us. Most of us chose to live, all the while wishing it were not necessary to do his bidding in order to avoid meeting dusk. We went from slavery of one kind to another. The general feeling seemed to be relief that it is over, gratitude that real choices are being offered now."

Ron rubbed his stubbled chin. "That makes a lot of sense. But if all of that is true, why wasn't there an internal uprising? Why was it up to us to get rid of Kai'Memna?"

Pio didn't answer for a long moment. "I can only speak for myself. It felt... impossible. He seemed so strong. And we saw—he made certain we witnessed—him killing our defenseless brothers and sisters. I felt hopeless and complicit." She went quiet.

They were all silent.

"I didn't feel hope until I spoke to Jane, until I watched her fight him, heard Brai speak of her care and compassion and say that she was human and different. I couldn't stand by and watch Kai'Memna destroy her. That was when I acted. Perhaps that sort of encounter was all any of us would need to conquer our fear."

Pio continued, "I think, perhaps, that was why it was so easy to defeat him, even with thirteen ships to back him up. They all knew we'd come very close to defeating him before. I had said no to him and survived. We'd slain his best lieutenant, who was instrumental in keeping the rest in line. They said he'd become unstable after that. Reckless. Consumed with revenge. The idea that he could be beaten had already been planted. Their greatest fear was that they would meet dusk with him when his time would come."

That was all Pio had to say. After that Ron set up shifts so that two crew members were always on the bridge, ready to raise the alarm. Alan got the first shift off, but he knew he couldn't sleep right away, so he headed down to Tech Deck to work for a while. He hoped that if nothing happened for a few hours, he might be able to catch some sleep before his shift came up.

As he walked, Pio gave him that little shiver in the back of his brain that was her warning that she was about to contact him. "Alan? Do you have a moment?"

"Sure."

"There's something I'd like to tell you, but I didn't want to embarrass you in front of the others."

He stopped in his tracks. "What? Did you find a calculation error that we didn't catch in the simulations?"

"Oh, no. Nothing like that. Quite the opposite."

He sniffed hard and resumed walking. "Okay. Then what is it?"

"I thought you should know that your inventions were the primary reason why those who decided to stay chose that course of action. You. Your inventions helped them make that decision."

He halted again. "Me?"

"If a kuboderan needed any proof that humans were different from sectilians, you gave that to them to an infinite degree. You gave them hope."

He shook his head. "That doesn't make sense. Ron offered them freedom."

"But how could they blindly trust that after what they'd been through? Kai'Memna offered them freedom as well."

"I still don't understand. You're going to have to explain."

"You create things out of ideas. Very quickly. Most of the time that the kuboderans and I spent talking, the topics were related to these projects you took on—the anti-anipraxic devices, the blink drive, the gravitational sling. Of course I didn't delineate how any of them actually work. They were more curious about the process you underwent. How you took the things from idea to finished object."

"But sectilians invent things."

"They do. Over decades, centuries. They are slow to act. Rigorous in debate of theory, slow to reach experimentation which is extensive in the extreme. They would never have thought to use an untested blink drive in battle. They would have died first. That gamble proved to them that humans are different."

"Huh."

"Over these many months since I met all of you, I have often contemplated what the yoke was for. To my knowledge there were no historic examples of kuboderan officers wreaking havoc on sectilian ships. I have come to the conclusion that the yoke was there to prevent the chaos we *might* have created. We were never given the opportunity to prove ourselves. We were too much of an unknown factor, so they did all they could to mitigate what was seen as a potential liability. Stories coming from outside sectilian space about kuboderans who had rebelled only reinforced this notion. They clamped down harder on us, took a little more of what we were. Are."

Alan rubbed his neck. "And that led to the birth of Kai'Memna."

"But humans are different. I've seen that firsthand. These kuboderans wanted more than just my thoughts and memories. I was able to show them a great deal. Even Lira, which astounded them. But you were the reason the four joined us. The reason seven more may yet join us. I thought you should know this."

Alan got to the deck transport, and his fingers hovered over the symbols. They came to rest on the Crew Deck after all. He was going to retire to his quarters to do nothing but think for a while.

40

JANE HAD BEEN on edge for days, waiting for word from Darcy. As time went on, the fear congealed in her stomach and she could barely eat or sleep, worried that something had gone horribly wrong and that both the *Oblignatus* and the *Vermachten* had been so badly damaged in an encounter with Kai'Memna that they were beyond repair. And that maybe the people she cared for so much were too.

All she wanted to do was flip the bird at the Decatribunal, at all of Terac, and fly to Pliga That Was. Instead she was getting ready for a party.

Jane and her multispecies crew were about to celebrate the completion and subsequent broadcast of the first six episodes of Jane's video series about Earth by tasting delicacies sent from Terac by drone, many of them gifts from other cultures that were actively courting Jane, clearly hoping to curry favor with Earth.

It was Feig's idea. She thought it would take Jane's and Ajaya's minds off of what was happening at Pliga That Was. Jane didn't think it would help, but she humored Feig and was doing her best to pretend it was working.

Jane wished Alan could be there so she could watch his reaction to the strange new foods. He always had some quip or dry, crotchety comment that made her struggle not to giggle. She loved that. She missed him terribly.

Feig placed twelve bowls of food in a line down the center of the table.

Pledor leaned forward, peering into the nearest bowl and sniffing suspiciously. "What's this?"

"It's called glil," Feig answered as she picked up the bowl of the small, bright-red, heart-shaped fruit and handed it to him. "It's from Sebapen."

Next to Pledor, Murrrsi grabbed one and popped the morsel in her mouth. She made a delighted expression.

"What does it taste like?" Pledor asked. He scrutinized the fruit minutely. Pledor had clearly become more than friendly with the pelimarians. He spent a lot of time with them and had begun to be included in their more intimate caresses before they retired from ship society, which Jane gathered was customary whenever pelimarians were in a multispecies situation, out of respect for other cultures.

Pledor's inclusion made her uncomfortable, and she really wasn't sure why. Why should it matter? The truth was, he seemed happier, which meant he'd hopefully cause less disruption. She reminded herself that it was really none of her business whenever her thoughts strayed to the topic.

Jane and Ajaya had fielded a lot of oblique questions about human sexuality. It was a topic that came up far more than Jane was comfortable with. She'd done her best to be direct, to satisfy their curiosity.

"Bright and sweet and a little sour. It explodes in your mouth," Murrrsi replied enthusiastically.

Pledor cautiously took a single tiny fruit and passed the bowl to Celui, who then passed it to Jane. Pledor watched her with narrowed eyes as she selected one and bit down.

It was a sudden burst of flavor, flooding her mouth. Her salivary glands gushed painfully in response. Once that uncomfortable feeling passed, she chewed slowly to pick up all of the intense flavor components. There were lingering notes that reminded her of stone fruit and berries, a potent alcoholic kick, and even a hint of something like balsamic vinegar. It was unusual, but she liked it.

Ouvaq took the bowl from Jane. "It is a berry with a tough pericarp and a watery interior. It's sold in three main types. Fresh-picked glil is very sweet, but doesn't have a lot of flavor. The second type has been left on the shrub to ferment to the stage when alcohol is present, and that form is very popular. The third type has been left on the shrub even longer, reaching a second stage where some acetic acid forms from the alcohol, rendering what might have been a relatively bland fruit delightfully complex. This was a very expensive gift."

Pledor gently bit the fruit in half, slurping at the squirting contents. His eyes widened, and he peered at what was left of it in his hand. "There are many small seeds. I wonder if they are viable?"

Celui smiled at Pledor and stroked his arm. "Let's dry some and find out, shall we?"

Pledor absently patted Celui and rose from the table, clearly already taken with the idea. He vaguely aimed his next question at Jane, still squinting at his fruit. "May I be greedy and ask for another?"

The bowl was full. "Take as many as you want," Jane said.

The fruit had reached Ajaya. "Remarkable!" she exclaimed and held it up for Pledor. He grabbed a large handful and left with Celui, the rest of the tasting forgotten.

Ajaya asked, "Are fermented alcoholic beverages common? On Earth we ferment a variety of fruits and grains."

"Such beverages are available, though other intoxicants are generally preferred because they have fewer side effects," Feig replied.

Brai's voice rumbled in Jane's head. "Qua'dux, a message has just come in on the *Vermachten*'s secured channel."

Jane thrust her chair back with a screech. "Put it on-screen here in the dining hall."

It came up nearly instantly, which she was grateful for. Ajaya moved to stand next to her. Jane grabbed her hand.

Darcy looked calm, with one corner of her mouth turned up.

Jane felt herself relax a small fraction. Darcy wouldn't be smiling if she had bad news.

"Well, I don't know what you were so worried about. I got there shortly before Kai'Memna, and your folks didn't need my help at all. The threat to your experiment out there, whatever it is, is taken care of. Kai'Memna will not be bothering you anymore. Not only that, you may be adding a few more ships to your fleet. I've just transferred a packet of text addressed to you and Ajaya Varma from your Captain Gibbs. Oh, and by the way..." Darcy's face broke out into a full, toothy grin. "Your boy Einstein says he misses you, and that you'll know what that means. I'll be in touch. You can contact me anytime on this channel. Seems like you have no trouble finding me. Just yell if you need anything, especially if it will help Earth."

Ajaya squeezed her hand. It was over. They were safe. She would love to know a lot more information than Darcy had supplied, but she could send a video message with more questions tomorrow. Now she actually felt like celebrating. She spontaneously hugged Ajaya, and they returned to the table.

More special foods made the rounds. Jane sampled each with gusto. Next was a small, salted fish. It didn't taste terribly different from similar foods on Earth. It was rich and oily, with an earthy flavor. Most of these foods were familiar to the pelimarians, Murrrsi, and probably Imadua, but novel for Jane and Ajaya.

"I'm glad to hear the pligan project and your people are safe," Feig said.

"It sounds like an effective treatment," Ouvaq commented as she broke off a piece of a dehydrated vegetable that looked quite a bit like potato.

Murrrsi took the bowl from Ouvaq. "Deceiving the Swarm to protect a planet is all well and good, but something must be done to decrease their numbers, weaken them, or even send them to another galaxy."

Imadua held a piece of the vegetable just in front of his mantle. His flat appendages moved with a flexible grace, cupping the food as adroitly as a human hand and passing it under his hood where it disappeared from view. "They must be eradicated. They have nothing to offer but death."

The group grew more somber. Jane bit off a small piece of the fragile dehydrated vegetable. It dissolved on her tongue instantly, and surprisingly tasted more like melon than anything else. "Have any of your worlds been affected by the Swarm?"

Feig had a far-off look in her eyes. "No civilization has been untouched by that menace. Colony worlds and farming worlds are the most vulnerable, because the populations are small and these planets are often quite distant. As a result foods like these are quite dear, because few people are willing to take such risks."

Murrrsi laid another sheet of the vegetable on her tongue. "Overpopulation and famine are a constant problem."

Imadua said, "Wex instituted population-control measures centuries ago. We do not experience famine. But the people are dissatisfied that only a few selected by lottery may be allowed to procreate."

Ajaya reached for a bowl of what looked like a very soft, oily nut. "And is there no definitive line of defense?"

Feig looked down. "When the Swarm comes there is always great loss of life, no matter how well fortified a world may attempt to be. It is a sad fact."

Jane noticed that Imadua didn't partake of many of the offerings. After sampling a few things, he made excuses and left quietly. Imadua was a subdued individual, only speaking when he had something vital to offer. He always made an appearance at these social events, but rarely lingered long.

The wexian had worked tirelessly to make the recordings for her broadcast and happened to have a small camera that hovered in the air and moved around smoothly. As part of the wexian diplomatic delegation, it had been his job to record any sessions of the assembly that would affect Wex for news broadcasts on his world. The recordings he had made for her were simple, but done well. Jane had footage that had been created by NASA about Earth's cultures and people for the *Providence* mission. Imadua converted it to a new format appropriate for galactic distribution and weaved it into the final production along with Jane's voiceovers. The result was, Jane hoped, professional and interesting. They'd made six episodes, each about an hour long. If there was interest, they'd make more.

The pelimarians helped her with the scripts for the videos, pointing out potential cultural misunderstandings. She appreciated the experience they brought with them in these matters. The pelimarians and the wexian were fitting in fairly well with the rest of the inhabitants of the ship. There hadn't been any conflicts, though the overt sexuality of the pelimarians did add some tension, at least from Jane's point of view.

Feig leaned forward in her seat in the way that Jane had come to understand meant the woman was about to broach a subject that might be uncomfortable.

Jane started to stiffen, caught herself, and made herself relax.

"We were reviewing your programming, Qua'dux, and found ourselves curious. If we may ask? We shall certainly be fielding many questions about the content."

"Go ahead," Jane said. She tasted a slice of a large, crispy fruit that was like sweet celery. It was salty with a hint of anise flavor, but had the consistency of a juicy apple.

"There are many images of you, Ajaya, and other female humans in the program you will broadcast in which your facial features appear quite different than they do now. Is this a function of age? Or some other factor?"

Jane frowned and glanced at Ajaya.

Ajaya nodded. "I believe the differences you note are due to cosmetics." The word "cosmetics" had no direct translation, so Ajaya used the English word.

Feig looked from Ajaya to Jane and back again.

Ajaya continued. "It's a cultural practice. On Earth some people, mostly women, apply color to their faces to enhance physical beauty."

"It's an affectation?" Feig asked.

Ajaya shrugged. "I suppose it is. It's expected in some circles. Many women reject the practice or are uninterested. It's relatively benign. I suppose it makes women feel better about themselves. Some treat it like an art form."

"And do the different colors signify anything? Estrus, availability, pregnancy? Why do only females practice this?" Feig asked.

"Colors used are personal preference and don't signal anything. As for why it's mostly women who use cosmetics—that is rooted in historic cultural norms. Some males do use these products to express themselves, or to look a certain way for recorded media or theater, though that's a little more rare."

Ouvaq looked enthralled. "But neither of you use these enhancements now—why not?"

Ajaya smiled. "A very simple, practical reason. Weight. Our ship was quite primitive compared to what is standard here. Everything aboard had to fulfill a pragmatic purpose. And we were far too busy to indulge in something quite so fanciful."

Murrrsi sniffed a piece of dried meat before tossing it into her mouth. "It's not unheard of to enhance one's looks artificially. My people pride themselves on maintaining impeccably clean and shiny hair. Some people who can't achieve that naturally use products to make themselves more attractive to others."

Jane nodded. "Humans do that too."

"Do the Sectilius?" Ouvaq asked.

Jane thought about it. "Sectilian women sometimes elaborately plait their hair. It seems to be an intricate and time-consuming endeavor. My impression was that it was intended to make one more beautiful."

Ouvaq smiled and rubbed her hairless head with a rueful look. "That sounds lovely. Can you show us?"

Jane said, "There must be images in the ship's database."

Ouvaq stood up immediately. "I think I'm going to go look right now."

"Do pelimarians use any enhancements?" Ajaya asked.

Feig looked a little surprised. "No. We've no need of them."

Ajaya looked hesitant, then asked, "Not even scents?"

Feig tilted her head to one side. "No scents. We wouldn't want to alter or mask our personal aroma. It's very important to us, to our identity. It signals that we are healthy and fit, among other things."

So that answered that question.

Murrrsi rose. "My eyes don't want to stay open anymore." She yawned and stretched, then padded slowly for the exit.

Ajaya scooted her chair back. "I'm going to go do some reading before I sleep."

Jane smiled at Ajaya. She knew she'd be reading the messages from Ron.

It seemed as though the evening's festivities had come to an end. Jane was about to push back and excuse herself when Feig touched her arm.

"I wanted to ask another question."

Jane raised her brows and steeled herself.

Feig's fingers lingered on her arm in a familiar manner. Jane resisted the urge to pull away. This was just friendly affection, she was sure. Nothing more. A human friend touching her like this wouldn't have bothered her in the slightest. She silently berated herself for the biases about the pelimarians that she had not yet completely let go of. They had done absolutely nothing but good since arriving on the ship. They'd respected her. She had no reason to react that way.

"It's about Ei'Brai. It is a delight to swim with a kuboderan, and a rare opportunity for those who aren't shipbound. We have inquired and found Ei'Brai is interested, but he requested that we ask your permission before indulging."

Feig turned Jane's arm over and lightly traced the blue veins under her skin. Jane was beginning to feel strange about the contact. It felt very intimate. And Feig's scent was particularly noticeable, especially after talking about it. First, she would answer the question, and second, she would extricate herself.

Except she was speechless. On the surface, it seemed an odd request, but hadn't she thought about it herself many times? Was there any reason at all to deny it? And then there was the sensation of Brai, who had maintained only a tenuous connection to the preceding conversation, perking up and opening his channel wider, suddenly very interested in both the question and her response.

She stammered, partly because she didn't know what to say and partly because Feig had moved on to gently kneading her palm, which felt insanely good but also wrong. And that scent. It was heady. It was surprisingly hard to think of anything else. "Oh, I... Well, if Ei'Brai says he'd like to... I see no problem..."

Feig studiously kept her eyes focused on massaging Jane's hand, no expression crossing her face. "Will you join us?"

"I don't know..."

"We have a breathing apparatus that will fit nearly anyone. It may certainly be used by a human. This exercise is most properly attended by the entire crew."

Jane didn't say anything. She just watched Feig sensually manipulating her hand. She couldn't seem to break free of the moment, but she knew she needed to stop it before Feig got the wrong idea.

She had thoughts of asking Brai to inspect Feig's intentions, but did not allow those to bubble into the areas she shared with Brai. That would be wrong.

Feig lifted her eyes to meet Jane's. "You isolate yourselves so much, Jane. Aren't you lonely?"

Her face felt flaming hot. This was exactly the kind of conversation she'd been dreading from the pelimarians. Her fingers clenched and the muscles in her arm tensed. Feig's ministrations ceased, but she didn't remove her hands from Jane's. They rested lightly on her, still soothing despite the subtly implied rejection. "I miss Alan, yes. But I'm not lonely. This kind of separation from a partner is sometimes unavoidable, but bearable."

"We could not be without family. We would waste away."

Jane shook her head. "But my family is here."

"But you don't—"

Jane leapt to cut her off. "We don't. No. Our concept of family, of a support network, of friendship, is different. That's true. We separate our community from our romantic lives, but that doesn't mean it's any less valuable."

Feig looked confused. "Your community seems so tenuously connected. It seems fragile to us. Without the daily reassurance of touch..."

Jane moved her hand to cover Feig's lightly. "Touch is very important to humans. We need it to be healthy, but it doesn't have to be sexual in nature to fulfill that need."

Feig tilted her head toward one shoulder in a manner that looked uncharacteristically helpless for her. "We don't understand. Full skin-to-skin contact is—"

"We don't normally engage in casual contact with people we don't know well. Extensive amounts of touch are generally reserved for relationships with special people, like a parent or child, close family members, devoted friends, people who care deeply for each other."

"What kind of touch?"

"Like this." Jane nodded at their clasped hands. "Sitting close together. And hugging—that's probably the most important in my culture."

Feig looked down at their hands, clearly not grasping what a hug was. Then she looked up, that unmistakable questioning expression on her face.

Jane stood. "I'll show you."

Feig rose to her feet as Jane stepped close and wrapped her arms around her, squeezing gently. "Like this?" Feig mimicked what Jane was doing.

It felt nice. Feig's scent was even richer and more potent at this proximity. The moment stretched out longer than it probably should have.

Jane wondered suddenly if this was something Brai also needed. Was he missing Pio just as much as she was missing Alan? Perhaps the swim would relax them all.

Jane pulled away slowly. "Yes, I'll swim with you and Ei'Brai."

Feig continued to cradle Jane's arm and hovered over her, forcing eye contact. Her voice was soft and pleading. "Will you also consider joining us in our rooms? We could show you the joys of pelimarian friendship as you have shown me your lovely hug."

Jane resisted the urge to break Feig's gaze. The moment of forced refusal had come and she would be clear and honest. "No, Feig. I'm very sorry. I'm in a monogamous relationship and I will not betray his trust. Please don't ask me that again."

Feig managed to smile and look mildly chagrinned at the same time. "We were hoping we could tempt you. I couldn't let this moment pass. Please remember that this is our nature. We long to learn about human intimacy, but it is not to be with you. We will try to understand your reasons and will respect your decision. We hope this doesn't create any negative feelings for you."

"Thank you." It was all she could say.

Feig released Jane and turned and walked away.

41

BRAI TRIED NOT to let his excitement bleed into his connections with anyone, though Jane sensed it, of course. She was on her way for a session of what she designated as 'one on one' time with him. He treasured these moments with her.

She would stand on the other side of the transparent enclosure and they would discuss a variety of topics, from mundane to urgent. When these conversations went on for lengthy durations, she would eventually seat herself on the platform. Often she wore warm clothing or brought blankets with her because his environment was so different from what was optimal for her.

The crew swim would be held soon, immediately after the daily work was complete. In fact, nearly everyone had begun preparations for the event. It enlivened his senses to note that every crew member was not only interested in participating, but that they were experiencing the same sort of rousing excitement.

Life had already returned to its standard rhythm. He was once again lodged in his enclosure. Nothing had significantly changed within its boundaries, and though he worked hard to keep himself distracted, once again the only sensory input he experienced came from outside, from others.

He could almost believe that Pliga and Pio were just a dream, or a memory experienced by another crew member, not one of his own.

And yet he ached for the lost freedom and for her. He wondered if their lives would ever twine that same way again.

And yet if they did, that might mean not having Jane in his life.

Maybe it had been wrong to deny Pio the chance to produce his offspring. When his life ended, Jane, with her short lifespan, would be long gone. Who would be left to remember him? To know that he'd existed? Who would tell stories of his life the way Jane read stories of the lives of other humans on her portable reading device? Would there be stories of Jane and Brai? Or would there be stories of Jane and Alan or perhaps of Jane and Ron?

Perhaps he should devote some effort to writing his own stories.

Jane arrived, her mouth set in a closed-lip smile. She was very apprehensive about the group swim, but she noted his eagerness and found it amusing. He sought to ease her anxiety.

Brai jetted in a loop, arriving opposite her to bob in place. Her mouth opened to let out a delighted laugh, the smile broadening afterward. He liked eliciting these responses from her.

"You're smiling too," she said. "In your own way."

"Indeed. A chimerical smile."

Her brow knit together slightly. "Do you know what to expect? The pelimarians are being very mysterious."

"Not in the slightest."

She found that answer less than adequate.

He regarded her tense expression. "Kuboderans occupying pelimarian ships were shunned, Jane. They were other, too different for sectilian kuboderans to tolerate. Any contact was brief and related only to docking procedures or general navigation."

Jane frowned.

"Retrospectively examining my own brief encounters with pelimarian kuboderan individuals leads me to venture that they are perhaps more expressive and, though I cannot be certain, happier."

Her eyes widened. She quickly drew the same conclusion he had. "You think they don't use anything like the yoke to force control?"

"Perhaps not. It's certainly possible."

"Have you asked Feig or the others about it?"

"Not yet."

She tilted her head to one side. Humans were very expressive with body language despite being confined by the rigid structure of bones. "You never hesitate to ask me questions. Why are you being so shy?"

He gazed at her solemnly. "It seemed disloyal."

"What? Why?"

"You are still wary of them."

The small crease between her lightly furred brows deepened. "That's about me. I know that you and Murrrsi and probably everyone else have had a good laugh at my expense regarding my reaction to the arrival of the pelimarians. But what no one seems to understand is that infidelity is not a threat. That's not what has bothered me. They're helpful. I'm glad they're here, but they're also a distraction. I worry about unintentional misunderstandings. If I make a mistake in my interactions with them, I could very well prevent Pelimar from assisting Earth should that need arise. And that's the last thing I want." She sagged a little. "But that's my problem. And I think with time it will resolve and I can be at ease. You can cultivate any kind of relationship with any or all of them that you want."

He felt contrite and resisted the urge to move into a servile position. "As you wish."

She placed her hand on the glass. "Brai, bring me these issues when they come up."

"It is not an issue."

Her eyes rolled around in their sockets. They were remarkably mobile.

He changed the subject purposefully. "This clothing is special for the swim?"

She looked different. The garment was like a second skin and the colors were vibrant splashes—very different from her normal attire.

Jane glanced down, making a wry face. "I borrowed this from Ouvaq. I wouldn't have chosen these colors for myself. It's made to conserve heat. Humans can easily get hypothermia in cold water. I haven't put on the hood to cover my head yet."

"You were very busy today. It seems as though your presentations have been well received."

"Too well. The number of messages is overwhelming. I can probably do about ten to twelve more shows just answering questions about Earth."

He pointed out the positive, in an attempt to redirect her thoughts. "The interest bodes well. You are suited to teach."

"I should be. That was my profession. But it all seems so... fruitless. I'm just entertaining them. I feel like I'm not making any headway. I'm no closer to protecting Earth from the Swarm. I just don't know what else to do."

"You are doing what you must. You are doing what you can."

She sighed. "Is everyone ready for the swim?"

He sent out tendrils of thought and the queries were quickly answered. "They have begun to gather in the medical chamber, with the intention of entering through the newly fashioned access portal there."

He felt her anxiety triple. "I'd better get going then. I believe we'll be learning a lot more about the pelimarians today, as well as their kuboderans."

"Indeed."

He waited until she was out of sight, then surged toward the medical-access chamber giddily.

42

A MANTRA RAN through Jane's head as she walked toward Brai's medical suite. "This will be different."

Jane had been a strong swimmer since early elementary school, but had managed to avoid recreational swimming since preadolescence. It brought up too many memories. It simply hadn't been worth the painful ache in her chest. The same ache that was close to paralyzing her right now.

However, in this case she wouldn't stay away for several reasons. Curiosity, primarily. But the prospect of the group swim was also breathing new life into Brai, who had clearly been bored and somewhat dispirited of late. She hadn't seen him this excited in weeks and didn't want to disappoint him. Even now, Brai waited just outside the diagnostic bubble that they'd be using as an airlock, his limbs curling and whipping around in uncontained exuberance. The rest of the crew had decided to participate. She was their leader. Not going just didn't seem to be an option, so she'd tough out the bad feelings.

The headgear Celui handed her was nothing like anything she'd ever seen before. In fact, the first thing she asked him was where the rest of her gear was. He smiled, demonstrated how to put it on, and reassuringly described how it worked.

It was startlingly simple and small. A full face mask, seemingly composed of plastic, it remodeled itself to fit the user when placed on the face, creating a flexible seal which even allowed her to talk into a tiny mic. It detected not only facial structure but also where gas exchange was occurring and adjusted to accommodate. The straps that went around the head could be configured to suit different species, and a pair of tubes led to a book-sized device that attached to her clothing on front or back, specifically tailored to recycle the user's exhalations, cleaving CO_2 to produce more oxygen when needed and storing the excess carbon for disposal.

Jane pulled down her ponytail and quickly braided her hair so she could slip the wet suit's hood over her head. Celui helped her attach it to the neck of the wet suit. When she put the mask against her face, Celui and Ouvaq helped her mold it around her ears so she'd be able to hear the rest of the group speak. Then both of them turned to assist Murrrsi, whose mask fitting was a little more complex due to all her hair. They parted her fur just behind her ears and helped her hold it in place as the mask was coaxed to settle into these furrows. It elongated to cover her projecting muzzle and nestled against her upper throat in another part in her fur. Murrrsi acted as though she'd done all of this before and seemed unconcerned about the seal.

Jane had been dreading putting on any kind of face mask, but this was so light and transparent she barely knew she had it on. Her view didn't fog up at all, so it handled moisture as well. It felt nothing like the SCUBA gear she remembered wearing as a youth in Australia with her parents. That went a long way to relieving some of her anxiety.

Imadua had his own gear, which was even more compact. If she hadn't happened to be looking she would have missed him manipulating a small, dark object and then inserting it some-where under his mantle.

Jane glanced around. Everyone seemed to be done fiddling with their masks.

Feig stood in the middle of the room and spoke up. "If there's a problem with anyone's gear, don't panic. Just return to the airlock. It cycles quickly. Ouvaq will join you to help you. We'll stay close at first since some of us are inexperienced."

Jane nodded. She had no problem with Feig being in charge. She was doing a fine job so far.

Jane focused on breathing evenly and staying calm. There was a faint sour smell in the mask from her breath, but she breathed easily enough. So far so good.

Feig gestured at Brai. "And now, let us clear our minds and join with Brai as we enter the airlock in pairs. Ouvaq and Imadua will go first." She tapped the console, and the portal, newly constructed by the pligans to be nearly identical to the one on Brai's side, glided open silently. Imadua gracefully stepped over the threshold toward the center of the chamber. Ouvaq joined him silently. They turned toward Brai together as Ouvaq reached out to trigger the water to fill the chamber.

Jane's heart beat a little faster.

The globe quickly filled.

Jane swallowed hard as it went over Ouvaq's head.

Imadua looked like he belonged there. His limbs ceased to remain vertical. He pulled them up and they mostly disappeared under his mantle. He floated in place, looking very much like a pink jellyfish. Then the portal on the other side opened and they both glided out to hover near Brai. The chamber emptied and Feig triggered the portal again, motioning to Ajaya and Murrrsi. Another cycle, then Pledor and Feig herself went.

Everyone seemed just fine out there, floating in place. There was no localized artificial gravity in Brai's enclosure to pull them

341

in any direction. Nothing to drag them down. But no *up* to escape to either. Her fingers tingled.

Finally, it was time for Celui and Jane.

Celui looked at her searchingly. "Your skin has lightened in tone. Are you cold?"

She laughed nervously. "Oh, no." She was actually sweating a little in the wet suit Ouvaq had loaned her. She gritted her teeth and stepped inside.

He cocked his head to one side as he reached for the controls. "Ready?" he asked gently.

She didn't reply for a moment. She'd been underwater many times in her mech suit. That hadn't seemed as nerve-wracking. She felt safe inside the suit. It was made to protect soldiers at war and seemed nearly indestructible. Now she felt like she was nearly naked, soft and squishy, exposed.

"Jane?" Brai's voice rumbled in her head. He drifted closer to the examination chamber, his limbs slowing their curling motion. "Ah. Jane, you should bring me these issues when they arise."

She huffed. "Very funny," she replied to him alone. He was attempting to lighten her mood. He knew why she was so afraid. She had once shared the memory of her father's death with him.

He pushed a soothing blanket of thought toward her through their narrow private channel. She grabbed ahold of it and let it in fully. It helped. A lot.

She licked her lips. "Ready," she said firmly.

Brai stayed close, eyes locked with hers, as the water rose. The bubble filled quietly. When the water reached her chin she couldn't help but raise herself up on her tiptoes and lift her head, gasping for air.

Celui grabbed her hand. "It's okay," he said.

She breathed rapidly and closed her eyes. Her ears popped from the pressure change as the portal opened. She couldn't move. Not yet.

"Shall we go back?" Celui asked.

She opened her eyes again. Her vision filled with Brai. She focused on him, on shedding the panic. Finally she would get the chance to actually swim with him. She was not going to let this stupid fear keep her from doing that. "No, I'm okay." She let go of Celui's hand and paddled forward awkwardly toward Brai. He reached out an arm, hooks pointing away, and held her steady. It was exactly the right thing.

She took a moment to acclimate. She could feel the pressure of the water all over her body, but that was soothing rather than frightening. The water was completely calm. She had no trouble breathing and concentrated on doing just that, slow and steady. She was okay.

She looked around. It was dizzying how large his enclosure was. Seeing the ellipsoidal shape from this side of the glass was very different. In some ways it was like a massive clear-glass skyscraper with fire escapes wrapping around the outside.

"Welcome to my home," Brai chuckled.

"Shall we begin?" Feig's voice said over the small communicator in the face mask. "First we must all open our thoughts to Ei'Brai, as well as each other through him, so that we may coordinate our activity."

Jane cleared her mind of her trepidation as well as she could and connected to the rest of the group. Their overall sentiment was eagerness and curiosity.

Feig's mental voice was soothing. "I will lead us by projecting our movement. It will begin simply, and as we become comfortable I will increase the complexity. Do not focus on perfection, just relax and enjoy moving and sharing. No assumptions will be made. No judgments about ability. We are here to commune with as few words as possible, just using our bodies and our emotions."

Feig conveyed a rudimentary image of their bodies equally spaced around Brai. The swimmers moved into position without much difficulty. The mental image gradually morphed to show them all from Feig's perspective. And then one by one each swimmer's viewpoint, including Brai's, was incorporated into the whole, creating a new kind of point of view that anchored each individual. Simultaneously many of their minds experienced surprise and wonder at this new way of seeing.

Through Feig's mind's eye they began to move, circling Brai. Hesitantly, they sought to mimic her projection. Their first movements were uncoordinated, and a few were confused about which direction to turn. But soon Feig's expectations and reality were not so very different. Jane pushed herself through the water with relative ease.

Now Brai was incorporated into the movement. He pulsed toward one end of the enclosure with the ring of swimmers spiraling around him. Then he began to spin, steadily, in a circle.

Jane saw him, seeing them through each other's eyes. His brain took in the data from all of them and integrated it into something utterly new.

They reached one end of the tank, twirling, whirling together. A kaleidoscope of sight and motion. As Brai spun, he offered each member a different arm or tentacle. Every swimmer reached out in turn with whatever appendage they had to touch him. Jane marveled at how perfectly they were spaced. No one had to swim forward or even stretch. It was just right. She could feel each caress from giver to receiver.

And now a rush. Together they dove as fast as the slowest among them could go toward the other end of the ellipsoidal shape, always sensing each other's movements, spacing, and limitations. Jane didn't even have to think about which way to go. It seemed to just flow naturally through this method of communication.

She forgot her fear completely and concentrated on the whole.

Gradually they converged into a cone, bodies close, undulating like natural sea creatures. They slowed and drifted to a stop with Brai at their center. Hands and other appendages reached out with featherlight brushes against his mantle as he spun.

Inside and outside of each other's minds they bloomed with pleasure. Their senses were multiplied, stacked. Taken altogether it was exhilarating.

Then they turned away from Brai, spreading out like a slowly exploding firework until some point, predetermined in Feig's mind, was reached. They curled into a ball and hugged themselves, then burst, expanding their limbs fully. She, they, felt like something larger unfurling.

Brai darted up, and one by one they followed him. A spurt of motion and then drifting, hanging suspended in the water. They chased him until they reconvened into a new shape, this time a rotating sphere with Brai tumbling at their center, passing each other narrowly, each in their own orbits.

Someone began to tire. Jane could no longer pinpoint who in the elated fog of reaction and response. Feig signaled it was time to draw the exercise to a close. Like children called in from play too soon, they protested in wordless echoes.

Feig chided them gently, directed them to say their goodbyes, and one by one they left through the airlock, also leaving Brai's collective channel.

Jane stayed behind. She faced Brai and took off the warm gloves of the diving suit. The water was cold, but she didn't mind. She was warmed through from the exercise.

"May I?" she asked.

"I should be offended if you did not," he replied.

She placed her hand on one of his thick arms. He moved it to wrap around her and she nestled against him, beside one of his enormous eyes.

43

ALAN LIKED HUNA. He did. But the dude had been raised on a world where no one understood the concept of time. So when asked how much longer something would take, his standard answer was, "It's not ripe yet."

Irritating, but it was what it was. Alan just kept working on his blink drives and so on. He tried to keep as busy as possible while he waited.

However, once Huna's first test pods ripened and were harvested, they all had a much better understanding of the time involved. Huna tested these pods extensively and decided that his idea would work. He wanted to grow three more experimental sets to work on further optimization, but when he and Ron sat down and calculated the time required to complete all of the experiments as well as the final crop, they realized that it would take way longer than the two standard years that Jane was stuck in the Terac system, under quarantine. They compromised on two large experimental sets followed by a single worldwide crop of *particulos oscuros*.

JENNIFER FOEHNER WELLS

When they harvested the first of the large experimental sets,
it was time to work out the details of containment and delivery.
The particles were grown inside a football-sized organic husk. If
that husk got too dry, the end opposite of the stem started to curl
back and open, prematurely exposing the contents, which were a
fine, light, shimmery powder very easy to scatter. So Alan
converted cargo bays into enormous humidors to maintain the
pods optimally. It was a good project. Lots of challenges but not
impossible. Just like he liked it.

The next issue to tackle was delivery. On New Pliga, the
Tree held billions of these pods evenly distributed in a sort of
suspended animation just at the brink of full viability. When
they detected a Swarm pod on the approach, a dehiscence
protocol was activated. All over the planet, the particles were
released in the turbulent winds, spilling them into the
atmosphere to do the work of hiding the planet.

He, Huna, Jaross, and Ron sat down and brainstormed ideas
for release into Earth's atmosphere. They came up with a drone
system that would perform the final drying of the pods and
release the particles in the upper atmosphere simultaneously. Pio
and Brai would be able to orchestrate their movements easily.
After the design work, they made a few prototypes and tested
them. When they had the system optimized, they went into full
production. Their first order of business was manufacturing more
3-D printers and setting up factory staging. Then it took all hands
to keep production going around the clock so they could manufacture enough units by the time the final pods reached maturity.
When they ran out of raw materials, another step was added:
breaking down components of nonessential materials. In a ship
that big, there was plenty of that, but it was time consuming.

To say they were busy was an understatement. Once they
were going full bore, the time slipped by quickly. And now things

348

were coming to a close. The final crop was on the vine. Preparations to harvest and store the pods were nearly complete. The delivery system was in manufacture. They'd have a massive payload ready to put in Earth's atmosphere in just a few weeks.

He'd be going home to Jane soon.

44

ZARA GAVE THE NASA ADMINISTRATOR, Dr. Kenneth Lin, a personal tour of Jane's not-so-secret file two days later in Dr. Sakey's office. She'd caught up on sleep the night before, but she still felt clumsy and stupid with nerves, though she did everything she could to not let that show.

He never brought up the controversy, but the offices and labs were buzzing with it. She was sure Lin suspected she was the source of the opposition to his takedown. He had to. Who else could have been responsible? It was very unlikely anyone would notice that file disappearing when no one else had noticed it to begin with. Her roommate Dominica had instructed her to suggest someone had probably set up a macro to monitor any tampering with the sectilian files online. That would give her plausible deniability. It was never necessary. She wasn't about to bring it up if he didn't.

Lin leaned back and exhaled heavily. "I'll be briefing the president on this information in person tomorrow."

Zara nodded and kept her expression blank. She was sure that was unnecessary. Though the situation had gotten very little coverage, there had been enough that the government had to be aware of it.

"Dr. Hampton, I'm aware that you were the very first MSTEM Scholar. I wanted to thank you for your service and personally hand you your next assignment. Many of your peers will be receiving these today—right now, in fact." He handed over a pale blue envelope.

She took it from him, perplexed. "My next assignment?"

Lin's expression was grim. "Earth has built twelve starships. The time has come to see them fully manned and operational."

"Manned?" She tore open the envelope so fast she ripped off a corner of the letter inside.

She'd been commissioned to serve aboard the *Aegis*, the fleet's flagship, as a second lieutenant.

She glanced up at Lin, not making any attempt to conceal her shock. Then she looked back down. The paper went on to say in some kind of legal language that any rank given was a rank within the Earth United Fleet and contained a brief description of her rank's seniority and responsibilities. The Earth United Fleet's newly devised ranking system used ranks drawn from all of the most easily recognizable ranks in the proud tradition of Earth's many military services.

She flipped the paper over, but it didn't say anything else—not the position she'd occupy or the department in which she'd serve. She had to report for duty early the next morning.

This was exactly what she'd always wanted. But it was sudden. She had to abandon her work, her home, her family and friends. There was no time to prepare. No time for proper goodbyes.

There were more shocks to come when she got home. Every one of her roommates had been conscripted as well. Ben would be with her on the *Aegis* and the rest of her roommates would be scattered across different ships.

Zara cleared off a spot on the living-room sofa and sat down to check a few more things off her list, the butterflies in her stomach growing stronger by the minute. The house had been ransacked as all six of them scrambled to find everything they'd need to take to their postings and to tie up loose ends. There was stuff scattered everywhere—clothes, luggage, toiletries. The ancient washing machine chugged in the background, baskets full of washed and unwashed clothes clogging the floor in the adjacent kitchen area.

Charlotte flopped down beside her, ignoring stacks of white T-shirts, underwear, and socks someone had left there, and heaved a heavy sigh. "There's so much to do. They aren't giving us any time. I wonder why? What's the big rush? And what the hell are we going to do about the house and all our stuff in it?"

A loud *thump* came from upstairs and they both reflexively looked up at the ceiling.

Zara frowned. "I hadn't thought that far ahead yet. I was about to call my parents and tell them the news. I guess it's silly to pay rent on an empty house, especially since we haven't been told how long we'll be gone. But we don't have time to move out."

Charlotte said, "I'll set out some boxes for all of us to put things in that we really want to keep. Maybe someone can put them in storage for us. That'd be a lot cheaper than rent. The rest of these treasures can be donated." She waved her hands around to indicate the shabby, mismatched furniture and piles of computer components and gaming systems.

Zara's phone rang. It was her dad. He'd probably heard about the assignments and wanted to know if she'd managed to get one.

She held up the phone with a smile. "I'll ask my dad if he'll handle it."

Charlotte hopped up and jogged upstairs, several pairs of socks and a pile of underwear tumbling off the sofa in her wake. "I'm going to ask Danny if he knows what he's going to do with Buster."

Zara blew out a heavy breath. She hadn't even thought of the cat. She slid her finger across the screen, mentally shoring herself up for what was going to be an emotional conversation. Her dad knew this was her dream, but he would be worried about what it meant. "Hey, Dad."

Zara was flown to the base of the space elevator on a tiny island in the Pacific, where she was vaccinated, then handed a rucksack containing three dove-gray uniforms and told she'd have ten minutes to change. She wouldn't be allowed to take anything with her that didn't fit inside that bag. Most of the careful packing she'd done the night before had been a waste of time. She barely had room for undergarments, a few toiletries, a laptop, and her e-reader. She packed the sack until the seams were tight and she had to struggle to get it closed.

Then they were crammed inside a windowless capsule and strapped in, standing shoulder to shoulder, for the long trip up the elevator. In the chaos she'd been separated from all of her roommates. To pass the time, the new recruits introduced themselves to each other.

It was necessary to use Mensententia. The crews of all of the ships were international, the total number from each nation proportional to the population of their country of origin and distributed evenly over all twelve ships, officers and enlisted alike. Seeing faces of every color and ethnicity imaginable, nearly all sporting purple hair, buoyed her spirits. NASA had been a multicultural place, but this was something altogether different.

The nervous energy and excitement were contagious. They'd all known this day might come. The general consensus seemed to be happiness that they had been chosen and trepidation over what they might have to face in the coming years.

The mood was buoyant until someone wondered aloud if a threat had already been detected. Then everyone went silent for the remainder of the trip to ISS-2, tethered at the other end of the elevator.

She would have liked to explore the ship a bit, take it all in, but there was no time for sightseeing. They were handed papers, then told to dump their rucksacks in their quarters and report for duty. The main thing she noticed was a ubiquitous presence of the recently commissioned Earth United crest. Most people called it the green pretzel. It was three interlocking triangles made of one continuous forest-green line, superimposed over a simplified cloud-covered Earth.

Zara followed the crowd to a bank of deck-to-deck transports, scanning the blue slip of paper she'd been handed. Her quarters were on deck thirty-seven. She was to report to deck six, conference room three, on the Command Deck. Her heart did a back-flip. She searched the slip for more detail, but they were still keeping her in the dark. She'd find out what she was here to do soon.

She'd worked on the blueprints of sectilian ships for years. Walking through one that had come to physical fruition was more than a little strange. She couldn't help but try to spot all the changes that had been made from the original design. The corridors were definitely narrower and not as tall. She wondered how many more decks they'd been able to squeeze in by doing that.

The decor was Spartan. Like the Sectilius, they'd used a composite for most visible surfaces. She didn't know what colors were used on a sectilian ship aside from the odd green color she'd seen in the background of Jane's videos, but here it was matte white everywhere she looked. Even the lighting felt stark and industrial. Only the impatient hordes of new recruits provided contrast, with their pale gray uniforms, purple hair, and varied skin tones.

This column of deck-to-deck transports ran through the entire ship. It could easily handle the comings and goings of personnel under normal workday circumstances, but this influx all at once had bottlenecked flow. The person next to her turned and was close enough that their backpack grazed Zara, shoving her sideways into someone else and nearly knocking her off her feet. She apologized to the person she'd nearly toppled into and looked up, expecting to get an apology from the person who'd pushed her, but they'd already disappeared into the crowd. She got into the transport, mindful of the space she and her pack were taking up, then sighed. Not everyone was as thoughtful as she was. And cultural norms would come into play in interactions all over the ship. That was surely going to lead to misunderstandings if people didn't keep cool.

Her quarters were as small as she'd expected. There was room for two twin beds and not much else. Every eight rooms opened into a central communal bathroom. The *Aegis* was immense, and every sectilian on a similar ship would have had small private quarters, but the humans had repurposed most of the crew decks as hangar bays to hold armored sectilian shuttles, redesigned to serve as fighters. She couldn't complain. She was lucky enough to be an officer, though the lowest rank possible. She'd overheard someone say the enlisted had to share rooms with ten bunks and had no privacy at all.

She slipped off the backpack and set it on one of the beds

next to a stack of bedding and towels. She'd unpack later. She took only the blue slip with her and headed toward the nearest deck transport.

When she got to deck six she noticed right away that she was the youngest, lowest-ranked person in sight. As she passed the door to the bridge she had a strong feeling that there'd been a mistake. She'd expected to be assigned to engineering, repairing and maintaining things. That was what she'd trained for.

She stood outside conference room three for several minutes, rereading the blue slip and looking around to verify that she was in the right place. When it seemed to be indisputable, she tapped the symbol for *open* on the wall next to the door. The door slid up, revealing an austere room with one long table surrounded by eight chairs. Occupying one of the chairs was an older gray-haired man.

She blinked.

That was Thomas Compton. He was one of the *Providence* Six. He'd been the pilot on that mission. He knew Jane Holloway. Oh, goodness. This had to be the wrong room.

She was appalled that she'd disturbed him.

He looked up from a laptop, his lips immediately turning up in a warm, welcome smile.

Zara opened her mouth and ducked her head. "I'm so sorry. I must have the wrong room, sir. Please excuse me."

"Dr. Zara Hampton?"

She almost didn't hear him in her haste to back out of the doorway, close the door again, and get away. But when what he'd said sank in, she looked up to be sure she'd heard correctly.

He was nodding. "For the record, I don't like how they're handling assignments. If you're Hampton, you're in the right place. Come in."

She moved forward hesitantly, still not sure how to behave. That was Tom Compton in front of her. *The* Tom Compton.

He stood and extended a hand. She took it, awestruck. He was seventy-nine years old and still didn't look any older than he had when he'd left on the mission that discovered the *Speroancora*. He wore the bars of a colonel on his shoulder. "Tom Compton," he said. "I'm the XO of the *Aegis*. To be fair, you almost ended up in engineering."

She barely remembered to grip his hand firmly like her dad had taught her. "I did?"

"Have a seat. I'm not going to beat around the bush. You deserve to know where you stand. The powers that be are of two minds with regards to you. I think you know why. Domestically, there were many who advocated to keep you grounded. Internationally, you have many powerful friends, especially among your peers who have already moved up in rank. Your proponents prevailed, and so here you are. The compromise was to keep you on a ship with American leadership."

She swallowed hard and nearly choked. She'd been the subject of international debate? She sat down across from him, feeling very ill at ease. She was amped with nerves and the butterflies felt like they might erupt up and out of her at any moment. "What *is* my position, sir?"

"You're going to be busy. You'll serve primarily as an interpreter for senior officers who aren't fluent in Mensententia. In addition, you'll consult on any matters that relate to the sectilian download. We may need information quickly. We want someone experienced with it. No one is more experienced than you are."

"But I *am* an engineer—"

He held up a hand, a rueful expression on his face. "I'm aware. But you're more valuable to the fleet in this capacity. The truth is, Zara, you don't fit well into military structure. I've decided that means you should be perfect for command. Please don't make a fool out of me."

She clamped her mouth shut. Arguing with one's senior

officer was not a good idea. That had been driven into her in the M version of basic training. Twice. Her role was already decided. She had no recourse. She'd accept it and do her best.

He shuffled some papers around. "I've read your file carefully. You've been practicing your leadership skills at NASA since you were thirteen years old. It's time you were rewarded for it. I'm officially promoting you to first lieutenant. You'll lead a team of twelve other interpreters, scheduling shifts, handling conflicts and disciplinary actions. You'll report directly to me daily for briefings. In time, you may be given more responsibility, but that's a good place to start. My secretary will get you settled. Then we'll need you to get to work translating some speeches."

She nodded. It didn't sound all that different from what she was used to doing at NASA.

He gave her a very direct look. "These speeches are for your eyes only."

She cringed internally and hoped it didn't show outwardly. "Yes, sir. Thank you, sir."

"And Hampton? It's time to get rid of the purple hair. You're an officer now. You have to look like one."

Her fingers started to lift to touch her head. She made a fist and slammed them back to her side. She'd worn the MSTEM purple for years, even after being told the secret code for turning it off. Most MSTEMs had done the same. Her father had been right. It was a symbol of unity that instantly made a peer visible no matter where they were in the world. That had come in handy more than once. She was reluctant to turn off the nanites, but she'd do what she was told.

"Yes, sir."

"Dismissed."

45

July 29, 2020
One month from the end of the quarantine period

CELUI TURNED IN HIS SEAT, his dark gray, glabrous features drawn into a frown. "Qua'dux, I've just received a message from the miremon delegate of the Teracian Decatribunal requesting that you pick up a specific call."

Jane, who had been answering messages and taking call requests all day, mirrored his look. They'd fallen into a working routine in the early months that had long since become habit, and it was near the end of her shift. She'd just been about to get up and attend to some of her other duties.

Jane worked with the pelimarians every day, managing communication with the greater galaxy. They helped her understand societal norms and expectations as she navigated an ever-growing network of people who were interested in learning more about Earth and how it might fit into intergalactic commerce and defense. Jane had to dance delicately around a lot of subjects to indicate interest without committing to anything. She was most

361

definitely not an official emissary, but these talks would pave the way for the future.

The days were long and filled with work, which had kept her distracted. The time since Alan had left had flown by in some ways and crawled by in others, but thankfully their time in quarantine was coming to a close and *Oblignatus* was due back soon.

The miremon had made an unusual demand. She looked down at the screen in front of her. There were dozens of call requests listed. She could never answer them all. "Which one?"

He leaned over her and scanned the list, then pointed. "Uobuc of Miremon. They ask that you have patience with her and just answer her questions."

Jane raised her eyebrows. "What's this about?"

Celui had already gone back to scanning through correspondence. "It doesn't say."

Jane scowled and stabbed the name Uobuc on her screen. The screen went dark, with patches of gray going in and out of focus. She waited. People often wandered away from their call requests, especially if they left them up for a long time. She knew that on the other side there was some kind of alert going off. It was a very frustrating system.

A light came on and a miremon slid into view, fumbling around for a few moments. Miremon were covered in tiny projections that moved. Not tentacles, exactly. They were like stubby, rounded hairs about the size of a human finger. They might qualify as cilia or something. Jane wasn't sure. Uobuc was a soft, peachy pink color. "Yes? Is this Jane Holloway of Terra?"

Before Jane could answer, Uobuc squinted into her monitor. "Yes, of course you are."

Jane couldn't see much of the room Uobuc occupied. Heavy mists floated in and out of view.

"I was asked to take this call by a member of the Teracian Decatribunal," Jane said. "How can—"

"And about time. I've been issuing call requests for ages," Uobuc muttered.

Jane blinked. "How can I help you?"

"This is an official query into the nature of terran society."

Jane glanced sideways at Celui. "I've been producing programming to illustrate that for nearly two standard years. Perhaps I can direct you—"

"Seen it. We need more information."

Jane strove hard to keep her voice neutral. "If I may ask, who has requested this information?"

"The Solar Confederacy of Miremon has requested it. It won't take long. It's a standardized scientific assessment. I'll be recording your answers and will score the questionnaire subsequent to this call. You may receive a copy if you put in a request. I'd prefer to simply begin, rather than chat, if you don't mind."

"Perhaps it would be easier if you sent the questionnaire in a message?"

"That would not be easier."

Jane looked up. Feig, Ouvaq, Ajaya, and Celui all were watching curiously.

Uobuc raised an ultrathin tablet, scrolling and tapping. "I'll issue the same assessment to the rest of your terran crew when we've finished."

Jane inhaled slowly, exhaled just as slowly. "I've only one other human crew member aboard at the moment."

"Ajaya Varma. Yes. I see that here. And there are two more on a mission. I'll have to speak to them when they return. Question one: Have you ever committed murder?"

"No!" Jane replied sharply, aghast that this was the line of questioning.

"You've never killed anything, ever?"

She nearly choked on her surprise. She didn't know how to

reply to this and felt the urge to just hang up. "I would define murder as killing a sentient person in a premeditated fashion."

"So you've never murdered a sentient being, but you have killed?"

Jane blanched. "I... yes. In self-defense when being attacked."

Uobuc continued dryly, as though counting cans on a shelf. "How many?"

Jane made eye contact with Ajaya. Ajaya had a look of utter distress on her face. The pelimarians seemed equally dismayed, though Jane couldn't be sure if it was from the questions or her answers.

She shook her head. "Is this really necessary?"

Uobuc leaned back, looking bored. "Was it one? Five? Ten? Multiples of ten? Hundreds? Thousands?"

Jane gritted out, "Multiples of ten. These were dire situations."

"Would you kill again?"

"Only if absolutely necessary."

"Did you enjoy any aspect of it?"

"I did not."

Uobuc tapped her tablet. "All right. Did you suffer any remorse about these deaths?"

Jane's mouth had gone dry. "Yes, of course."

"In your own words, what is the primary reason for this remorse?"

"Well, I... I wish that circumstances had been different so that it hadn't been necessary to do those things in order to survive and to protect other people. I wish that I could have found another way. I wish I'd had more information, better tools, or other options. It's an act of desperation. Of last resort."

More tapping on the tablet. "What do you consider your primary emotion?"

Jane didn't reply for a moment.

Uobuc was unfazed. "Would you say you are angry, depressed, apathetic, confused, afraid, helpless, sad...?" She sounded like a telephone pollster.

Jane waited for more suggestions, but they weren't forthcoming. "Those are all negative emotions."

Uobuc looked over the top of the tablet at the camera. "You believe your primary emotion is positive?"

"Yes."

There was a pause as Uobuc seemed to be scrolling. "Would you say you are peaceful, relaxed, interested, happy, loving, strong, positive...?"

"I am peaceful."

Uobuc shifted in her seat and continued blandly. "Is it acceptable to strike a romantic partner?"

"Absolutely not."

"How about subordinates in your work? Is it acceptable to strike them?"

"No."

"If someone strikes you, is that justification to strike them back?"

Jane frowned. "No."

"What is your typical response when someone strikes you?"

"People don't—"

Celui interrupted. "Qua'dux, I'm very sorry, but you have an urgent message you will want to see immediately."

Jane could have kissed him.

"I'm sorry, Uobuc, but I'll need to continue this another time. My apologies."

Uobuc put down her tablet and stared dully into the camera. "Just put me on hold. I'll be here when you're finished."

"I'll see what I can do," Jane replied, and punched the key to put the call on hold so that the camera and sound were off. She shook her head and turned to Celui. "Goodness. Thank you."

Celui gestured at his screen and a message popped up on Jane's console.

"Oh, I really do have a message?"

He looked confused. "Yes."

Jane chuckled. "I thought you were rescuing me."

He still looked bemused. Jane ignored that and glanced at the screen. Then she sat up straight. "It's from Ron."

Ajaya perked up. "May I?"

"Of course."

Ajaya crossed the bridge to come read over her shoulder.

Jane scanned the message. "It's brief. This is dated two days ago. They're on their way back. It took so long for this message to get here... I think they could be back any moment now."

Ajaya squeezed her shoulder.

Jane widened her connection with Brai. "Please do some long-range scans and let us know when they jump into the system."

"Already begun, Jane," Brai replied.

"Urgent incoming call request from Yliriu of Sebapen," Celui said.

"What?" Jane said. "Surely this isn't about the miremon questionnaire?"

His head dropped to one side. "Perhaps? It seems unlikely. But maybe."

Jane let out a sigh and tapped the screen. "Greetings, Delegate. If this is about the miremon questionnaire, I assure you I was just about to return to the call with Uobuc and finish it."

Yliriu's bushy brow furrowed. "What miremon questionnaire?"

Jane faltered. "That's not why you're calling, is it?"

"No."

There was a sinking feeling in her stomach. "It wasn't officially sanctioned by the Decatribunal, then?"

"Definitely not."

Jane's jaw locked down hard. She'd been duped into answering the questions because of the miremon delegate to the Decatribunal's message. It was an entirely miremon inquisition and had nothing whatsoever to do with the Decatribunal. She had to put that aside, for now, and discuss that with Feig and the others when she had time. "My apologies for the confusion. What can I do for you, Yliriu?"

Yliriu looked uneasy. "As you are aware, there has been a lot of discussion on the floors of the Greater Assembly regarding the process of choosing a delegation to begin talks with Earth."

Jane nodded. "Of course."

"You may not be aware of a subassembly that was formed to expand our communication-relay network into that sector in advance of a party being sent to Earth. It's a remote region. There weren't any relays there. This was a routine procedure."

Jane nodded again.

"Because of the evidence you presented regarding the kuboderan called Kai'Memna, a standard set of Swarm pod detection equipment was deployed in the vicinity of each relay station. Again, all very routine."

A wave of cold spread out from Jane's stomach. She clutched the console, her fingertips going white.

"I'm sorry, Jane. I just got the report moments ago. I've read it at least five times to be sure I have the information correct before I pass it on to you. I hate having to tell you this. There is a Swarm pod in the sector."

Jane's hand flew to her mouth. Her eyes began to water.

"Now, there's no immediate danger. It's at least twelve to thirteen standard years away, but it's definitely on a course for Earth."

Kai'Memna had done it.

He had given the Swarm the location of Earth.

Jane stood. She needed to pace. Or scream. Or cry. She'd seen what the Swarm could do to a world firsthand. Brai had shown her through her predecessor's eyes—Rageth Elia Hator had narrowly survived a Swarm pod attack on a sectilian colony world. It was as vivid in her mind as if it were her own memory. She couldn't let that happen to Earth.

She tried to do the math quickly, but had trouble concentrating. She knew a year on Earth was approximately nine-tenths of a standard year in the USR. That was just over a decade. Would that be enough time?

She realized Yliriu could no longer see her face. She sat back down. "I'll have to go back. Immediately. We don't have the technology that you have. We don't have anything. We aren't ready."

Yliriu's soft brown eyes drew down with worry. "Yes, I remember your testimony about this. I have faith that you'll find a way. There are a few other things we need to discuss."

Jane broke out in a cold sweat. "Okay."

"Your quarantine term is nearly complete. Have Murrrsi do one more scan and on my authority, considering the situation, we'll call it done. I may catch hell for not following the letter of the law, but I'll take that risk. After that scan, assuming the results are negative, you may release the non-terrans in your care to return to their lives elsewhere."

"Yes, of course. Thank you."

"I'll immediately begin the work to muster support for you here. It's so early in your relationship with us, though, Jane. We have to be realistic. This is not the entry into galactic society that anyone expected for Terra. Our roles were supposed to be reversed. I don't know if help will be forthcoming, but I will do whatever I can to get it for you."

"Thank you. I—"

"Jane," Brai said softly, breaking into her scattered thoughts, "the *Oblignatus* has just jumped into the Terac system."

46

July 29, 2020

ALAN CLOSED his eyes and inhaled deeply. Jane was draped over his bare chest. Her hair was all messed up, pressing against his chin and lips. She smelled wonderful. She felt just right against him. Yeah. He was home.

"What was it like, while we were gone?" he asked. The *Obli* had jumped close enough to a comm relay point a few times solely for the purposes of exchanging messages with the *Spero*, but that had been far from enough communication to have a clue about what had really been going on.

She lifted her hand limply then let it fall again. He grabbed it and clasped it.

"I spent nearly every day writing messages and answering calls. Nothing very interesting actually happened."

"Are you still a celebrity?"

She looked up at him and rolled her eyes. "I'm still pretty popular. When they aren't trying to figure out if I'm a monster."

He tilted his head, trying to see her expression better. "What do you mean?"

"It seems like there are two main fears about humans. It's rarely overt, but I know there's a lot of gossip. Usually they steer a conversation so they can try to decide for themselves. Some people want to know just how aggressive we actually are. I think those people are afraid we'll invade their planets and subjugate them, rather than protect them like they feel they were promised. Then there are the people who are worried that the Cunabula's human experiment failed and that we aren't aggressive enough. These people often say things to me like, 'But you're just so nice!'"

He stared at the ceiling and thought about it. "It's understandable. I gotta admit, I wonder the same things sometimes. I worry that either we're gonna go extinct or go mad with power. People are crazy."

"I know. But it's hard being the object of all that scrutiny."

He squeezed her gently. "Have you stayed in touch with Darcy Eberhardt?"

"Yes. I've been making inquiries for her. Doing research. I don't know that I've been much help. It's not easy finding someone who was sold into slavery. Most people are reluctant to admit the slave trade even exists."

"That's some fucked-up shit."

She plucked at a stray thread on the sheet. "I know. It's hard to believe that it goes on. I hope she finds him soon."

"Have you sent her a message about the Swarm?"

She slid off him and nestled against his side. "Not yet. I'll wait until I have more concrete information. I don't want to pull her off her search for Adam Benally until we actually need her. The galactic communication network has been extended to cover the Sol system, so I'll be able to send a message to her from there when I know more. We're going to need all the help we can get."

"What's the climate like? Do you think the data we pulled from Kai'Memna's ship will clear the sectilians?"

She tipped up her face to him. "Is he really dead?"

He curled his lip with disgust. "He's really dead. I saw a dead squid with my own eyes." He shuddered a little at the memory. "Do you think the USR will be willing to lift the quarantine and give the Sectilius another chance?"

She breathed deeply. "They might. Sectilian products are missed in the marketplace. I heard that mentioned a lot. But there's a lot of residual anger, even all these years later, about the squillae virus. If they find out it wasn't them, that might change. I just hope that sentiments don't turn against the Kubodera."

"I wonder how other races treat their kuboderans. Did you learn anything about that? Is it pretty much the same deal they got from the sectilians? Or are there people who treat them better?"

Jane shifted slightly. "I think it varies a lot even between individual ships. Feig has told me that pelimarians don't use any systems that resemble the yoke. They work hard to build good relationships with their kuboderans and even give them vacations in a safe ocean on Pelimar."

"Huh. That's cool."

"I want to do that too, if we can. Brai was so happy on Pliga."

"You said you swam with Brai? That it's something pelimarians do? What was it like?"

She nodded against his chest. "Kind of amazing. At its heart, it's a community-building exercise. We've done it many times since. You'll like it. It's fun, good exercise, and I think it really builds trust and cooperation."

It sounded kind of woo, but he wouldn't break the mood by saying so. He stroked her hair. It felt cool and silky between his fingers. "Are you disappointed that we have to leave before you get a chance to physically meet all these people you've been talking to?"

"Maybe a little. I wish I could say I'm excited to go home, but I don't really know what we're going to find there. I don't know how they reacted to my messages. It's such a huge unknown."

"Yeah. I hope they weren't jackasses." He paused. "So, um, since you mentioned them... pelimarians?"

She chuckled. "What about them?"

"Where do I start?"

She propped herself up with an elbow on the bed, smiling.

"I read a little bit about them. Wow."

"Mm-hm."

"I half wondered if I was going to come back and find you had a harem."

She snorted.

He ran his free hand up and down her back. Her skin was so smooth. He couldn't stop touching her. "Were you tempted?" He was only about ten to twenty-five percent serious.

She sighed dramatically. "They do smell really good." Her voice was husky and sensual. Then she slapped him playfully and kissed him.

He smirked. He guessed he'd deserved that. "You aren't kidding. Am I allowed to notice that too? What the hell is that? Cologne or something?"

"They say it's their own natural scent. I did read something about them producing copious amounts of pheromones. Maybe that's part of it."

"I noticed Pledor was all up in their business."

"Oh, yes. It's been interesting to watch all that develop. It was painfully awkward at first. Now it just seems normal. For all I know Murrrsi may be as well. If she is, she's more discreet."

He reached up to scratch his nose. "Huh. So no problems with them, then?"

"I didn't say that." She flopped on her back. "Their primary delegate Xua has been very unhappy that Ajaya and I didn't join Feig's 'family.' He went so far as to intimate that if we aren't obliging we shouldn't expect good relations with Pelimar."

Alan blinked. "Crap. That's harsh."

"It is. It's so strange. They're very powerful and a lot of other cultures follow their lead in political matters. There may not be help coming for Earth."

He looked down at her. She was working her mouth around, blinking, and flaring her nostrils. She was trying not to cry. He reached for her. "Hey..."

She swiped at her eyes angrily. Her voice sounded strained. "I failed. All this time here, working so hard... and I failed."

"You didn't fail. They're assholes." He felt helpless to console her. He didn't know what to say, but he would really like to punch that guy Xua in the nuts. "I bet that was an empty threat."

"Well, we'll find out soon, I guess."

He could tell she didn't want to talk about that anymore. She was pursing her lips and still dashing away and occasional tear. Maybe a change of subject would help. "What's the wexian like? He didn't say much."

She sniffed. "He rarely does. It seems like we don't have a lot in common with him. Or perhaps this is just his way. I don't know."

A low tone sounded that slowly increased in intensity, and a soft yellow light came on near the open doorway. Jane inhaled sharply and began to extricate herself from him.

"What is it? What's wrong?"

"Someone's at the outer door." Her expression went blank for a second, then she said, "It's Feig. I better go see. It could be important." She pulled on a robe and padded through to the large outer room and the door.

He pulled his pants back on and grabbed his shirt, slipping it over his head as he moved to lean against the wall at the end of the hallway between Jane's private rooms and the public space.

Jane let Feig in. Feig was tall with a large frame, and exotic looking. She towered over Jane. No hair but that hardly mattered —she was sexy as hell. If he weren't happily in a relationship, he'd definitely have wanted to climb that mountain. He rolled his eyes at his own ridiculous thoughts.

Feig said something soft, and Jane gestured for her to come in. Feig's eyes flicked over to him in an assessing, curious way, then back to Jane. "We're sorry to interrupt your reunion, but we wanted to relay some news. We thought you might already be anticipating your next moves, thinking and planning, and we wanted to let you know that we'd like to remain aboard for whatever that may be."

Jane looked surprised. "Oh, I—"

Feig took Jane's hand in both of hers. "Jane, we feel like our journey with you is not over. We believe we can continue to be of help to you, to your people, in this difficult time ahead. In fact, I have also spoken with Murrrsi and Imadua and they feel the same way. Will you have us, Jane?" Feig's hand had moved up Jane's arm and she was kneading and stroking. Alan couldn't look away.

"Of course. I'd be honored for all of you to stay and help us. Thank you."

Feig dipped her head and moved in close to Jane. For a second he thought she was going to kiss her, but she pulled Jane into a hug. "Wonderful. Wonderful. We'll tell the others. When you need us, let us know."

Feig slowly pulled away, her fingers lingering. She cast another long look at Alan before sashaying her way out the main door.

Jane followed to the doorway and pressed the symbol to close the door.

Alan cleared his throat. "Well, Feig sure likes you. That might go a long way on Pelimar."

Jane shook her head. "They're very touchy-feely. It's nothing. Don't make it into something it's not." There was a note of warning in her voice. Just a small one. But it was there.

He held up his hands. "No, no. No. Not gonna do that. There's always my imagination, after all."

Jane huffed. "You're awful."

He grinned. "Yes. Yes, I am."

She slipped into his arms. They swayed together.

"So tomorrow we start the jumps back to Earth," he said against her hair.

"Yes. Tomorrow we head home. Brai has already plotted out the jump sequences."

"And the four kuboderan ships waiting just outside this system?"

"We're bringing them along, if they want to come. I suspect they'll be needed."

47

JANE SAID goodbye to Terac without ceremony, leaving Yliriu to make her apologies and explanations. The *Speroancora* and *Oblignatus* moved a safe distance from the planet's gravity well before opening a wormhole and jumping to the spot where Ron had left the four ships he had brought with him from Pliga That Was.

Jane spoke to these kuboderans frankly. They were under no obligation to continue on to Earth. Kai'Memna had started this war and she made it clear that she thought they were every bit as much the victims of his despicable, twisted regime as the sectilians who had died and the humans who were fated to fight the Swarm. Ron had promised them freedom. They would be free to choose.

All four decided to accompany her to Earth.

She now commanded a fleet of six ships.

She wasn't sure if that was going to be an asset or liability when she returned to Earth. It all depended on what had happened during the time she was gone. On a human time scale she'd left about three years before. There was no way of knowing what had transpired since then. Either they'd listened to her or they hadn't. Either way, there would be plenty of work to do.

They had the pligan Hiding particles as a potential defense. They had six ships and Alan's new blink drive that could be used offensively. They had access to the galactic communications network and an extensive and updated database of information about the Swarm and weapons technology. They might even have allies that they could call upon.

The trip back to Earth was far easier than the trip away had been. Even with six ships utilizing a single wormhole generated by the *Speroancora*, each jump was quick and easy. They needed only a few minutes to coordinate the movement and position of each ship before they could jump again. It became routine by jump number four. By jump number eight people were bored.

Jump number eleven was different.

Within moments of arrival at their target location, a comm alert went off.

Celui tapped his console. "It's a distress call from a planet in the nearby system."

Jane sat up straighter. "What's the nature of their problem?"

He listened for a moment. "It's a farming colony called Vendal. They've got a Swarm pod on the way. There are just over 100,000 farmers on the planet and they're defenseless. Their early detection system failed and now they're calling on anyone who can help them."

"Well, fuck," Alan muttered.

Ron connected via anipraxia. "You're hearing this?"

She replied, "Yes. Gathering information." To Celui: "Can you get someone in charge for us to talk to? Maybe we can coordinate an evacuation."

"Hailing now."

Murrrsi said, "I'm pulling up long-range scans now. There's no time for evac. That would take weeks on a planet of this size. People on farming colonies are spread out. This Swarm pod will be here in just over four standard days."

"Brai, let the rest of the fleet know about a change in plans. We're going to see what we can do to help. Or if they even need us. Maybe they have help coming and we'll just be in the way."

Jane spoke to the governor of the colony. That was not the case.

No one was coming to help them.

"They waited too long," Murrrsi said. "Trying to fight a pod of this size, this close to a planet, is suicide."

Ouvaq looked distressed. "They've got little more than farm machinery. They can't fight the Swarm with pitchforks and plows."

Governor Panciklau was nintergertehunt. He wore a big, floppy hat that shadowed his pale face. It looked like he was speaking directly from the barnyard. His clothes were threadbare and stained, white hands cracked and lined with dirt. He spoke slowly, his voice thick with emotion. "We knew the alert system went out some time ago. But we had to bring in a crop, process, package, and sell it. We planned to send someone to go up and work on it, but by then it was time to plant the next crop. We're simple people. We're peaceful. We live by the cycle of the land. I should have delegated the job to someone else. I never thought... I take full responsibility." He broke off and turned away from his camera.

It was a multicultural world, home to six different species, but the cities were just small ports for trading. The population was evenly distributed over the globe in small farming enclaves. There was very little organized government in place. It didn't seem to be needed.

Ron initiated a private connection with Jane and Brai via Pio.

"I've spoken to Huna. We can give them the particles and go back to Pliga That Was and grow more. We've got years to get ready for Earth's defense. We can use this as a case study, measure its effectiveness, make sure our delivery system works. This could be a good thing. We should try to help these people."

"Agreed," Jane said. "What do you need from me?"

"Alan, and any other hands you can spare."

The entire *Speroancora* crew, including Jane, transferred to the *Oblignatus* to get the drones ready for dispersal, transfer the pods to the drones, and load them onto shuttlecraft. It was back-breaking physical labor and they worked around the clock until everything was set.

And Alan had one more idea up his sleeve. Because the Swarm pod was so close, it likely could already see Vendal. It was going to take some theater to make the Swarm believe it was gone. He proposed detonating a series of really spectacular bombs around the planet, just as the particles were activated, that would hopefully make the Swarm believe that the planet had been destroyed. The hope was that they'd turn around and go home or find another target, preferably on an uninhabited planet.

No one knew what level of cognition the Swarm operated under. But it seemed worth a try. The timing was going to have to be absolutely perfect for it to work.

Between the two crewed ships, only eight had been trained to fly shuttlecraft. Each pilot delivered drones into the atmosphere over Vendal and came back for more until all were dispatched. Pio remotely moved the drones so that they were equally spaced planet wide. They kept their ships visible to the Swarm so it would look like the planet had been under attack. Alan created a series of big dirty bombs that would create a lot of debris and attached them to small blink drives.

Jane spoke with Governor Panciklau after everything was in place and she was back aboard the *Speroancora*. Panciklau had his hat off, stiff white hair standing straight up in places, mashed and swirled by the hat in others. Velvety crimson crops swayed in the breeze behind him, belying the potential violence to come. His pale blue eyes were fierce with determination. His voice was gruff and commanding. "You have sacrificed something to us that you needed for your own defense. You don't see that kind of generosity every day out there." He gestured toward the sky. "No one else would come to our aid. If we'd had early warning, it might have been different." He hung his head, composing himself. A large piece of farming machinery rumbled by behind him. Even with the impending threat, the people of Vendal kept working. "You've given us a great gift. You've given us a chance. I know I've no right to ask this, but I have one final request."

Jane frowned. "What is your request, Governor?"

"I don't know if your particles will work. I surely hope they do. But we don't want you to stay here and fight and die for us. It's not right. What we ask is that you get the Swarm's attention and lead them away from here."

"But—"

Panciklau spoke over her. "You leave. You leave the second those bombs are detonated. You make it look like you blew this world up and just flew away without a care in the world. Don't worry about what happens to us. This isn't your fight. It never was."

"What if it doesn't work? We can save some people. There's still time," Jane pleaded.

"Who would you save? Not me. I don't deserve saving. And the rest... How do you pick one over the others? What kind of outrage would you incite if you picked up a miremon and nintergertehunt enclave and not a gaerwyn or pelimarian? The fallout from that politically would damage your reputation. You can't afford that, Quasador Dux."

"What will be the fallout if I leave you?"

"With all due respect, no one even knows you're here."

Jane went quiet, thinking of what she could say to convince him to let her try.

"We need you to draw them away. That's all we ask. Just get them to change their course and then jump away. Nothing more." He cut the connection with a gesture.

The bridge was quiet as a tomb.

"We need to start the process if this is going to work, Jane," Alan said softly.

Jane nodded. "Start the dehiscence sequence."

Alan tapped his console. "Dehiscence sequence initiated. Putting interior drone images up on-screen."

The viewscreen split into eight images, each showing the interior of a different drone filled with pligan pods.

Pio said over the shared anipraxic link, "Drones are functioning within set parameters. We've lost only a few to malfunctions."

Huna chimed in. "Internal drone sensors indicate the pods are drying quickly, as expected."

On the screen Jane could see the pods changing in real time. The ends curled back and shimmering contents began to spill out.

Huna said, "Dehiscence is nearly optimal."

Alan rapidly tapped and scrolled through data. "Pio, can you confirm that we've got similar figures all over the globe?"

"Confirmed. Drying cycle is uniformly reaching completion."

Alan glanced at Jane.

Jane nodded.

Alan said, "Triggering vibration and opening release ports."

On the screen the pods rumbled and the fine particles spilled out, filling the air with glittery dust which began to sift through small holes that opened in the drone casing.

Jane leaned forward. "Let's see Vendal on-screen."

Murrrsi tapped her console. "Vendal on-screen, Qua'dux."

The entirety of Vendal began to sparkle as the particulates in the atmosphere caught the light.

Pio said, "Particle deployment complete."

"We've got good coverage!" Alan crowed.

"Confirmed. Coverage is uniform," Pio said.

"Pods are empty. It's time to blow the bombs and activate the Hiding protocol," Alan said.

Huna chimed in. "I can verify that is the case. We are ready for signaling."

Jane took a deep breath. "Blow the bombs."

Alan punched at his screen with one fingertip. "Bombs going 'boom.'"

One side of the large screen whited out, then continued to flare over and over. Alan had done his job enthusiastically.

"Activate the Hiding protocol," Jane ordered. Alan's bombs continued to go off.

"Activating," Alan said.

The drones were now giving off a signal that would polarize the suspended particles and broadcast an image over them, depicting the space on the exact opposite side of the planet.

As they watched, Vendal disappeared.

"Holy fuck. It actually worked!" Alan exclaimed.

Feig said, "The fleet is taking minor damage from the bomb debris."

Alan looked sheepish. "I may have overdone the bombs. I wanted it to look like a planet was really blowing up."

"I'd say you did a convincing job of it," Jane said. "All right, let's honor Governor Panciklau's request. We'll draw them off.

Way off. Let's make sure they change course. Put us on a vector to intercept, full speed. Form up into a wedge formation. Every ship, continuous active scanning of the Swarm. Let's get their attention and hold it."

The bridge was silent as they closed the gap.

"In visual range now, Qua'dux," Celui said.

"On-screen, if you please," Jane replied. It was about time she saw these creatures with her own eyes.

"On-screen and magnifying, Qua'dux."

The viewscreen flickered, and the star field they'd been looking at was replaced with a churning column of black insects trailing a great distance away. Their abdomens glowed with a reddish light that reflected off their lustrous outer shells and their vacant alien compound eyes. They looked as sinister as their reputation. Jane recoiled, as did every member of her fleet via the anipraxis link.

The command-and-control engram set that Brai had placed in her brain just after they'd met allowed her to assess the data streaming between herself and Brai and make quick decisions based on the collective knowledge and experience of every quasador dux that had gone before her on this ship and its name-sake before. She knew that lasers and missiles from a single ship would do very little damage to an adult *Confluos giganus*, but it might make them angry enough to follow her.

"Murrrsi, warm up the laser cannons and arm missiles."

"Aye, Qua'dux."

Jane stood and walked down to the viewscreen, examining the individuals at the tip of the Swarm pod's spear. She pointed at one of the largest adults, then another as she spoke. "Lasers on this one. Two missiles on this one."

Murrrsi said, "Lasers and missiles ready."

"Fire."

Murrrsi bent over her console. "Firing now, Qua'dux.

Missiles away." She looked up at the viewscreen with hope in her eyes.

Jane returned to the command chair. "Fleet, change course, bearing three-thirty mark twenty. Stay in formation. All ships, continue active scanning." Now they would see if the Swarm would follow.

It did.

And more swiftly than she'd anticipated. None of her predecessors had ever attempted such a maneuver. She was traversing new territory here.

All along the column, Swarm beetles flipped, and the burn that had been slowing them down in advance of landing on Vendal now pushed them toward Jane's fleet.

"Oh, you got their attention," Alan called out. "They're closing in fast."

Ron said, "We just took their meal ticket. They're highly motivated."

The thrill of success and primal terror warred momentarily in Jane's brain.

Ei'Yin, one of the four crewless kuboderans, said, "The *Scholaffecti* is taking plasma damage. May I return fire?"

"Yes, return fire at will," Jane answered. "All ships disengage active scanning."

"I've got a visual on a bug attempting to land on the *Lumenfuga*," Ron said.

"Confirmed," said Do'Nii, the kuboderan on the *Lumenfuga*.

"*Lumenfuga*, break formation and take evasive action," Jane commanded.

She had miscalculated. She needed help getting them out of this situation and connected privately with Ron. "We've bitten off more than we can chew. Recommendations?"

Ron replied, his mental presence calm but concerned, "We can't outrun them. We can try coordinating firepower and picking off individuals. But that might backfire if they turn back toward Vendal."

Jane gritted her teeth. "All ships break formation, but maintain general heading. Let's put some distance between us to maneuver. Ei'Brai will assist with coordination. Take orders directly from him unless otherwise specified."

"Brai," Jane said, just to him, "get creative."

"Affirmative."

"That bug is dogging *Lumenfuga*," Ron said.

"Show me the fleet on-screen," Jane said. Celui put a feed up instantly from the aft of the *Speroancora*. They were still in a roughly arrow-shaped formation, but more spread out, with the *Speroancora* at the tip. She had little tactical knowledge and was feeling that lack now. The Sectilius simply didn't engage in these sorts of activities unless their hand was forced.

She was just a linguist.

The *Corgnomon* and the *Scholaffecti* were closest to the *Lumenfuga*. "Ei'Tial and Ei'Yin, synchronize fire on the bug on *Lumenfuga*'s back. Train your lasers and fire missiles. Keep firing. If you can't get a good angle that avoids collateral damage to the *Lumenfuga*, hold fire."

"Two bogeys flanking the *Spero* and closing in," Alan called out.

Jane looked up at the screen, looking for some kind of way out. They had to do something the bugs wouldn't expect and get out of there. They couldn't win this fight. They just had to survive to fight another day.

Panic streamed from Ei'Rew of the *Decuscien*. "Multiple plasma hits! Hull breach!" Brai, Pio, and several other kuboderan officers blanketed Ei'Rew with calm.

The *Speroancora* shuddered.

"Contact," Feig said.

Ouvaq whimpered.

Jane stared at the tactical display. Two bugs that had been pursuing Pio suddenly turned to join the assault on the *Decuscien*. The *Oblignatus* was clear.

Jane swallowed. *"Oblignatus*, spool up your wormhole drive. Confirm when the drive is ready."

Every kuboderan made a wordless cry of dismay.

"Aye," Ron said.

"On my mark, every ship—except *Oblignatus*—disengage engines and employ reverse thrust for a count of ten aepar. At ten, reengage engines and set course for a new vector. We will converge, in standard wormhole sequence, on the wormhole produced by *Oblignatus*."

Brai said, "It is not recommended to open a wormhole so near a gravity well."

Jane took a steadying breath. "I know. We're out of options. We can do this."

Pio began the calculations. Jane felt every kuboderan in the fleet lending her mental support. The calculations were far more complex this close to a planet.

Jane's heart thudded in her throat. This was a huge risk. Closer to a gravity well, a wormhole had an increased chance of losing symmetry. Losing symmetry would mean that the laws of physics could warp in unpredictable ways. They might come out on the other side of the galaxy, or they might simply disappear the way some early warp-science pioneers had. Theoretically they could become displaced in time, or the wormhole could collapse before they could traverse it, leaving them trapped with the Swarm where they would surely die trying to fight them off.

She hoped they'd at least convinced the pod that Vendal was gone.

"Murrrsi, continue tracking the Swarm pod's movements until the last possible second. I want a report on the other side."

"Aye, Qua'dux."

"It's a good plan, Jane," Ron said.

Jane couldn't respond. She refused to concentrate on anything but getting them out of this. This was on her.

While they waited for the drive to spool, Brai put the fleet through bizarre machinations to evade and throw off the bugs. Ei'Tial and Ei'Yin had managed to dislodge the solitary bug on the *Lumenfuga* by firing on it. Now Brai ordered the *Lumenfuga* and the *Corgnomon* to flank the *Decusian* closely, leaving just enough clearance for *Decusian* to roll on its lengthwise axis while maintaining course and velocity.

Do'Nii was less experienced and balked at moving in so near to another ship, but Brai coaxed him through it. *Decusian* rotated. Through the anipraxic link with the *Decusian*'s Ei'Rew, Jane heard the *Decusian* groan, protesting the strange maneuvers. These ships were not made to move like this, especially at this velocity, but Brai knew them well. He pushed *Decusian* to the farthest threshold but not beyond. It worked. Three Swarm beetles were thrown clear of *Decusian*.

Meanwhile, Brai changed course again and again, narrowly evading the second beetle that was trying to land on the *Speroancora*. It shadowed the ship mercilessly until it managed to land. Brai opened a cargo bay door beneath it. The rush of the venting atmosphere knocked it away. The second bug would be harder.

"May I have your consent to utilize one of your blink drives, Alan?" Brai asked.

Alan made eye contact with Jane. "Hell yeah," he said vehemently.

Brai continued to orchestrate the fleet's evasive maneuvers while he simultaneously powered up a blink drive in a cargo hold. Jane watched him carefully calculating then, decisively, he activated the drive. A split second later the last Swarm beetle burst away from *Speroancora*'s hull in a million pieces.

It was working. They were holding their own.

She praised Brai privately. Given free rein, he was all she could want in an officer.

"Confirmed. The *Oblignatus*'s jump drive is ready," Ron said.

"Open the wormhole," Jane said. Then, "Mark!"

The *Speroancora* vibrated violently and Jane was thrown forward against her straps. She silently counted to ten along with the rest of the fleet as the reverse thrust worked against their forward momentum to slow them dramatically.

The bugs, unprepared for this tactic, flew out in front of them.

Then the engines reengaged and each ship veered away on wild arcs toward the wormhole, just as Brai had plotted out for them. Jane watched as the *Oblignatus* slipped through. Then *Corgnomon*, the *Lumenfuga*, the *Decuscien*, and the *Scholaffecti*. All five of her charges were safely through.

The wormhole was open before the *Speroancora*, a swirling matrix of space-time and gravity. It would lead to a haven from this chaos.

Jane held her breath.

They jumped.

48

THE ALL-CREW assembly took place in an empty cargo hold. A platform had been constructed at one end, dominated by a podium featuring a large Earth United crest and a row of chairs behind. Big screens lined the wall behind the platform, and projectors had been set into the ceiling.

The rest of the fleet was about to find out what Zara had learned just a few days before, when she'd translated the speeches Compton had given her. Nearly every member of the *Aegis*'s crew had been pulled off a long shift of system checks, drills, and simulations to listen to the brass speak.

When her group got the signal that it was time, she followed the command staff, most of whose shoulders displayed high ranks within the Earth United military, onto the platform and stood in front of the seat she'd been assigned.

Brigadier General Mark Walsh, the commanding officer of the *Aegis*, strode in shortly after that. The entire room came to attention. Walsh took his place behind the podium, followed

closely by Tom Compton, who stood slightly behind Walsh and
to one side. This was her first glimpse of Walsh, the man who had
commanded the *Providence*. Like Compton, he hadn't aged much
since that expedition. Zara fidgeted slightly and she was
suddenly filled with a feeling of intense pride to be serving with
them. To have contributed to them getting to this place.

Walsh stood surveying the crowd as the lights dimmed.
Behind them, in Mensententia, the words At Ease flashed on the
screens. Then General Gordon Bonham, the former NASA
administrator who was serving as the current coordinator of the
Earth United fleet, filled the screens. Everyone on the platform
turned sideways to look up at the projection. Bonham looked
grim. As he began to speak in English, Zara's translation of his
speech in Mensententia displayed prominently near the bottom
of the screens.

"The time has come for us to call you to action. You've been
trained well. You are the best of Earth." His eyes shifted away
from the camera and he gestured to someone off-screen. Bonham
disappeared. A series of images of the solar system from different
vantage points began to play.

Bonham went on. "As you know, six Americans visited a
sectilian ship fourteen years ago. As a result, we've been warned
about threats that may come from beyond this system. We've sent
probes throughout our system to monitor strategic points. Three
weeks ago, one of these probes recorded these images."

A chorus of strangled gasps went up from the crowd. Zara
had read Jane's text file many times, but even she was shocked by
the pictures. The gleaming black shells of enormous beetles.
Confluos giganus. The Swarm. There had to be at least one
hundred in this pod. The camera angle changed to a much closer
image. The bugs' faces were pointed away from the sun, their
bodies oddly shaped—short and wide. Then she realized they
appeared to be foreshortened due to their velocity. They'd

flipped and were burning their organic anatomical drives to slow their momentum in preparation for reaching Earth. Such creatures should have been impossible, but the evidence was right there for them all to see.

"This is the Swarm. They've just entered our solar system, crossed the orbit of Pluto yesterday. We estimate they could reach Earth in just over five weeks." Bonham's face filled the screen again. "Dr. Jane Holloway and the sectilian database have told us that they're capable of consuming every living thing on Earth if we don't stop them.

"Look around you. What you see is one people, wearing a single uniform, united with one purpose: to preserve our world. We are the guardians of Earth. We are the beacon of hope in a dark and dangerous universe. This fleet is the pride of Earth, outfitted with the most advanced technology that two different civilizations can offer. In seven days you will be using the sectilian artificial-wormhole drives to jump to the Swarm's location in the space between the orbits of Uranus and Neptune. There, we will engage the enemy and we will defeat them. I am confident that you'll each do your part." Bonham nodded and looked down. The screens went dark for a moment.

The screens lit up again, now displaying Walsh as he stood before them. "You all know who I am, where I've been. You know that this ship is the flagship of our fleet. Now you know what we face. We will *not* allow even one of these bugs to reach Earth, to escape, or to transmit any information about Earth and our defensive capabilities to another pod." He scanned the crowd for a few moments, then gestured at Zara, indicating it was time for her to come forward. "I will take a few questions."

He was running this more like a press conference than a typical address to the troops. Zara moved to his side, doing her best to look calm and poised, though she was nervous as hell. It wasn't like she hadn't translated for important people before. She'd done that all the time at NASA. But for *Mark Walsh*?

A few people raised their hands. Walsh gestured at a young Asian woman. She spoke in Mensententia. "I've been trying to text my husband and my texts aren't being delivered."

Zara translated her words into English.

Walsh nodded. "As of thirty minutes ago, all personal communication with Earth has been terminated, as a measure of security. I assure you that when we complete our mission, the populace will be informed of our success. But until then, we will protect them from needless worry." Walsh watched as Zara translated what he said into Mensententia, and then he gestured toward a small dark-skinned man with his hand in the air.

He also spoke in Mensententia. "What is our estimated chance of success, Captain?"

After she translated, Walsh looked at the man disdainfully. "We will not fail." He pulled back from the podium for a second, then leaned in to say, "Your department heads are fully informed and capable of answering any further questions. Dismissed."

The screens went off, and the lights in the cargo hold came back up. Walsh, Compton, and the rest of the command officers left the platform and walked out of the cargo hold.

The crowd immediately began to move toward the exits.

Zara stepped down from the platform and scanned the crowd until she spotted Ben. He pulled her into a bear hug and introduced her to some of his team members. They all stood around fidgeting and looking uncomfortable. She hoped it wasn't because she outranked them or because she'd just been standing on the dais.

"You holding up okay?" Ben asked.

She nodded. "I'm fine."

"That was short," one of Ben's teammates remarked in Mensententia.

"That's why it's called a briefing," Ben retorted with a wry look, no mirth in his voice or expression.

A woman in a dove-gray hijab that matched her uniform moved past their small group. "I wish I could say I was surprised. They got us all up here in a hurry. I knew something had to be up."

Zara looked around uneasily. She was glad everyone knew now. Most of the faces Zara saw were expressionless or displayed little more than determination. A few people looked paler than usual and drawn, probably scared or worried. Everyone would deal with the news in their own way.

Zara felt a sense of vague anxiety. She was more than a little numb. She'd known about the contents of this announcement for two days, but she'd been kept so busy that she just dropped dead on her bunk at the ends of her shifts. She hadn't had time to think about any of it. Everything was happening so fast that it didn't seem real. Her main emotion was grief over leaving behind her entire support network. Maybe if she'd had someone to talk to about all of this, it would feel different.

Ben put his hand on her shoulder. It felt so comforting. "Hey, we've got a lot to do in the next seven days, so we better get started. Text me if you have time to grab some chow, okay?"

"I'll do that." She tried to smile, but her lips just wobbled a little. She watched Ben depart with his teammates, then hurried to return to the command deck.

49

IMMEDIATELY, Brai knew something had gone wrong.

Every kuboderan in the anipraxic network knew something had gone wrong.

Hot panic flooded every cell of his body. Quickly he checked and rechecked Pio's calculations, his thoughts speeding with a rapidity he'd never experienced before.

Then they turned to sludge.

They were all checking the calculations, simultaneously. He sensed them all reaching the same conclusion. This shouldn't be happening.

He drifted between thoughts. He was aware of a stillness punctuating his mental impulses in arrhythmic staccato sequences. Communications with the others in the anipraxic network pulsed in and out of phase. He felt his blood pressure rise as he attempted to overcome the disturbance through sheer force of will. It was insurmountable.

Until it wasn't. His brains surged, as though his body had stopped but his mental momentum had not. The voices in his head were screaming, discordant wails of fear.

Every kuboderan feared this.

A wormhole failure.

The non-kuboderans only knew incomprehensible wrongness. They had yet to understand that they were caught in the open mouth of the wormhole. He tried to explain to Jane but was cut off midthought. Nothingness. Surge. He tried again.

What had gone wrong?

Pio, repeating: "Look to below starboard of the *Oblignatus*. A mass." Again. Then again. She was trying to get through to the rest of the group.

Every eye turned. Every tentacle reached out like a whip to adjust a monitor to view the *Oblignatus*'s exterior cameras.

The out-of-sync periodicity returned.

His hearts quit beating for long moments.

He sucked in great gulps of water, desperate to achieve enough gas exchange, anything to compensate for these interruptions.

Jane burst inside his mind, larger than life. "What do we do?"

All he could say to her was, "Working."

There was an additional mass that had entered the wormhole with them. A Swarm beetle? More than one? It was anchoring them just inside, because it had not been part of Pio's calculations.

Someone said, "Can we recalculate?"

That didn't make sense. Were they proposing opening another wormhole within a wormhole? The mass was unknown. He could not calculate for that. No one could. He'd never heard of a wormhole generated from within a wormhole. The laws of physics changed on the inside. It was impossible. He could not make that calculation.

"No."

"No."

"No."

Would they remain stuck there, skipping in and out of reality for eternity?

"If we destroy the mass, the conversion to energy might momentarily allow us to pass through. The wormhole might absorb the energy, freeing us."

Had he thought that? Said that? Or had someone else?

He grappled with reality, to not fade away.

Jane said, "Pio—fire laser cannons at the mass."

Blankness.

Pio fired.

And missed. The space-time distortion bent the waves of light. The beam scattered and collapsed.

"I can't aim properly!"

"Keep trying."

She fired again.

The laser bent back upon itself.

"Stop firing! The *Corgnomon* has been hit!"

Alan's mental voice, raging with insight. "The blink drive, Pio. Create a warp bubble around the mass—surround it with normal space-time. Then fire."

Calculations. Cross-checking. Readiness.

Emptiness that stretched on and on.

Implementation. Pio fired again and again, relentlessly.

The mass disintegrated. Pio dropped the warp bubble.

And they were through.

50

ZARA SPENT every waking hour of the next seven days translating correspondence and communications for senior officers and looking up information in the sectilian database. Then there were the conferences held on the *Aegis* because it was the flagship. They were long and the atmosphere of every meeting was charged.

Every scrap of information about the Swarm and every detail about every documented encounter with the enemy the Sectilius had ever recorded was picked apart in excruciating detail. Arguments often broke out about the age of the intel, the veracity of any particular data point as it compared to another, and whether information should be trusted or ignored.

The weight of the world was on her shoulders. If she missed some crucial bit of information, if she were inaccurate in the most minute shade of meaning, it could mean life or death for too many people for her to comprehend. She worried she wasn't good enough. That they hadn't had enough time to prepare. There were new ships in the shipyards, but they were months from completion. There wouldn't be time to get them ready to defend their world. The crews had been trained, but the bulk of them were inexperienced in battle, aside from simulations. It all felt too fast.

The upcoming fight could mean a future for Earth or no future at all.

Her only solace was that she wasn't the only person combing through all of this. There were dozens of interpreters of the highest skill level working right alongside her from all over the globe. Surely they'd pick up on anything she missed and vice versa. When they looked at each other across the table, she saw the kinship of their shared misery and fierce determination in their eyes.

The most frustrating part of the process was that every conversation between the leaders of the Earth United military went through several rounds of translation because few of the fleet's officers were proficient enough with the language for this level of discussion. Questions would start in the speaker's native language, then be converted to Mensententia, and from there they had to do interpretations in Mandarin, English, Russian, and more, until everyone was up to speed. Then the replies were orchestrated in reverse. It took forever, and the process got on everyone's nerves. Tempers ran high and the opinions expressed became increasingly pithy, disregarding all nicety just to save time and effort. The process bred misunderstandings and on occasion nearly led to blows.

One of the major differences between the *Aegis* and a sectilian class-six dreadnought was the absence of a kuboderan to control navigation and communication, among a host of other things. While she didn't think a kuboderan normally served as a translator, having one would probably speed up this process in some way.

A German colonel stood up and shouted in English, "We need a break! We just spent fifty-seven minutes discussing a battle for which we do not know the precise number or types of ships involved, the number of casualties, or even how many adult *Confluos* were present. We're wasting our time. Please. Let us take a break." He collapsed back in his seat, and all of the translators began murmuring to their officers.

Zara glanced at Walsh and Compton. Walsh, who as fleet admiral ran the meetings, nodded. "Call for a break."

She stood and made the announcement in Mensententia. Almost instantly the doors to the room opened as the occupants fled. Zara, Walsh, Compton, and Bonham were the only ones left in the room. Bonham rose slowly and leaned against the table. "Wagner's right."

Walsh shook his head. "If we don't turn over every stone... There's too much at stake."

Compton's lips were pressed together in a thin line. "It's tedious, but we can't leave anyone out of the loop or we'll be accused of taking over. This has to remain an international effort in every respect."

No one had any better ideas, so they continued on, analyzing, interrupting, and clarifying until they'd come up with a final battle plan.

The days seemed interminably long as they passed, but when they were finished, she realized another precious day had slipped through her fingers. What kind of life would she have led if she hadn't stolen the files from her dad's laptop all those years ago? Would she be blissfully unaware of all this taking place in orbit around Earth? It was strange to realize that it was entirely possible that none of this might be happening at all if not for her.

And where was Jane Holloway? Why hadn't she come back with help or fresh information? What could be keeping her away from her home for so long? Was she in danger or dead somewhere out there? Had she been able to get to the United Sentient Races and let them know that Earth was real and they needed to work together?

If Earth were truly a seed planted by the Cunabula that was meant to save the rest of the galaxy from the Swarm and others like them, surely the United Sentient Races would see that humanity was just in its infancy. It needed to be nurtured, helped to grow. If the galaxy's other sentients left them to die, they were sealing their own fate. The Swarm would nip humanity in the bud, and any chance for the rest of the galaxy would die on the vine.

The download just wasn't enough.

On the last day before the fleet was due to leave, Zara finished writing her notes from the final planning session and closed her laptop. She looked up, expecting the conference room to be empty. Compton still lingered. He rose, looking weary, and closed his own laptop. "You've done well, First Lieutenant. Several of the officers have recommended you for a commendation for your patience and competence."

She didn't deserve such praise. She wasn't working any harder than anyone else. Couldn't they see that? They were all just doing their best. All of them. As a team.

A surge of emotion welled up inside her, fatigue making it impossible to control. She should just say thank you and gather her things to go. She looked down and bit her lip, willing the feeling to subside. That seemed to make it worse. A tear fled down her cheek and she was sure the struggle must have visibly played over her face. She was mortified at the display. What was wrong with her? Why was she acting so stupid? She didn't want him to think that she was crying because she'd been waiting to be noticed. That was the opposite of how she felt. She stood and turned away from him and breathed deeply, looking up at the ceiling until she could master herself. "Thank you, but the teams work well together. It's not just me."

When she glanced back at Compton, he had a kind and understanding look on his face. "It won't always be like this. When your generation fully comes to power, Earth will have become a fully Mensententia-speaking world. These are growing pains, Zara. But until that day comes, sadly, you need old codgers like us."

It was an attempt to lighten the mood, to help her get through this. He'd understood. They'd chosen the perfect XO for this ship.

She couldn't say the things that were actually on her mind: that she was terrified they'd never have the chance to do what he said. Saying them would mean that he'd have to comfort her further, and she couldn't lay that at his feet, knowing all the responsibility he bore already. She tried to smile, but she didn't think she was very successful.

He rubbed his face. "Go get some sleep if you can. I'll see you on the bridge in a few hours."

She plodded toward her small, sterile room. Her roommate was on an opposite shift and wouldn't be there. In the corridors people gathered in small groups, talking in hushed tones, sharing meaningful touches, even kisses. In twenty-four hours some of these people might not be among them anymore. Everyone was painfully aware of that, and they were saying whatever goodbyes to each other that they needed to.

She absently checked her phone. She didn't expect there to be any messages, and there weren't. She'd never gotten together with Ben for a meal. There just hadn't been time. She wished now that she'd found a way to make time. A friendly face might have helped these last few days feel less lonely.

Inside, a new ache formed around her heart as she dwelled on the lovers she'd seen in the corridors. She was twenty-seven years old and had never had a serious relationship. She spent ninety-five percent or more of her waking hours working. She'd had crushes but never acted on them for many reasons, none of which seemed good enough in this moment.

Most of the people she worked with were twenty to thirty years older than her, and the taboo against fraternizing with MSTEM scholars had lingered even after she'd grown past the age of consent. The most intimate relationships she had were with her roommates, and while they'd fooled around from time to time, trying nearly every sexual configuration in a vain attempt to blow off steam, it had never led to anything because there just weren't enough hours in the day to maintain anything serious. All their lives were devoted to the cause—to preparing for the very thing they were about to do. They hadn't had the opportunity to be teenagers or young adults in the historic sense.

Now she regretted that, as much as her exhausted mind let her.

Her experience wasn't unique. Her shipmates had been as busy as she'd been. There'd been quality-control checks all over the ship and simulations, seeking more speed and accuracy in response times and developing protocols. They had to know how to handle all kinds of frightening scenarios—hull breaches, power failure, system damage. The lives of the rest of the crew depended on their ability to seal off decks, repair broken equipment, and reroute power. Very few people had the time to indulge in the gatherings she'd seen on her way back to her quarters.

She lay down on her bunk, fully clothed. She was too tired to change. She'd shower in the morning. Probably. It hardly mattered. No one would be sniffing her or commenting on her appearance.

She stared at the ceiling in the dark. Hours ticked by. Sometimes a few tears leaked out. Her mind was too full for sleep. It just wouldn't come.

She wished she could talk to her parents one last time.

Eventually she got up, showered, and dressed mechanically. She sat on the edge of the bed to collect herself.

There'd been a service set up on the fleet's intranet to collect messages for loved ones back on Earth, set to transmit once the lines of communication were opened again. It seemed like such a final act. Using it meant that a person was admitting to oneself that they might never see those people again.

She logged on to the service and filled out the form with her parents' cell phone numbers. She sent them each a single sentence: "I love you with all my heart."

51

THE *SPEROANCORA* FELL over the lip at the other end of the wormhole and for a split second Jane felt like she was tumbling. Disorientation and fear gripped her, plunging her stomach into the seat. Then it was over.

They were still.

The viewscreen showed dark space, littered with stars. The phase shifts had ended. Her thoughts made sense again.

She gasped for a breath. "Show the fleet on-screen," she rasped.

Instantly the viewscreen changed and she saw the other ships waiting. She counted five and allowed herself to exhale.

We made it. We all made it through.

"All ships report in," she said.

One by one every ship in her little fleet acknowledged her request.

"Have we arrived at our target location?" she demanded, more sharply than she should have. Her fingers trembled from the adrenaline.

Brai was already analyzing star maps. A second later he said, "Confirmed. We have reached target coordinates."

Through the anipraxic network, every mind was trying to reel itself in and assess whether they were okay, performing system checks.

Jane slumped in her seat. "We're going to take a break. No more jumps for a full standard day. Everyone get some rest. That's an order."

Alan was hunched over his console, half out of his seat. He held a hand up in the air. "Hold on. Nobody go anywhere."

His voice sounded strained.

The adrenaline reignited.

Jane cleared her throat. "What is it?"

He looked up at her. "We're not where we wanted to be."

"Brai just confirmed—"

Alan's face had lost all color. "We're in the right place, physically. But we are *not* in the right time."

52

February 9, 2031

WHEN ZARA ARRIVED on the command deck an hour earlier than her appointed time, things were deceptively business as usual. All stations were manned with quiet, industriously working individuals, most of them much older than her.

She checked in with Compton in his office to see if he had any last-minute duties for her. He looked like he hadn't gone to bed. His eyes were bloodshot and his skin was gray with fatigue. He sent her to the bridge to man her station.

She relieved the first communications officer and took her seat. She was the primary liaison between the *Aegis* and the rest of the fleet. There was already a lot of chatter, but nothing critical yet.

There was a countdown clock at her station, at everyone's station. The minutes were going by far too quickly.

When it was time, it would happen fast.

The fleet had had already jumped to the approximate location of the battle and built the velocity necessary to match the

Swarm's. Now they were getting into position. When the Swarm came into range they would form what the tacticians were calling a three-dimensional defile.

There would be three sizes of ship in play. The eight cruisers —smaller, much more agile, maneuverable, and able to respond quickly to changing conditions—had gone out to surround the Swarm. They would reach the outer limits of the Swarm's ability to detect them at the same time that the Swarm arrived within range of the Earth United's four dreadnought-class ships.

The dreadnoughts would position themselves in a diamond shape around the Swarm's projected vector, and would reach maximum velocity just hours before the Swarm passed through the defile. While the dreadnoughts opened fire, the cruisers would work to squeeze the Swarm down to a narrow band. As the Swarm reached the dreadnoughts, they'd release fighters, physically corralling any stray insects back into line, picking off stragglers, and chasing down any survivors one by one.

They'd be hitting them from all directions. There would be nowhere for them to go. The dreadnoughts would kill as many as possible, using missiles and laser fire until the Swarm outran them. The individuals that made it through the defile would continue to be squeezed by the eight cruisers until every last one was dead. The hope was that it would be like shooting fish in a barrel. If it wasn't, they would jump ahead of the Swarm and try another tactic. They could repeat this jump-and-attack sequence as long as there were ships left to fight, if necessary. Hopefully it would never be down to Earth's orbital and dirtside weapons.

When it came to warfare, there were so many more variables in space than on a planet. Humans were new to thinking of three-dimensional combat on this scale. Zara worried that they were just adapting ground-level techniques to space. She hoped that there hadn't been any egregious errors in their assumptions about how the Swarm would move or react.

There were one hundred and twenty-one adults and sixteen subadults in this pod. That meant each ship had to take out eleven to thirteen individuals. *Aegis*, being one of the four dreadnought-class ships, was slow to accelerate and lumbering to change course, but had lots of firepower and plenty of fighters. It would likely make the most kills in the first volley, but the eight cruisers would be doing the cleanup.

The *Aegis* was also tasked with coordinating the movements of the rest of the fleet and the fighters, as well as collecting sensor data that could be analyzed and used in future battles.

"Captain on the bridge!" someone barked. Everyone stood at attention until they were put at ease to resume work.

Walsh moved from station to station, speaking in hushed tones to every officer. When he got to her, he said, "First Lieutenant Hampton. Report."

She gave him a concise briefing on the comm chatter, the gist being everyone was ready and in place.

He nodded. Eventually he came back to the central command chair and sat down. "Ready missile bays. Warm up the lasers."

The bridge was absolutely silent for the next ten minutes as they waited for the bugs to come in range.

Walsh said, "Open a channel to the rest of the fleet, on speaker. Ask for a report. Be ready for translation."

Zara completed the command. "Aye, sir."

There was a brief moment of static, then a crystal-clear connection. She spoke into the mic in Mensententia. "Every vessel, report."

"The *Yoroi* stands ready."

"The *Zirh* stands ready."

"The *Pingbi* stands ready."

In turn, each ship sounded off. The *Bronya*, the *Dhaal*, the *Ritter*, the *Caballero*, the *Bouclier*, the *Guardião*, the *Paladin*, and the *Vincitore*. Each one replied in Mensententia and Zara repeated the phrase in English, though after the first two it was clear what they were saying.

Zara waited to see if Walsh was going to give a speech. He didn't. He said, "Standby, until my signal."

Long minutes passed. The countdown was closing in on zero. The fight would begin as soon as the Swarm came into missile range.

When the countdown reached two minutes and eleven seconds, Major Sokolov, the sensor specialist, calmly said aloud in English with a thick Russian accent, "Contact. First target is coming into missile range in ninety seconds." She knew from their talks that the extremes of their range were quite far because there was no air resistance to slow anything down or cause missiles to veer off course.

Walsh pointed a finger at her. "Repeat that for the fleet."

She did. She didn't know how many seconds had passed, so she repeated it verbatim. Her heart beat erratically in her chest.

Walsh leaned forward. "Can we get a visual?"

"Yes, sir. It'll be grainy, sir."

Walsh waved a hand. Zara translated the conversation into Mensententia for the rest of the fleet.

The big screen zoomed in from the star field that had dominated the space for the last few hours. Zara squinted. Occasionally she could see stray reflected light off of the carapace of one of the insects, but that was all. She wished they could see them better, to put a face on the evil that wanted to use them as food.

"Any deviation from their original trajectory or travel pattern?"

"None, sir."

She translated that. Someone on the *Bouclier* forgot to mute their mic as they translated the *Aegis* conversation into Mandarin. Zara fumbled to take them off speaker for a few seconds, then brought them back on the line when they finished speaking. She sent the *Bouclier*'s communications officer a quick text to remind them to turn off the mic during translations. She didn't bother with pleasantries. There wasn't time for worrying about hurt feelings right now.

"Fire missiles at your assigned sector of the pod on my mark," Walsh said. Zara translated. It would begin soon. Her breathing sounds seemed so loud in her own ears. She hoped the mic wasn't picking that up. She swallowed against a dry mouth, getting ready to translate the moment Walsh spoke. She had to sound crystal clear and not hesitate.

"Fire," Walsh said.

"*Jiacti,*" Zara translated, her voice as clear and true as she could have hoped.

She could hear the distant vibrations of the missiles in their loading tubes. The atmosphere was tense and absolutely silent as every head craned forward, watching the main screen in an attempt to see what was happening. Zara couldn't see anything but blobs. The fleet fired three separate volleys.

Zara's fingers trembled. She breathed shallowly. How many had they killed? How would they react?

Walsh leaned back in the command chair. "Major Sokolov, report."

Sokolov shook his head. "Sir, I register one hundred thirty-seven objects maintaining velocity."

Zara looked down at her hands on the console. Her heart sank. Not even one?

Walsh rose from his seat. "What?"

Compton stood up too. "They dodged every missile?"

Sokolov remained impassive. "That appears to be the case. There were momentary minor deviations in their courses but their overall trajectory is unchanged."

Walsh slammed his body back into the command chair.

Zara's earpiece chirped. Someone was reminding her to translate. She turned to the mic and translated the conversation word for word, except for Walsh's colorful muttering. She hoped they couldn't hear that.

The Brazilian scientist Lieutenant Colonel Rossi said in Mensententia, "The Sectilius never mentioned their eyesight was so good."

Zara translated quietly. She didn't think the timing was great.

Walsh glared at Rossi, then turned to Zara. "Announce a video-conference call in two minutes."

A room full of physically present officers had been difficult enough to manage, but a video conference of those same officers was ten times worse. Without a physical room to contain them, they spoke over each other. They accused each other of assuming this fight would be simple. One of them said little more than, "This is a disaster," over and over again. Another repeated, "I told you all that long range was a bad idea and none of you would listen to me."

Everyone quieted momentarily when the Swedish captain of the *Guardião*, who was normally very soft-spoken, said, "We would not be scrambling in the face of this threat if we had simply worked together from the start. I wish to go on the record stating this disarray is the fault of a lack of cooperation between nations. The attributes that the Sectilius believed made us strong have also splintered us, putting our very existence at risk."

The quiet didn't last longer than a moment's hesitation, and they were back to yelling and sniping, no matter what Walsh said to try to hush them. Eventually Walsh growled at her to mute anyone who hadn't been given the floor and she did so gladly. The conference suddenly became easier to manage, though the silenced officers looked angry enough to bite.

After everyone calmed down, the consensus of the conference was that it would be best to save ordnance until the pod was much closer. The insects wouldn't be as likely to dodge something coming at close range—and there was no dodging something you couldn't see. Lasers would be their best offensive weapon. They had time to change tactics. It would be an hour wait until the pod came into laser cannon range.

Since they would be forced to use more laser power than they'd anticipated, that hour gave them time to get every ship's engineering department working to divert power from anything that wasn't absolutely necessary in order to recharge the laser cannons as quickly as possible.

The conference call ended more calmly and more positively than it had begun. They had a new plan. They knew from analyzing historic encounters between the Swarm and the Sectilius that they had a tough road ahead. The long-range missiles had been an experiment that hadn't been found in the sectilian logs. Now they knew why. It must have been common knowledge among the Sectilius that it wouldn't work.

Some analysts reported they just barely had enough resources to give them a seventy percent chance of defeating the Swarm. Other analysts were more pessimistic. An average of all the predictions gave them a fifty-fifty chance.

Zara reminded herself, when she started to feel really scared, that the bugs might be resourceful, but humans were too.

And no one could calculate an average for that.

53

ALAN PINGED the nearest communication relay point to get an accurate date and time, something they did with regularity. It wasn't unheard of to lose a few seconds inside a wormhole. The ship's clocks would reset automatically when the ping bounced back.

He waited for that to happen, rubbing the back of his neck self-consciously. All eyes on the bridge were on him.

He heard Jane unlatch herself and stand. "What do you mean?" she asked.

"I can't tell yet," he said brusquely. "All I know is that the ship's computer is very confused about the time and date."

"That happens sometimes with rough transits," Murrrsi said. "It's normally minor. Nothing to worry about."

Ouvaq turned in her seat. She looked terrified. "That didn't feel minor to me."

Feig reached out to touch her reassuringly. "We're all here together. We survived. That's what's important."

The ping came back. The ship's clock reset.

Alan bellowed involuntarily when he saw the readout. "Holy fucking shit!"

Jane was at his side in an instant. "Oh, no." She sat down in his seat, her eyes wide with disbelief, staring at him.

"Eleven point eight-nine standard years. Stolen from us inside that goddamn fucking wormhole." He instantly started converting from standard years to Earth years in his head, though why that would matter now, he didn't know. That was ten point five-eight years on Earth.

The entire anipraxis network was stunned. Alan was glad for the internal silence.

"Yliriu said the Swarm was twelve to thirteen standard years away. There's still time to make a difference in the outcome on Earth," Ron said via the anipraxic link.

Alan shook his head in disgust. If Yliriu was right, the Swarm might hit Earth any fucking minute. There might not be time to grow another crop of particles. They might have wasted their best defense on those stupid fucks at Vendal. *Damn it.*

Feig said, "Excuse me, please, for my ignorance. Is it possible to reverse the wormhole, reproduce the effect, and go back?"

No one answered her. It was a stupid question. But Jane was looking at him expectantly so he kept his face blank and just said what anyone with any knowledge of the problem was thinking. "We don't know which thing caused the time dilation. It could have been that we were too close to a gravity well, or it was the extra mass that snuck in, the warp bubble, the laser fire, the explosion, or all of it together. We don't know and we have no way of knowing unless we devote about five lifetimes to studying wormhole anomalies."

Celui spread his hands. "Those moments when it felt like we were winking in and out of existence probably had something to do with it. We were skipping through time."

Alan shrugged. "Maybe. That was just our perception of an

event beyond our sensory comprehension. For all we know, we could have been jumping through parallel universes. We might not even be in the same universe we started in."

Ouvaq stifled a cry of fear and covered her face in her hands. Feig and Celui surrounded her, touching and grabbing. Bleh. Alan turned his back on the room and indulged in rolling his eyes.

Brai broke in for the first time, his voice soothing. "We are exploring possibilities. Such a jump has never been documented. It is at the extreme end of what we believe could be possible. There is no need for fear."

Ouvaq sniffed and straightened. Brai was probably sending tranquilizing mental waves her way. More power to him on that.

"I want complete system checks," Jane said. Rest wasn't an option anymore. "I'll put together teams to inspect damage on the unmanned ships. The *Decuscien* and the *Scholaffecti* have first priority. Once we're certain we're secure, we'll continue our jump sequence toward Earth. Murrrsi, before you leave your station, I want that analysis from Vendal. Everyone get to work."

54

BACK ON THE BRIDGE, it was as if they'd never left. Walsh settled back in his chair, and the fleet communication channel was reopened. A new countdown clock was posted that read twenty-seven minutes.

Gradually, on the viewscreen, they watched the Swarm develop from abstract-looking, pixelated blobs to real, larger-than-life nightmarish monsters. Zara began to avoid looking at the viewscreen and focused on her own console as the clock ticked down to zero. It was too hard to look at them and not be possessed with paralyzing fear.

They just were so unnatural. Their abdomens glowed bright orange from their bizarre organic drives. She wondered how they survived the heat the drives surely generated. Without air to dissipate that heat, they must have some organ or chemical reaction to compensate in order to keep them from burning alive.

Bugs had never particularly bothered Zara. She'd never been squeamish, but there was something primal about these creatures that screamed wrongness. Maybe it was because they were organic but looked anything but.

The countdown reached five minutes.

Every ship reported in. The lasers were ready to go.

Sokolov called out, "Targets within laser cannon range...now."

"Fire laser cannons," Walsh said, his nostrils flaring.

Zara translated.

Visually, nothing happened. The movies got laser weapons wrong and she couldn't blame them. It was more dramatic on film if they used colorful lines of light that people could see. The reality was that laser light traveled at the speed of light—faster than the human eye could perceive.

Lasers did their damage through rapid heating with a lot of energy. They could burn through ship hulls, airplane skins, armored plate, human skin, and then anything behind or within, igniting explosives or fuel tanks, if present. The US military had just begun to use them to take down incoming artillery shells in war zones when Holloway left the database behind. The sectilian blueprints furthered human knowledge of the technology, made these new lasers more efficient and more powerful, and opened up the use of more wavelengths.

The major downside to the use of lasers, even these efficient sectilian models, was that they generated vast amounts of heat that had to be shed between firings for safety reasons, even when outfitted with extensive cooling systems. So while the lasers cooled, Sokolov and his team gathered data on how much damage the first volley had done.

Most pre-sectilian lasers on Earth had been in the thirty- to one-hundred-fifty-kilowatt range. The lasers on the *Aegis* were two hundred megawatts. Zara kept reminding herself of this power while they awaited the results.

All eyes were on Sokolov, and he seemed agitated. He

appeared to be arguing with his team. He pushed one of them out of their seat and took over their station, shaking his head, one hand gripping his short-cropped hair.

Walsh stood. "Report, Major Sokolov."

Sokolov gathered himself. He stood and faced Walsh, his face blank. "Sir, we've recorded no appreciable damage to the targets."

Zara started to translate the conversation for the fleet, but Walsh swung around and pointed at her. "Cut the connection."

"Aye, Captain." She did as told, translated for the bridge crew, and waited for further instruction.

"They don't need to listen to this. They're seeing the same results." He shook his head. "I want to hear some theories. How can this be possible? We're using the same wavelength the Sectilius decided was most effective."

Lieutenant Colonel Rossi stood and looked at Zara. "It's possible that's why it's not working now."

Walsh glanced from Rossi to Zara. Zara translated.

Rossi continued, "A lot of time has passed since that database stopped accumulating new information. If the Sectilius used that tactic for a while, and a few individuals survived sectilian attacks, it may have been because those particular individuals had some advantage. If most of a pod was killed and only those with the advantage survived to reproduce, the new pod that formed around them would *all* have that characteristic. It's basic evolutionary science. It's how populations change over time. Small mutations that confer a survival advantage become dominant."

When Zara finished her translation of Rossi's statement, Walsh nodded. "But what's the advantage this pod has? How can we work around it?"

Rossi shrugged.

Walsh glanced around the room.

Zara tapped her finger on her console, feeling the urge to

speak but afraid she'd sound stupid. Walsh glanced at her and raised his eyebrows.

She bit her lip. "Sir, they *are* awfully shiny."

Someone snorted.

Zara grimaced. "No, hear me out. We know mirrors are the best defense against laser fire. Maybe this pod is more reflective. I mean, I don't know if we can measure their albedo. I don't remember seeing anything in the database that mentions that the Sectilius measured that characteristic, but I can look."

Rossi spoke up. "That's a good working theory. If this turns out to be the case, then we need to switch wavelengths away from near infrared toward ultraviolet."

Walsh swung around. "Any other theories?"

Zara took a step forward. "Sir, I have a second theory, but that one would be worse for us."

Walsh harrumphed. "Let's hear it anyway."

Zara glanced at the screen. The glowing objects were steadily getting larger. "Their... rears are pointed at us at the moment." She closed her eyes for a second. Couldn't she say anything that didn't sound childish? "What I mean is—their abdomens contain their organic drives, right? Which have to generate insane amounts of heat. They must have some very efficient method of dissipating heat in vacuum or they couldn't survive. We're aiming at the part of them that can probably take the most heat. Sir, if we want to kill them, I believe we'll have to target the other end."

Walsh rubbed his cheek, which was bristling with white stubble. He glanced at Rossi.

She nodded. "According to the database, most sectilian defense took place just outside of atmosphere and with ground-level weapons. If they never went out to meet the Swarm like this, they wouldn't have encountered this problem, so it wouldn't have been recorded."

"We made new problems by being more aggressive," Compton commented.

Walsh raised his chin. "Tactical, conference room one. Now. Hampton, you too."

Major Zhang stood and gestured at Zara to go first.

55

WALSH MET with tactical and went over alternatives that took their current theories into consideration. Then he videoconferenced again with the leadership of the rest of the fleet. This time he didn't give options, he gave orders.

They would continue with the defile maneuver, but the lasers were reset from nine hundred nanometers to three hundred nanometers, a wavelength which was less susceptible to mirror defenses. They'd wait for the Swarm to pass by—to fire on their front ends, instead of their back ends. They'd be forced to hold the fighters back for now. There wasn't enough time to reconfigure all of their laser cannons, though crews were scrambling to do just that.

Their position in this encounter had changed dramatically from just hours before. They were weaker against the Swarm than they'd ever anticipated. Their success seemed far less certain. With each failure, the tension on the bridge crept higher.

Once again, the countdown clocks were reset.

Once again, every ship checked in, verifying their readiness.

The moment came for Zara to say, *"Jiacti."*

Then, during the cooldown period, they fired missiles again. They repeated this pattern several times.

Sokolov hunched stiffly over his station. He glanced over at Walsh. "Damage verified, Captain." He hesitated. "But not as much as we hoped. We're seeing some minor course changes... and a few *Confluos* are clearly dead."

Walsh's face went red. "Dammit! A few? I want to know *exactly* what made those bugs dead, Sokolov. Was it two lasers hitting them at the same time from two sides? Was it laser plus missile? Was it contact time? Don't say another word until you know the answer."

Sokolov turned around and got back to work.

Major Tinibu, a young Nigerian woman at the helm, said, "Do we continue pursuit, Captain?"

They could match the Swarm's velocity only as long as the Swarm didn't deviate from its current trajectory by much. The dreadnoughts couldn't easily change course at high rates of speed.

"Yes. Pursue the targets. Formation Eta Tau. Power down weapons. Until we understand this data, no one fires again." He turned to Zara. "Translate that and cut the comm for now."

Compton frowned. "It's a damn good thing they're moving too fast to turn and engage us. Those must be some angry bugs."

Walsh blew out a heavy breath through tight lips. "That won't be the case for much longer. They're slowing down and eventually they'll turn and fight if we don't kill them first."

"It was a good plan."

Walsh shook his head. "All that stuff in the database...it didn't help. It's old data. None of it applies to us, here and now. We have to treat these bugs like we don't know a damn thing."

The new-new-new plan was to release all the fighters. Sokolov uploaded an animation to the fleet's intranet and it played on the bridge of every ship while Zara translated his narration.

He explained that it took sustained laser fire from two ships or sustained laser fire from one ship plus ballistics to kill an individual. On-screen, these options played out. Then Sokolov gave the kill stats for the last battle.

Most of those that died had been subadults. Their dead bodies would continue to hurtle toward Earth until they were caught up in an orbit somewhere along the way. Some would surely be collected for study, but they weren't going to be fighting, at least.

Four down, one hundred thirty-four to go.

At Rossi's suggestion, thirty percent of the fighters were going to use a variety of different wavelengths. Work crews continued to retrofit them with the appropriate laser gain media, and necessary adjustments were being made. In addition, these ships were being fitted out with more-sensitive sensor arrays. They needed to know if there was a particular wavelength that was most effective.

When everything was in place, they closed in and released the fighters. The dreadnoughts would form a cap shape behind the bugs while the cruisers continued the defile formation, and each ship was assigned specific bugs to target until it was sure they were dead. Walsh warned all the captains it might seem chaotic, but to stay calm and keep their ears on. Orders were likely to change from minute to minute.

It went well, for a while.

They killed nine more, all adults this time.

Then all hell broke loose.

Thirteen bugs veered off, each in a wildly different direction, escaping the defile and swinging around to come up behind the EU fleet.

Walsh divided the fleet. Eight ships and their fighters continued to pursue the majority of the pod toward Earth. The remainder—the *Vincitore, Caballero, Bronya,* and *Aegis*—would fight the bugs that had left the defile and were crawling up their backsides. Even minor course changes at such high speeds were stressful for everyone on board due to the sudden, intense g-forces. As her stomach was being pulled through her spine, Zara hoped they were also stressful for the *Confluos.*

Each individual bug had gone off on a different vector. The *Aegis* was incapable of chasing them around the solar system, but the three smaller cruisers were more versatile, and Walsh used that versatility. He was clearly fearful one of the Swarm would escape to relay knowledge of human defense capabilities to another pod. He barked orders off rapidly, swinging from navigation to helm to sensors to tactical and weapons, consulting frequently with Compton, who remained close at his side, and shouting for Zara to translate.

But now they weren't firing on defenseless creatures.

These were clearly experienced adults. They flipped and burned unpredictably and with apparent ease, maneuvering with a flexibility that no ship in the fleet could match. As they passed by one of the Earth United ships, they shot off bursts of plasma, possibly from their organic interstellar drives. The plasma meted out horrific damage to the Earth United ships. The bugs also landed on the ships and physically clawed and bit at them with their enormous pincer-shaped mouths, seeking any vulnerability. The ships rocked under the onslaught. Damage reports came in. The comm panels lit up with people wanting to relay urgent messages or queries.

Zara became robotic, efficiently answering calls and making instant judgments about who to route them to. Three minutes in, the *Bronya* was disabled and losing air. They went critical at six and a half minutes. There was no time to get anyone off. The only survivors were their small number of fighters.

She felt like she'd failed them somehow, though she knew that in her minor role in this event, there was no way she could have done anything to save them.

Her heart swelled painfully, but there was no time to mourn the lost. Not yet. Maybe not ever.

The eight ships in pursuit of the main pod were still picking off individuals slowly, with painstaking precision. Then six more adults turned to fight. Walsh ordered the *Paladin* and the *Bouclier* to turn and fight them. That left ninety-nine bugs still on a trajectory toward Earth and only half of the EU ships still in pursuit of the pod at large.

Zara and the three other communications officers struggled to handle the queries and reports from the *Aegis's* fighters in addition to the communiques from the other captains.

Then the *Paladin* was lost. A few people were ferried to the *Bouclier* on fighters, but not many. The *Caballero* went a few minutes later. They'd lost one-third of their ships in less than half an hour.

The tide was turning against them.

All *Bronya* fighters were reassigned to the *Aegis*. A blue light representing requested communication came in from one of these fighters. Zara took the call.

"This is Captain Olivia Cote in BRO-37," she said in Mensententia with a French accent. "My husband just died on the *Bronya*. I have nothing left. I'm going to *mortevindahipt*." Zara took the word to basically mean kamikaze or self-sacrifice in the name of revenge, but that particular word didn't exist. Cote had just made it up, using fragments of other Mensententic words.

Zara felt paralyzed for a split second. Was she supposed to talk Cote out of this? She turned to the screen, but she had no idea if any of the dozens of fighters she could see was Cote. "Captain, we'll find a way. We have time. You don't need to do this."

Cote sounded calm. "I have eyes, First Lieutenant. We're losing. Cote, over and out."

Zara realized that Cote had opened the channel to broadcast that exchange to every fighter in the fleet. Her hands trembled just above the console as she stared down at it. In the chaos, she hadn't noticed until Cote cut the signal.

She stood. "Captain!"

Walsh glanced over his shoulder at her from where he was hovering over the navigation console next to the nav officer.

Zara moved between the rows of consoles until she reached Sokolov. "Where is *BRO-37*?"

Sokolov looked up at her, questioning. Walsh strode over. "Show us. What is it, Hampton?"

"The pilot in *BRO-37*, Captain Olivia Cote, says she is going to... kamikaze one of the *Confluos*, sir."

Sokolov said, "She's in this sector." The field of view zoomed in, and one of the small fighters was highlighted with a red dot. "She's heading straight for the largest adult. She's firing lasers. It appears she's overridden the laser cooldown period from the cockpit, sir."

"Put me on with her," Walsh said, putting a hand on Zara's arm. "Broadcast fleet wide."

Zara went back to her station and tried to open a channel. She had to force herself not to pound on the touch screen in an attempt to make Cote answer. "She's not responding, sir."

On-screen, the large bug swung in a wide arc, but Cote stayed steady in her pursuit.

"*BRO-37* still firing constant laser, sir," Sokolov said. "It's reaching critical levels."

"Then just broadcast. She'll hear me." He gestured at Sokolov. "Broadcast the tactical feed too."

VALENCE

Cote was closing in. If the bug didn't change course again, she'd have it.

Zara input the command. "You're broadcasting, sir."

Sokolov said softly, "The feed is up, sir."

Walsh stood tall. "Olivia Cote, we honor you. You are a true Earth patriot. There will—"

There was a bright flash where BRO-37 impacted the insect. Its abdomen swelled. There was another flash, larger than the first, and then the bug broke apart in glowing fragments that quickly went black, still streaming at high velocity in the direction the insect had been going. It was nothing more than space debris now.

The bridge and all communication channels went silent.

After a moment, Walsh spoke, his words slow and measured. "Rest in peace, Captain Olivia Cote. Your sacrifice will not be forgotten."

Zara translated that, struggling to keep her voice crisp and clear and devoid of emotion.

Why had this worked when the missiles and lasers hadn't? She couldn't be sure, but there was the mass of the fighter, the remainder of the fuel, the laser going critical. Surely Cote had armed any missiles left on the rack before impact. Then there was the extended laser fire, concentrated at close range, a human pilot's ability to react to the insect's dodging swiftly and keep that laser precisely on target. With all of this at once, Cote had been able to break through the tough shell better than uncoordinated laser and missile fire. She'd packed a bigger punch.

Instantly Zara began thinking of how to design a remote-controlled drone that could do the same thing. Or maybe something that could latch on and drill through before delivering a payload. They'd have to scrutinize this footage minutely and figure out at which point Cote broke through, analyze all of the Swarm fragments they could find...

435

The maelstrom of the fight returned like a fist slamming down.

Only a minute later, the communications officer next to Zara stood. "I have another volunteer. Fighter *CAB*-22. First Lieutenant Davi Sousa."

Davi Sousa's last words were that he had a sister with three little girls in Brazil and he had to make sure they lived.

Blue lights lit up across the comm console.

No Earth continent went without sacrificing at least one of its own. Walsh allowed them to broadcast a final statement to the fleet. Most of the fighters who volunteered made statements about the survival of the species or mentioned specific loved ones by name whom they wanted to protect. They sacrificed themselves for the greater good. Zara had to wonder if she would have the courage to do the same in their place.

She sat there, whole. Able to go on. She could hardly process it.

In the end, they eliminated every *Confluos* threat. The majority of the kills went to *mortevindahipt*. Four of the fleet of twelve ships were lost in total. Two were completely disabled but holding air, and one was losing air slowly, but between fighters working as rescue ferries and repair crews, it looked like they'd soon have that situation under control. The *Bouclier* lost its jump drive.

The *Aegis* was badly damaged but was airtight and could jump. It took on the majority of the fighters from lost ships and as many other rescuees as possible.

Some people were celebrating, but Zara couldn't join in. She sat dumbly at the comm station, watching the others speak to each other.

The last thing she'd heard was Compton murmuring, "What if that was only the tip of the spear?"

56

March 3, 2031

EVERY JUMP SET Jane's teeth on edge, but the anomalous wormhole experience did not repeat itself. The ships themselves were unharmed. Her people were tense and moody, but otherwise fine.

She didn't blame them. She felt the same.

She'd failed them.

Her body ached with guilt. It had been a mistake to get so close to the Swarm pod, to taunt them, to underestimate them.

She would never do that again.

They jumped into the Sol system between the orbits of Uranus and Neptune. No planets were in sight. Just vast empty space. Sol itself was too far away to be distinguished from other stars. Earth was, of course, invisible.

Jane wanted to give the powers that be on Earth plenty of time to notice their presence and recognize her ship, assuming they were even looking out that far. Their arrival was going to create some waves. Better to give them time to think before they could act.

"Qua'dux, long-range scans are picking up organic debris ahead in a planetary orbit. And industrial debris. It's spread out over a vast distance. Something happened out there," Murrrsi said.

Jane frowned. "Let's investigate."

"Course laid in, Jane," Brai said.

"Let's go. Forward cameras up on-screen."

When the debris field came into view, Jane said, "Magnify."

The lower-left corner of the screen blew up, and the image refocused. Jane stared at the corner of the screen, trying to make sense of what she was looking at.

"Those look like bug parts to me," Alan said. "Big bug parts."

He was right. Now she could identify a leg, a piece of shiny black carapace...

Her stomach flipped over. The sick feeling spread through her body.

They were too late.

The Swarm had already been here.

Jane darted a glance at Murrrsi. "You said you also detected industrial debris?"

"Ahead," Murrrsi said.

Brai navigated through the orbiting bug graveyard until they reached the industrial debris.

Ships. Or what was left of them. There'd been a battle here. Several ships the size of the *Speroancora* had been lost. Jane was so shocked and dismayed that she could barely register any other emotion. She wasn't sure she had any emotions left.

"They look sectilian, with modifications," Alan said. "Earth built a fleet based on the plans we gave them."

Feig leaned over Ouvaq's console, pointing out a sector and enlarging the image. "Look here. See the evidence of catastrophic impact on the front of the ship? Did this pilot sacrifice themself to kill one of the Swarm?"

Jane leaned forward, squinting. "Send that image to the *Oblignatus*, please. Ron, what do you make of this?"

"That was definitely a suicide run," Ron said. "And that's not the only one. I've seen at least three others. These small ships look like they're based on sectilian shuttlecraft."

Jane swallowed hard. She'd thought it couldn't get worse. It had. "It must have been bad if they resorted to those sorts of tactics."

"The wreckage just goes on and on," Ouvaq whispered.

Jane made eye contact with Alan. His expression was bleak.

She felt hollow and empty inside. She'd failed them. All the time and energy she'd put into finding a way to help Earth build a defense of some kind...

"Who do you think won?" Alan asked.

She was afraid to speculate.

"We have a contact," Brai said.

"A ship just jumped in," Celui said. "I don't recognize any of the markings or identification beacons. It must be of terran origin."

Celui pushed an image of the recently arrived ship onto the main viewscreen. It had clearly seen some action. Sections of the hull were black with damage. Emblazoned on one side in bold red letters was its name: *Aegis*.

Jane sat up straight. Someone had clearly survived. A small burst of hope bloomed inside her. "Open a channel in the terran range we discussed earlier. Be ready for anything."

"Channel open, Qua'dux," Celui said.

"*Aegis*, this is Quasador Dux Jane Holloway of the *Speroan-cora*." She broke off then. She didn't know what else to say.

A familiar voice echoed across the bridge. "You're late."

Jane would recognize that voice anywhere. She'd heard its

gruff tones for more than ten months in that tiny capsule. "Walsh, is that you? Celui, on-screen."

It was Mark Walsh. On a bridge very much like her own. He was safe.

A hint of a sad smile snuck into his expression. "You're a sight for sore eyes, Holloway. You know, you missed all the fun just a few weeks ago."

Her heart thudded out of rhythm. How could she have let this happen? "Weeks? Really? I'm so sorry, Mark. It may be hard to believe but I've been trying to get back here for nearly twenty years."

"Well, you're here now. Looks like you've rounded up a fleet and made a few friends along the way." His eyes roved over his own viewscreen, and he frowned. "You're missing a few faces."

"Ron commands the *Oblignatus*. Ajaya is with him over there."

"I'll be damned. Ron's got his own ship. You hear that, Tom?" Mark turned sideways so that Jane could see behind him. Tom Compton stood and approached the camera.

"Tom! It's good to see you." Tears sprang to Jane's eyes. It was so good to see her old friends.

One corner of his mouth crooked. "You too, Jane."

Alan piped up, "So you were able to eliminate the threat?"

Walsh nodded. He looked down. "With heavy losses."

The silence was deep and long. Jane's throat ached, empty phrases of condolence and regret lodged there. Nothing she could say was good enough.

They'd done it. She was fiercely proud of them. But they'd suffered greatly. Not long before Feig had said that when the Swarm came, there was always great loss of life. Would it have made a difference if she'd gotten there sooner?

Walsh cleared his throat. "So you've come back home. Will you be staying awhile?"

She faltered. "Am I welcome?"

He looked incredulous. "Of course you are. You're a goddamned hero. The entire planet knows your name. They'll probably throw parades for you."

Jane shook her head. She wasn't a hero. She was just a linguist. "No parades, please. I think I will stay awhile. As long as you need me."

Walsh huffed. "You damn well better. I'll tell you straight— we *do* need you. We don't know if another flock of these bugs is on its way."

ABOUT THE AUTHOR

As a child growing up in rural Illinois, Jennifer Foehner Wells had the wild outdoors, a budding imagination, and books for company.

Her interest in science fiction was piqued early on when a family friend loaned her a collection of Ray Bradbury shorts. That was all it took to set her on a course toward a lifelong love of science and science fiction. She earned a degree in biology in 1995.

Jen's first novel, Fluency, was a virally successful best seller. Her second novel, Remanence, was nominated for the Goodreads Choice Awards of 2016.

Jen currently lives in Pennsylvania with two boisterous boys, the geekiest literature professor on the planet, three semi-crazed cats, and a five-pound Pekingese/Chihuahua mix that steals hearts and takes names.

If you enjoyed this book, please consider leaving a review on your favorite online site and tell your friends about it, both in person and via social media. Help other readers find it! Support the authors from whom you crave more stories.

ALSO BY JENNIFER FOEHNER WELLS

Novels

Fluency (Confluence Book 1)

Remanence (Confluence Book 2)

Inheritance (Confluence Book 3)
(formerly titled The Druid Gene)

Short Fiction

The Grove

Symbiont Seeking Symbiont

Anthologies

The Future Chronicles—Special Edition

The Future Chronicles—Alien Chronicles

The Future Chronicles—Z Chronicles

The Future Chronicles—Galaxy Chronicles

Dark Beyond the Stars

At the Helm Vol. 1: A Sci-Fi Bridge Anthology

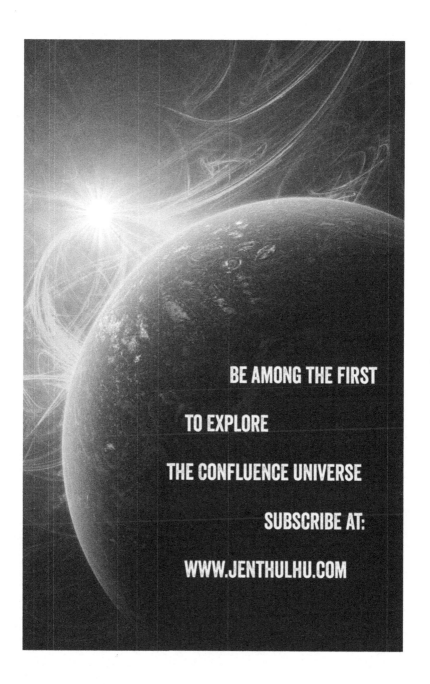

BE AMONG THE FIRST

TO EXPLORE

THE CONFLUENCE UNIVERSE

SUBSCRIBE AT:

WWW.JENTHULHU.COM

Made in the USA
Las Vegas, NV
11 February 2022

43729649R00267